YOU ARE THE
AUTHOR OF MY
STORY

SUNIL KUMAWAT

First published by 2018

Becomeshakspeare.com
Wordit Content Design & Editing Services Pvt Ltd
Unit - 26, Building A -1, Nr Wadala RTO,
Wadala (East), Mumbai 400037, India
T: +91 8080226699
Wordit Art Fund helps deserving authors publish their work by
providing monetary support. To apply for funding, please visit us
atwww.BecomeShakespeare.com

Cover design – Yuvraj Bhatnagar
Editing – Sunil Kumawat
Author Photograph – Manmohan Kumawat
Copyrights © 2018, Sunil Kumawat

ISBN - 978-81-937634-0-7

Dedicated To,

All the struggling spirits, who dare to dream.
May universe bless you to find path of your heart.

Acknowledgement

Describing this book as writing journey would be injustice to itself. This book is life that I have lived when I first held pen in my hands. Every day, I born and died on the same time in this journey. This book has provided me the truth, which I was seeking for. I have lived a new era with this book. It has given me the essence of myself. I found my existence with this book in this huge universe. It's the process of self emancipation for me. But as dreams take sacrifices.

I have sacrificed my sleep, time, and peace for it. Dreaming something was my biggest mistake that took away everything, my family, my friends, and happiness. I was like what the hell I have done to my life. But there were people who grabbed my hand when I was falling down. I would warmly like to acknowledge all of them. I belong to a small village that made me introvert, weird boy, having no expectations from life. But my Dad, small farmer, sought something special in me. He believed that I would be something in life. He wanted me to dream something that he couldn't. This journey is about completing my father's dream but not mine. He didn't show me the path but he walk along with me in this path. He presented his feet prints so that I could easily walk on impression of his feet on stony path. In this jaunt, everyone would lose faith in me. And I would be the first to lose faith in myself, but he would be alone who would gripe faith in me. I don't dedicate this book to my father, he dedicated this dream to me. I couldn't express my love to you Dad. Today I'm gonna take this moment to simply thank my Dad. Thank you Dad.

Now I want bow to the mighty universe that is the source of origin, and destruction of everything. I'm blessed to have realization of all your mighty power that turned me fearless, positive, and filled with serenity by merging my incomplete into you. You are within me; I am within you.

My eternal gratefulness to my mentor Raghvendra Bhaiya, who

enlightened my soul and gave different vision to look the world. I could find all my answers through you. Adhar Chaturvedi, once you said to me, 'I may not fix your problems, but I promise you won't face them alone.' You proved these words man. Love you so much.

I wanna pay my gratitude to Ravi Jiju, big man with bigger heart. I found 3 AM friend in you. Mannu, It would be your insult if I thank you. You are another part of mine like my soul, so I just want you to be with me always, that's it. And here comes my cousins who turned my best friends, who knows all the secrets of my diary. Gopal Dada, Ravi, Pawan Kamawishdar, Rahul Challotra, Rahul Kapse, Ankit, Maya, Bhawana, Ishwar, Deepak(both Deepak), Arjun Choudhary, Devendra, Manish, Prakash Choudhary, Jayant. You guys are amazing. You helped me, took care of me 24 hours, and made me laughed every time. Most important, mid night discussions with you are stimulating and enlightening. Thank you for unflinching faith that I could be a writer. Special thanks to Anand Gupta and Nitesh Gupta. A big thanks to team Becomeshakspears for the encouragement, and believing in my work.

At some point, we would be lost in our path, then some special people cross our path and put us on the right path. There are two people who crossed my journey to say that I should write, and then they left and never came back. Thank you for finding the real me in this messy crowd.

Amish Tripathi Sir, and Paulo Coelho Sir thank you for introducing me to the spiritual world through your words. I could see eternal hope through your books. And I offer greetings to Bhagwat Geeta, the granth that holds answers of every questions in the universe.

Anil, Ram has Laxman in his Vanvas. I found my Laxman in you. I'm stunned that how could you do so much for me without any expectations. You would awake whole night to do my things even when I am sleeping. Thank you.

And now last, but certainly not the least, you, the reader. Thank you for holding this book, this is your story. Your story of love, friendship, dreams, struggles, and hopes that everything will be good one day. May the universe bless us.

About the author

Sunil Kumawat is a son of poor farmer, lives near Indore, graduated in Arts from DAVV, Indore. At present, he is preparing for Civil Services from New Delhi. Belongings to village that holds cruel thinking scared him. He turned introvert that forced him to hold pen and paper to express his emotions. To dream something is like a crime in his village. Nevertheless, he dares to dream. He chose the endless path of writing to find his voice. This book is the dawn of the Revolution to awake the people of his village, to live the life the way they want, to break the boundaries of their own. By this book, he is presenting example to youth of his village, so that they could dare to dream, as that's how they can find their real Karm on earth.

He has dedicated his soul to help people of his village in helping them to find the right way to live the life, to fight for the truth, to set theory of Karm, to know their own souls.

Sunil has dwelled himself in spiritual world. Moreover, he accepted the writing journey to find the truth of the universe, he is wondering about from years. This is his journey to merge his incomplete part into the all mighty universe to become Purn.

Inspired by the words of Amish Tripathi and Paulo Coelho he began his jaunt to awake all the spirits and to find true essence of his own soul.

CHAPTER ONE

"Hey! Man....," I greeted with wide smile, as I entered into a barren, prison type room. However, my smile went dull, as he didn't respond to me. He was lying over his stomach on his bed, legs cycling in air, and completely lost in his Temple Run. He was totally disoriented about where he was and what's happening around him. I ignored him, and pulled my trolley bag inside my new room.

"Shit...., fuck yourself." He groaned and threw his iphone 6 on wall. He dug his head in his pillow

"Now this is too much. I will fuck you now," well I didn't actually say that, but that's what I was wondering.

"Better luck next time," I gave him fake smile to make him aware of my presence in the same room, which had dull grey walls.

"Huh?" he sounded puzzlement on his face.

"Hiiii….. I am Shourya Sharma, your new roommate," I said forwarded my hand to that unknown boy in blue shorts and grey T-shirt said Lee Cooper.

"Oh my goodness," he shouted and jumped off from his bed, "Thank God, finally you came dude. I was dying in this hell," he said enthusiastically and buried me in bear hug.

"Ok, ok, it's fine. Now leave me, I am not a gay," I sneered.

"May be, you are. Who knows?" he quipped and cocked his eye at me and laughed himself.

"By the way I am Rohan," he beamed at me.

"Which department?" I asked. Head titled questioningly

"MA- Sociology," he responded promptly.

"Whooaa..! It's awesome. Me too," I said, my face lit up in a wide smile.

"Dude, I am telling you, we are going to fuck whole college," Rohan bellowed in over confidence, and clapped his hand against mine.

Unearthly, but it's true that we boys need only 0.08 seconds to become best buddies. It means we are faster than MS Dhoni's wicket keeping. Therefore, I was not surprised to find me becoming good friend with Rohan. In addition, we didn't have any option left but to become friends, as staying together in a confided space for hours left minimum leeway.

"Hey! Man. Wake up, where are you dreaming," Rohan shook my shoulder and fetched me back out of my thoughts.

"Oh! Sorry ....," I whispered, rubbing my neck, trying to hide my silly.

Soon Rohan and I found ourselves, sharing our secrets about first crush at school, and about how many girl friends we had from school to college, and about our experience of watching first porn movie.

"By the way Rohan, why did you are here so early? I mean, college will start after more few days." I asked, my eyes narrowed questioningly as if searching for answers in his eyes. However, I was just trying to make our conversation longer.

"Ugh," Rohan sighed and scattered on his bed, "It's all because of this fucking college and its staff. They warned me to come early. But when I approached to them, they denied that they didn't call me." Rohan snapped.

"Disgusting It is." I murmured with Rohan, but soon I got busy in arranging my books, clothes, cricket kits, shoes and all daily use stuffs.

"Shourya, I think you should rent on one more room for your

luggage. I will not allow you to destroy my room with these fucking useless things," Rohan freaked out.

"Just shut up Rohan," I smacked, "and what are looking like nuts, just help me out man," I hissed at him.

"It's too heavy. What's in it?" Rohan exhaled heavily, lifted my suitcase.

"May be a dead body," I giggled.

We both flopped on the bed, facing the ceiling, where a dull white fan was revolving slowly as if he was forced to do that. I moved my gaze here and there in whole room. And what I could find was just two wooden beds, two study table, one cupboard with two partitions. The walls were painted dark grey, and window were hitting terribly with fast wind. The room was as good as like cage of a prisoner, sentenced for whole life.

We hostlers have the worst life one could ever afford. We have to sacrifice all the luxury of home as like soft foamy bed, TV, vehicle, parents, younger ones and more. But the most painful is not having 'Maa ke hath ka khana.' However, we have to do it, as it's the rule of nature. Like birds don't learn to fly in their nest, so as we don't.

"Rohan, I didn't think we can survive even a single day in this trap," I muttered.

"Of course we would survive," he said, "just come here, and have a look to this heaven," he excited with wider smile and bigger eyes. He opened window next to his bed.

"What the F____," I stopped abruptly and sighed, "Dude its breath taking. Isn't it?" I gasped.

That window would give direct pose to the girl's hostel, just besides of boy's hostel. We could see even into girls' room through their windows. At least we have got the medicine to blur our whole day frustration.

"Lucky bastard, Rohan you are," I amazed, "Rohan please give this window to me," I pleaded like a beggar.

"Just fuck off," Rohan grumbled, "I would rather die," he showed me his middle finger straight.

"Fucking man..," I murmured to myself, "I am tired. I wanna a deep nap, so just don't disturb me now, else I will swell your ass," I said rudely, and shattered on my bed, buried myself under white blanket.

****

CHEPTER SECOND

"Phir le aaya dil mujboor kya kije.....," the song called of today's most melodious, romantic singer Arijit Singh. It was my alarming tone since last few days. My phone was trying hard from 20 minutes to interrupt me from deep sleep. Although, I love that song but now it was irritating me. So if you want to hate any of your favorite song, just set it as your alarm tone, and you'll find yourselves hating that number.

Anyhow, I stretched my hand out of my blanket and shuffled my hand to find my cell. I dismissed the alarm and hid under blanket once again for more sleep. Next Moment, my cell rang, it was my Mom.

"Mom, can't you just keep patience, I was sleeping, and you broke my sleep," I heated, under my blanket. I was sounding gruffly.

"Shut up Shourya. I just want to confirm that you reached safe or not," Mom bellowed.

"Mom, I am 23 now. And I came to Delhi, I mean, now I am studying in DU. I can take care of myself. I am not a kid now," I hit back to Mom.

"Of course you are still kid for me, and will be always. You have no idea how much I am missing you. But why would you care for me. You never cared for me, you never loved me," Mom gasped in cry.

Sometimes we talk to our parents rudely and later feel like shit for behaving like this. I could picture my Mom busy in kitchen, and also wiping her tears at times.

"Sorry Mumma, really sorry," I whispered, "and I love you Mumma, and I am also missing you. Please don't cry," I kissed my cell.

"Ok, ok, stop buttering. I love you too. Take care of you," she sobbed.

Our parents know us so well. They have spent much time than us in this world. They are always right. But we don't listen to them and at last we feel we should have listened to them.

I got up hastily, sat on my bed, wrapped my arms around my legs as if, i was holding myself. I was pacing my dark room like fool. There was tension, and awkward silence in the room. I was feeling suffocated, I just wanted to run from there.

Journals 555

"Shifting to the new place is quite sorrowful. Few days back I was living in the place, where I could feel like the whole world is mine. Every road, every building, every street, is like holding some part of mine. And every people there could express me better than myself. I love to live in small town where I would know every corner and that makes me happy.
I am afraid of big metro city like New Delhi. I just feel like I have lost in that messy crowd. I think here is tension in the atmosphere itself. I don't get positive vibes when I travel in Delhi. It's like the insecurity that I would lose if I go out. I feel like I would forget my soul, which is dying within my body. I couldn't accept the roads, the buildings, and the people. As if I am standing in the middle of the greenery that is so beautiful, but as I step forward in that grass cobra insert his all poison in my right foot."

****

I texted Rohan : *whr d hell, u r getting fuckd, i m dying here alone.*

He texted me back in five minutes : *jst cum upstairs on d terrace n hv d pleasure of beautiful evning.*

It was little after six in the evening, and the sun was ridding low. I exhaled deeply in fresh air, arms stretched. The evenings after a rainy day are really pleasant. I found half rainbow above the reddish sun.

"Bhai.., where were you. I was dying there alone," I waved my hand to Rohan. He was sitting on edge of the hotel roof.

"Come here, I will make you breathe," Rohan said wickedly. Rohan was a handsome hunk, with wide chest, abs, and biceps, with his muscular body. He looked hot in beard shave. Every girl wanted to be his Gf. "What are you doing here?" I asked, and sat next to Rohan.

"Enjoying the hotness in cold evening," he said and pointed out towards girl's hostel terrace.

"Gorgeous...," I whispered, as I gazed towards terrace of girls hostel. Whole terrace was buzzing in beautiful butterflies in red, pink, yellow, white, and so many colored sleeveless short tops and shorts. They were busy in books, cell phone, mirrors, and badminton. Even some of the fairies were dancing and singing too just to seduce all the boys.

We bastards were not innocent. Every boy tried to impress girls by singing, dancing, with guitar, flute and by passing vulgar comments to girls. And many assholes pulled out their T-shirt just to show their muscles, and abs to girls. And they tried stupid ideas.

And why didn't we try, because all girls were responding to us by their cute smile, giggle. Even some of them were blowing kisses to us.

"Who is she? She is too hot dude," I asked to Rohan, about the girl, waving her hand to Rohan, and then text in her cell.

"Bastard, don't try at her, she is my GF, Ashvini," Rohan hit on my head.

"What!.....," I shocked, "I mean, how can you have a GF?" I sneered and patted his back.

"Idiot," Rohan hit back, "she is my GF from last four years. But I had to propose her 20 times, and then she accepted me." Rohan said and smiled at Ashvini.

"Say hey to her." Rohan ordered me. I obliged him, and gave a wider smile to Ashvini.

"Ok, ok. It's enough now. She is your bhabhi," Rohan ruined my smile. But I was happy as that is prideful to say Bhabhi to our best friend's GF.

"Hey! Guys," I heard a weird voice from behind, "so which one is 10/10 today?" he asked and looked towards girl's hostel.

"You mother fucker," Rohan snapped, "where were you?"

"Did you miss me?" That boy kissed Rohan.

"By the way, Shourya, meet Yash, the genius boy. He has solution of every problem." Rohan introduced Yash, "and the worst thing about Yash is that he was my ex-GF," Rohan kissed back Yash.

Yash was a fatty, short height and looked like a dwarf or hobbit. He had curling hair, and small eyes with big spectacles like Albert Einstein. I said 'hey' to Yash.

"Rohan look at her. She is damn sexy. Look at her buts. Wow! What a figure!" Yash exclaimed with surprise, "I can't control, I am dying," he added.

"Ohoo....," Rohan said loudly in weird sound, "come here babe I will take you to heaven," Rohan whispered to Yash and grabbed him from behind.

"Disgusting, you guys are," I irritated.

******

"So Ashvini, tell me, why did you take so long to accept Rohan?" I asked impatiently, and raised eyebrows to her. We were in hostel mess, doing our dinner. Ashvini was a simple girl, she had good knowledge and experience of life, and she could read people around her very well. And that's why she became good friend of mine. She had a natural glittering smile on her face. She had chubby hairs in which suited her small round face.

"Actually, I also have fallen in love at first sight with him, but I wanted to confirm that is his love is real or he is just cheating me for benefit." Ashvini cleared her throat, and took a bite of Rajma chawal.

"So what did you find in Rohan? True love for love for benefits," I shrieked and looked at Rohan.

"Benefits," Rohan quipped and we laughed out.

"What? you.... cheap...," Ashvini slapped Rohan with love.

"Guys, I am so much happy to see your cute love. But I am little bit confuse about love," I said, "I don't know, what is love?" I shrugged.

"Shourya, love isn't a theorem or law like gravitational law, there is no definition of love. It's just a feeling of care, just a belief for someone. Love doesn't need a qualification or criteria to be happened. It happens at anytime and with anyone special. You don't need reason to love someone, it just happens," Ashvini kissed Rohan, and armed him tightly, I felt so happy to see them.

"Ok, ok. But how one can know that he has fallen in love," I asked, stupidly.

"Dude, no one teaches you how to fall in love likewise, no one teaches you how to move on inn life. It's so simple yaar..., when someone special will appear in front of your eyes, and you will fall in love by her first glimpse. At that time, the whole world around you would seem to be stopped. Everything, everyone would start to disappear. And you would see only that special girl. A soft music would blow in your ears. A cold breeze would start blowing around you. And you would fly in sky. And in just one second you would decide that, she is your life, your aim and your everything. You would be always ready to die for her. This is love Shourya," Rohan sighed. Ashvini and Rohan looked and giggled at my half parted mouth.

"Oh my god, what the fuck it is?" I exclaimed in shock, "I can't do and die for anyone."

"Shourya, you are so mean. But one day you will also feel the same. Certain things in life simply have to be experienced and never explained. Love is such a thing," Ashvini said barely control her love for Rohan on her face.

"Don't worry. I will not fall in love. No girl can impress me. God have to take long time to create such an extra ordinary girl for me," I said and laughed proudly. They glared at me.

"Ashu, now I don't need you. I have got new GF." Rohan said.

"What, who?" I snapped.

"You, my bebo.. Darling." Rohan said and kissed on my cheeks.

******

"What are you doing Shourya?" Rohan asked and sat near me on my bed.

"Nothing..., just writing my daily journals," I said meekly.

"Wow! You sound so good. But tell me what and why do you write?" he again raised his brows.

"I write the precious Moments of my life. And I write because, I want to treasure these beautiful Moments till my last breathe, so that when I will read it in future, I could live every Moment once again," I said, appearing so ecstatic.

"Great dude..., now I have to check your beautiful Moments," Rohan said in mischievous tone and tried to snatch my diary.

"Just get lost, you lunatic," I freaked out and kicked him off my bed.

That was the first lie I said to Rohan. I didn't write the happy moments, I write the pain of people. Because the whole world see the smile on faces, and I see the pain into deep hearts. I want that pain to cover the pages of my diary. I am waiting for the day when I would stop writing, as that day I won't have any pain to tell to myself. I don't write the story of success, but the story of failure. I write the tell of struggle as that would tell the spirit of faith.

"Journal-556

It's my first night in Delhi. And I already have find three friends Rohan, Yash and Ashvini. All three are awesome. Though they are very different from me, but I am surprised why I find myself within them. Friendship is so weird_ you just pick a human you've met and you're like, 'yup I like this one,' and you just do stuff with them.

And everyone who comes to our life is like a book. They teach us something, we didn't know before. Today Ashvini made me aware of love."

"Shourya come here bro, look at her, she is damn hot," Rohan groaned. He was checking out every hostel girl on facebook.

"Whatever. I am not interested. And you moron, you just wait. I will tell Ashvini about this," I said grumpily.

Suddenly, we heard a sever knocking on our gate. But quickly sever knocking went louder. And it started stroking on our door, and in 3-4 strokes, our door broke down. Rohan and I exchanged our gaze in fear. Four boys, looked like unruly mob flooded into our room. We got up and looked at them like helpless puppy. So this was time for our ragging. We were thrown out of hostel to survive in severe cold night. Our Senior Atul has irrigated animosity with me.

****

"You bastard, can't you be silent. See because of you, I have to suffer now," Rohan rattled on.

"I didn't tell you to help me. You can go and say sorry to Atul," I giggled.

We were in garden of hostel basically. I had to spend my first night in garden. That was so cold night. We were shivering. We didn't have any blanket, and my shirt was already torn. Therefore, Rohan and I slept on same bench in garden, and held each other tightly to survive in cold night.

"Come here Bebo, I will make you hot," Rohan sneered and got over me.

"Get away, you gay," I hissed and kicked him down the bench.

So whole night, I was shivering, I couldn't sleep whole night. We kept fighting whole night for blanket. Whole night I cursed Atul.

And I checked time it was 6:00 o'clock of early morning. I had only caught a few hours sleep. The morning was beautiful, with the sun rays bouncing into park through trees. I was silently looking towards main gate of hostel. Rashly, I saw a girl entered through gate with a pink Scooty. She was in shorts and pink sleeveless top. She had fair complexioned skin. She had braided her long hair up to her waist in mermaid tail style. She had thin, curvy body, with smooth waistline, which were bare in short top. And I was starring at her long waxed, soapy legs. She had seductive beauty.

She was driving speedily towards parking, and I noticed that she lost control over her Scooty, and she bumped into a harsh accident with a luxury R-One-5. That harsh sound of collision woke up everyone.

"Rohan get up..," I patted him and got up quickly. Unexpectedly, a boy, owner of destroyed R-One-5 rushed out of hostel. And in next second, he started shouting on that girl. And that girl looked scared.

"Rohan get up," I shouted, and hit his buts.

"Don't trouble me Shourya...," Rohan mumbled sleepily

"Get up bastard. Look that girl, she is in trouble," I freaked out and made him to get up hastily. Rohan looked at that girl.

"Idiots, she is fucking bitch, she is a cat girl of college. She only looks for reasons to fight with anyone." Rohan muttered, rubbing his eyes and again slept on bench.

"Fuck off," I again kicked his ass, and strode hastily towards that girl.

"You idiot, what you did with my bike? You moron girl," that boy was shouting, and his shouting increase with his temper.

"It's not my fault, why did you park here? It's my place," she shrugged dramatically, and turned around to leave. But that boy grabbed her hand angrily.

"You bitch," he became abusive, "what do you think of yourself?" He roared, and glared her.

"You bastard, how dare you say me bitch, I will gauge you," she shouted and hit his chest.

"You Xanthippe! You need only single chance to fight with other. But today I will not leave you, you ugly girl," he ranted on.

"You bloody transgender," she said furiously, "I will ruin your dick," she grabbed his hair and shook violently.

"Stop it, guys. What are you doing?" I interrupted, "take it easy, you should have solved it silently," I said and looked into her big black eyes. Her face was red in anger. Her long braid was lying over her right shoulder.

"Dude she can't understand silent talk, she is cocky bitch, she don't have any quality of womanhood. You trumpet," that boy muttered.

"Shhhh....., I will kill you now," she grinded her teeth, and again scratched his face by her sharp nails. That boy was about to slap her, but I defended her, and took that boy aside.

"Dude, what are you doing? You are not supposed to hit a girl, leave her yarr...," I tried to convince that boy.

"Bhai, you don't know, she is a bloody Daayan. She would kill anyone. We can't let her go," that boy muttered and turned to hit her. But I stopped him, and tried to persuade him, and turned him back.

Hurriedly, we heard a cracking sound, and we turned to her.

"Oh my God!" I whispered in shock. She had destroyed head light of R-One-5. She showed her middle figure to us. We ran to catch her, but she had already rushed inside of girl's hostel. I was looking at her like helpless puppy, and she was laughing, jumping, and enjoying her victory.

****

CHAPTER THIRD

"Get up, you idiots," Yash said, and kicked us. Yes! On the second night we had to survive in harsh cold again on the bench of garden area, as Atul has thrown us out last night also.

"What's your problem Yash, let us sleep, you bitch," Rohan mumbled grumpily.

"It's our first day of college, you bastards," Yash snapped, "and it's already 7:45 by my clock. And Raghav Sir will take the lecture at 8:00 am," Yash added.

"What?" I got up hastily, "can't you wake up us early," I huffed. And Rohan and I ran into our room. We skipped shower. We just sprayed water on our faces, and ran to college. We were running unsteadily, half running half falling and colliding with other guys.

"You are stinging," everyone gave us awkward look, as we entered into campus.

DCAC is scattered in huge area 50,000 meter square. It has so many large and well decorated building for each department.

The main building was at center, surrounded by other large building. Every building was made up of red stone just like red fort. And every department was circled by garden, play ground, basketball courts, etc. There was a big library in front of art department, and a beautifully maintained canteen looked, like a restaurant. And in front of canteen there was a hanging garden for love birds. I could picture boys and girl holding each other's hands. Some boys have wrapped their arms around waist of their girls. Few Romeos were smooching lips of innocent girls. And yes. Rests of the nerds were holding books as they had no girl.

Behind the Art department, there were so many residency quarters for faculty and dean. Our building was most luxury and awesome, which was of 4 storey's. It was painted in red Gerua.

There was a courtyard inside of building, which was center of building. And building was shaped in circle around the courtyard, which gave open look to sky. Rohan and I strode through corridor. Suddenly I saw that Hitler girl, again arguing with a cute boy.

"Rohan stop, look that girl," I was saying. But he interrupted, "it's 8 O'clock, idiots, let's run. We are already late," he irritated.

"Noooo….. I am going to her," I said.

"Go to hell, you rascal," Rohan rushed inside.

"What's the matter?" I frowned, as I reached to her. She was in pink and white printed top, blue skirt. She glared at me, and touched her long mermaid tail braid.

"Sir, she is hitting me badly," that boy said, adjusting his big spectacles. And I fixed my eyes on her. She felt feared and nervous.

"This stupid nerd collided with me intentionally, pushed me harshly, and broke my phone," she snapped. Her big black eyes became more wide in anger. But her voice was so sweet like honey. She appeared so innocent, but she wasn't.

"No Sir, she is lying," that boy exasperated, "I didn't push her. Actually she collided with me, and now she is blaming me for her broken phone."

"You bloody liar," she roared and pushed aside her long braid, "I very well know all boys are sick. They just want and look for chance to strike with a girl," she glared at me, and then lifted her hands to scratch that boy's face. But I stopped her hands.

"How dare you touch me? And why are you following me from two days? You all boys are same dog," she spat out each word loudly and clearly. Indirectly, she condemned all boys.

"Look, I am just helping you," I said in serious tone, "see it's already late, and so tell me fast, what do you want?" I asked to her.

"1000 bucks. For repairing of my phone," she stifled, and turned her face away. I asked that boy to give her 1000 bucks. And that innocent boy respected my words, and gave her money.

She took the money, and I turned towards metal gate, to leave for class. But quickly, that girl pushed that boy on me. And I fell down in mud.

"You absurd, you kaminiiiiiiii," I shouted from, lying in mud, "you destroyed my favorite shirt," I said and strode to washroom to clean my shirt.

"Oh my god," the words caught in my throat, as I checked, it was 8:20 by my watch. I ran through stair case as fast as I could. As I padded towards class, a feeling of nervousness swelled near my heart with every step I moved forward. All my excitement ruined by that girl. As I reached to class, I leaned against the gate of classroom, I was panting high, my hairs were ruffled, and my shirt was wet and dirty, and not properly done.

"May, I come in Sir?" I asked, still panting and resting on the gate. Whole class turned to me, and fixed their eyes on me. That girl was also there, she was shocked as I was her classmate. But literally I was much shocked that she was my fucking classmate.

"Who am I to permit you, to let you enter into class? This is all yours." A man frowned, and glared at me. He looked so unhygienic, his grey striped shirt was in dust, and his face was dull. He looked old and tired even on first day of college.

"Oh!" I surprised, "so you are not Prof. Ragav. Thank God, Sir still hasn't come. I am safe," I was blurting stupidly, and walking inside in over confidence.

"So, you must be a peon, right?" I asked to him and went close to him. And the whole class burst into laugh.

"Shut up," that old man yelled to class, and banged the desk in his front. And everyone stopped their laugh. I was still looking to him in fear and bit of shock cum confusion.

"And you. How dare you interred into class? Get lost from here," he pointed me out of gate, his eyes were flaming in anger.

"Sorry Sir, it's misunderstanding, please forgive me," I stammered nervously and lay on my knees, and pleaded. Again whole crowd giggled.

"Just get out of my class, you are late, you can't be seated today," he barked furiously.

"Sir please, Sir," I was close to cry, but he didn't allow me.

"Get out my class," he roared. I got up and looked like helpless puppy. I was about to leave the class. Nimbly, my eyes met with that idiot girl, because of whom I was late.

"I will kill you," I murmured under my breath.

****

CHAPTER FOURTH

It was 11 of late night. Rohan, Yash and I were sitting on the edge the roof of hostel, our legs dangling precariously from its edge. We had already poured ourselves with one bottle of 'BLENDERS PRIDE', and opened one more. We were drunk as a shrunk.

"Bhai, you were right, she is bloody bitch. She ruined my first impression in front of whole class," I murmured in weird voice, as we were intoxicated by alcohol, "actually all girls are fucking bitch. They use us first then kick on our ass," I shouted.

"Shut up Shourya," Rohan annoyed to me, "Ashvini is not like other girls. She loves me a lot, she takes care of me, she understands me, and she has faith in me. Everyone wishes that there should be someone special in their life, who takes care of them, ask them, *'did you eat, did you complete your work, did you get up, I love you etc'*, and in my life Ashvini is that person. Whenever I am in pain, she comes and hugs me to say, *'don't worry, I am with you.'* She makes me feel alive. All my pain and grief vanished away when I see her. I love her so much," Rohan blushed like girls, and I saw true love on his face for Ashvini.

"You are so lucky, bhai, I love you too," I mumbled and kissed Rohan.

"Not much lucky dude. I am from a middle class family. And you know when we born in middle class family, our parents, and society murder our dreams and then teach us to smile for whole of our life." Rohan said, and laughed himself.

I mused for a second, and said, "Bhai, I am not lucky like you." I looked down in the courtyard of the hostel. "I am always surrounded by problems and bad luck. At first, these mother fucker seniors have fucked my life, and now that girl shattered me. They all made my life hell," I snapped and threw empty bottle on roof. Rohan and Yash starred at that rolling bottle.

"khali ho gyi yaar," I sighed.

"Bhai..., please don't be hopeless, your life is not empty, we are with you," Yash announced and put his head on my shoulder. His face lit up in a wide smile.

"Bastard, I mean bottle khali ho gyi," I sniffed.

"I love you, Ashu," Rohan said to himself, third time.

"Guys, I swear, I will destroy bloody Atul," I sounded bitter.

"Yeah.., I am with you, I will fuck that moron Rahul," Yash said violently. And we both looked at Rohan. He looked feared, he ignored us.

"Yash, I don't believe, coward Rohan will be with us. He is afraid of Atul," we laughed at Rohan.

"What did you say?" Rohan said furiously, "look at you first, you were like bheegi billi, when Raghav Sir fucked you," Rohan screamed at me.

"Ok, so you want to see my power, just wait and watch, tomorrow I will smack Ragav Sir."

"Don't even dare to think anything fucking about Raghav Sir. He is a good man," Yash frowned. Rohan and I gazed at each other in shock, and then turned to Yash.

"What? Why are you staring me," Yash whispered in fear.

"Shourya, I think Yash loves Raghav Sir," Rohan sneered, "yeah Rohan.., look our Yash is a gay," I laughed out and clapped with Rohan.

"Dude you are crossing your limits," Yash exasperated.

"So, you wanna fight, come on let's fight then," I pushed Yash, and got down on roof, braced myself for fight like a boxer.

"Guys, I am referee," Rohan got up, "come on Shourya show him your feet," he announced in empty bottle of 'BLENDERS PRIDE'. Then, I started punching Yash, and in 4th punch, he was on ground.

"You, cowards, why are you fighting your anger on me, if you have guts than smash that girl," Yash muttered from floor. Suddenly, I saw that girl on terrace of girl's hostel, and my blood went boiled, I stood up on edge of wall of roof. I was nodding with waves.

"Hey! You white witch, you are enjoying there, after screwing my life," I shouted, waved my hands to her to get her attention. She was staring at me. I started walking unsteadily on that short wall. Many times, I was about to slip down, but Rohan held me every time.

"What do you think of yourself, you jerk? I just wanted to help you, because I found a familiar relation with you. But you blamed me that I am flirting with you, you arrogant girl. My life has been fucked up. I paid 2000 rupees for your wrong did. And despite of that you didn't even thank to me. You are just a selfish. Fuck on you. You brawler girl," I over reacted, but I felt peace as I vented out my anger, frustration on that girl. That girl pushed back her long braid and ran inside.

"Hey! You idiot. Why are you shouting? Just get down, or I will kill you," Rahul snapped from courtyard.

"You monster, I will kill you too," I inflamed, while wobbling and showed him middle finger.

"Yeah, you just come up. I will shove your hand into your ash, I am not a coward of you," Rohan also braved himself. Actually, it's all because of power of one bottle of BLUNDER'S PRIDE.

"You are gone today," Rahul grinded his teeth and went towards staircase to reach us. And in few seconds, Rahul with other pimps, stumbled out of the staircase, they all were armed with hockey.

"Rahul, please forgive us. It was Yash, who forced us to abuse you. Please let us go," Rohan and I lay on our knees and begged to Rahul and saved ourselves from smash of hockey. We went in a corner and pretended like innocent kids.

"You pimp," Rahul snapped to Yash. He was going close to hit Yash and at that Moment, Yash started vomiting on Rahul. And we all ran leaving Yash on his own.

"Journal 557

Night is the clock time where my heart dawns to beat. I love to live in the dark sky. The around me would fell so silent that makes the presence of nature more noticeable. As if the cold wind and the moon light has just arrived to meet me. It's like I am the king of the night and every single creation belongs to me.
Night is like open theater to me where I am the director, actor, and writer. And I have awake to paint all my imaginations, my emotions, and my characters all over the sky. It's like the darkness is pushing me more ahead of my limitations. There is no one to see me, to judge me. And no one could stop my dreaming. I know whatever I would do in that dark heaven I would love it. And there won't be any murder case of my dreams."

****

On next morning, I was late again for class because of harsh hangover. I ran to class, while panting. I was glad as Raghav Sir was also late today. The class room was so big. But it was already packed. I was searching for a place.

"Hey! Come here," I heard a melody voice, and turned towards that voice. She was that arrogant girl, who was my bad luck. She waved her hand again to me, and whole class turned to her first and then at her. Everyone glued their eyes to us, as if we were the alien. Although I didn't want to respond her, but that was the last seat, so I had to seat next to her, on the 4th bench of second row from right.

I didn't look even at her, I was angry, and I was feeling uncomfortable with her. Even I was doubtful of her intensions.

"Sorry, I really troubled you a lot, please forgive me for my rude and stupid behavior," she regretted, and I saw guilt on her face. She looked like innocent kid; she had bright face, and long black hair, made into long mermaid tail braid. Now I noticed that she was so beautiful.

"I want my money back, and then only I can forgive you," I said rudely. I looked at her with deadpan on my face, my voice flat and dull.

"Oh yeah, of course," she searched her purse, but didn't find. Her purse was fell down yesterday when she pushed me on ground. And I had got that. I was smiling surreptitiously.

"Is it your purse?" I smiled to her. She looked in surprise, and her smile became more glittering, and her eyes became more wider.

"Thank you," she said politely.

"Anytime," I nodded with smile, a smile of condolence.

"So, we are friends now. I guess," she shrugged, gleefully.

"Only if you will stop fighting with others," I quipped.

"Ok, done. I will not fight with other. As now I will fight only with you," she laughed out loudly, and got the attention of whole class.

"Shut up," I muttered to her.

"Ok, ok," she said, "by the way, I am Ruhi Sharma," she forwarded her hand to me.

"Shourya Sharma," I shocked her hand.

"Wow….. It's amazing. We both are Sharma," she excited with more big black eyes.

"Yeah…., but I am not your type of Sharma," I said and pulled her big braid aside.

Raghav Sir entered into class, and started first chapter of sociology. We all were so much excited and curious to know about our subject we put our hands under our chin, and looked at Sir with a big smile. Raghav Sir wielded the black marker like a samurai, and no one saw, how it happened? But the white board was completely filled by definitions. And in few minutes our curiosity, our excitement, our happiness drained by boredom.

Then one by one Prof. Came and filled board and gave dull lectures. Every definition was bouncing from our head. We were just listening, what they were saying and then vented it out by other ear. Some students were snoozing, sleeping on bench. Some were yawning other were busy in their iphones. After every lecture, strength of class was getting shorter.

In our 4th lecture, only 15 students were left. Then a girl in black sari entered. She was Miss Aasha, our English teacher. She was hot and stunning in black backless blouse. She charged every boy of class. Everyone was staring at her. And I too had fixed my eyes on her low thin and fair waist.

"Shourya... are you checking her out?" Ruhi muttered, shaking me out of my dirty thoughts.

"No, not at all," I quipped, but my eyes were still on Aasha ma'am.

"Don't lie, I noticed you, you heaved a leer at ma'am. Shame on you," Ruhi pinched me.

"Oh! Come on Ruhi. Don't be jealous of her beauty," I said in mischievous tone. Straight away, Ruhi slapped me and we both started fighting and shouting.

"You both," Aasha ma'am pointed at us, "you both just get out of my class."

We stumbled out of class, and now only 4 horny boys were enjoying Aasha ma'am.

"Shourya, I am dying of starvation. Let's go to canteen," Ruhi annoyed like kid. And we padded to canteen. Canteen is the best place one could ever want to go. As almost every college, love story starts in canteen. It starts with a coffee, and remembers a lot can happen over a coffee. Even every canteen cafe is surviving just because of love birds. The only place where boys don't do bargaining is the cafeteria, as we don't want to ruin our image in front of a girl.

"So Shourya, You are from Delhi?" Ruhi asked and reclined on her chair. She took another sip of her cappuccino.

"Nope. Mumbai..., I am Mumbian," I replied on impulse, feeling proud of being from city of super stars.

"Wow! Yaar, Mumbai...," she amazed with big black eyes,

"but why are you here, leaving such beautiful city?" she looked cheerful.

"Long story," I said and finished my coffee, in attitude, trying to impress the gravity of situation upon me.

"Tell me. I have so much time," she raised her eyebrows.

"But I don't have time," I said rudely.

"Ok, what your father do?" she asked.

"He has huge business empire," I said.

"Oh my God, then why are you doing master in art?" she furrowed her eyes.

"I hate his business," I spoke loudly, "and will you please stop asking so many questions," I prayed to her.

She giggled. She took last sip of coffee. The bubbles clung to her upper lip.

"Ruhi, your lip...," I pointed.

"What?" she raised her eyebrows in confusion?

"Bubbles on your lip..," I repeated. She down her eyes, tried to flash at her lips. Then she licked them off delicately. But there were still remains of bubbles on the right Side. I traced my finger on her upper lip and rubbed it right ward to clean bubbles.

Next Moment, she beamed at me. There was glint of teasing in her eyes.

"Damboo...," I mocked at her, and wiped my finger on her purple barred shoulder top.

"You idiot, you collapsed my new top. You____," she agitated, and got up furiously to hit me. But abruptly she stopped. She picked her bag and turned around to leave.

"Hey! What happened? Where are you going?" I squeezed her hand to stop her.

"Your friends are coming. You should have fun with them,"

she said and I followed Ruhi's gaze towards Rohan and Ashvini, coming to us.

"Ruhi, don't be so rude. You should talk to them at least. They are so good," I said.

"No, I hate people, I don't want friends," she tried to free her hand, but I didn't leave her hand. And they approached to us.

"Hey! Shourya," Ashvini gave me hi-fi.

"Rohan, Ashu meet Ruhi," I introduced Ruhi with smile. But they all three were so rude.

"Who don't know her? The cat girl of college," Rohan grumbled.

"What did you say," Ruhi said heatedly. Immediately I pleaded to Ashvini to handle them.

"Shut up Rohan," Ashvini scolded Rohan, "you can't like this to my friend," Ashvini chucked under Ruhi's chin.

"Ashvini, you don't know one day he called me bitch," Ruhi complained to Ashvini like a kid.

"Now you don't worry Ruhi, we both will screw him," Ashvini armed Ruhi.

"Ashvini, I just want to slap him once," Ruhi grinded her teeth and glared Rohan.

"Just touch me, and I will show you," Rohan frowned furiously. They were close to kill each other. I got fear, but Ashvini controlled them cleverly.

"Ruhi, you can slap him anytime, but right now I have some doubts about today's class, will you help me" Ashvini held Ruhi's hand and left. Rohan was like statue, he was baffled. He didn't get, what just happened?

"Coffee?" I sneered at Rohan.

****

CHAPTER FIFTH

Next day We all went to a restaurant to mark the memory of our first treat paid by Ruhi. Though I fail to recall how much efforts I did to convince Ruhi to be in our gang. We enjoyed a lot, we fought hard, but we had started loving each other soon. Rohan was an extrovert personality. He could easily adjust with anyone. He always is ready to help other like an altruist. But he was a strong and aggressive man too. He didn't fear of anyone. Although, he wouldn't trouble people, but if someone would hurt him. Then he would collapse him. He was a gold-hearted man, he could die for me, and he could fight for me with anyone. And because of his such good qualities, God had given him a precious gift, Ashvini. She was a sweet and simple girl. She was so kind to other. She cared for us a lot. And she would always effort to bring smile on other's face. For her, her friends were her life. She would love Rohan a lot and they both would love and respect each other. And they both would always trust me blindly. They only cared for me.

Now we had Ruhi too in our gang. I couldn't figure out her character. She was so much different from others. She was an introvert personality. She would always remain in silence. She would talk only sincere, and matured. Very soon, she had become boss of our gang. She was so much more intelligent than all of us. She was so much close to me, I really found a familiar relation with her. She would always care for me. She knew what was good and bad for me. But I could realize that she was in pain. She was hiding a big secret from all of us. Although, she always pretended as if she was so much harder and stronger, but I knew she had a fake smile. There was so much grief, she had buried in her heart. I knew there was more that she held deeper and closer to her heart, and I wanted badly to uncover her secrets.

Although, I couldn't read her silent face, but could conclude that, she might had a worst past, which had destroyed her, which made her feared of people, so that's why she wanted to look harder, to save herself from evil and betrayed people. She had lost her faith in love, emotions, and relations. I thought she might has been cheated by someone, or it might be her family problems that forced her to be so isolated and afraid. She would laugh rarely. She became a living dead body. But I had decided that I have to give breathe to her dead body.

******

Finally, our gang was completed, and our friendship was at its zenith. We were so euphoric and blissful together. We would take care of each other. We would hang out together, we would go to movie together, we would eat together, and we would study together. We can't live without each other. And specially, I was so much fascinated with my friends. They were only my life, my dreams, my happiness, my sorrow.

Everyone would feel envy of our friendship. And many would try to collapse us. But it was our unity, our faith in each other that gave strength to our friendship. No one could touch us as we were together. We would always stand for each other at anytime.

But it was also true that we would fight a lot, and many times we would scratch each other's faces. But there was love too in our fight. Even God might be jealous of our friendship.

"Journal-557.

Life is kind of like a party. You invite a lot of people, some leave early, some stay all night, some laugh with you, some laugh at you, and some show up really late. But in the end, after the fun, there are a few who stay to help you clean up the mess. And most of the time, they aren't even the ones who made the mess. These people are your true friends in life.

Today Ashvini taught me a life lesion that if someone is trying hard to be your friend, hold their hand and never let them go. We don't meet people by accident. They are meant to cross our path for a reason. And If you have power to make someone happy, do it! The world needs more that.

People cross us to teach us, to makes us powerful, and to enlight us. We all are connected by that might power in the universe. Universe sends people in our life so that we can get on the right path.

People come in our life and take us to journey of their life and put examples of their life. Sometimes it good to take a break from our journey so that we can find path of our journey.

We are always in a journey, and that is the purpose of our life. And by that journey we fulfill the goal of universe. We are only a medium."

CHAPTER SIXTH

"You minion, you cheated me, it wasn't Ashvini's b'day," Ruhi said in aggression. We were sitting on 2nd bench of middle row. Raghav Sir was giving his boring lecture as usual. And half of class was snoozing as usual. I lied to Ruhi about Ashvini's birthday just to have treat from Ruhi on behalf of Ashvini.

"Hey! Idiot, actually you should thank me for that," I bellowed.

"Oh! Really, Shourya," she made weird face.

"Yeah, if I wouldn't have lied, then you wouldn't have come with us, and you wouldn't have got such good friends," I shrieked at her.

"Disgusting," she irritated, "you all boys are bloody dogs, I shouldn't have trusted you, you just get the hell away from my bench," she smacked. She hit on my head with by her book and pushed me.

"Are you stupid? You just can't stop fighting, you cat girl," I responded heatedly, "and you just get the hell away from my seat. It's my bench, I came here first," I pushed her grisly.

"How dare you hit me?" She spat out each word loudly. And she threw me down the bench forcedly. I got up, glared at Ruhi by flaming eyes. I threw her bag on floor. Her books, pens, her body lotion, her lipstick, face powder, and all the stuffs were ruffled under the table. I am shocked why girls carry their makeup kit in their bag instead of books. And whenever they get time, they get busy in doing their makeup. She snatched me by hair, and shook my head violently with both hands.

37

"Idiot, leave me," I groaned in pain and removed away her hands. But quickly she snatched my phone.

"Collect all my things in my bag fast, or I will destroy your phone," Ruhi snorted.

"Noooo, Ruhi, no, please, don't do that. I am doing," I exasperated, obeyed promptly, and went under the table to collect her things.

I was assembling her things under the table. At that Moment, I heard harsh clapping sound of running high heels towards our class room.

Whole class was waiting for those heels to enter into gate. And suddenly two legs strode inside the class. They were of girl. She was panting and walking inside. I could see only her legs as I was under the table. She had smooth, slippery hot legs done by yellow heels.

"Stop, how dare you enter into class?" Raghav Sir shouted angrily. And because of sudden shout of Raghav Sir, she froze for a Moment. Books and purse slipped down and scattered from hands of that feared girl.

And in next Moment, swiftly, she bent down on her knees to collect her books. I saw her light yellow skirt up to her knees. I don't know, But I really wanted to see her face. But her hairs were falling again and again over her face. I was amazed by her flossy, curly hair with hint of brown in them at the end.

"Gorgeous...," I whispered under the bench. She was collecting her books by her soft, milky hands. Her skin was glittering like sun. Her little-little cute fingers, polished by yellow nail paint, were trembling in nervousness and fear.

I was peering at her sleeveless white transparent top. But I couldn't see her face. I wanted to remove away her lock of hairs, which was disturbing her. She shook her head vehemently, her hair tickling her nose. She pushed the hair back from her face and tucked it behind her ear. Her fingers were still behind her ear. She kept collecting things by one hand.

I don't know, what happened in me. Something was wrong with me. My heart started beating high. She was appearing so much special to me. I just wanted to know her, without any reason. I had a feeling that something was wrong with me.

She just pushed away lock of hairs by finger and I was near to capture glance her. But she got up hastily. "Shit...." I muttered under my breath.

There was something that was connecting me with her. I got under the table just to have one look of that pretty woman. But Ruhi again pressed my head under the table.

"Do it fast or I will destroy your phone," she snapped.

"Sorry Sir," that girl whispered.

"Oh! God, you killed me," I mused as I heard her soft melodious voice. My heart was yearning to get her just single glimpse. It was for the first time that I was getting so much attracted towards a girl.

"You are late, you can't sit for today," Raghav Sir said rudely

"Sir please. It's my first day. And I was stuck in traffic, so I got late," she pleaded in sweet and low tone like an innocent girl. I felt like someone had poured honey in my ears.

"That's not my problem. You are late and you can't get in," Raghav Sir said in piercing voice.

"Sir please," she said, choking on her words. But Raghav Sir interrupted, "just get out of my class." I could hear she muttered something abusing to Raghav Sir and she turned around rudely to leave. At that Moment, I really wanted to chap Raghav Sir. But I had to see her first. I got up under the table and shoved my books in my bag.

"Hey! What are you doing?" Ruhi shrugged as Raghav Sir turned to board. Slowly, slowly without making any sound I started walking out. But Sir caught me.

"Hey! Shourya, where are you going?" he asked and looked at me with pondering face. I too looked at him in bit of fear. Then I gave a jerk smile to him and ran away as fast as I could.

I was running to catch that girl. I passed through balcony and I saw that girl in yellow skirt white top yellow hair belt, her hairs were waving in air. She was going towards parking. I could see only her back Side. I ran through corridors while pushing everyone on my way. I jumped from stairs and collided with walls just for her glance. I don't know, why? I was doing such stupid. I was doing what my heart was saying to me. But before I could reach parking, she had already left.

****

CHAPTER SEVENTH

"Stop it, you idiot," Ruhi screeched on me, "it's enough now. You have asked 10times in 10 minutes about that unknown girl. Now I will kill either you or myself," she relented.
We all were in PUB late night. It was Saturday night, the night to which people come to PUB, to party whole night.

"Huh...?" I asked evenly, as I was not present there mentally.

"Nothing," Rohan frowned, "just go and get some vodka and squash for us."

I followed his order like robot, without any argument. The PUB was fully crowded, and decorated by dim blue, red and yellow lights, hanging from refer. Waiters were serving Beer and Vodka.
In one corner some couples were dating each other by wine. In other corner some professional employees were busy in their boring conversation of whole week office work.
The DJ was playing remix on jukebox at first floor and so many boys and girls were dancing there on ground floor, under the DJ. They all were dancing out of tune.
I was walking towards Beer bar and my mind and heart were still swimming in dreams of that pretty girl. I wondered briefly why that girl was still flashing in my eyes, in mind, and in my heart, but tried not to think about it.

And quickly, I collided with a drunk man. And so he pushed me back aggressively. I lost my balance. And I was just trying to hold myself, but by mistake I put my next step on a skate. I don't know, why and who the hell had brought that skate in PUB. And I started wobbling on skate, and that bloody skate started moving speedily. I was waving my hands like wings of bi rd. I stretched my arms to break my fall.

Suddenly, I looked at my front. There was a girl standing at a distance. She wore a half blue and white pencil skirt, half blue and white sleeveless top. She had put a pretty brown leather jacket on her. I was facing her back.

I realized that I was too close to strike with her.

"Yeppieee....., I will have pleasure of falling over a hot girl...," it was the first thing that popped in my evil head.

Impulsively, my heart revolted against my head__ "Noooo...., move away....... move away......no.. no.... no...," I was shouting. But she didn't hear me.

"Fuck...," I sighed and closed my eyes, and surrendered myself to collide with her.

In next second, I fell down with her. But for few seconds, I couldn't feel myself. Then what happened next with me was unbelievable.

That girl and I were completely lying on floor. I was all over her. My one hand was on her barred, thin and soft waist. My other hand was on her right shoulder. I opened my eyes in slowly. And I found my face too much close to her sparkling face.

I was shocked when I saw her. "Heaven," I could whisper only when I gazed at her big brownish eyes. I was swimming in her alcoholic brown eyes. I was mesmerizing by her beauty or heavenly beauty.

Something weird and unusual started happening with me. I never sensed like that. She smelled familiar to me.

When I observed her thin eyebrows and glowing face, at that Moment, a cool wind started blowing faster. Whole world around me went silent and motionless.

The DJ, dancers, waiters, couples, drunker, and everyone became statue. And in next second everything started disappearing. I could see only that pretty girl.

And suddenly, flowers, roses, and butterflies started revolving around us. A soft and romantic music started to play in my ears.

My heart started beating so faster while making loud noise that was giving a good rhythm to that soft music.

I was looking into her brown eyes, and she was too gazing into my eyes innocently. She blinked her eyes quickly thrice in surprise or may be in shock. But I didn't blink once. I didn't want to miss a single second to praise her beauty.

Her face was glittering even more brighter than diamond. She vamped me by her charm. I don't know anything but she was giving me so much peace. I found her so much special that in few seconds, I gave her my life, my dreams, my happiness and everything to her. I didn't want to get up. I wanted to spend my whole life in her arms. I would like to die just for single glimpse of her pretty face. I decided to fight from whole world only for her. One glance of her took away all my pain and remorse.

She gave me the reason to smile for my whole life. She gave breathe to my dead body. She was the girl I was made for.

We both started breathing heavily, and panting. Our breaths were merging into each other's. I felt a sweet fragrance of her breathes. We both felt so much seduced by each other. I went more close to her, and noticed her lips. She had hot and juicy lips, done with red lipstick. They were getting more sexy and seducing by drops of squash on them.

I was getting out of control. And she was too. We both were seduced. I tucked a strand of hair that had fallen on her face behind her ear. I rested my palm on her right cheek, and rubbed my thumb on her cheek. I could feel her breathe were getting louder, my own heart was pondering inSide me.

I went close to her parted lips, I lingered just above her lips for a second, looking at her, and then let my lips touch her. I moved them gently, holding her lips between mine, pulling in before releasing. My lips felt the drop of vodka sticking to her lips. She closed her eyes. She was breathing faster now, shivering lips. We went for another short kiss I sucked her upper lip twice. She put her one hand on my left cheek and rubbed it. And she smooched tightly my lower lip, pressing my head more cruelly towards her. I felt weightless, and my arms were stretching. I was almost close to fly.

But in next second, she got sensed. She opened her big brown eyes. My lips were still on her. She glared me and pushed me aside aggressively. And we got up.

"How dare you touch me? You fucking bastard?" she held me by collar. And she burst into shout. She was furious and I was silent, lost in the world of love. I checked her from toe to head. She was looking like fairy in that blue and white short dress.

Her curly and brown hairs, at the end were flying in slow motion. She was continuously pushing them away by her blue nailed fingers. I could saw many butterflies revolving around her, to offer crown to her. It started showering of red rose on her. Little-little stars started twinkling to praise her.
And moon shrouded itself by clouds, as he was feeling jealous of beauty of that fairy girl.

She was squealing and fuming at me, but I couldn't listen her, I could see her lip sing in slow motion. And I was smiling at her like jerk, when she was scolding me.
She narrowed her eyes in irritation, she pushed me by her both hands. I stretched my arms, and started falling back in slow motion. Instantly, Rohan held me. Some girls stopped that girl from hitting me by her heels.
My friends anyhow solved the matter and took me in a corner and they showered their anger on me.
"Are you mad? What you did?" they shouted. But I was still giggling surreptitiously. I could still sense her soft lips on mine.
"Do you know? Who is she?" Ruhi frowned, "she is our classmate, she is that girl, you were asking about," Ruhi blew a fuse.
"What? She____," I freaked out but I stopped, as I noticed a soft hand on my shoulder. I turned around, and shocked. She was that girl to whom I kissed few minutes ago. I skipped a heartbeat, as I saw her.

"Excuse me! Actually I want to say sorry to you," she said in low tone, "actually it was an accident. You didn't do it deliberately. But I over reacted to you. I shouldn't have done that, I insulted you. Please forgive me", she regretted and looked in my eyes.

I couldn't get what she was saying? And what was in her mind?

"Can you come with me please? I want to correct my mistake," she said and held my hand in her soft hand. She pulled me away towards her friends. I couldn't protest her. Actually who the hell don't want to go with a girl in PUB. And if anyone don't, then he is an idiot.

She took me to her evil friends and introduced me. Then they all poured so many shots of vodka in my mouth. I still couldn't protest, I was drinking without any protest. Although I had realized that, they were with eyes of devil. But I wanted to see that what they will do with me?

So again and again they forced me to drink.

And in few minutes, I was tanked. My head was spinning. I couldn't recognize anyone's face. But I noticed that they were punching me kicking me, slapping me by their sharp nailed hands. The last punch was of that pretty girl. And I was on floor. After that, I don't know what happened to me.

****

CHAPTER EIGHT

Next day, when I opened my eyes, I found myself on my bed.

"Uth gyi meri jaan," Rohan spoke mischievously, and jumped all over me, and kissed me.

"What happened last night?" I mumbled, rubbing my eyelash like a kid, and my eyes on him again, "how did I come here?" I asked and pushed him away. But he again got over me, and looked into my eyes.

"Last night, you slept with me," and Rohan burst into laugh himself.

"Bastard," I said sternly, and kicked him out of my bed.

Then in a second, I noticed a guy sitting on Rohan's bed. I looked at him by squinted eyes. Then I raised my eyebrows to Rohan and shrugged.

"Oh yeah!" Rohan got up and went to that guy, "Shourya, he is our new roommate Sidharth," Rohan put his hands on shoulder of Sidharth.

"Hey!" I smiled to him. He looked nervous. Sidharth was an idyllic, decent boy. And he was too cute to live on earth. Anyone could easily cheat him, as he was from backward village near Allahabad. He was in black shirt, grey trouser. And he had put a red jersey on his black shirt. His hairs were done like an innocent school going child. But he was a tough guy. He had such strong muscles and body. But by heart, he was too weak, he was like a saint, and would live an ascetic life. He was shy but a good human being and best ever friend of mine.

"Sucks, my head is bursting," I grinded my teeth and held my head tightly.
I was in hangover of last night over drunk.

And my face, jaw and teeth were paining, because of last night punches by the hands of that pretty girl. I leaned forward and rested my head on my table, and closed my eyes to lost in dreams of that girl.

Then few minutes later, I heard clattering sound of high heels, running towards my room. And instantly, someone pushed door by hard force, so it collided with wall, made a harsh noise.

Rohan and I, we both looked at gate in shock, Sidharth was already in washroom.

And we caught Ruhi and Ashvini at the gate. *'How could they enter into boys' hostel?'* I started talking to myself in a very low murmur. And all of a sudden, whole boys hostel was wandering outside of my room, and they started checking out Ruhi and Ashvini. And many of the idiots, leaned against the my gate, so Ruhi kicked the door on their faces to give a smack.

"Damn it. You scared me. And what are you doing here?" I asked, increasing size of my eyes. But they dodged my question, and rushed to me, sat by each Side of me, and they started teasing me.

"Thank God, you are alive Shourya," Ashvini said in fear or I should say in teasing way.
I dug my head on my table again. They were giggling and making fun of me about last night humiliation..

"You don't know Shourya, we were so much scared last night. Even I had lost my hope that you will not survive anymore," Ruhi sneered, and held my chin and made to look at her.

"Yeah... you are right Ruhi," Ashvini surprised, "But I am still in shock that how could he survive. Let me check your pulses Shourya," Ashvini pressed my wrist and winked at Ruhi.

"Ashu, look at these marks, how cruelly those bitches ruined our Shourya's face," Rohan put salt on my pain.

"Ohhh..," Ruhi buzzed, "is it hurting Shourya?" Ruhi whispered and chuck under my chin.

I was getting so much irritated and I was close to lose my temper and to burst out on those morons.

"Shhhh...," Ashvini threw away, "are you mad Ruhi? How can it hurt Shourya. These are marks of first love. And that girl is first love of our Shourya," Ashvini shrieked and patted my back.

"Guys... you don't know, Shourya was going to kill that girl. But I stopped him. So don't think that our Shourya is a coward ok. He is so brave. Although he has been beaten by girls but he isn't a coward," Rohan taunted again and again on me.

Now I couldn't control anymore, I banged my desk cruelly.

'Stop it right now or I will kill all of you," I shouted grumpily. They all feared but looked at me still giggling. "And get lost from here you fools," I exasperated, and let out a frustrated sigh. Briskly all three of them rushed away, and sat on Rohan's bed. They glared at me and I too for few seconds.

"Seriously, you're scaring me now, kutteee," Ruhi cringed. Then, they ignored me.
Ruhi and Ashvini opened laptop, which they had brought with them.

"Ruhi, look at her, she is so pretty," Ashvini excited in happiness. They were talking about that girl, to whom I kissed and again started torturing me.

"Yeah....., Ashu, she is gorgeous. Just look at her. She is alluring in this yellow outfit," Ruhi said and they both kept stealing eye on me. I too peered at them from the corner of my eye.

"Ruhi see here is her name. OH! GOD HER NAME IS MORE PRETTY THAN HER," Rohan said and looked at me. They were provoking me, and I was dying to see her. I couldn't help and I surrendered to them and strode hastily.
"Show me, show me, guyss.....," I excited and tried to glance into laptop.

"No, no, why you came here? You wanted us to get lost. Now you get lost, I will not show you," Ruhi and Ashvini showered angrily on me, and hided laptop from my eyes.

"Maaf kr de meri maa....," I begged to them. But Ruhi closed the laptop, clutched close to her chest. Now I had to snatch it. I held it, and tried to snatch it from Ruhi. But she had completely got over the laptop, and Ashvini defended Ruhi while pulling me aSide. But I grabbed Ruhi by her big braid and threw away. And finally, I got the Lapi, and ran to my bed.

"Kaminaaa....," they muttered. Ruhi and Ashvinni had already found that girl on facebook. How easy and exciting it is that we can find anyone on facebook. Thanks to Mark Zuckerberg for Facebook

"Oh God....!" I stopped abruptly and sighed, "She is bewitching," I whispered while taking pause at each word. She was so pretty in those pictures.

Ruhi came and put her arms firmly around me from behind.

"She is charming, just like a fairy," Ruhi whispered in smile, and leaned against my back.

"Hmm..," I nodded and smiled at her.

"And her name is, "Aahna. Aahna Kapoor." Ruhi said.

"Aahna....," i pronounced it again and again. I was feeling heavenly peace only in her name.

"Ok, now you get lost, leave me alone with my love," I snorted to her.

"So mean haa, Shourya," irritated, but she kissed my cheek and stamped towards gate. And at that instant Sidharth came out of washroom, and they both stroked harshly.

"Aaaauuuuuchhhhh...," Ruhi fumbled holding her head and she was close to fume but she remained with parted mouth as she met to Sidharth's eyes. They gazed at each other they looked at each other in caress. They were lost in each other. And soon their faces turned into red and then pink, the sign of love.

"Oh shit....," I got down, and went close to them, "she is blushing," I froze at the mid-sentence at the expression on Ruhi's face. Ashvini pulled me aside. And we observed Sidharth and Ruhi carefully.

I couldn't believe my eyes, I never saw such expression, and emotion on Ruhi's face before.

Ruhi was a strong and a girl with attitude, no one could affect her. But today when she stroked with Sidharth, she started shying she explored all the qualities of womanhood. There was love and feelings on her face only for Sidharth.

They were looking into each other's eyes silently. There was a creepy and stupid smile on their faces. Even I could hear their heartbeats, which were going faster and faster.

I found definition of true love on their faces. And I was so glad that, finally my little Ruhi had found someone, who would give her love, life, and her smile back. Someone, who would care and save her from all the evil. Sidharth had also felt so much love for Ruhi. I saw honesty on his face for Ruhi, and that was the only thing that forced Ruhi to believe in Sidharth.

A girl just wants love and respect from a boy. Suddenly, Rohan dropped a glass to break their love.

"Huh?" Ruhi hesitated; totally unaware of what was happening with her.

"Ruhi, he is Sidharth, our new roommate," I just opened my mouth, but Ruhi held Ashvini's hand, turned around and shuffled away without giving me a chance to speak.

****

CHAPTER NINE

It was cold night of Sunday. I was sitting on edge of hostel roof, completely soaked in emptiness of campus. I was swimming in thoughts of Aahna. I was smiling stupidly, while looking at the stars and moon, shining in dark night, clutching my diary close to my heart. {I was figuring out the brighter one stars, and trying to sketch images by the scattering smog. All I was doing was just stupid. And that's because I have fallen in love, I guess.

I was feeling so much loved. Although I didn't know much or anything about love, and what I knew, was that, love is so special and so pure form of relationship that exists on earth.

Love is the precious gift to humankind by God. Love is a best way to worship God. One can easily find God, only by spreading love. And the true lovers or one who is in love is blessed by God. Only love makes us realize that we all are good in same way. Love is a lovely place to find ourselves.

I saw people defining love in different ways. But I personally muse that love has no definition. Actually there is no need to define love. Love has no mean. And the love which has a mean, then for me it's not a true love. Love is just a feeling, a special feeling, we feel when someone special in our front. Love is that peace, and glad that we observe when our lover hold our hand and smile at us.

Love has no place for demands, conditions, and proof. Love just needs a trust, a caring and a faith in each other. Love is something that goes beyond the existing world. We cross all the limits in love. Love is the feeling of craziness. We smile like an idiot while remembering our beloved and Moments we have with her. We behave like mad and do all the creepy and crazy things with our beloved, just to make her laugh. Love is about the comfort that she and we feel with each other.

We are always ready to die for her. But I think that love is not about to die for her. It's about that how much good time we spend with her.

We wait for hours, just for her single glimpse. And when she comes in our front, our heart started breathing faster. We walk miles, while holding hands of our beloved. We don't care for other, we just want to spend our whole life in our beloved's arms.

Actually, love is something so much strange. How ominous and unusual it is that suddenly we strike with someone stranger and in next second we give our everything to that stranger.

Instantly, we start liking that person even when, we don't know anything about that person.
We love her or him blindly, without caring about anyone and anything.

But I want to add that, if we start loving someone blindly, then just love him or her blindly for whole of your life.

We shouldn't open our eyes. As if we open our eyes, we would start thinking, judging and doubting him or her. And it will lead to distrust and hatred. So it is good to love someone with closed or blind eyes.

People always say that love has both negative and positive Sides. But I wonder that love has only one Side, the good Side, the positive Side.

Love never leads towards destruction, it is we, the human being who lead love towards destruction love lead us towards only progress. Love is combination of two pure souls.

I was also feeling same for Aahna. I found her, so much pure hearted. On that whole day, I kept my eyes on Aahna's pics. I couldn't realize the world around me. In such sort time, Aahna became my world. She meant a lot for me. She became reason for my happiness and for my sorrow too.

She was my soul, and she was my body. She was my heart, and

she was my beat. She would make me feel alive. I was still thinking about her, her face was not getting away from my eyes.

Sudden, I realized a hand on my shoulder. I turned around. They were Rohan and Sidharth. They sat by my each Side, on the edge of roof.

"What are you doing here, alone?" Rohan asked and forwarded beer bottle to me.

"Aaj mood nhi hai yaar," I shook my head.

"Thinking about Aahna?" Rohan asked mildly and looked into my eyes.

"Yup," I nodded, and blushed.

"Yehhhh.....," Rohan put his hand on my shoulder, "launda sudhar gya, sachha pyaar ho gya launde ko," he laughed with Sidharth.

"May be or not, still confuse," I said, and looked down towards courtyard, "you were right Rohan, love is so much special and complicated too. I am not getting over of Aahna. She has completely captured my mind. I can't concentrate on anything, except her. I am getting mad dude," I elaborate.

"Huh?" Rohan narrowed his eyes.

"I mean how smart she is. How easily she hit me last night, and I couldn't do anything except smiling," I smiled to him again, "I always wanted such girl."

"Hmm... hmm.. I can see what you wanted?" Rohan shrieked, "it is just a beginning my boy, you have to suffer a lot. I am seeing you turning into a helpless dog. If you love deeply, you're going to get hurt badly. But it's still worth it," Rohan talked like philosopher, and then they both burst into laugh.

"Why are you laughing idiot? We know what you did to Ruhi?" I snapped to Sidharth. And he got scared, as I talked about Ruhi. I cocked my eye to Rohan, and we started ragging Sidharth.

"What you mean?" Sidharth's eyebrows burrowed together to form a mountain between his eyes.

"Don't play smart, we have seen everything, you were checking out Ruhi from whole day," Rohan smacked him back.

"No, no, bhai... it's not like that," Sidharth surrendered, he was gasping in cold feet.

"How dare you glare my friend? I will kill you, and throw you down," I flamed at him.

"Sorry, sorry, guys. Please forgive me. I will not show my face to her again," Sidharth pleaded like thief, who had been caught by police. Rohan and I looked at each other and turned into evil laughter, and patting Sidharth. His eyes were wet.

"Relax dude, it's ok, we are just torturing you," I said, and laugh again. Sidharth was almost nearby to cry. I could detect a tinge of tears in his eyes.

"Dude, we have no problem, if you stare Ruhi, we know you like her," Rohan laughed.

"No, no, I don't," Sidharth blushed. I smothered Sidharth hand in mine.

"Look Sidharth, I don't know what you feel for Ruhi. But I want to add that Ruhi is so different from other. She is so deep-rooted person. She is much more than a friend for me. She is my life. She is a pure soul, but she is in pain. But today when she faced you, there was a peace on her face. So, I think she needs you. So I will be so happy, if you will be with her. Sidharth, life is too short to worry about stupid things. Have fun. Fall in love. Regret nothing and don't let people bring you down," I said emotionally. Sidharth looked down, he couldn't speak a word. He dared to look up, mostly out of nervousness. I tried to figure out his face, was with blank expression. I freed his hand and turned away.

"Shourya, I like her too," Sidharth said in calm and composed voice, and shied, he turned his eyes away from us.

"We knew it bastard," Rohan hit Sidharth, and then armed him, "ye launda bhi gya kaam se," Rohan again hit Sidharth and laughed.

"Sidharth," I again whispered and held, squeezed his hand, "promise me, you will not cheat her ever. You will take care of her, and you will not leave her at any cost," I looked at him in expectations.

"I will never leave her alone. I promise to you Shourya," Sidharth squeezed my both hands. And I pulled him in a warm and faithful hug. I patted his head.
Suddenly Yash strode unsteadily towards us. He was wobbling, as he was fully drunk.

"You bastard, you cheater, she is mine. I love her deeply from one month. I will kill you if you ever looked at her," Yash shouted in funny voice. Rohan and I grabbed Yash by his neck.

"Sidharth he is all yours, you can throw him down right now," Rohan frowned.

"No, no, leave him guys. He is my GOLU MOLU sa friend," Sidharth held Yash's face in his palms, "and Yash don't worry, Ruhi is yours only," Sidharth said.
Suddenly Yash's expression changed, he starred Sidharth with big eyes. And he pulled him into his chest,

"Dil jeet liya bhai tune. Ruhi is all yours only," Yash whispered, Still wobbling. And then kissed Sidharth's cheek.

"Bas kr pgle, ab rulayega kya," Sidharth patted Yash's back and giggled.
Rohan and I sneered at Yash. He hit my head.

"Laugh, laugh, idiot but soon you will cry," Yash said.

"Huh?" I asked to him, completely startled.

"Aahna's Dad is an MLA, HE WILL KILL you, if you even looked at her," Yash shrieked.

"No, he can't, he has to kill me before Shourya," Sidharth looked at me. I was so much touched by his words.

"I love you Bhai... tu hi mera sachha dost hai," I said and kissed Sidharth. And we all cheered up for Sidharth.

It's queerer that often most of the important conversation starts with the bottle of beer; a bottle of beer gulps out every bullshit emotions that we boys hide deep in our heart from our friends. So i am telling you just don't drink with your best friends as sometimes it's dangerous too, as we might vomit some big secrets to our friends.

"Journal- 558

I think I am in love. It's my first experience, and guess what? It's so cool. I think I am changing myself. I can't write my feelings right now.
Hey! Aahna, this is first time I am writing for you. And now I will write only because you exist.
Aahna, I like you. And the reason why I like you?
There is no reason. There should be no reason. If you love someone because of a reason, when that reason is gone, your heart will change too.
I like you without a reason. I like you because you are you.
Aahna, the one time the writer in me fell short of words was the one time I saw you.
And your smile is much sweeter than a box of chocolates.
Your eyes say more than your lips even could and your hands touch part of me I didn't know existed.
Aahna, I will love you in all of the way you should have always been loved, I will love you."

CHAPTER TEN

That whole night, lying on my bed, I went over the whole Moments with Aahna. I could still feel her hands on my neck and her lips on mine. Though, marks of her lipstick had been vanished. Thank god, she didn't use too much lipstick. It was next morning, a beautiful morning as I dreamt of Aahna whole night. I got up so early and got ready for college. I was so excited jubilant, as I was going to see Aahna.

Rohan and Sidharth were still fighting for the common blanket in their sleep. I felt pity for the poor blanket that was being pulled here and there so often. They were looking so cute in sleep. I couldn't resist to indulge between both of them. I jumped over them.

"Fuck you Shourya..," the only sound I could hear of Rohan and Sidharth.

"Get up bastards, it's too late. I am leaving for college," I bellowed and kicked both of them out of bed. However, they had no trouble falling asleep again. I strode towards college 30 minutes early. I was waiting for her in corridor near balcony of our classroom.

"Shhh....," I muttered as time was running so fast. Everyone had already got seated in class. And I was still waiting for her. But there was no sign of Aahna.

"Shourya, last time we are asking. Are you coming or not?" Ruhi and Rohan screamed at me. But I didn't respond, I was looking on the way for her.

"Go to hell," Ruhi stormed, kicked on my foot and they left for class.

"Aaaauuuchhhh.., it's hurting you silly girl," I cried, and I held my foot. After that, I saw Aahna entertaining into corridor with her two friends, holding books in one hand and cell phone in other.
She was looking damn cool and pretty in pink sleeveless top and white short skirt up to her knees. She had put yellow white hair band on her light browned hairs; they were waving furiously when she strode towards me.
She was moving slowly in white moccasin, making a clattering sound. She was glittering like moon of full night.

She was about to pass through me.

"Aahna, look he is that boy, we screwed last night," one of her friend whispered to her. And Aahna turned her face to me.

"Oh God save me," I mused, when I looked into her brownish eyes.

Therefore, I again fell in love, again lost myself in other world. Again cool wind started blowing very speedily. Again whole world around me started disappearing, and I could see only her.
She started walking towards me in slow motion. I was like flying in sky,

"Shourya, class is on," a boy said, shaking me out of my thoughts.

"Shit......," I whispered, and looked around fiercely, and hesitantly.

I saw Aahna passing through, and crossed me. She tried not to look at me as she walked, but found herself stealing glances. She moved her fingers on her hair and tucked a curl behind her ear and she smiled at me before entering into class room.

"Dazzling," I sounded with big eyes and opened mouth, "she has twin dimples," I said. I noticed her cute little-little dimples on her both cheeks. They really killed me. I was breathless; I leaned against the pillars, and smiled absurdly.

And I don't know, after how much time I got back in world existing nearby me. And I realized that i had to go to class. I ran towards class and again I was 20 minutes late.

"May I come in Sir?" I asked to Raghav Sir while panting.

Raghav Sir barked at me, "when will you come on right time, get inSide fast."

And as usual whole class giggled at me. But Aahna didn't. She was stealing her eyes from me.
She was sitting on 2nd bench of first row and I sat on 3rd bench of second row with Ruhi.
Raghav Sir, Aasha ma'am and other professor gave their drawling lectures. And whole class would listen to them while nodding.

But whole day I was looking and stealing glances at Aahna. She also kept stealing glance at me time to time. Many times our gaze struck with each other and at that Moment, we would turn away, cleverly, pretending innocent.

"Shourya, look at front, Ma'am is glaring you, and you will also take me out of class," Ruhi sniffed slowly while looking at front, and pinched my waist.

"Ummm?" I shrugged, innocently, lips twitched to one Side a hint of a smile.

"Nuts," she snapped and hit on my head.
During lunch break, Aahna and her friends went out towards canteen.

I planned something crazy. Actually it's Rohan's idea. I wrote a sorry letter and asked Ruhi and Ashvini to place it in Aahna's books, before her return back.

"Have you gone mad?" Ruhi glowered at me as if she wanted to eat me.

"Oyeeee...... Don't try to be my M'om ok. Just tell me whether you will do it or not," I glared at both of them.

"Aahna will kill both of us. I am still in fear of that night," Ashvini surrendered, stuck out her lower lip to Ruhi.

"Guys, please, please, maan jao meri matao.....," I pleaded, and emotionally blackmailed them.

"Ok, ok. I will," Ruhi muttered, forcing herself to sound

cheerful, "but if she says anything to me, then I will kill you. I swear," she exasperated and left, after pushing her long braid behind the shoulder.

After break, Aahna came back and took out her books, so that that letter slipped from book, and fell down on her lap. She took that card, and read a big sorry. She narrowed her eyes in suspense; she looked here and there with puzzling face. And quickly she caught me, she looked at me, i gestured to her that I had kept that card, and I held my ears, to say sorry to her.

She smiled at me, with her cute dimples. Her smile was glowing more and more prettier.

"Yeah...," I excited in victory, "she accepted my sorry," I shook Ruhi violently. However, nothing of that sort happened. But in next second Aahna gave a ridiculous smile to me. She tore that card into several small pieces, and she threw them towards me.

I looked at her with half opened mouth, flaming eyes. I was like statue, I didn't even blink. I was just looking at Aahna. And Aahna showed her soft fingers to me with aggressive look.

"HA... HA .. HA.. that's the spirit Aahna," Ruhi burst into evil laughter and now she shook me   violently, "you slay girl. I love you Aahna," she teased me.

So finally Aahna rolled water on my over excitement. Aahna and I had started off on the wrong foot.

Everyone was leaving for home. Aahna also shoved some books in bag, and some held in hand, and left out after giving a look to me. I couldn't let her go easily. I jumped out of bench, and rushed out to catch Aahna.

She scared as she noticed me. She clutched the books, she was holding closer to her chest, and she strode so briskly. Consequently, she stumbled with the staircase.

Books slipped from her hands. She stretched out her arms to break her fall, scraping her palms in the process. She was near to fall down, but hastily I held her hand in mine, and pulled her into my chest. I held her tightly in my arms. A sweet fragrance, I felt of her. I touched a strand falling over her eyes and pushed it back, letting my fingers linger in her hair. Her hair smelled so good.

But she pushed away me desperately. She glared at me, and in next second, she knelt down to gather her books.

I followed her, and picked up the last book, which she already had held. She eagled eye to me. She moped.

"Aahna, listen I'm sorry, I really hurt you-----," I was saying but she cuts me off.

"Don't follow me," she spat out each word like poison.
She snatched her book vengefully from my hands, and turned to leave.

"So cruel you are. What do you think of yourself? I just want to talk to you. And you have no right to do this to me," I smacked at her back.

She stopped her feet, and turned to me back.

"Ok fine. Lets meet me at star bucks cafe, at CP, at 5pm," she uttered softly and left.

In evening, I was so excited. I got ready with new black cotton shirt, navy blue jeans, so much perfume.
On the way, I bought a gift, some chocolates and red rose for Aahna.

At accurate 5pm, I entered into star bucks cafe. She was already sitting on table on in one corner. She was in light low sky blue jeans up to her knees, and a short sleeveless white t-shirt. She was busy in her iphone. Some locks of brown hair were falling on her face, but she didn't effort to push them away. She waved her hand to me "Hey!" and smiled with cute dimples. I strode and smiled at her. I slid in her front.

"This is for you." I said and forwarded that gift and rose to her. Instantly, two body builders stood by my Sides.

"Thank you," one of them said and took that rose and twisted it.

I looked at Aahna in confusion. I raised my eyebrows to her. And she gave a creepy smile to me.

And those guards picked me up like a ball and strode away from her.

She was giggling and waving her hand to me, making funny expression, "Bye-bye Shourya, have a good date. Take care," she sounded.

Those bastards took me in a dark room and screwed me.

****

CHAPTER ELEVAN

"How cruelly she hit you Shourya. Such an inhuman she is," Rohan said in bitter flavor, "fuck on you Aahna," he said hatefully, pushing a big bite of Malai kofta, today's special on the occasion birthday of hotel manager.

We all gathered in mess for dinner.

"Oyee....., mind your words, it's not Aahna's fault. Shourya is lattu for her. Shourya tortured her, so she revenged. That's it," Ruhi frowned, "and why do you eat like Janwar."

"Oh! Here you go," Rohan exasperated, and swallowed whole bite without chewing, "so you are showing care for that girl, you want to prove woman power and unity," he grumbled.

"What do you mean? And why are you shouting at me?" a frown creased on her forehead.

"Actually, you all girls are same. If a boy likes you, then you have a problem. And if a boy don't like you, then also you have a problem," Rohan shrieked.

"Shut up, you bastard," Ashvini said angrily to Rohan. Shidharth and i was looking at them in surprise. Although, we didn't says a word to girls. We didn't want to mess with those furious girls. We were in no mood to contemplate on it, so tried not to dwell on it. We concentrated on Malai Kofta. Rohan looked at Ashvini in hatred.

"Why should I shut up? You silly girls, you all very well know how to use a boy and then how to kick our ass?" Rohan banged the dining table angrily.

Suddenly Ruhi and Ashvini stood up hastily, banged on table aggressively.

"Now you are crossing your limit," Ashivini muttered, "I will shove your hand in your ass," Ashvini wasn't like that. She herself couldn't believe she actually said it aloud, but it slipped out before she could put a leash on her tongue.

"So what will do?" Rohan slammed, "you wanna hit me, come on hit me," Rohan snickered at them.
And in next second, all three of them got in fight and became abusive. Everyone turned to them, and enjoyed the fight.

"Hey you! Stop it or get out of here," mess In-charge shouted to them.

Ruhi and Ashvini grabbed Rohan's collar and dragged him out of mess. And then I was so feared of what I saw. Ruhi and Ashivini started hitting Rohan. They shook his hair violently, kicked him again by their sneakers. They grazed his face by their sharp nails.

Shidharth and I exchanged our gaze in alert. We were filled with dread. We didn't even say word in protest for Rohan, we didn't want to be hit by girls. Although I was already hit a lot by Aahna. Amid, Rohan escaped away from the evil girls. And Ruhi and Ashivini came back on table. And boys were starring at them in fear. And all girls were clapping for them in proud.

I couldn't stop my giggle at them, "shut up you absurd, or I will kill you too," Ruhi banged the table.

****

It was late night, and I was searching Rohan since hours. I went on terrace, and found him there. He was sitting on the edge of the roof. He was so much drunk.

"Rohan, what are you doing here? It's late night. Come on, let's sleep," I said, and put my hands on his back.

"Leave me alone on my own. I am just trying to cure my pain and frustration," Rohan shuttered, and removed away my hands.

"Rohan, don't be serious. They are our friends, it was just a masti...," I was saying, but he killed my words.

"Fuck on of such friends," he irritated, feeling disgruntled, "they insulted me on eyes of everyone, and you are defending them. Just get lost you also. You monster," Rohan again panicked at me.

"You are totally tanked, we will talk later," I said, but he again cuts me off.

"Oh! There is nothing to talk about this fucking bullshit," he laughed, and held me close to his drunken mouth, "you bastard, I was fighting for you, and you didn't save me, when they were hitting me," Rohan complained to me like a kid. I could barely control my laugh,

"Fuck......," I mused under my breathe, "you are right Rohan. I shouldn't have done this. Sorry bhai....., let's come with me, I will slap them in your front," I lied to Rohan to console him. But he was more fucking clever than me.

"No, first you come here, sit with me, and drink," he fumbled, firmly pulling me down towards him and made me to sit with him on edge, legs dangling. And in few minutes I was too drunk as shrunk like Rohan.

I saw Rohan was trying to climb up on short boundary wall of hostel roof.

"What the fuck, you are doing?" I howled, trying to hold Rohan.

"Shut up, and help me out," he whispered, almost inaudible. And in next second, he stood up unsteadily on that boundary wall. He was wobbling on that wall.

"RUHIIIIIIIIIII........," he shouted in queerer voice, sounding funny, "come out you bloody girl."

"Monster, why are you shouting? Rakesh Sir would fuck us. Just get down," I muttered, and hided myself behind that short wall.

"Just shut up man," Rohan glared at me, "bloody Rakesh is busy with girl's hostel warden. So don't trouble me now," he threatened me. He was holding bottle in one hand, grinding his jaw by other, and his eyes were red in toxicity.

"Fuck up," I buzzed and lay on roof like a panda.

"Ruhi...... where are you? You snotty girl," Rohan shouted, "come out, I will ruin you," he threw empty bottle on roof of girls hostel. And it's cracking sound broke sleep of every girl.
Ruhi, Ashvini and many other girls rushed out on their terrace.

"Rohan, what are you doing there? Get down, you will fall down," Ashvini cared for Rohan. That's the spirit of girl. She always cares for her love, even if she is fighting with her love.

"Fuck off, don't order me. You selfish girl, I will kill you," Rohan snapped while walking unsteadily on that wall.

"Disgusting, Rohan you so drunk, how could you?" Ruhi frowned, her eyes narrowed questioningly.

"Yeah! I am drunk," Rohan said proudly, "I am drunk because you made me to drink. You ruined my life. You egoist girl, you hit me in front of everyone. You made my jock but now I will take revenge," came the dreary response from Rohan.

"Fuck off," Ashvini grinded her teeth, "where the hell, Shourya and Sidharth?" Ashvini called out my name. And fleetly, I climbed on that wall with Rohan. As if I was doing my attendance in classroom.

"Hey! Guys, here I am. What's going on?" I waved my hands to all girls.

"IT's ridiculous, I can't believe Shourya, and you are drunk too. I didn't expect this," Ruhi and Ashvini said, while shacking their head and lips pursing.

"Oh! Shut up you cocky girl. What do you think of yourself? That you will beat us like dogs and we will not say a word," I shouted angrily and looked at dark sky. I gasped on my knees, collected myself and continued.

"You all girls are same. Aahna you are also so arrogant. Why did you hit me, just because I like you? Is there no mercy in this world for boys? Come answer me Aahna. Where are you? Answer me," I snapped out my frustration, while nodding. Suddenly, Sidharth and Yash ran to us. They grabbed us.

"I will kill you bastards. Such an embarrassing you are," Ruhi roared and threw her heels on Rohan and me.

"Shut up you morons, greedy girls. We will kill you. Why did you hit me? And why did she hit Shourya?" Rohan smacked.

"Because you deserve it, you fool." Ashvini snapped. She clenched her fist and hit on the other palm.

"Oh! Just shut up, you dizzy. I loved you a lot, but you hit me, because of influence of this bitch Ruhi. She brain washed you against me," Roahn frowned and eagled eye to Ruhi.

"Rohan, it's enough. Don't say a word against Ruhi," Ashvini hit back.
Sidharth was looking silently to us and then at Ruhi. He was feared that how vulgar and evil friends he had have got.
Although, he was trying to stop us but every time we would push him away. Bastard Yash was drinking our left beer.

"Oh! Not again," Rohan irritated, "again you want to show your bloody woman power. Ashvini you are leaving me for this idiot girl. Ok then, it's over now. I just want to get rid of you and your Ruhi," Rohan blabbered, words stumbling over each other to escape his lips.

"Really Rohan! I also want peace. And I want to get rid of you Ruhi," I shrieked absurdly.

"Come down and I will kill you by my own hands," Ruhi and Ashvini grinded their teeth and showed their nails to us.

"Yeah, it's time to action now. I will gauge your blood," I agitated.

"HA HA HA..," Rohan laughed like evil, "I will kill you all girls. Today I will collapse your woman power. You all use boys, you all are selfish, you all are bloody strumpet. Fuck-on-all of you," Rohan panicked and blurted out on every girl standing there.
I alerted him that he was over acting. It might cause us to pay hard. And yeah, it happened. Every girl on terrace started roaring like a hungry lioness. There occurred stampede in all girls.

"Come down. You coward, we will kill you," they shouted.

"You both just come down, I will happily see your body in blenders," Ashvini shouted.

"You all have gone today," Rohan leered. And we clumped unsteadily towards down stairs. Sidharth tried to stop us but we approached in courtyard of hostel. And we shouted and waited for Ruhi and Ashvini there.

Unexpectedly, we saw so many girls stumbled out of girls' hostel gate. They were armed with hockey, knife, sticks, stones, heels and other so many dangerous weapons.

I looked at Rohan, we both were so much frightened. A dead weight was stuck in my throat. Rohan and I padded back slowly. We looked concerned, ruffled, even frightened. It ruined our hangover.

"Bhaag, Shourya," Rohan louded, and we ran so fast to save our lives. We locked the hostel gate channel and we locked ourselves on terrace.

"Bal, bal bach gye yaar," I panted to Rohan and Sidharth.

All lionesses were roaring in courtyard, outSide of our channel gate.

"Ruhi this is cheating. We had thought that fight would be between you and me. That's not fair, the war should be equal," I shouted in fear and looked down to all girls.

"Oh really, you are so brave naa. What happened now?" Ashvini laughed.

"Ok Shourya, you just come down. I swear, no one will touch you except me. I can kill you alone," Ruhi thundered. She looked so furious.

Rohan and I looked at each other. And shook our head.

"Hey! Girls, we dropped our plan. We changed our mind. Now we will not kill you. We forgive all of you. Now you all go and sleep," Rohan and I said politely. Our voice was meek.

"You bastard, you coward, you will forgive us!" Ruhi laughed, "you just come down once, I will make your chatani by this hockey," Ruhi crumbled her teeth in pain.

And all girls started throwing their weapons to us. Many of them hit with us, so we had to hide ourselves. We lay down on roof. We were gasping. Rohan and I bit our tongue, realizing the mess we had created. And then suddenly we laughed out. Sidharth looked at me in fear.

"Shourya, sorry bhai. You are right. Ruhi is harpy. I can't love her. She would kill and eat me on our first day of love." Sidharth whispered in cold feet.
And we all again broke into boisterous laugh.

"Ok dude, don't mind. I will love her, I will bear your pain," Yash mumbled.

"Bastard, don't even dare to think about it," Sidharth smacked and got over Yash. Rohan and I jumped over them and we hit each other. I don't know when we got asleep.

******

"Journal-558

Sometimes I am scared of new things, I am scared of innovations, I am scared of new changes. I don't know why? But I feel that I would forget myself, the inner me in race of change. Even sometimes, I am scared of the truth that I was searching from years. So it's better to live in illusion of darkness. At least, that provide me moment of relax, and easiness. As I know if I would follow the truth, that would only bring storm. That would turn my life upside down. That would throw my life in the courtyard of struggle."

****

On following morning, we opened our eyes and found ourselves surrounded by so many boys. On that day, no one of us went to college. Rohan and I were so ashamed of last night.

I was feeling so embarrassing. I couldn't face Ruhi. I really had have hurt her. A part of me wanted to apologize to Ruhi and Ashvini, for what we had done last night.

But Sidharth forced me and Rohan to say sorry to our Ruhi

and Ashvini. Anyhow, we approached to them. They were sitting in hostel garden.

We went and lay our knees, held our ears and prayed to them. They would ignore and turned away and so on we would follow them.

"Ruhi.... sorry naa.. It's all because of that bloody beer. But we promise, we will never do that again. Please forgive us," we pleaded.

They didn't even give a look to us. We begged for half an hour and then sat silently to their feet.

Suddenly, I saw, Ruhi and Ashvini's eyes were shining with unshed tears. They looked very subdued. Ruhi's face was red and lips were trembling. She was biting her lower lip to keep from breaking down. She was green grass by her blue polished nails. She was letting out her frustration, anger on innocent grass. On the other hand, maybe it was giving her strength not to lose her tears, I guess. A hell of things scampered in my mind.

"Ruhi....," I heaved softly and touched her hands. And thereupon nimbly, she pulled me into her chest. And Ashvini hugged Rohan.

"Stupid, idiot, gadhe, you hurt me badly," she sobbed, "Please don't do this ever," Ruhi caress me and kissed my right cheek.

"Ruhi, it's all because of Aahna. I vented out her anger on you. But now I promise, I will not say her name. I hate her," I said.

"Shut up," she hit on my head.

"Huh?" I prodded.

"You absurd, are you mad? Why are doing this?" Ruhi held my palm, "I know you love her. And now we have only one mission. We have to complete your love story," Ruhi smiled.

"Yeeeeppppieeee.....," Rohan excited, while holding Ashvini, "it should be named as SHOURYAAHNA."

"I love you guys, you are my life," I was saying but they stopped me and we had group hug. Sometimes all you need is a warm hug from your best friends.

We all were so happy together. That was the best day of our friendship. No one could separate us. We had a strong faith in each other. For us our friendship was our God.

"Journal-559

Dear best friends,
you're stupid. You fail. You're weird. You're not perfect. But.
That's okay. I'm like that too. We laugh at the random things. You
know my ugliest Side. Even though we disagree at time and fight,
it never lasts long. When I'm sad, you were always there to make
me laugh. I thank you for that.
I love you.
Dear friends, friendship is strange. When we collect Moments and
tuck them into our soul, they never have a chance to rust. They
are preserved and pampered. They grow more magical with time,
until they cease to be a memory and take on an illumination that
is more perfect than when we placed it there for safe keeping. I
just want to collect so many such Moments with you, so please
allow me."

****

CHAPTER TWELVE

Aahna was not present from last one week. I was missing her badly. Every day I would go to college in hope that she would come. My eyes were thirsty for her single glance.

I reluctantly admitted to myself that I missed Aahna. I thought it was just an attraction but it was more than just an attraction.

On next day, again I would go to class in desire to see her.

I was sitting on my seat as usual with Ruhi. One by one everyone entered into class. And in everyone's face, I could see Aahna's glittering face.

And yes, suddenly, the real Aahna entered into class. She was dressed in sleeveless causal white outfit up to her knees. And there were so many yellow flowers on her white dress. She had white hair band with a white rose on her head. And her neck was decorated by thin golden chain, her right hand was glowing more with so many pink bangles, which were giving bristling sound. She was so magnificent. She sat hastily, on her place. My smile became more wider. I automatically fixed my eyes on her. She was gleaming in whole class. So her beauty enchanted me. My eyes were stuck at her. I felt like moon had come down on earth itself.

Raghav Sir started the lecture. She was looking into her book, and playing with her hair. She shoved her index finger in one of the brown curl, falling over her face, and kept twisting it unkindly.

"Oh! God...," I let out my tortured breathe and slumped back on my seat and inhaled heavily.

Immediately, she gossiped in her friend's ear. To that Moment, she turned around and again said something to her friend.

She was looking for me. So I threw my pens and pencils at her to get her attention. Although I had wasted 4pens and 3pencils but I missed every time. Now I had only a five star chocolate.

"Yeahhhh, I did this," I excited as my chocolate struck with her back. She picked the chocolate. Her head shot up, her eyes narrowed, as if searching for the fucking dog who threw that chocolate to her.

I waved my fingers and smiled. She looked stunned, she smiled, her lips barely stretching in a tight smile. And she smooched that chocolate slowly by her juicy pink lips.

"Damn it, you are taking my breath," I said after gazing at her pink dimples.

And our conversation began in signals. And it captured attention of many girls and boys.
But I don't care ever for other, that's the rule of my happy life.

She raised her brows of brownish eyes. At the end, she touched her right eye, left cheek and lips ad she pointed to me. In fact, she was talking about my injuries that she had given.

Then she made her fingers into sign of awesomeness. I looked with dull face at her.
So she smile and chuckled with twinkling dimples. I put my both hands on my heart, closed my eyes, slumped back on my seat, kept out my tongue.

"Aahhh....," I sighed. I said that she snatched my heart and killed me.
She glared at me with bigger eyes and ordered me to shut my mouth.

After two lectures, she rushed out of class.

"Go Shourya, talk to her now," Ruhi said. And I jumped out of class and followed her towards library.

She took out a book from bookshelves, and got herself on a

table in one corner. There was so much peace, and silence. Everyone was swimming in the books.

I too went towards queue of wardrobes, and took out a book from bookshelves. And I flopped down in the chair in her front on same table.

She shocked, when she looked up at me. I gave her a creepy smile like a fool. But she flamed at me, murmured something abusive, and flipped page of her book cruelly.

Since, last few minutes, we would do same irritating things. We would keep stealing glance at each other. Consequently, she would flip the pages harshly. I could barely keep the silly smile off my face and it was driving Aahna crazy.

Now it was over, so she closed her book with loud noise. She raised her eyebrows twice in manner of questioning to me. I also did the same to her.

"Ugh....," she groaned in frustration, while furrowing her eyebrows. She got up hastily, and hit my head by her book and whispered, "stupid."

She went to wardrobes to search another book. I followed her from others Side of bookshelves. And as she picked out a book from shelves, I appeared in her front with a stupid smile.

"Excuse me!" she sounded robotic, stretching, pressing, pausing at each word.

"Yeah..," I nodded, gleefully.

"You are not supposed to do this," Aahna said, clearly, pausing at each word, her voice was gruff.

"To do what?" I shrugged innocently.

"Idiot, don't mess with me. You don't know who I am? I would, I would____," she paused, "I would kill you," she snapped and broke the silence of the library.

"Hey! You both," librarian pointed at us, "get out of here, you fools," she said sternly.

"Fuck off," Aahna hissed at me, while grinding her teeth. She left the library and thus I followed her to canteen.

"Bhaiyya, one cold coffee please," she ordered.

"Bhaiyya not one, two coffees please for both of us," I said and smirked at Aahna.

"Go to hell, I don't want coffee, I hate coffee," Aahna strode towards garden.

I followed her while holding coffee in my both hands. Sometimes she would walk; sometimes she would run after glowing at me. Immediately, she stopped and turned to me.

"Why are you following me? What's your problem?" she asked, "I hit you twice and despite of that, you are torturing me. So come on please tell me, what you want?" she braced herself and pushed back her brown hair by her right hand, completely packed with pink bangles, which made jingling sound. Quickly, I lay down on my knees, joint my hands, "Aahna I want to do friendship with you. Please, please, please, give me a chance at least," I prayed to her like devotee to God

"Ok, ok calm down," she cackled, "but tell me first, why would I do friendship with you? What's special in you?" she quipped and raised her brows twice.

"Ummmm...," I mused and ruffled my hairs, "you tell me, what I should do for you?"

"Ok, let's have a game. You have to prove yourself better than me. You have to win by me in every field, in classroom, in the eyes of professors and in all other activities," she excited happily.

"Ok, done," I agreed to her and touched her feet, "bless me, so that I can win by you," I said.

"Tathasthuuuu, ghonchu....," she shrieked and ruffled my head softly, "God! I don't know why I am even talking to you," Aahna said, shaking her head and left.
But I again followed her.

"Now what?" she asked, inflamed.

"Nothing," I neglected her. I collided with her intentionally, so books slipped from her hands.

"Yehh.. I got one point," I laughed at her.

"Bastard, this is cheating," she stormed.

And there up our game began. We would fight to win in all spheres. Literally, we both were ambitious. We both wouldn't accept defeat. We fight hard to prove ourselves best in front of every professor.
I don't know until that why we were doing such crazy. We were not friends, neither enemy. And we were not lover too at all.

But I can mention only that there was something between us. There was cuteness, craziness, love and caring too in our fight.

Our relation had no name. And I knew she hated me. She wanted to kill me. But it's also true that she had found something unique, something special in me. That's why. She was connecting and coming closer to me. Although, she was getting attached to me by the way of fighting but it didn't matter. She was interested in me and that gave me peace and excitement to do for her.

I had already made my own interpretations that God wanted Aahna and me to be together, to come closer. God had fixed our destiny. So I knew that we had to meet at the end by any way and in any condition.

What so ever is happening around you is rooted in the mind. Mind is always the cause. It's the projector and outside there are only screens- we project ourselves.

****

"Where is Sid? Is he not coming?" Ruhi asked with concern. We all were going for movie.

"Oh my God!" I amazed. We all babbled.

"What?" Ruhi scared and assembled herself.

"What did you just say? You said Sid, on the place of Sidharth. When did it happen man?" Ashvini said, there was hint of teasing in her eyes.

"Excuse me!" she tried to be innocent, while raising her big black eyes.

"No, why should you?" Ashvini taunted her.

"What rubbish?" Ruhi frowned, arranged her long braid, "I said by mistake." She looked feared as if she had done a sin.

"Oh well, we all know your by mistake. Such a cute mistake," Ashvini and I quipped at Ruhi.

"Bastards, darn it, I shouldn't have talked to you about Sid," she snapped.

"Damn it, look at her. She is blushing pink," Rohan was inspecting her closely, trying to read her expression, "I don't believe this," Rohan burst into louder laugh.
And we all hugged out innocent girl Ruhi.

"Ok, ok I rest my keys," Ruhi threw her hands in surrender.

"By the way Sidharth____," I cleared my throat, "oh sorry, I mean Sid," I said and peered at Ruhi, "he is not coming."

"Ruhi, why don't you go and ask him. He will not say no to you," Ashvini uttered to Ruhi.

"Are you mad? No. Never. I can't," Ruhi waved her hands crazily.

"Ok then let's go. Why would we care for Sid?" Roahn taunted Ruhi, and we continued to prompt Ruhi.

"Ok, you morons, I am going," Ruhi smacked and went to Sid. He was lying in garden. But as Ruhi approached him, he got up hastily.
And in few seconds, we saw Ruhi and Sid coming back towards us. I was bumped, how easily Ruhi got him ready. This is all because of love. I genuinely saw power of love in them.

They were looking so cute together. Although, they wouldn't speak to each other but it were their eyes, which would speak and tell everything to each other.

77

Their shyness, their blushing, their honesty, their silence would speak much about them and their love.
They had pure and silent love, as they themselves were the pure souls.

They always loved each other without any commitment. They very well knew that, they had no destiny. Instead of that, they loved blindly. They knew they couldn't be together forever. Yet they loved and cherished each other for seemed like their small infinity.

It's not important that every love story should be completed. And if the love story which doesn't complete, then it doesn't mean that it's not a love story.

We should love someone without any expectations that he or she would also love us.

We should just wait. Love is also about that how much we can wait for someone.

And at last if we don't get our love, then also we shouldn't forget our love.

We should still love her for our whole life.

Love isn't about to get our lover. It's about to wait, to love, to have faith in her till our last breathe.

****

CHAPTER THIRTEEN

"And nd our battle went on. We troubled each other. We fought in mischievous ways like kids. Our classroom, canteen, library and garden were our battlefields.

Sometimes she would hit me and push me intentionally to make me fall down. Consequently, I would pinch her naked waist sometimes, and she would graze my face other times.

In whole college Aahna and Shourya were famous as funniest cartoon Tom and Jerry.
I was sitting on mid of the staircase with Rohan, Sid and other Matos.

Quickly, I saw Aahna coming down the staircase with her friends. She was so spectacular in black casual short sleeveless dress, which had a good floral work by red and blue flowers. And also a pink ribbon around her soft waistline.

And pink yellow scarf around her neck made her more classy.

Her curly brown hair at the ends, were waving as she stepped towards me.

At an instance, she noticed me. She waved her fingers to say hey!. And she smiled with her twinkling dimples.
I waved her back in slow motion and in under a spell of her heavenly beauty.

Unfairly, Aahna used to use her beauty as her weapon to seduce me to take my benefits. But I wasn't a lallu. I was bit of clever. I would always smack her back.

I stretched my legs to irritate her, to interrupt in her way.

She stopped her feet, gave creepy smile to me. I smirked back to her with a wider smile. But in next Moment, she kicked on my legs powerfully by her black heel.

"Aaaaaahhh....," I groaned in pain, held my ankles, "it's hurting dumboo," I snapped.
She crossed me while laughing aloud, "one more point."

I actually want to conclude that, whenever she would laugh, it looked like twinkling of stars. It always took away my pain, and I remained with peace only.

And that was the reason that, I was genuinely letting her win most of the times.
Because whenever she would win, she would enjoy her victory, she would fly; she would laugh at me loudly. She would be so happy. And that was only heaven I wanted. I wanted to see her happiness. My happiness, my victory was only in her.

Every time, when she would win, she would give me pleasure to see her cute dimples. She was knowing me more and more by her victory and my defeat.

Sometimes things that appear ridiculous at first are actually fabulous.

Next day, I was sitting on adjacent bench to her. It was Raghav Sir's lecture on sociology. Everyone was snoozing as usual. I leaned forward on my bench, resting my cheeks upon my hands, praising her beauty. As much I was trying to look away from her, more my eyes were sticking at her.
Sometimes, she would copy down from board. And sometimes, she would chew nib of her pen by her killing soft pink lips.

I gasped deeply, it really killed me.

Nimbly, she noticed that I was starring at her. She turned to me and knitted her brows twice. I pursed my lips and blew on an air kiss to her. She flamed at me in anger, mumbled something and the pointed me to look at front by her brownish eyes.

"So class, tell me. What is the definition of an idol society?" Raghav Sir asked and broke our romance.

Suddenly, whole class turned into statue. Half of class was sleeping; Raghav Sir's loud voice shook sleeping nuts out of their nap. We everyone was looking at each other's faces. Happiness drained out from our faces. Rohan tried to hide under the table. I beamed at Sir surreptitiously, not to meet his eyes.

"Such an embarrassing! No one can tell me," Sir said. He looked disappointed. Soon he turned red in anger, he reclined on his chair, threw marker on his desk, leaned back on his seat. And he gasped. He looked frazzled. His nose curled up as he took big breath. It was the only glint of life in him that I could see.

"Excuse me Sir," Aahna got up swiftly, "I have the answer," she said with attitude and gave a look to me. Rapidly, Raghav Sir got his breathe back.

"Very good. Go on," Sir smiled.

"Sir, a society is a social organization of human beings, where people come together to live with each other," Aahna said and braced herself.

"Good Aahna, at least some one is studying," Raghav Sir said. Aahan smiled proudly and showed me her thumb down.

"Excuse me Sir, I have more proper answer then her," I said loudly and glared at her.

"Excuse me! What did you say?" Aahan barked, "What do you mean by proper answer," she spat out each word clearly while pausing at each word.

"I mean that, you have just muttered, what is in book, like a rattu poppat," I sneered and whole class burst into laugh.

"What rubbish it is?" she irritated, "do you mean that books are wrong? Do you know more than books?" she bellowed and puffed me.

"Oh! Yeah!" I exasperated, "you just muttered definition. But you should have described the actual meaning of society. You silly," I quipped at her, "am I right class? Did you get, what she said?" I asked to whole class.

"Noooooo.....," everyone buzzed like bees.

"Shut up you dizzy. You vampire," she pounded her teeth.

"You bi___," I was saying but Sir chopped my words.

"Shut up, both of you," Raghav Sir thundered, banged his desk. We looked down, "Shourya go on your words."

"Sir as a matter of fact, Society shouldn't be described as an organization. As she did." I gasped and looked at Aahna. "Sir society is a mutual agreement of an organization, where people from variety of region comes together to share each others' cultures, principles, customs and languages.
Actually, society is a mutual integration of diverse cultures and distinct people. And when these people adjust themselves with each other, they share feelings of unity, brotherhood and kindness. There exists equality, respect and a name to every individual in society," I elaborated for 10 minutes and then sighed.

Raghav Sir and whole class shocked with parted lips. Even though, I was too shocked. I didn't know, I really know much more about society.
"Excellent! Brilliant! Unbelievable! I am proud of you my boy," Raghav Sir exasperated still in bit of shock.

Everyone clapped for me, except Aahna. She stood, sullenly. She irritated to me by showing her big sharp nails.

"Come here, Shourya," Sir said politely, "I want to bless you."

Quickly, I jumped off bench, and marched towards Sir. But cleverly, Aahna stretched her heel in my way. I stumbled with her leg. And I was near to fall down but I held myself and approached towards Sir, wobbling.

After class, I was walking through corridors. Immediately I noticed Aahna running towards me and collided with me brutally. I slipped down on floor.

"Hey! You dumboo..," I shouted. She turned back and picked her tongue out in funny way to taunt on me.

****

CHAPTER FORTEEN

The memories of Aahna were more sweet when they would awake me early in the morning. They would lit up my face so bright with the first ray of sunlight. I would miss her, and I would just want to do all the stuffs that I would ever wanted to do in all. I would smile in my bed, but my mind would travel back in all her moments to find out which one was sweetest. But I would fail hardly as each moment wouldn't get back to prove itself the sweetest. On next morning, I was walking through corridors. Abruptly Aahna and her friends stopped my way. She eagled eye at me. They girdled me from all Sides.

"Where is my scarf? Give it back to me," Aahna said furiously.

"Which scarf? What are you talking about?" I said innocently.

"My yellow scarf idiot," she smacked, "which you snatched yesterday evening. Now don't play smart with me. Give me my scarf, it's my favorite scarf," she hissed, and grabbed me by my collar.

"Are you kidding? I didn't do that. I don't know anything stuff," I said, "and you can't blame me. Do you have any proof?" I shrugged, wisely.

"You whelp. Fool yourself." she bristled, "I don't need a proof. Give me my scarf easily, otherwise I would chap you___," she showered angrily, pausing at each word. She grazed my face. I was threatened.

"Ok, ok relax, I surrender," I put my hands up, "but I could return it tomorrow, the scarf is at hostel," I gulped in dread.

"Fuck off," Aahna muttered, and threw me away. In quick Moment, I rushed away from them.
Suddenly, I stopped, and turned back to her.

"Aahna......," I shouted and picked out her scarf from my bag, I kissed it and waved to her.

"You monster, I will kill you," she pissed her teeth and ran to catch me.

Later, I was sitting in Raghav Sir's cabin with Ruhi and Sid.

As I had already succeeded to come into good books of Raghav Sir, so he treated me with special assignment, which was going to benefit my marks in exams.
So I was completing my assignment in that empty cabin.

Hurriedly, Aahna strode into that cabin. I could see her evil eyes in revenge. Therefore, I briskly covered my assignment by my arms, to save it from devil Aahna.

"Why did you come here? Just get out of here, don't come closer to me," I exasperated while collecting all my pages.

But immediately, she approached to me, and bent over me and waved her curly brown hair on my face. She started breathing heavily near my ears. I was getting enthused and seduced. My body started shivering.

"Aahna...." I whispered softly in her ears.

"Ummm..," she nodded and rubbed her soft cheeks on my cheeks and she kept panting on me.

"What are you doing? Leave me please," I mumbled. But she cradled my face in her palms and moved her fingers on my face softly, sensationally.

"Shourya...," she mumbled while panting, "Shourya.... actually, I want to say something to you," she whispered in sexy, seducing voice. Her lips however dangerously close to my ears. I couldn't protest her. I was rapt by her. And soon my body was frozen in that chair. A sensation ran into my body. I was excited furiously. My breathing got heaver. I realized a sense in my organs.

I harshly moved my hand in her hairs and rolled down on her shoulders.

"Shourya.... I was saying that I..., I..., I...." She mumbled in my ears, pausing after every 'I'. I nodded my head, just a trillionth of a fraction, even a slow motion camera wouldn't catch the Moment. And she held my face close to her, and gasped on my face. I was totally captured by her.

"Just close your eyes, Shourya...," she said and got up from my lap.

"Shouryaaaaaa.... Noooo..........," Ruhi shouted and stretched me out of her seduction.

Acute, I opened my eyes, and saw that Aahna took out a bottle from her bag and emptied it on my papers.

"Nooooooo....Aahnaaaaa," I hollered as loud as I could, echoed whole cabin, and rant to stop her. But she had already poured whole bottle on my assignment. And she ran out while laughing before i could catch her. I had to suffer a lot because of her lunacy. I was drying those papers in sun light sometimes, and in cool air sometimes.

Aahna approached to me with her friends.

"Ohoooooo... hooooo hooo! What happened Baby?" Aahna said in awkward sound, "oh baby ke paper gile ho gye, who did such evil to my shona," she teased me, chuck under my chin, and give a weird smile. Her smile pissed me off.

I pushed her hands away and glare at her with burning eyes.

"Oh! My God..., mele baby ko gussa aa rha hai...," she mumbled while doing a hard googly, pulling my both cheeks by her both cute fingers. I couldn't do anything, but bearing the torture of Aahna like statue.

****

85

CHAPTER FIFTEEN

"Good morning class, today I have something important," Raghav Sir stopped his words as we all fixed our eyes to him in fear, "don't give me such gawkily look, I am just talking about the matter of class representative." Sir exclaimed with thrill. It was first time that Raghav Sir's face turned into so many glows.

"Ooooooohhhhhh...," we all buzzed together, and exhaled.

"On keeping in mind your performance, I decided that Shourya Sharma would be the CR," Sir said excitingly.

Thereupon, whole class went into COMA. No one had expected that, even though I had never expected that. Everyone looked at me in envy.

"Come on guys, give him a big hand," Sir raised his brows and started clapping himself. Yes! My two idiots Ruhi and Rohan volunteered Raghav Sir. And then whole class clapped. They looked as if they didn't want to do that. It was like they all have awakened up through a worst nightmare.

"Excuse me Sir," Aahna interrupted as always. She got up and blazed at me.

"Yeah..," Sir responded.

"Sir, sorry to say, but I am not agree, in fact no one is agree with your decision," Aahna braced herself, as if she was the prime minister of India.

"Huh?" Sir shocked, grudgingly, "what are you saying?"

"Sir, everyone wants that there should have equal opportunity for all. Even I also want to be the CR," Aahna leaded whole class just like a politician.

I stood up, furiously, "have you last your sense. You are blaming Raghav Sir that he is doing partiality," I boiled over and looked at Sir.

"Shut up, dick," Aahna bellowed in animosity, "I am not blaming Sir. I am just saying that CR is a big responsibility. So there should be a responsible one to execute as CR," she frowned.

"Such embarrassing it is. You are saying that I am not responsible, while Raghav Sir has found me responsible," I quipped.

"HA, HA, HA," she laughed, "we all know, how much responsible you are, you bloody drunker," she abused me, and we both became abusive.

"Mind your tongue, you slut, I know well what I can do?" I hissed.

"Oh! Really, but I also know that you can't even tie your shoes," she shrieked and everyone laughed.

"Such a bitch, she is," Ruhi muttered near me.

"You vamp girl, you just love yourself. How could you be CR? You should go and waste your time in front of mirror," I snickered.

"Shut up, shut up, shut up," Raghav Sir banged the desk thrice, "this is not your battle field, this is my classroom," Sir steamed. There was pin drop silence after the killing storm. Aahna and I were headache to Raghav Sir. We had ruined his peace. We were like cohorts of devil for him.

"After 2 hours, election will be conducted between Shourya and Aahna for CR. And these are my final words," Sir roared and left.

After 2 hours, we all gathered for the election. Everyone had already made slip of name to whom they wanted to be CR. One by one they dropped the slip in metal box.

"Fucking bullshit," I moaned. I saw that everyone smiled at Aahna and showed middle finger to me after completing their vote.

"You lost, Shourya beta," Ruhi said in concern to me. But there was whole day and night left for me to change my defeat into victory. As Raghav Sir was going to announce result next day

****

CHAPTER SIXTEEN

"And the CR is, Shourya Sharma," Raghav Sir announced on the next day. I stood up with bloomed chest and waved my hand in ego just like a super star.

Aahna and the whole class went in sudden shock. Happiness drained out of their poor faces, as if they have woken up from a nightmare.

"Disgusting...," Aahna pursed her pink lips in hatred. She seemed so somber upset like a helpless puppy. Her face was noticeable. I could picture that she would break in tears in few seconds.

"Congrats, you won," Aahna said in low and sad voice. We both were in canteen, having our first coffee together.

"How generous, thanks Aahna," I giggled at her. She was dressed in white sleeveless short casual dress, which had 'O' neck and it's printed with yellow, green, red, pink leaves on its front.

"Aahna, literally, it was your win, but I had to turn into my victory," I said and plunked my hands on the table.

"What? What do you mean," she stammered, while sipping her cold coffee.
Hence, I don't know why I told her about the whole stuff that how Rohan, Yash, and I had unlocked Raghav sir's Cabin last night.

We had ruined all her votes and placed my votes in the voting box. I think I wanted to irritate her. As I always found fun to irritate her.

"You asshole, I will chap you," she hissed like snake, "how could you do that, how could you betrayed me."

"Everything is fair in love and war," I cheered and blew air kiss to her.

"Bug off," she looked at me in red eyes. Her blood was up.

"Ale bap le... mere Babu ko gussa aa rha hai...," I giggled while doing googly, stretching her both cheeks.

"Ugh!" she moaned in pain. And in next second she chuckled, and with every micro seconds her laughter touched high.

"You are a genius bastard, Shourya...," Aahna laughed and held my shoulder.

"Kind of," I said.

"Look there," she said and pointed her finger to open sky. Swiftly I followed her fingertip. And she played again. She pushed me, and I was lying in swimming pool. She started laughing herself. I was stunned. I ruffled my wet hair and slapped water waves.

"Such an idiot, you are Shourya," she cackled, and forwarded her hand to lift me out of pool.

"Only for you Aahna," I beamed at her and squeezed her hand.

And on being optimistic, I wondered that that was the spirit that would lead our relation longer and stronger It was first time that we met with each other with such cute love. She knew that I would fight with her, I would hit her, and I would tease her. But I would never ever hurt her. She had a belief in me that I would never do anything humiliating to her. We wait for each other for class to do masti. The days were boring when anyone of us was absent.

"Journal-560

Aahna, i have realized why it feels so good to be around you.
I don't have to be anything other than me.
Nothing to prove and no comparison to measure up to. I can forget about myself, and fully inhabit the Moments, simply enjoy being."

****

CHAPTER SEVENTEEN

"Shourya, you lied to me," Sid assailed furiously, "you told me that we are going to Jhande wala temple. And you brought me to such embarrassing place," he said irritatingly as we entered into BLUE BAR. We were at G. B. Road. We came here to celebrate my victory over Aahna.

"Bhai... if I wouldn't have lied to you, then you wouldn't have come with us," I sneered with Rohan and Yash.

"Damn it, I will still not come with you. You just wait here and I will get Ruhi here," he smacked and stumped out of bar.

But we stopped him, "Bhai.. please bhai, for me only, please come once. And if you don't like, you can leave," Rohan begged to Sid and we dragged him inSide.

The BLUE BAR or Roshni club was fully crowded. it was decorated with blue and red dim lights, which created a chromatic atmosphere there. A weird and fainting smell, I could sense there. The DJ was playing loud on jukebox. Girls and boys were dancing closer enough totally out of tune.
Everyone was intoxicated by alcohol and everyone was moving unsteadily.
In right Side of bar counter, girls in less clothes were dancing like vamp, on a high platform.
They had to seduce everyone present there. And spell bounded people were dancing with them, and showering money on those girls. Waitresses were serving beer and wine to customers.
In one corner, some couples were smooching each other's lips. But there was stuff in environment because of smoke of hukka.

We chose one corner and sat on black fabric couch. Waitress served us with beer. Rohan, Yash and I took their pleasure. But Sid was so nervous and uncomfortable. He riddled his thumb nervously.

"Hey! guys, may we join you," three hot and sizzling girls in miniskirts, colored blue, red and black asked to us with bright smile.

"Yeah.... of course! Why not?" Rohan spoke politely and gave them hands and they adjusted with us. They talked with us, enjoyed with us. They were from Lady Shri Ram College. They poured a glass of wine in our mouth by their soft hands.

"Please, don't force him," I sighed to the third girl in blue skirt. She was forcing our saint Sid. He felt uncomfortable. He was such a coyly boy. For a second, he moped at me.

"Let's dance," they said in enthusiasm and pulled Rohan and me to dance floor.

I danced softly, slowly moving my hands on her waist.

"Excuse me! Can I dance with you?" the voice travelled from the behind. It was a girl in black skirt and white top, with dark red lipstick, flossy hairs waving slowly.
I turned to her and bomb shelled.

"Oh My God! Neha. What a pleasant surprise!" I beamed at her in over excitement. She was my classmate, a hot classmate.

"Can I join you?" she asked politely. And without giving me a chance to speak, she held my hands and put them on her thin smooth waistline. She held my face in her palms. I was feeling so awkward and uncomfortable. She was looking into my eyes. I was quite cold feet.

"Who is with you?" I asked to divert her attention.

"Anshul and Atul," she answered. Atul was the bastard senior and Anshul was my bloody classmate. He was a bloody pimp of Atul and they both always used to trouble me.

I don't know? What Neha was doing with that betrayer Atul?

"Excuse me! Neha," I said to get rid of her. I didn't want to mess with Atul and Anshul. So I found it good to be away from her.

But suddenly, Neha clutched me tightly too closer to her body. She tried to kiss me.

"Neha, what the hell you are doing?" I frowned and pushed her away. I marched away from her.
But she pulled me in one corner and threw me to a sofa. She got over me. She was horrible. She was panting and waving her hair on my face.

"What are you doing? Stop it right now," I protested. But she ignored my words and began kissing my face madly.

"Get lost, you trumpet," I grinded my teeth and threw Neha away. I got up hastily to leave. But she stopped my feet.

"Shourya, don't this, please. I love you so much," she said furiously.

"But I can't love you," I was near to complete, but she cut me off.

"I know you are crazy for that bitch Aahna, I will ruin her," she snapped.

"Don't ever try to come close to her," I grabbed her by her hair, and pushed away and rushed.

"You have to pay for this, you bastard," she shouted in pain. I was muddled, unsure of what just happened. My heart was hitting fast. I was so feared and panic. I got towards bar counter and drank three to five shots rashly.

"Rohan, where is Sid?" I announced in his ear and pulled him out of dance floor.

"I don't know, last time I saw him, sitting there," he said and pointed towards a couch.

"Get him fast, idiot. We have to leave," I cringed.

And then, we searched Sid in every room, every corner. But he wasn't at anywhere.

I was so feared and terrified about Sid. My ear grew warm. I know, I was panicking, needlessly, but I couldn't help. He was a simple guy. He didn't know anything about such advance life. He was so innocent that anyone can cheat him easily. He was my responsibility. I had to take care of him always. Rohan and i strode outSide of the Bar.

And we saw Sid in parking. But I was shocked as I noticed Anshul and one other guy had griddled Sid by his hands. Neha was forcing Sid to gulp the bottle of beer.

Sid was protesting desperately, but Atul hit Sid and pocked his face. I couldn't believe my eyes. I became furious, at first, my breaths stuck in my throat. My blood went up. My body started burning in anger. I felt like I would blast in few seconds.

"You mother fuckers," I roared and galloped towards them. Rohan was so fast that he collided powerfully with Atul and fell over him.

I clutched Anshul and other guy by their hairs and threw them on ground. And I slapped Neha while pushing her away. I held Sid in arms like a kid. He was gasping heavily. He was drunk. He looked baffled for a Moment, rooted to the spot, his hand on my shoulder. Then he released a troubled breathe and gasp for air.

"Shourya, it's just ragging. You should stay away. It will be only good for you," Atul and Anshul snapped.

"You vamp..," I pounded my teeth in aggression and kicked Atul's belly harshly. He groaned in pain. The other guy pinioned me by arms, and Anshul punched me on my face.

Sudden, Rohan hooked Anshul and pushed him aSide. I dug my elbow in that guy's ribs and escaped myself.

Meanwhile, Atul hit on my legs by rod and then was near to hit on my head. But hastily, I cracked beer bottle on his head, blood ran out abundantly from his head. Rohan was hitting Anshul and the other boy by that rod.

"Get lost or I will kill you." I barked at Atul and cracked his head on a stone.

"Bastard Shourya, you have gone now, I will show you my dick now. You have to pay hard for this," Anshul bowled in pain, while running like a coward.

CHAPTER EIGHTEEN

Next morning, I got up early. My head was bursting. My body was aching because of fight of last night. Although, Sid was safe, he didn't get any kind of injury.
I got ready for college and padded slowly towards college. Although, my feet were not allowing me to move forward but i was forcing them to move. I felt something queerer and tension in the atmosphere. Whole environment of campus was so silent, the silence which occurs before a terrible storm, the silence which blows after a destructive storm. My mind was until captured by so many evil thoughts, about last night.

The cold wind, birds and leaves of trees everything were saying that something was going to happen worst.

How strange it is that, our heart comes to know about such storm even before us. And our heart alarms us about fucking bullshit, but the problem is that we never listen to our heart, and then we pay hard for this.

Whole class was busy in cell phones. But they all turned to me and giggled at me as I strode into the class.

In next Moment, they all broke into laugh. But some girls were flaming at me as if I have called them ugly or snatched their makeup kit. I sat on my seat and wondered about the class.

"Yehhh.., bro awesome haa.. it is," a voice rushed from last bench. That was a boy showing me his cell phone.

"Shourya, can I too get her number?" another boy shouted.

I was seeing them like statue. I couldn't get what was going there. And why they were looking in their cell phone.

"What the hell is this? Don't you have any sense," Ruhi screamed and threw her cell phone at me.

"Haaaiiinnnn, now what I did?" I prodded.

"You nuts check your facebook, what the fucking you did," she irritated on me. I shoved my hand in my pocket to pick out my phone, but I didn't find it. i was shuffling my hands in my pocket, then in my bag, but my phone was lost.

"Look here. You bastard," Ruhi smacked, and showed me her phone.

I was like stone when I saw at her screen. It was something like.

Shourya Sharma posted on his timeline:

'HEY! mother fuckers. I have a treat for all of you.' And below it there were nude faked scandals of Aahna in two piece.
'hi, this is Aahna kapoor, the fucking slut. She wants to fuck all the bastards. So who is interested contact me.'

"Fuck.....," I moaned in shock. My body went frozen and dead weight was stuck in my throat. My heartbeats started giving up in reverse order. i was losing my breathe. I felt like someone was garroting me.

I mused fiercely that how could this happen? Who did this? Suddenly, Anshul and Neha crossed by me. They both showed me middle finger. And i didn't need a second to get that it was those bastard's shit.

They had already planned everything. They very well knew my every move. i rushed angrily towards them, my anger had reached tipping point. I wanted to kick on their ass.
Rapidly, Aahna padded into the classroom. And whole class starred her, sneered at her, laughed at her, abused her and passed comments at her.

Aahna was glaring silently, still musing in confusion. Then, Sanaya,

Aahna's best friend, took Aahna aSide, vomited whole stuff, and showed that scandal to Aahna.
Although, I had no guts to look at Aahna, I was so ashamed. i downed my eyes in contrite and disgrace. I didn't meet her eyes, but when she persisted, I had to look up. My body was trembling. She looked at me. Her almonds brown eyes shined by unshed tears. She rushed out of there- all hurried and hassled while crying, wiping, and escaping from all bastards.

I followed her. However, my feet were giving up, but i protested against their wish.

"Aahna.... Aahna......," I was shouting her name, while running behind her, "please listen to me, Aahna," I caught her and held her palm and squeezed into my both hands. She was in light pink short casual sleeveless outfit, which was flared at bottom, printed in violet leaves and flowers. She had made her brown hair in Bohemian Side braid, which looked mess at the end.
She turned her face to me. Her brownish eyes were filled with tears, her face was red. She was sobbing. She looked more pretty and lovely with that innocent face.
She closed her eye lids pressed in deep pain. A single teardrop escaped the corner of one eye, rolled down on her red cheeks, then on her pink lips abundantly. I wished to kiss her lips to touch that tear by my lips.

I looked deeply into her brown eyes. Her eyes were regretting to me that why I had done that. Why I hurt her? Why I had broken her trust on me?
I wanted to reply that, "Aahna, I love you so much. So how can I do that? How can I hurt you? You are my life, so how can I see you in pa in?"

An unknown force was pilling me down; I found it difficult to stand in her front. I was gasping. I was trying to frame the sentence in my mind. But my words caught in my throat. Amidst, I gathered courage in me and spoke, "Aahna please listen to me, please give me a chance to prove myself. I have to clear this," I said to her, "Aahna, I didn't do this. I know who did this?" I grinded my teeth held her hand and marched towards Neha and Anshul. She didn't resisted, she just sobbed, her nose turned red as she heaved.

I glare Neha, as I reached her, near garden.

"Aahna, I didn't do that. She did that," I snapped, "Neha tell her, what is the truth?" I roared at Neha.

"Are you mad?" she frowned, "you ruined Aahna's life, you did such embarrassing with her. And now you are blaming me, you asshole," Neha lied confidently.

"You bloody cock, don't lie," I spat out each word angrily.

"Oh! Shut up, you bloody sick," Neha smacked.

"Aahna, let me tell you the truth," I said in low tone and held Aahna's soft hand, "Aahna last night I met to Neha in a Bar. And there she forced me to abuse her. She tried to kiss me. She wanted me to love her. But when I refused to her, she messed with me, and cleverly she stole my phone and posted that MMS by my ID to take revenge," I sighed after explaining about last night. And I looked at Aahna.

"Oh! God, it's hilarious," Neha hissed, "good story Shourya. You are awesome. But Aahna, let me tell you the real truth. Yes we met last night. But it was Shourya, who wanted to kiss me. He forced me to kiss him. He abused me. And when I denied as he like Aahna so why is he doing that to me. But he said, he is just playing with you. He would ruin your life," Neha said emotionally, tried to get Aahna's sympathy.

Aahna looked at me. She didn't let a single drop flow out. She kept blinking to hold them back. A strand of her brown hair was falling on her tearful eyes, but she didn't dare to push that strand aside. She was frozen, and frazzled.

"She is lying Aahna, trust me," I begged to Aahan, "You bitch, how much you will lie," I grinned at Neha. And turned to Aahna, "Aahna, this is a trap of fucking Anshul and Neha. Trust me, Aahna," I was blurting, panicking, fuming and panting all together. I was proved as criminal. I was helpless. I clutched Aahna's hand.

Aahna pulled out her hand and jerked my hands cruelly. She was biting her lower lip to control her cry. She gazed at me in so much pain in her eyes. Her nose flared as she sobbed. I held her gaze. I could feel the pang in her eyes. I urged to pull her into smoother hug.

I wanted to hide her in my arms to console her grief that everything is ok. don't cry Aahna.

Aahna gave up and let the tears flow freely down her face. She ran way briskly. I couldn't stop her. I was seeing her helplessly. I felt so chagrined of myself.

I couldn't sleep whole night; I was twisting and rolling on my bed in pain. I thought I had lost Aahna. I broke her trust. She had a faith in me that I would never hurt her. But I proved her wrong. I made her to cry. I mused that God was not going to forgive me as I broke heart of such pure girl.
We boys have no idea that how much painful and disgraceful for a girl that we play with their emotions. We broke their trust. We abuse their soul and respect. But only they have to pay hard for our misdeed.

Self respect is the most precious ornament of a girl. By humiliating their respect and soul, we collapse them physically and mentally both.

I had no idea that what she was suffering from only because of my silly. I had almost lost her forever. But I couldn't accept that. I had to prove myself.

I didn't ever care for other, I cared for Aahna only. She mattered for me.

****

"Ruhi, please believe me," I pleaded to Ruhi. We were gathered in mess for dinner.

"Shut up, Shourya, and get lost," Ruhi hissed, "I didn't expect this from you. I called you my brother, and now I am feeling guilty of myself," she muttered, with sullen face.

"Stop it Ruhi, will you ever listen to me? You don't want to hear the truth," I exasperated, "on that night, Rohan, Sid and I went to blue bar...," I mumbled, and then I explained her whole bullshit, that how we forced Sid to come with us, and then how we got messed with Anshul and Neha.

"What?" Ruhi roared, "Shame on you Shourya, shame on you," Ruhi irritated, pursing her lips. And got up to leave.

"Ruhi, please..., I said sorry to Sid also," I bellowed and held her hand.

"Fuck on you," Ruhi burst in anger and threw a glass of water on my face.

But that didn't hurt me; I knew Ruhi loved me a lot. And she also loved Sid. She just wanted us to be safe. She cared for both of us. But I was hurt for Aahna, I couldn't breathe freely without her. I tried to call Aahna but she didn't receive first, and then blocked me. Then I flooded her facebook inbox with so hundreds of massages said *'I m sry Aahna, tlk to me, I need to clarify dis'* Sometimes, the love of your life comes after the mistake of your life.

****

CHAPTER NINETEEN

Again, Aahna was missed in college from one week. I was dying day by day. And my post of that bloody MMS got viral in whole college. Soon, it reached to DEAN Mr. Sanjeev chopra. Thereupon, he fucked me. He warned me to rusticate next day. But I was saved by Raghav Sir. He had belief in me that I couldn't do such shit.

And after all, Aahna came to college. She was heavy hearted. I would effort a lot to talk to her, but she ignored me and rushed away every time.

Although, I didn't had such braveness to face her anymore but they were my friends, who charged me. They were my best buddies; they were my energy source, which could never end.
I always had a belief and confidence that my friends will stand with me not only in my good time but in dangerous situation too.

"Go, you have to talk to her," Ruhi and Ashvini forced me. We all were sitting in garden of the campus. Aahna was also there, standing at a distance with her friend Sanaya. I padded slowly towards her back. Although, my feet trembling they were refusing to move towards Aahna. Anyhow, I approached to her, facing her back. My legs started shaking and giving up always. They are my first ever-worst enemy. I willed them to stop oscillating. I padded to her.

She was astonishing in light pink and black sleek chiffon blouse top, with transparent visual effect. There was vintage floral pattern around the neck, sleeves and waist. Her shoulder was open by one Side. She had put blue denim damaged jeans. She was catching my eyes. I could saw her barred waist by one Side. I wanted to stroke my fingers on her soft naval.

"Aahna......," I said in hesitation. She didn't respond to my voice. Again I whispered her name. But she didn't answer.

So, I put my hand on her barred shoulder and bellowed, "Aahna, I want to talk to you."
Straightaway, she turned to me, dreadful, her hand came rushing to meet my face, and flat cheeks reverberated with her impact. She gave me a harsh slap.

And in next Moment, I was in severe shock. I couldn't get, what had just happened? I put my hand on my slapped cheek, harsh sound still reverberating in my ears. My body, my mind was numb.

The world around me felt silent, I became strongly aware of all my body parts. My breathing became more labored with every second.

Whole garden burst into sneering and giggling at me.

I looked towards my friends for help with unshed tearful eyes, and helpless poor face. I was in need of them badly. I thought they will help me. But they ran away so quickly that I couldn't even see their reflection.

I was wrong that I had best buddies. Indeed, they were the bastards. They were with me in pleasure time. I assembled myself to look up at Aahna in fear. She had rushed already. I was seeing her back. I felt like someone was snatching Aahna from me. I sensed as if someone had tinched my heart by a sharp knife.

I padded slowly in guilt towards hostel.

After that worst humiliation, I chose isolation as my company. I gave away my friends, college and everything.

I would spend my time with loneliness. I would spare whole night looking at dark sky. I didn't go to college, as being slapped by a girl is a shame for a boy.

But I don't believe in such bullshit. I only cared for Aahna. Now I genuinely felt bad as she hurt me. She broke my heart. I loved her that much that I had started dreaming of her. I had already made so many plans for both of us. But she swept away all my dreams, plans and hope in a second.

Although, I knew that she was not culprit. It was me, who hurt her, abused her. But I didn't do that intentionally. I loved her, so how could I do anything wrong with her.

But she didn't understand me. She didn't give me chance to prove me right.

And she insulted me in front of whole college. And she did this intentionally. I would effort a lot to clear our misunderstanding, but she was not ready to listen me. She had already believed in that bloody stuff. And that misunderstanding created a feeling of envy and hatred between us, and led us towards our end. Although, I loved her more than my life but now I was exhausted. I had no energy to suffer from any kind of pain.

Though, I wanted to let it all out, but couldn't help, but feel that no amount of tears would be able to quench the intense feelings of helplessness and hopelessness.

I had to accept the truth as God's wish. I had to say, *'it's all over.'*

Finally, after worst pain, I decided to move on while screwing all my feelings for her. She had given me the reason to hate her, to move forward.

Every day, I would endeavor my hardest to forget Aahna, and to never think about her.

But in spite of all torture she did, in spite of that she drain out my happiness, my heart was not ready to hate her. I was confused that I should listen to my heart or my brain. As they, both are constant enemies.

But it's surprising that even being such soft, heart always win by mind. So I texted her, but she didn't reply. Love is when even after you fight, you still wait for her message and call.
There was a single day, single second that I had never missed her. As much more I wanted to hatred her, much more I was swimming in her love.

But I couldn't let it happen. I indeed wanted to erase her from my eyes, as I had no option left.

I wondered I would need time. So I wanted to spend time with myself. I went in silence. Sometimes we need to be silent to find answers that are buried within ourselves.
I would spend time, while walking listlessly through empty corridors.

Albeit my friends attempted to get me back in the present world but I had already showered my frustration on them. I didn't speak to anyone.

While I had to share my room with Rohan and Sid during night.

If you want to be strong, learn how to fight alone. I separated my bed, my clothes, my books, and my everything from their things. Rohan and Sid would try to mock on me, try to mend things with me. But every time, I ruined them.

It's strange that whenever I get hurt I do three things only.
First, I would sleep a lot. Rohan and Sid could easily find me completely sank into my bed, hidden in white blanket.

Second, I read everyone's whatsapp status, and then upload the most heart breaking status on my profile with sad DP, just to show other that I am broken heart.

Third, I listen Arijit's heart breaking numbers. It's a therapy for me. I feel like every song is composed for me only.

It was 9pm, and I was wandering in courtyard. Rapidly, my friends surrounded me furiously. I was scared, that they would hit me now. But in next Moment they lay on their knees, joint their hands.

"What?" I said rudely and raised my brows.

"Sorry..... Shourya.....," they begged together.

"You coward bastard. You left me alone, when she slapped me. I was in need of your. But you stabbed my back," I snapped and tried to move. Briskly, they all held my feet and started to pray violently, absurdly.

"Ok, ok... stop this notanki...," I shrieked.

And in next Moment, Ruhi pulled me into her chest and we all had furious group hug. I felt the peace of heaven in that hug. I felt alive after long time. I was so lucky that I had friends, only who could make me smile in such worst remorse.

My friends were my strength, my energy. I can win whole world if they are with me. And the best part of them was that, they would always forgive my mistakes and would pull me into hug. A best friend is someone who loves you when you have forgotten how to love yourself.

I always thanked God for honoring me with such true friends.

"I missed you guys a lot," I whispered emotionally and held them more tightly.
"Shourya, did it hurt? When she slapped you?" Ruhi asked and touched my slapped cheek.
"Yeah..., so much. Aahna slapped so powerfully," I annoyed like an innocent kid. And they all merged into laugh.

"Stupid...," Ruhi shrieked and kissed my forehead.

"But now what about Aahna?" Ashvini shrugged.

"Who is Aahna? I don't know any Aahna," I braced myself, "I know only myself, Shourya Sharma, the CR," I bellowed in attitude. But my heart only knew how badly I was missing Aahna.

"Journal-561

Aahna, why you think that I hurt you. How can I hurt you Aahna. I love you Aahna, and I don't want to be the one who hurt you. When will you understand? I want you on your good days and on your bad. I want you on the days where you can't make yourself get out of bed. I want you on the days when you are dancing, and on the days when you are crying. I want you on the days when you will put your head on shoulder, and fall asleep instantly. Why don't you understand? Every time when I tell you to get home safe, stay warm, have a good day, or sleep well that I am really saying is I love you."

****

CHAPTER TWENTY

Aahna and I too were present in class. But we didn't even gaze at each other.

We both were blood thirsty of each other.
She had dressed herself in short causal sleeveless black dress with o neck, which was printed with a big sun floral effect at her chest.

She was looking angelic and sparking in that black flared dress.

She had bound her brown long hairs into double braid messy hairstyle.

Admitting, that I had decided not to look at her, I had decided to hatred her. I couldn't control myself. My eyes were sticking at her. And I was spell bounded by her cute dimples. How awkward, after break-up girls turn out to be more hot; and boys turn out more dull with big beard, and messy hair.

"Good morning class," Asha ma'am greeted with so much energy, as she strode into class.

"Good morning ma'am," we buzzed, and glared at her stunning yellow transparent law waist saree.

"Guys, I have something exciting for all of you," she gave pretty smile, "your seniors are organizing a welcoming party for you. The event will be held after 5 days. This is going to be so much exciting. As this time, they have done something innovative. This time there is a theme for the event, and which is 'prom night'. I mean you all have to prepare an awesome performance with your partner," Asha ma'am sighed, and looked in so much enthusiasm, and ecstatic more than all of us.

In a Moment, whole class turned into bustle. Every fucking bastard had already approached to the hot girls. And rest of the nerds were still hesitating to ask a girl for prom night. I had already chosen Ruhi.

"Wait, wait, I have more surprise to tell you," Asha Ma'am banged the board, so her bangles made jingling sound, "your partners will be selected by me, as like lucky draw," she shrieked, loudly.

Hence, Asha ma'am gave us hoops, and we had to mention our names on those hoops by marker pen, and had to drop it into the bowl.

Ashu Ma'am was going to attaché one hoop of girl with one hoop of boy, and they would be coupled with each for fresher party.

****

On the following day, Aasha ma'am came to announce couples. She was announcing from last five minutes. Ashvini was going to dance with Rohan. How surprising it was that the love birds were coupled by ma'am also.

Sid was going with Aahna's friend Sanaya. And Ruhi was going with fatty Yash.

When I heard that announcement, I couldn't control my laugh. I started teasing Ruhi. She was so furious, for the reason that, Ruhi badly wanted to go with Sid. And now she was greened eye for Sanaya.

"And the next couple is, Shourya Sharma and Aahna Kapoor," Aasha ma'am sniffed and smacked on my smile.

"What the hell?" I couldn't complete my words, as my mouth remained parted.

My temper was at its zenith, I wanted to shut Aasha Ma'am's mouth for that stuff. I looked at Aahna with squinted eyes. She was too shocked; she glared at me with flaming brownish eyes.

Thereupon, after Aasha ma'am, everyone left with her to argue with her for not giving right partner. Specially girls, as they didn't got their crush as their partner. Boys are so cheap, as they can dance with any girl.

I was sitting alone in empty classroom, Aahna padded in hesitation towards me.

"Oyee..," she said rudely, braced herself, and looked away in attitude.

I didn't reply to her, and got busy into my phone.

"Oyee.., I am talking to you," she shouted and banged my table.

"What ?" I steamed and flamed at her angrily, with frustrated eyes, "MY name is Shourya, don't you know?"

"Whatever, but I don't want to go with you in party," she muttered rudely, her voice was gruff.

"Oh really! So don't come, I am not insisting you," I grinned at her.

"You bad mannered, can't you just talk properly," she frowned.

"Oyee, don't shout at me," I roared, "and even I am also not dying to dance with you ugly girl," I slammed at her.

"Same here," she sneered gawkily, "I would like to die rather than to dance with you absurd," she gulped, making funny face.

"Ok, then go and die, you bitch, I would enjoy a lot, if you die," I hissed.

"Shut up or I will tinch your face," she pissed her teeth, and tried to tinch my face by her sharp blue nails.

"Hath to lga ke dikha," I stood up terribly, so she got scared, she moved back.

"Look I don't want any fight, I am just saying, I don't want to dance with you, so do something," she said, grumpily.

"Ha ha ha, So funny, Miss Kapoor," I laughed, "I am not your maid," I snapped.

And here we became abusive again.

"Stop, stop, you guys, stop fighting like kids," Sanaya and Ruhi ran to interrupted.

"Why don't you go to Aasha ma'am and solve it," Sanaya and Ruhi explained us.

"Why I would go? She will go," I complained to them like kid.

"I am not so stupid," Aahna said in funny and weird tone, "why will I go?" she bellowed.

"Meri maa...," Sanaya irritated, "dono sath jao."

We marched towards Aasha medam's cabin, and we stumbled into it. I was amazed by Aasha ma'am. She was checking out something in the cupboard.

Her yellow sleeveless, backless blouse was mesmerizing me.

"What?" she asked meekly, as she turned towards Aahna and me. And she waved her black hair by her right hand.

"Damn it," I muttered with big eyes and opened mouth. She was stunning and sizzling in that yellow saree.

"Ma'am I want to change my partner, I can't go with Shourya," Aahna uttered.

"Oh! Hello, excuse me. Even I don't want to go with you egoist girl," I hissed at Aahna.
"What did you just say," Aahna shouted, "you bloody." But Ma'am interjected.

"Shut up, both of you," Aasha Ma'am roared, "what is your problem?"

Rapidly, a fast and cool breeze blew from window, which waved Aasha madam's saree briskly. I saw her glowing low waist. It was so much inducing.

I glued my eyes on her low waist and starred her novel. Aahna noticed my vulgar eyes. Aahna glared at me first then kicked harshly on my left foot. And I braced myself and looked away from Aasha madam's navel.

"Ma'am, genuinely she is storage of problems. She is bad luck for me. She will eat like a hungry dayan," I complained ma'am.

110

"You bloody pimp," she grinded her teeth, "Ma'am I would dance with anyone, but not with this dog," Aahna grinned at me.

"Shut up..........," ma'am burst out her anger, "this is not your home that everyone will work for your pleasure. You both have to dance together, and that's final," ma'am smacked.

"But ma'am," we both agitated together. But Aasha ma'am chopped us.

"I want both of you at practice hall," ma'am quipped, and threw both of us out of her cabin.

"You bloody sick, what you were doing with ma'am?" Aahna chuckled, "you are flirting with a teacher."

"What? When? Where? And how?" I played innocently.

"Ugh! Fuck yourself," she irritated, sighed and continued again, "look I will not dance with you at any condition," she said rudely, with flamed brownish eyes.

"Then I have a solution," I said.

"What?" she said in robotic tone.

"Why don't you jump down from here? So that I wouldn't have to dance with you," I quipped, and shrieked.

"Oh god, please forgive me, I am going to kill him," Aahna kibbled her teeth and stifled her hands around my neck, and tried to smother me by her sharp nails.
I protested and we turned into ruse.
"Get lost from here, and die somewhere else," Aasha ma'am shouted inside of the cabin.

****

CHAPTER TWENTY ONE

It was already 5:15 pm by my clock of a dazzling evening. The evening sun was kind, scattering the reddish in low sky. I was enjoying the fresh air, waiting for Aahna at rehearsal hall in college campus.

In reality, I didn't want to go for rehearsal but it was terror of Aasha ma'am, who pressurized me to go for rehearsal. But I mused that Aahna wouldn't come.

Quickly, an awesome Audi Q5, my dream car stopped near my feet. Aahna stepped out in blue low waist denim up to her fair knees white dull sleeveless top and black goggles on her brownish eyes. There was 4 inch gap between her top and jeans.

"Spectacular," I mused not for Aahna but for Audi Q5 this time.

Aahna's Audi emerged me into confusion that I loved Aahna or her Audi more.

Thereupon, I concluded that I was ready to being slapped again by Aahna only if she gives me her Audi Q5

"Can't you be on time lazy girl," I bellowed at her.

"Shut up," she replied, curtly, pocked on my stomach, and walked in towards rehearsal hall.

I followed her briskly. And we entered into a huge, Abundant luxury hall, half heartily.

It was a rectangular marble hall.

Big mirrors decorated its walls. And three 40 inch LED were placed to learn steps. And every corner was packed by awesome sound system. Four choreographers were welcomed to make us learn to dance. Some couples were already dancing there with choreographers.

Sid was enjoying dancing with Sanaya they looked so happy with each other. But it hurt Ruhi, she was glaring at Sid and Sanaya with the feeling of hatred and envy, and cursing Sanaya and Aasha ma'am in one corner.

Aahna and I chose each corner, facing each other. We slumped to three floors, our back propped against the wall, legs stretched on floor towards each other. We both were looking with eagle eyes at each other. We were almost close to gauge each others' blood.

We would give creepy and freaky expressions to each other sometimes. And sometimes she would throw her purse, her bottle and her sneakers at me.

"Guys, what are you doing there come on get up, you are already late," choreographer Rahul and Shreya said to us.

We both chucked them even we didn't look at them, as if they were not present there.

"Hey! We are talking to you, can you hear us?" they huffed and fixed their eyes on us.

"Don't talk to me anything, talk to her," I frowned at them, but before I could complete, Aahna chopped my line.

"I don't know anything, I wouldn't dance with him," Aahna hissed and looked at Rahul and Shreya.

Aahna and I kept on irritating Rahul and Shreya. They would come repeatedly to us, but every time we would ignore them. They were startled at first

They were getting more and more frustrated. Indeed Aasha ma'am had already warned them about Aahna and me that we both were blood thirsty of each other.

So Rahul and Shreya had to take special care of both of us.

"Look, this is enough ok," Shreya bellowed at Aahna and me,

"now last time I am asking, will you dance? Or I should call Aasha ma'am," Shreya complete grumpily and left.
Suddenly, we got scared of Aasha ma'am, we both exchanged our gaze, gulped our weight. Quickly Aahna approached to me.

"Oyee...," she sighed.

"Tu hogi oyee... Mera naam Shourya hai," I quipped heatedly.

"Achha...listen," she said and knelt down on her knees in my front, "we have to dance. Granting all this that I should kill myself rather than dancing with you. But Aasha ma'am will screw both of us. So have to dance," Aahna muttered helplessly, and rolled her eyes.

"I would like to die rather," I mumbled, looking away from her brownish eyes.

"Ok fine by me," she shouted and got up hastily, "now I have an excuse for Aasha ma'am," she burst and padded away slowly as if she was waiting for my call.

"Wait, wait, I will dance," I hesitated.
While I was showing like that I was not interested to dance with her. But somewhere, a part of me was happy to dance with my crush.

We went to Shreya and Rahul. At first they showered their whole anger and frustration on us.

"Come now let's dance now," Rahul said.

"Actually, you both are special couple, so we have something amazing and breathe taking performance for you," Shreya said in over excitement, and in haste.

"So, first look at us carefully," Rahul said. He played a track 'Jiyein kyu..' from Dum Maro Dum, by awesome and soulful voice of Papon. It is an emotional and so much romantic one with deep feelings.

Rahul and Shreya started dancing. They had done creative and newborn things. They had choreographed that song in contemporary. They were dancing with so much ease and smoothness. But they had mixed some salsa moves. And they had mixed it with aerial freestyle dancing. In fact, they made it too much complicated. They used so many flips, spins, dips, tricks, swings and so many lifts.

But the breaths taking part was that Rahul and Shreya decorated that song by so much hot, sexy, seducing and sensational moves.

They were dancing while holding each other to close, in too much romantic way.

It was so much sensational. And Shreya made it damn sexy by her sizzling moves.

When I saw them dancing, I was shocked and panicked. My body was frozen, and my heart was surrendering. A cold weight was stuck in my throat. I was simply stunned.

Secretly, I looked at Aahna. She was shivering. She was almost near to burst into cry. Her face was steamed in cold sweat because of nervousness.

We both must that how could we dance like that?

On account of, few minutes ago, we wanted to kill each other. So now how could we dance with so much romance?

Our bodies had already started trembling. And sensational waves had already started in our bodies, only by watching Rahul and Shreya. So what would happen, when we dance like that? Even, the thought made me oscillate.
I beamed at Aahna, she kept twisting and squeezing her one hand by another, as if this was giving her strength to stand. She clocked at me with an expectation in her eyes, but I downed my gaze. She collected herself and stepped towards Rahul.

"Sir I can't dance like that with him. It is too scummy and awful," Aahna said to Rahul.

"Oh! Really," Shreya smirked and braced herself, "can you please tell me why?"

"It's too vulgar and sexy. We hate each other, I can't dance this," Aahna was blurting nonsense.

So Rahul raised his hand violently and angrily to interrupt Aahna.

"Shut up....," he shouted, "this is your performance, and you have to do it at any condition, otherwise I have to call Aasha ma'am right now," Rahul snapped, and left.

"Bastard," Aahna murmured under her breathe.

"Ok. Now get ready, you have to try it," Shreya said and guided us.

Aahna and I took our position. We held each other's hands. Our hands were shaking terribly. We both felt so much awkward, and uncomfortable. I had never dance with a girl before. And dancing with your crush is even more, worst.

We began dancing, while stepping forward, then two steps backward. Then I had to lift Aahna in my arms, when she would run towards me.

At that time, my evil mind woke up. I wished to take revenge from her. So when she came to me, while running, I lifted her for a second, and in next second I dropped her on floor.

"Aaaahhh....," she groaned in pain so loudly.

"Idiot, why you dropped me, I know you did it intentionally, you want to break my waist," Aahna shouted and cried like kid and held her soft, barred waist.

"Oh hello!" I slammed with creepy smile, "it's not my mistake, you are so heavy, I can't lift your fat," I gulped at her.

"What," she shouted, increasing size of her brownish eyes, "you calls me fat, hilarious. I am just___," she stopped her words, "Sir I will not dance with him, bloody bastard," Aahna grinded her teeth angrily.

Rahul and Shreya held their head and gave up.

"Kill each other by this," Rahul frowned and threw a knife towards us and they left. As it was 7p.m.

Aahna got up hardly, groaning, she glared at me, and padded like lamb towards her Audi.

"Ale baap le....mele babu ko chot lg gyi," I sounded funny and collided softly with her.

"kuttaaaaa.....," she squawked.

"Babu ko help chahiye, may I lift you Babu again?" I teased her.

"Fuck yourself." she shouted, ran to hit me, and hurled her sneakers at me.

I left quickly with my pulsar. I was driving slowly while enjoyed the silent and peaceful evening after whole day heavy rain.

Suddenly, I noticed Aahna, driving speedily her Audi towards me.

She was so terrible, and I was so scared. In next second, she overtook me, furiously, and gave killing cut to my bike. I lost my control and fall down in a gadda, fully filled with mud.

"Bitch," I shouted.

****

CHAPTER TWENTY TWO

Now we had only three days left for fresher party. As we had already ruined one whole day, so Rahul and Shreya called us alone for special and extra rehearsal in a separate hall. Aahna and I forget our personal stuff, and worked hard for those three days.

Whereas, Aahna and I both were good dancer, but we had suffer a lot, as the song was choreographed in complicated way. In contemporary style we had to move our bodies with so much ease and smoothness like butter. We had to do so many curves like smooth waves of river. We were dancing it, in so much sensational way. And in aerial freestyle part, we had to move with so much of energy and quick to do flips, swings and lifts.

Actually, the song is about love and anger for the beloved of the girl. The song expresses the fight, the frustration between the two couples or love birds that are fighting and hurting each other, and regretting with each other sometimes.
So while expressing our anger, we had to move our bodies with suddenness, quick jerk and jump like the electric current. Despite that fact, we had to express a cute and romantic fight.

But literally, Aahna and I would fight cruelly, and harshly. We were fighting like enemies from ages to explore our anger, and our frustration that we were hiding from months.

During rehearsal, Aahna was outfitted in gym kit, in black short, sleeveless skinned top, and black tight leggings. She was damn sexy and breathe taking. I was under a spell by her barred waistlines and curvy body. And her hot and sizzling moves were killing me.

I didn't let go the opportunity, so with every move i would touch her badly. I would roll my fingers on her, neck, chest, waist, hairs, navel and everywhere. She couldn't help, she would protest only by slapping me, tinching my face by her long sharp nails.

It was last day of our rehearsal. I would hold her palm and would make her to spin twice, and then I would pull her back, and so my chest would lean against her back. Hence, I would roll my hands from her barred shoulder to her palms, to assault her.

"Hey! Excuse me," she burst and pushed me away, "how dare you touch me," she snapped with big brownish eyes, gasping heatedly.

"Oh, relax, relax," I raised my hands in surrender, "I was just doing my step," I said.

"Fuck on the step," she roared, "don't fool me. I know you are taking my benefits," she sniffed.

"What happened now?" Rahul and Shreya asked.

"Sir, he touched me," Aahna complained.

"Look, don't behave like kid again you have to complete it today. And I want more and more romance and hotness, we are giving you such special treatment, and you idiots are still fighting like kids. I think, I should call Ma'am," Shreya bellowed and left both of us alone in that room.

After 5 minutes, Aahna realized her mistake, and we started it again. And we would do our next step. Now we would hold each other's hands and I would make her to do spin twice, to that end, I would pull her into my chest. Her brownish hair, were falling over my face. Her cheeks were rubbing against my cheeks. I would wave her hair smoothly, and kiss on her ears while taking a bite.

I would feel a sweat fragrance of her hairs. Her hair smelled so good. Briskly she pitted in her nails into my face and I pushed her away quickly. Then I lifted her, while carrying her by waist and swung.

Suddenly, I would turn towards her back, and grabbed her tightly into my chest. And briskly, I put my lips on her barred shoulder and licked her shoulder and, chucked my hand on her chest following towards her chest and after that on her soft navel. I moved my fingers on her barred navel, she couldn't be more strong. She couldn't control her emotions anymore. Suddenly, she started breathing hastily. I would smell her breathe. Her soft waistline was shivering terrible with her breathe.

There up, we stretched ourselves and strode while lying on our knees. Rapidly, she knelt on her knees; I marched to her back, and stroked my palms harshly on her opened back. Now I leaned against her back and kissed smoothly on her back, she had started panting.

On the ground, I lifted her in arms and moved round and round, then I lifted her by her one hand and one leg, and we made spins thrice. She was swimming in air.

Again I would carry her in my arms; her hands were around my neck. She pricked her nails on my neck. And it started bleeding little bit.

And moving on wards, I would stand at a distance from her. And hurriedly, she would run towards me and hugged me tightly from my behind; she would move her hands violently on my chest. Cleverly, she dug her fingers in my chest.

On our next move, I would remove her away to explore my anger, but she would slap me twice furiously and would pull me tightly into her chest, my face was red because of her hasty slaps.

Then I would grab her by her brown hairs and bent over her. I would move our upper bodies in a round, and I kissed on her waist and navel. She took a deep swoon and kicked me away.

Now it was her turn to hurt me. I would lie on my knees; she would grab me by my hairs from my behind. She would move my head violently, and threw me away.

Now we would do some salsa steps. We would hold each other's hands. We would step forward and then two steps backward again, while keeping our upper bodies straight. And she would put her one leg across my belly I would roll my hand on her barred flossy leg from ankle to her thighs and would lift her.

After that, I would hold her by waist and would bend my body over her body.

I looked into her deep brownish eyes; her face was flashing so much innocence. Her eyes were shining like stars by unshed tears.

Her pink lips were appearing so much juicy. I would chuck my hand on her soft cheeks and then on her trembling lips and then on her neck and followed on her thin waist.

Abruptly, she shook her hair horribly and hit on my face by her brown hair, which were curly and brown at the end.

Quickly in next Moment, I would drop her on floor and got over her body. I lay on top of her, resting my weight on her body. Our bodies touching from shoulder to knees. Our breaths were mingling. She smelled so good, I was about to ask her which deodorant she use. She shivered against me, her breasts heaving against my chest. I gently pushed a curl falling on her face, and tucked behind her ear. I moved my fingers to her cheeks, grazing her lips with my thumb and then pulling her bottom lip down. It almost killed her. She sucked my thumb. I captured her both hands in my one hand over her head; and pressed against floor.

"You are hurting me Shourya, please leave me," she moaned, taking a deep breath. She flashed so beautiful and innocent when she said that.

I moved close to her shaking lips, I could feel her breathes on my lips; I hold my lips close to her. She closed her eyes, and a tear rolled down on her cheek. I moved my lips on her cheeks and sucked that tear. Then I kissed on her forehead and released her from my cage. I sat near her. She was still lying by my Side, breathing hardly, eyes closed. I got up.

"Aahna....," I said softly. She opened her eyes and looked up at me without blinking. I forwarded my hand, she clutched my palm, and I pulled her in my arms.

****

CHAPTER TWENTY THREE

Finally the day of convivial came. Finally the day of fresher party came. The event was organized at St. Patrik garden little bit away from campus.

I was already waiting for Aahna outside of garden. She was already 20min. late, and after more 20 minutes, she stopped near me with her grand Audi Q5.

"Razzle-and-dazzle," I surprised with big eyes, this time also for luxury Audi.

"Can't you ever be on time Aahna," I showered at her as she padded out of her Audi, "God! How many hours you waste on make up?"

"Just shut up ok," she squelched at me, "and tell me how? I am looking," she asked, exhilarated, proud of her heavenly beauty, and padded towards gate of entrance.
"Patakaaaaaa...," I teased her. She punched on my belly and we shrieked.

"Excuse me, ma'am," a girl said to Aahna, who was there to welcome everyone, "you have to arm him,"

"No, no, we are fine," Aahna cut her off, waving her right hand.

"Sorry ma'am, it's one of rule of today's event," that girl pointed towards cameraman, "we have to capture both of you."

"My foot," Aahna fumed, glared at that girl first, and then grinded her teeth at me, and threaded her arms into mine rudely, half heartily, and gave a creepy smile.

Hence, we walked on red carpet, while holding each other.

The garden was a blazed so beautifully, many varieties of colored lights were flashing flowers, and by awesome curtains. I could smell sweet fragrance of saints.

It was fully crowded, even though it was so much fascinating. At the centre of the garden, there was a huge stage was decorated like stage of any bollywood award show.

And round dining tables were arranged for each couple. It seemed like candle light dinner.

Everyone was appearing so pretty and handsome. Every girl was dressed in saree and boys in blazer and trouser.

My table was arranged just in front of stage, as I was the CR, so I had some special privileges. Aahna and I walked towards our table through red carpet. Ruhi was by my left Side. The event had already gone on.

At first, our seniors welcomed us by a awesome performance, they pleasured us with live band.

Aahna was on my front, too close to my eyes. I was short of words to praise her beauty. But I have to do it. She wore a half black and half red thin and transparent saree with low waist. Whole saree was embellished with sequins or stonework or embroidery. She had covered herself with a thin stripped blouse. She was stunning and sizzling in that sexy saree. I was mesmerized by her breathe taking beauty.

Even, everyone was amazed by Aahna's beauty. She was the centre of attraction. Everyone was starring at her.

I felt so unsecure for Aahna at that Moment. I wished to fuck every bastard. But I was broadened chest, as Aahna, the most glamorous girl was my partner.

But I too focused on her barred navel. Her glowing fair body was glistering in that black -red saree.

Her brownish eyes were alighting. She was playing by her fingers with her long, untied brown hair that fell upon her eyes with a gust of wind. Her hand moving across her face, and moving her hair behind her left ear. She was charismatic. I wasn't able to take my eyes off her.

"Damn it," I gulped and took a long and deep breathe, and leaned back on my chair.

Little-little sequins on her black saree were twinkling to praise Aahna. She was glittering more and more, even that, moon itself felt guilt in front of Aahna. So he hid behind dark clouds.

Aahna had put a handmade crown of white and yellow roses on her head. It was so creative, that made her to look like princess of a royal kingdom.

She was eating chocolate ice-cream by her hot juicy pink lips.

Suddenly I noticed a bite of chocolate was stuck on her lower lip. It was killing me I was dying to put my lips on that small bite of chocolate.

I was continuously gliming at her, with wider eyes. I don't know, what went wrong with me. On that day again I ruined my anger and hatred for her. I felt so loving for her. I just wanted to sit on that table with Aahna, and just wanted to praise her until my last breathe.

She noticed my eyes she raised her eyebrows twice, and took another spoonful of that ice-cream.

I smiled, rubbed my neck, and shook my head.

"Don't glare at me like, I am feeling so nervous," she said and tried to escape from my eyes.

"Miss Aahna kapoor, today you are mine. No one can save you from me, even you can't," I sneered like devil and went close to her and pressed her left hand in my right hand.

"Ek thappad padega abhi," she frowned and pulled her hand away.

"Really, ok then, slap me; I will bear one more slap, as you have already slapped me a lot. I have been habitual of it," I said and surrendered my face towards her.

"Stupid..... Gadhe, tu nhi sudhrega," she raised her hand to slap me but she dodged me and laughed. She pushed me back on my seat.

And we turned towards stage. Now Sid and Sanaya were performing. They genuinely enjoying with each other. They looked so cute together.
But I knew, there was someone who was not happy to see them.

Quickly I turned my eyes towards Ruhi. I was amazed that, her eyes were shining in tears.
I raised my brows at her. Suddenly, she shook her head and wiped her tear in right eye. I blinked at her in console that it's ok. She smiled pretty at me. It's strange that somewhere we all hold a broken heart.

"And the next couple is Shourya and Aahna," host announced. We were already getting ready, and dressed for our song.

I wore a thin transparent sky -blue shirt and white pant. Aahna outfitted in sky -blue frock, which was flare, and had lots of layers at bottom, which bloomed when I made her to spin. She was looking like a Barbie girl, with white yellow rose crowned.

We went on stage, and I was so nervous in front of so large crowd. Admitting that I am an adult guy, so what? A boy can also get nervous.

Aahna felt my fear and hesitation. She came close to me, and squeezed my palm into her soft hands. She greeted me with her cute smile and dimples. And in next second, my fear, my nervousness swept away. And I felt so much Peace and loved just in her one cute smile.

We would take our position. We would sit opposite to each other, leaned against each other's back.
Our heads were buried under our knees.

Immediately, all lights went off, and only Shadow lights went on, which would move with our Shadows till the end of the song. So much of dim and silence was there. And finally the track played, in soulful voice of Papon.

"Na aaye ho......,Na aaoge......., Na din dhale....Bulaoge....., Na sham ki........,Karari chai....., labo se yun pilaoge..........."

Aahna and I lost ourselves in soulful and romantic song. We didn't know what we were doing.

We were completely unaware that how much love we had for each other.
We couldn't see anyone, we were letting go ourselves to swim in the world of love.

We would dance like love birds or I should say heroes and heroines of romantic Bollywood movie.

We destroyed all the anger, regretted and hatred we had for each other. We just loved more and more each other.

On first step, we would stretched our hands, moved them in vertical circle, and then we would face each other to hug violently.

We would get up slowly while holding each other's hands, and we would step in Salsa style.

Suddenly, I would push her away and rush away from her, in next second, she would run towards me and hug me furiously from behind. In reality, she was trying to stop me, she didn't want to letting me go, leaving her alone.

The song is about the fight, the cute fight between the two lovers. One is going away and others are stopping the first one.

Aahna and I were regretting to each other while dancing. We were expressing our anger, love and our regret we had.

Aahana would say, "Why did you leave me alone? Where were you? Why didn't you come early? You don't know how much I suffered in your love. How much I missed you?"

And I would protest, "I don't love you any more, just leave me, let me go."

Hurriedly, I would lift her in my arms, and she would wrap her hands around my neck, and I would do spins again and again.

To that end, I would drop her down, and would again lift her by her one hand and one leg, and I would swing in circle. Quickly I would make her to slide on sleepy floor and I would stride away from her.

But again she would run to stop me. I would grab her hairs, bend over her hand and would move our upper bodies in round violently.

Now I would hold her by hand, I would make her to spin thrice, and quickly she would hug me. But I would protest, so she would slap me horribly. And again she would hug me.

In next Move, we would stand opposite to each other. Our backs would lean against each other. We would stretch our hands. And squeeze each others' hands and would sit down slowly. Whereas, she would lie on my lap and I would roll my hands on her brown hairs and then I would cradle her face with love and I would kiss her cheeks.

Rapidly I would make her to roll on floor. Then she would run to catch me, but I would hold her by her waist and lift her up to my shoulders. She would stretch her hands in air and I would do spins and kiss her waist and then on her neck.

Since, in our next step, I would put my hand on her back, she would bend on my hand; I would move my other hand on her face, then. Neck, them on her thin waist, and then quickly I would throw her on floor and I would stride away while kicking her.

She would burst into cry furiously. She would scatter gifts and flowers, placed on a round table, which we had to use as prob. She would lay on her knees shake her hairs terribly.

Then suddenly, she would grab my legs furiously I would snag her by her hairs and I would drag her cruelly on floor. Her upper body was in air while her lower part was sliding on floor.

Harshly, I would throw her on floor, and rush away. Now she would act as might be she was injured. So prematurely, I would run to her, while sliding on my knees. I would pull her in my lap, I would cry furiously and would bury her in my chest, shadow lights went off, and we ended our song.

She was still in my arms. We gazed into each other's eyes. Her eyes were flashing in tears, more brownish. I was amazed that, how could we dance like that. Only true lovers could dance like that.

Aahna and I had created such romantic and loving atmosphere, by our dance. We danced to explore our love, which we were hiding from each other. We danced just as we were the lovers from last many lives. I contemplate that in this life also, God had made us for each other.

I mused that there was something, which was beyond the love that exist between us. Whole garden burst into claps, whistles and in praises.

I am damn sure that everyone must had felt loved and missed their loved ones. Aahna and I didn't know that what we had done. And how did that happen? We felt something strange we couldn't see at each Other. Quickly she ran backstage. After all the performance, a panel of jury announced Mr. and Miss fresher.

"And the winner are Shourya and Aahna," host announced in excitement," give them a big hand."

And I don't know when Aahna approached towards stage. She was more excited and enthralled.

Seniors labeled us as Mr. and Miss fresher. And I took out Aahna's handmade crown from her head, as some girls wanted to crown her. I cleverly hid that crown of white and yellow rose in memory of Aahna.

Aahna's enthusiasm was at cloud nine. She was the happiest girl of world. She was jumping like kid. And her smile was getting more and more lustrous. Her cute dimples were twinkling like stars. I never had seen her so much blissful. But literally I was much more happy than her. I felt so much peace and alive by seeing her smile and pretty laugh.

I didn't want anything from God, but I just want to see her glad always. And for that, I could do anything.

Aahna looked at me, she squeezed my hand, and blinked her brownish eyes to say, "Thank you."

After that, it was party time. We all danced out of tune with D.J. We stuffed ourselves with lots of dishes, and then we tanked ourselves with beer, and again we danced and tortured DJ.

And now it was 11:30of late night, it was time to leave. I wished that night not to turn into dawn. I was happy with her. Everything was going so good. And so I was scared that, when sun will rise. May things would be different again. But of course, good time passes so fast.

I was padding with Aahna while holding her purse in one hand, clutching her right hand in my left hand. Our warm palms steamed into sweat. We walked to her Audi, and I made her to sit on driver's seat.

"So, Aahna," I whispered slowly, and leaned against the open door of Audi.

"So, Shourya?" she raised her brows.

"Don't you think we should do friendship now," I asked, with lopsided smile on my face.

"Excuse me, Mr. Shourya Sharma," she prodded with big brown eyes, "Don't even dare to think about it. I was good to you only for this crown. I still hate you, you are my worst enemy, so just get lost now," she squelched and giggled.

"Soo...mean you are, Miss Aahna Kapoor," I said rudely and innocently.

"Just fuck off," she smirked and shut the door powerful that it hurt my fingers.

"kaminiii," I snapped.

****

CHAPTER TWENTY FOUR

After more 10 minutes, I walked towards my Pulsar, I was about to leave for hostel. And everyone and my friends had already gone.

"Shourya....Shourya.....," I heard a shouting of someone, briskly I turned around. He was Yash, running towards me with his fatty body. He leaned against my bike, he was panting badly.

"What?" I asked and patted his back, "Are you ok?"

"Aahna....," he stammered and continued, "Aahna is in danger."

"What are talking?" I asked in disbelief, "she had already left," I said in concern.

"After the event, I saw," Yash assembled himself and spoke, "Atul and Anshul screwed petrol tank of Aahna's Audi, and punctured also. And when Aahna left, Atul and Anshul hounded Aahna from main gate. I saw their green evil eyes. I am scared, they would hurt Aahna on the way," Yash said in fear.

When I heard Yash, my breath got stuck in my throat. My throat felt parched, and my mouth dry. My heartbeat went faster in fear for Aahna.

But at the same instant, my anger and temper was at its zenith for unworthy Atul and Anshul. My eyes went on fire. I was terrible.

"Today, you are gone, mother fuckers," I roared and kicked my pulsar towards bypass lane, the way towards Aahna's place, promptly.

I was searching for Aahna on dark and silent highway.

I was filled with dread. I was praying or I should say I was begging to god for Aahna. And yes!
Abruptly, every now and then weird thoughts popped into my head.
What If I don't reach on time?
What If they would have hurt her.
What If I can't save her? And so many fears crowded my mind.

After more 5 minutes, I saw Aahna's Audi lying on one Side of highway. I approached to her car and jumped off from my bike, nimbly.

I looked into the car for Aahna, but I couldn't find out her in car.

"Aahnaaa......, Aahna........," I started shouting for her, terribly and looked here and where an highway.

"Shourya....," I heard Aahna's voice. Agilely, I dogged her voice, which was coming from behind the trees and under brushes, at a distance from highway.

I was paralyzed as I saw Anshul had clutched Aahna from behind. And Atul was slapping Aahna unkindly, and he was forcing Aahna to kiss her.

They were fully intoxicated. Aahna was protesting desperately Atul, and spanking on Atul's face. That made Atul more contemptuous and violent.

Atul shattered her sky-blue frock and tinched her soft shoulders, and slapped her again. He tried to assault her sexually. Aahna was begging to them, to leave her. She was howling furiously. Her face was red, and her lips were stained in red blood.

There upon, Atul snatched her face and tried to kiss on her lips.

Tears rolled down on my face for that pity girl. My heart stopped beating for a Moment. And started beating again at twice the pace. But now I couldn't see anymore, my volcano blast in myself. I was blood thirsty, like a monster or vampire. I just want to gauge blood of those bastards. I wanted to shout as loud as I could.

"Mother fucker," I hissed, crumbled my teeth, and scampered towards them horribly. And I collared Atul by hairs, and shook violently, and threw him away. But Atul punched me, and braced himself again to hit my ribs.

Heedlessly, I defended myself by my elbow, and punched Atul's face. Suddenly, my fist crashed into his ribs, snapping them like dry wings and I collapsed his head against my knee. Atul was almost dead he fell down on ground.

Without wasting an instant, I strode towards Anshul. He was already petrified by terror. He threw Aahna towards me. Quickly, I clutched Aahna in my arms.

At sudden, Anshul kicked me, and punched my nose, and then squeezed his both hands around my neck and tried to throttle me. My nose started blooding. And I was continuously smacking Anshul's ribs to free myself. Consequently, we had to release me.

Rapidly, I clutched Anshul from behind, and smashed his waist again and again. And I threw him on a tree. He was sabotaged and fell down.

Then as I turned around to Atul, he attacked me by sharp knife. Blood ran out abundantly out of my face and hands.

He again attacked me, but I stopped his hand and twisted it, so knife fell down. Again I twisted his hand cruelly, and dug my elbows in his back, and threw him on big stone. Atul and Anshul were fully stained in blood. They were crippled, so they ran away.

Quickly I gazed for Aahna, but she was not there, I rushed out towards Highway.

"Aahna....," I called her name, and eyed towards Highway, panting on my knees.

I saw Aahna. She was sitting on the mid-highway, with dim Yellow Street light. Her legs were folded; her head was dig under her knees. She had wrapped her arms around her head and knees, as if she was holding herself together lest she shatter into a million pieces. Her saree was damaged; her black blouse was torn off from right shoulder. Her hands, cheeks and shoulders were injured, her hair falling around her face, hiding it from view. She was sobbing furiously and loudly. Her breathe was coming in gasp. She was so much terrorized. She was crying like a little girl, who had lost her mother. She might be felt so much of irreverent and guilt.

Although, I have no idea about her pain but I also felt the same grief. I felt like someone had piled into my heart. I was, just as if someone had cut my artery and left me to die slowly. I felt so much pang in my heart for that poor girl. I felt like my heart would jump out of my mouth. I could feel my feet shaking losing their grip on ground.

An unshed tear revolved in my eyes, automatically. I wasn't aware about how to deal with her, how to console on her malaise.

I contemplated that, should I have showed sympathy to her? Should I ask her that is she ok? But no, she was not at all ok. How could be she ok? Those devils had already destroyed her life. They would have abused her if I wasn't having been there in time.

Despite of that, they succeeded in assaulting her pure soul. They had made her to feel intimidate. As it is more worst to abuse someone's soul. Though, Aahna was so strong and straight forward, but regardless of that, she was totally broken, as those bastards really hurt her.

And I was a bastard too. I had also hurt her a lot. I dishonored her too.

'Loving a girl is a second thing, as we should learn to respect her first.'

Self respect is such a special and inestimable gift for a girl. By offering respect to a girl, we make her to feel so much special and happy. And we would feel heavenly Peace by seeing her in bliss.

But on that day, Aahna was not happy. I couldn't see her in such grief. I wished to die in place of seeing her in pain. An hour ago, Aahna was the happiest girl on earth and now she was the poorest girl. I was so much threatened; I was daring to touch her. But I had to do it.

I assembled myself, and padded slowly towards her. I lay on my knees next to her. But when that innocent heart sobbed, when tears rolled down from her eyes, it made me scared. I tried to speak, but my mouth was dry. I swallowed. I put my shivering on her hands, suddenly; she got panicked, and hastily rushed away from me, as though I would hurt her. She sank within herself. She was crippled with fear.

I held her face in my palm; and looked into her red eyes, dipped in tears. She gazed at me innocently, without blinking for a Moment.

"Aahna, don't worry, it's me..... Shourya," I whispered softly, and again wrapped my arms firmly around her shoulders; making sure not to scare her. And I started rubbIng her barred shoulders gently.

She gazed at me carefully. She was shivering and panting. I looked at her in sympathy.

"Shourya," she mumbled, and in next Moment, she buried her face in my chest. She didn't even try to control the sobs that were shaking her body. And she gave up and let the tears flow freely down her face. I clutched her more tightly in my warm chest. She breathed hard, her chest heaving. Goose booms raised on her body. Her heart was pounding in her chest. I could hear it.

While tears were running out of her eyes, it indeed it was my heart, who was crying. She grabbed me furiously, arms wrapped around my neck; digging her nails in my neck.

My shirt was dampened in her Diamond like tears. She was breathing in my chest, and I felt her warm hug.

I didn't want time to pass away; I just wanted to hold her in my arms for ages. I clutched her more tightly, rolled my palm on her back, ruffled her brown hair, and caressed her like my small newborn baby.

And as I closed my eyes and that revolving tear rolled down on my cheeks.

"It's ok.... Don't cry..... It's ok," I whispered, "they have gone, don't cry, and now no will ever hurt you."

For last 10 minutes, Aahna was in my arms, and we were lying in mid of Highway. She was still sobbing and I was silently patting her back. She was exhausted, and I don't know, when she fell into deep nap in my lap.

She was looking so cute, while sleeping. I removed a lock of her hair from her face and tucked it behind her ear. I kissed her forehead softly, not to disturb her sleep. The happiness for a boy is seeing his girl sleeping.

I didn't want to disturb her from deep sleep. So I waited her to wake up. For more 20 minutes, she was sleeping in my lap. It was best ever Moment of my life. I can still feel her warm breathe in my chest. I can still sense her smell, her tears, and her hands by which she had clutched me tightly.

Rapidly, she woke up with jolt. As if she had a worst nightmare. Her hair was sticking to her skin, strewn all over her face, neck and chest. Her eyes and lips were swollen. Her tears had dried up, scattering her eyeliner on her cheeks. I held her to calm her down. I wiped her tears, and blood on her lips. I covered her barred body by yellow scarf, which I had stolen from her earlier. She didn't protest. She was behaving like a good child.

I made her to seat on my bike, and I dropped her to her home. She was silent, she didn't say a word, and padded unsteadily inside her home.

Delhi is famous in crime of sexual harassment. It ranks no. 1 in cases of sexual assaulting. Girls are no safer. Even in capital of our country. How embarrassing?
People give so many excuses for this. And even, they blame girls for their sexual abusing.

But I want to know that why it is so? And what should we do solve this evil? In genuinely, I want to ask to people that, to whom we should blame for this. Is Delhi city responsible for this? Are people responsible for this? Is the modernization responsible for this?

But no, neither people, nor city is responsible. It is the cruel thinking of people, which is responsible. People are no more human, everyone is tending towards inhumanity. We, the people have lost love and respect for female figure.

Modesty isn't about hiding your body it's about revealing your dignity. It's that what we should learn.

Hell and heaven are within us, it's we decide what we want. Everything depends on us only. But the problem is that we don't want to do anything, we just keep silence. We have became habitual of living in crime.

The world suffers a lot, not because of the violence of bad people, but because of the silence of good people.

****

CHAPTER TWENTY FIVE

After that worst, Aahna wouldn't come college. It was 8th day, and she was missed. Atul and Anshul also didn't show their fucking faces to me. They were absquatulated.

I was so much bothered about Aahna. And upset too. I was missing her badly. And I was paralyzed too that she would be fine or not.

My friends were concerned about me, as they had noticed my silence and anxieties. They tried their hardest to make me laugh and to gulp out the truth from mouth.

But I didn't speak out a word, about that bullshit. I didn't want to cheat Aahna, and I didn't want Aahna to feel remorseful in front of everyone.

We were in canteen, sipping hot coffee.

"Excuse me! Shourya," Sanaya Aahna's best friend gazed at me, "can I have your two minutes," she said politely. Some time she pretended to be very polite, without any reason.

I nodded and, got up, and walked out of table.

"Hey! Sid how are you?" Sanaya smiled brightly at Sid and put her hand on his shoulder.

Sid smiled at her with wider smile. And that actually killed Ruhi. She muttered to us and left away.

"Shourya, Aahna sent a message for you," Sanaya braced herself, "she wants to meet you at Starbucks cafe at CP at 5 pm," Sanaya said and left, immediately, "and go alone," she shouted from a distance.

In evening, I was getting read, but I was scared too, as last time when Aahna called me to that Starbucks cafe, she hit me by two body builders.

But I was ready to be hit again. I just want to confirm that she was ok or not. So I reached to Starbucks on time. I took a corner table by the window and waited for Aahna. After few minutes, I gazed Aahna stepped out from Audi, and padded inside of cafe. She waved her hand with glittering smile as she beamed towards me.

"Sorry, got late," she said politely and slid in front of my eyes.

She was dressed in casual white sleeveless top with more whiter shorts. She had covered her barred shoulders by that yellow scarf.

I noticed her carefully; her eyes were swollen and drowsy, with dark shadows under her eyes. They were missing their usual glimpse; because she cried a lot from last few days. Despite of that, she was appearing so cute and innocent.

Even though. She had smiled on her pretty face. But I fact, that was a fake smile. She was pretending to be fine, but she was very shattered from inside. Laughing face does not mean that there is absence of sorrow. But it means that they have the ability to deal with it. But she had guilt that she had been abused, and touched by demons.

She was feeling embarrassed that what I would have been thinking about her. But I was not like those morons. I wanted to console her that, why she was feeling shamed. Even those bastards should feel guilt. It wasn't her fault, so she shouldn't punish herself.

"Coffee?" I asked to her. She nodded with short smile. I ordered cappuccino for us.

Therefore, there was on gawkily silence between both of us. We didn't know what to say? And how to start?

We were stealing glance at each other. And sudden, when our eyes would meet, we would give dreadful smile to each other.

Aahna riddled her thumbs nervously. Since lost few months, we both were fighting only. We were blood thirst of each other. But after that accident, we felt something strange for each other. There was love and emotions between us. An unknown relation started surfacing between us. Aahna also felt something special for me. We started caring for each other. And we had shyness as like the shyness that exists between two love birds.

Without any double, these all were the sign of trending love. We started behaving like newlywed couple she would blush and I would felt nervous.

Suddenly she started twisting her curly brown hairs in nervousness by her soft fingers, which were polished green and red. I pleaded my shivering lips to bring out the words I had kept for Aahna from months. And what I got was stupid.

"How are you?" we both asked together to break the awkwardness. And we laughed on our stupid.

"Go on," I said.

"I am good," she replied sweetly.

"I don't believe this," I prodded.

"Huh?" she fumbled nervously.

"If you are ok, then why are you not coming college?" I asked. Head titled questioningly.

"Ok let me be true to you," she said and looked down, "actually Shourya, I am afraid of those pimps. I am still in severe shock. I am scared that, they will hurt me again. I am feared that how I will face everyone, if they would have told everyone about that stuff. I am so much guilt," Aahna sighed, emotionally, stealing her eyes off me.

"Aahna. What are you doing with yourself." I whispered and smothered her palm in my both hands and kept holding for a while, "you are so brave; you slapped me in front of whole college. So how can you be afraid off bloody Atul and Ansul. Why are you guilt? They should be punished, and we will file case against them," I roared with flaming eyes. But she interrupted.

"No, Shourya I don't want to make it fucking issue. I am almost broken already. And even if I wanted to punish them, then I would have told to my Dad and he would have killed them. But I don't want to do evil like those demons," Aahna said absent-mindedly and exhaled. Her palm was still in my cage, which grew warm now.

How disappointing it is that, a girl has to be silent even after she is being assaulted by someone. Aahna easily said that she don't want to make it big issue. But she said that not because of fear of Atul. She kept silence because of our bloody society, where a girl is assumed as impure and shame, even when it's not her mistake. Aahna was terror that people will talk shit about her only, and not about those fucking culprits.

So basically, in our society the accused is praised for his crime, and a girl is guilt, just because she is girl. She has to bear all pain and molestation, just because she is a girl. By the law of our so-called society, it's natural that a girl has to be responsible for all the fucking shit, just because she is a girl.

So it is in the nature of girl that she is a shit, just because she is a girl.

"But Aahna, it's not a small thing, we can't let them go, they tried to harr-------," I stopped my words, "Aahna I don't know anything. But I will kill those bastards, I am just waiting for them," I pestle my teeth.

"Shourya, please try to understand," she sniffed, "let it go. And see, today the best part is that you are with me. Now I don't want anything. Now we are together here, only because of Anshul and Atul," she said and put her other hand on mine, but abruptly she removed away her hand swiftly. She darted her eyes on every corner, trying to hide her blush.

Actually, she was right, sometimes our enemies benefits us, accidently. And we finished our coffee. I was continuously trying to hide my wounds and injuries. I knew she would feel more concerned and disrepute. But amid, she clocked my wounds on my forehead and shoulders.

"What is it?" she asked.

"Nothing," I said and covered my face.

She leaned forward and touched my cheeks, forehead and

hands. I felt so smooth touch, she vanished away all my pain in just one touch.

"It's all because of me naa........," she whispered, and her brownish eyes shining by unshed tear. And a tear rolled down on her cheeks. I got up, and went to her and put my arms firmly around her.

"Aahna, It's ok..... I am fine," I said, rubbing her shoulder. And already tears were spilling over. She didn't try to stop them.

"How much evil, I am. You should slap me," I said grumpily.

"Why?" she asked.

"I came here to see your cute smile, and look I made you to cry," I said dreary.

"No, I am fine, I am not crying," she sighed, wiping her tears by her fingers

"Ok then, please smile for me. You really have such cute dimples, I actually wanna touch them," I said, looked at her expectantly.

"Nope......," she buzzed longer, and showed her big eyes.

"Please, Aahna," I begged.

"Shut up......, Shourya," she frowned again. I again slumped back on my chair rudely.

"You know Aahna, the greatest gift you can ever give me_ is to look at me and smile," I said, and captured her eyes. She slowly smiled with love, and flashing her twin dimples.
"Look Aahna, I got your dimples back," I excited, "now can I touch them," I begged abruptly.

"Stupid," she shrieked, "ok but only once," she said. And two cute dimples appeared on her pink cheeks, when I touched them by my fingers. I felt heavenly peace. Once again I fell in love of Aahna.

"Shourya, you are tickling me now, move away," she laughed, and pushed me away.
"So beautiful, you are Aahna," I said, and we beamed at each other.

I wanted to say so much things to her which i had buried deeper in my heart. But the most important things are the hardest to say because words diminish them.

But the things left unsaid, stay with us for forever.

"Shourya, I am really sorry. Shourya," she looked into my eyes," I always misunderstood you, I troubled you a lot, and I slap------" she was saying, but I cut her off, and held her both hands.

"It's ok, Aahna, it was our past, and I too hurt you a lot," I was saying.

"Really, then, you should say sorry to me," she chuckled at me.

"Ok meri... Maa.. Kan.. Pakde.." I yapped.

"Khush rho," she crackled and blessed me.

"Ha, Ha. Very funny," I annoyed.

"Ok listen," she got serious tone, "Shourya, I called you to thank you, if you wouldn't have come that night," she said I interrupted.

"Which night," I shrugged.

"That night, Atul and Anshul remember," she sighed, narrowing her eyes.

"Who are they? I don't know them. Do you know them?" I said and winked my eyes with smile at her.

Actually I wanted her to forget every fucking bullshits. I want her to smile, and to move on.

"Chill forgets all," I cocked again. She smiled in respect for me.

"Thank you", she said politely.

"Aahna, you look so pretty, when you smile so can you please always smile for me," I squeezed het hand.

"I will but, only for you," she said.

"So, you one coming to college ok," I ordered her.

"Ok, but only if you will be with me, to protect me," she said.

"I promise, I will be always with you, I will never leave you alone," I said mildly and patted her palms.

"Ok, now, I have to go, Dad will be angry," she said and stood up briskly

"But it has been only few minutes," I complained like kid.

"Don't believe like kid," she snapped, "we are catching in college Naa...," she raised her brows.

"So, Now I think, we are friends," I smirked.

"May be, how come you so sure," she mocked and laughed.

We padded to her Audi. And once again she held my hands.

"Thank you Shourya, you mean a lot to me," she said innocently. I saw a faith for me in her brown eyes. I blinked at her in that same faith. She sat in car.

"Aahna can I get my scarf," I pointed towards that yellow scarf.

"But it's mine naa, and what, you will do of it?" she touched that scarf and shrugged.

"Aaaiiivanyiiiiii..," I sighed, "ok rehne do."

But amid, she pulled out that yellow scarf from her neck and handed to me.

"Always keep it close to you heart," she said and left.

"Journal-675

when we irrigate the seeds of our dreams with the drops of Time, one day the plant itself shine to the world. It's all the cycle of Time that roots the base of any big achievements. That's what Aahna and I was doing."

****

143

CHAPTER TWENTY SIX

After that day, I would never ever leave Aahna alone. We both would walk everywhere, in classroom, library, canteen, and park. All places would hold our essence. And my hand would be always in company of her hand. And my body would be her shadow. We would talk less. We would just beam at each other absurdly. And sometimes, I would have to separate from her, at that time she would wait for me, and if I got late, she would cry, "Where were you? Why did you leave me alone?"

At other point, apparently, my love story overrode my friendship. This should not have been the case. I was getting away from my friends, as all time I had to be with Aahna. But my friends were bloody morons. They never left me alone. They followed Aahna and me everywhere. And they kept on taunting and torturing us.

"They are so crazy," Aahna would say about my friends.

****

It was dark night, my friends and I were doing party late Saturday night in hostel garden, with pizzas, drinks, cocktails, beers. Granting all this, I didn't drink, as I had promised to Aahna. She want me to be good, she wanted to remove all the beasts in me. And so that I didn't want to betray her.

"Dekh, yash Aahna ne do din me sudhar diya launde ko," Rohan shrieked. He was lying in Ashvini's lap.

"Kaminee... Tu kab sudherega," I snapped, "Don't drink now," I snatched Bottle from Rohan, and gave it to Ruhi, lying in my lap, my arms wrapped around her shoulders from behind.

"So........ Shourya...?" Rohan raised his brows.
"So....... Rohan....?" I copied him.

"Absurd, did you kiss Aahna, again?" Rohan Ridiculed.

"Shut up, you asshole, don't talk vulgar, I am not a bad mannered, like you," I bellowed.

"Oh really! Then why you kissed her in pub, you sick?" Rohan smacked back.

"Fuck off," I snapped, "Aashu.... Tell him to shut up," I complained to Ashvini.

"Shut up, Rohan," Ashvini giggled, and we laughed.

"Shourya, but seriously, you should thank Rohan and me. As because of us, Aahna and you are together," Ruhi said and laid her head in my lap.

"What rubbish?" I gulped, "why would I do that?"

"Oh! Hello, Mr. Shourya Sharma," Ruhi shouted hastily, weirdly and got up, and twisted her long braid, "you don't know, you were Aahna's partner because on that night Rohan and I unlocked Aasha ma'am cabin and attached your named hook with Aahna's name," Ruhi hit on my head.

"What?" I shocked, "how could you entered into Ma'am's cabin?"

"Dude, if you can unlock Raghav Sir's cabin, then why we can't unlock Aasha ma'am's cabin," Rohan and Ruhi said, and laughed boisterous.

"Such rogue, you all are," I said rudely, and pulled Ruhi's chaps.

"By the way Ruhi, you helped me to meet, to win Aahna's heart, so thank you so much," I touched her feet, "And I pray that soon you will get you love," I said and looked at Sid with squinted eyes.

"Oh! Hello, I have already got my love," Ruhi sniffed, and clocked at Sid.
We all were shocked; we looked at Sid and buzzed together, "who?"

"Yash....," she said and pulled fatty Yash in her arms, she wanted to make Sid jealous.

We all glared at Yash. And Sid's blood went up.

"Really Ruhi, are you serious?" Yash exasperated. Ruhi screwed his all intoxication.

"Yeah! Yash, I love you," Ruhi chuck under Yash's chin, "actually I wanted that someone will come and propose me. But I got that no one loves me. People love that bloody bitch Sanaya. So I have decided that you are my only love, I love you so much Yash," Ruhi sounded, gawkily. She kissed Yash's hands. She was taunting Sid.

She glared at Sid, we all were tittering. Sid looked so angry, as if he would kill Yash or Ruhi, either.
In a corner of heart, everyone holds sorrow.
 Once you have been hurt, you get so much scared to be attached again. You are afraid that everyone is going to break your heart.

****

CHAPTER TWENTY SEVEN

I genuinely have a very bad habit that, I don't get attached to someone easily. But once I got attached to someone, then I can't live without that person. I become addicted of that person. Aahna was like a drug, the most addictive kind of.

It was so much painful to spend, to live a single second without her.

"Hlo Aahna: I texted her, but she didn't reply.
"Hey! R u there: I typed again. But again she didn't respond.
"Wht's wrng wd u. Whr d hell r u: I continued to text her, and filled her inbox. But she didn't text back.

It was so hurting, I got upset, I placed my phone my front, and waited. My urge to talk to her was increasing with every second. I was getting panic, I was missing her, and angry too at the same time. I wanted to fight with her, and wanted to hug her all together. Love is such package of mix feelings.

How strange it is that when we text to someone special, we wait for her/ he is massage for hours.

And every time when our cell beeps, we get excited, we assume that it is her/his massage. And we check our phone again and again. At the end, we got sad when we find telecom companies massage about fucking special offers.

Every time, when my cell phone's screen flashed, I jumped from bed to check it. I was so enthusiasm. But in next Moment I all my happiness drain away, as I saw they ware Sid and Rohan, texted me to torture me.

Being mad at someone when they couldn't help the situation was childish. 'Ok fine, I am child, I agree," I murmured to myself.

It was 11:30 p.m. I stood outside in the balcony in partial darkness.It was quite, and the light breeze held just a tinge of coolness. I rested my arms on the cold metal railing and leaned forward. I could see half bright moon, and dancing stars making the same wish on each other.
Loudly, my phone beeped, it was Aahna.

"Sry sry sry sry sry .... so sry..., stuck bsy so couldn't hlp" : said her message.

"Jst get lost, nt in d mood to tlk" : I replied quickly.

"sry Shourya, plsssssss" : she said.

"Wht sry Aahna, wht sry. You knw Naa_ I don't feel gud wdout tlking to u" : I typed longer.

"Yahhh I knw bt was jst": she said.

"U knw wht Aahna, you hv tym fr everyone bt not fr me. U dn't care fr me. so jst good bye, dn't msg me ever" : I texted.

"SHOURYA.... sry na baba pls...., last tym,": she kept massaging me, but I didn't reply now.

Though, my heart wanted to text but my mind denied. I kept reading her messages.

"Shourya... I m cryng now...plss.. tlk to me pls pardon me" : she sent.

"Hey! R u awaking" : I replied after 30 minutes.

"Idiot, kuttee, kamineee..., jst get lost, I dn't wanna tlk, u made me cry today" : she angered.

"sry Aahna....., it was your eyes who cried, but it was my heart who bleeded,": I texted wisely.

"Sht up... missing u idiot, dn't use to tlk me so mch, I miss u when u left, I cn't sleep, I jst wnna tlk to u whle nght,": she messaged.

"Tht's so romantic," : I said.

I could paint an image of Aahna in green top, pink sort, lying on her foamy bed, sank into her comforter, a pillow clutched to her chest, smiling while reading my messages.

We chatted whole night until our phone breathed last. It's such

148

a painful, when you are chatting with your love, till late night, and your battery says I am low.

And, even more worst is that, you don't find charger. At that time I would like to throw my cell on the face company's owner. We talked nonsense about new movie, new song, new TV show. We talked much about bollywood stars and their current affairs. We would tell what we had in dinner. She would send me pics of her new clothes, shoes and everything.

"DDLJ is my favorite one" : she texted.
"Namaste London" : I said.
"I love Alia batt," : I texted.
"Ranbeer kapoor" : she said.
"Sonu Nigam" : I texted.
"Shreya ghosal," : she messaged.
"Robin Sharma and Paulo coelho," : I texted.
"Charles Dikken's plays," : she massaged.
"Wanna see Paris," : she said.
"Same," : I texted.
"Dinner....,":I Texted.
"Yeah, I like Dinner, lunch, Breakfast. Indeed, I love to eat every time. I am glutton," : she texted.
"No, I was saying that can I have pleasure to do dinner with you," : I said.
"No, can't. Dad wouldn't allow,": she added.
"Please...,": I pleaded and sent smiles.
"Noo...," : she denied.
"I don't know, I will wait for at hotel royal palace, tomorrow evening, 7 p. M." : I mentioned
"Go to hell, I wll nt cm," : she messaged last. Now I was lying on my bed, scrolling up and down whole chat and smiling like nuts. The best part of love is reading whole conversation once again.

****

CHAPTER TWENTY EIGHT

"Kamineeeee.... Sale.... De na teri new shirt," I shouted at Rohan, and pulled out another shirt, and tried one more another shirt. I was getting ready for hotel Royal Palace.

"Kamineeee...... You have already destroyed my 2 shirts of mine 3 shirts of Sid," Rohan barked, and with eagled eyed at me.

"How's it?" I shrugged my brows at Sid, ignoring Rohan.

"Sexy lag rha bhaiii.... Ummmaaaahhhhh," Rohan cocked and shrieked.

It was already 7: pm of beautiful evening. I was already sitting on table, which I had already booked for Aahna and me at Royal Palace in Nehru Palace. I was waiting badly for her; I knew the time was running so fast. But I suppressed my urge to check that watch.

It was 7:30 p.m., I was dying with every second. I was losing my hopes. And with every second my heart beat was going off. I felt that my body started burning in sever fever.

But as says "if *you have a single hope in your heart than you can even win the world.*"

I also had last hope that she will come. And suddenly I saw Aahna's Audi stopped on front of Restaurant. And quickly my messy face turned into flashing weird smile. My heart beat started going faster. I jumped out, and rush towards Aahna in full trepidation.

She stepped out of her car and padded towards staircase. Immediately, I appeared in her front, and gave my hand to help her. She held my hand in her soft hand.

"Hello!" she said politely and with twinkling smile, giving half hug to me.

"I knew, that you will come," I said with a beam.

"Oh really, and how did you know that?" she gleamed and raised her eyes brows.

"Because, my heart was saying that Aahna will come," I quipped and touched my heart.

"So clever Shourya," she chuckled, and leaned against my arms, snuggled close to me and we walked inside.

"And, if I would have not come, then?" she Shrugged,

"Then, I would have eaten alone," I said, and she laughed, "don't laugh, I would have sent bill to you," I shrieked cleverly, and pressed her twin dimples.

She sat on my front, as I offered her chair to respect her. She welcomed me. Actually, to win Girls heart, we should behave well mannered with them, to make them feel so special.

Hotel royal Palace is amongst one of the best restaurants of South Delhi, and especially for couples.

There were so many couples dating each other, with candle light dinner on a round red dining table decorated with flowers. The atmosphere was so silent. Lights were dimmed with Yellow and red. Soft, and romantic music played by a band of awesome violin artists, they truly made the atmosphere more romantic and loving.

Today Aahna, was looking spectacular and pretty too. She dressed herself in short sleeved casual short dress, which was flared at her knees, and colored orchid pink. There was so much floral effect and butterflies with blue, red, black and violet colors. She was glistening in that dress.

Today she made her light brown hairs into bouffant Side ponytail braid, and crowned herself with handmade Yellow roses.

Some stands of her curly brown hair were falling on her forehead from both Sides. And she would keep continuously removing those lock of hairs by her fingers polished orchid pink. Often, she would puff air by her pink lips to remove her curl.

She was shining like Diamond. Word falls short to express her beauty.
I hardly suppressed my urge to hug her. It was my first untold date with Aahna, but I wished it should be a candle light date with the girl I loved.

So that we could eat while doing some romantic and lovely gossips, so that I could feed her by my own hands. And after dinner, we could eat same ice-cream, and then we would kiss each other. And after that, I could sleep in her lap. And when I would get up next morning, I could see only Aahna's glance. And she could give me cute good morning kiss.

"Hello Sir, good evening ma'am," a waiter welcomed both of us, shaking me out o my dream.

We ordered our dinner. Veritably she ordered our dinner. She ordered Paneer, some kofta, Dal fry, rice, cheese, custards, ice-cream, Chinese and so many. Aahna would eat so much.

After waiter left, again worst happened, we again went in silence, we were looking away here and there, we were trying that our eyes don't collide with each other, as we wanted to hide our nervousness, shyness, and blushing.

How much queer is that the person to whom we love a lot, if she is not with us at that time we miss her terribly, we want to capture her in our eyes for our whole life.

But when she or that person comes in our front, at that time we become so panic and nervous. We can't look at her. Our body started trembling. And we forget all the things, all the gossips, all the crazy stuff that we wanted to say to her.

Supposing, many times we want to open our heart to her, but our voice don't come out of our throat. Some of the best conversations are worthless, some soundless. Same happened with me and Aahna. I had prepared long list in my mind but when she appeared in my front, I forgot everything.

In spite of such gawkiness, Aahna and I both kept on stealing glance at each other, and smiling like jerks.

"Aahna," I assembled myself and gasped, "We talk a lot on massaging; we do so much masti, craziness like absurd. But today we are face to face, and we have nothing to say," I giggled.

"Yeah. You are right Shourya, we are destroying such beautiful evening," she exasperated. I could see concern on her forehead.

"So ....," I shrugged.

"So, let's start again," she said in elation, with big brown eyes.

"Sorry, I didn't get you," I asked in surprise.

"Shut up ....and just answer me," she started me, "how are you?" She asked politely.

"I am so good," I answered, mildly.

"Now you are supposed to ask the same to me ask me ghonchu..," she frowned.

"Ok, so Miss Aahna Kapoor, how are you?" I asked and grinned.

"Now, I am too good, "she shrieked and removed lock of her curly brown hair.

" Aahna.....This is for you," I said and handed gift to her.

"Wow," she buzzed longer, "gift! I love gift," she said with enthusiasm, "can I open it," she asked like cute kid.

"Of course," I couldn't complete my line, but she had already unwrapped that gift.

"Wow, it's gorgeous, I loved it," she amazed and kissed black long and flared skirt, with lots of unparalleled layers at the bottom.

"I am blissful Aahna, that you like it," I said politely.

"I loved it Shourya," she held my hand. And then we had our first dinner together. I feed Aahna by my hands, but she didn't do the same to me. After dinner, we had ice-cream outside of the restaurant.

"Shourya, it's too late, I don't think, I can make it to home alone," Aahna said licking her ice-cream, "can you drop me home."

"Yeah! Why not? Pleasure will be mine," I said politely. I was like on top of sky. I had the pleasure of long drive with Aahna. And guess what? In few seconds, I was in her Audi Q7, my first love. She drove to her home on dark and silent highway. I was enjoying Audi. And yes I was feeling proud, gleeful and shame at the same time.

I was proud that my crush was driving and I was sitting by her Side, in the dark and lonely night.
And I was shameful that a girl was riding and I was sitting by her Side all relax.

I was swimming in weird and funny thoughts, smiling within myself, completely unaware of Aahna's presence. But she had noticed me already.

Abruptly, she stopped the car, by the left Side of the highway. And that rapid action interrupted my thoughts. I was startled_ I beamed at Aahna. She placed her right elbow on the steering wheel and resting her chin on her palm. She faced towards me. She was staring at me without blinking. I couldn't read her expressions. I raised my eyebrows in questioning. But she didn't make any move. She glued her eyes at me. She was scaring me now. I looked down in my lap. I swallowed my weight under my throat.
The silence in the car persisted, tearing me apart. I didn't dare to meet her eyes, but her presence persisted me to look up at her.

"What? If I rape you here," Aahna said in threatening voice, as if she was a ghost. And here I shuddered, my face steamed in sweat.

"What," I collected myself and said.

"Yes.........!" she said.

"No! You will not Aahna...," my voice throbbed.

"Yes! I will Shourya...," she said and gave eerie look.

She moved close to me, leaning over me. I closed my eyes, heartbeat went twice the pace, and I waited to be attacked by her.

"Open your eyes Shourya...," she yelled.

"No I won't," I said.

"Look at me Shourya," she grabbed my face, and as I opened my eyes, I clocked Aahna holding red rose and a gift in her hands with twinkling dimples.

"Idiot, you just have killed me," I panted heavily.

"This is for you you," she handed me that rose and gift.

"Thank you Aahna. You are so sweet," my face lit up in a wide smile.

She leaned on me, and licked my right cheek. My words felt short to describe my feelings at that very Moment, as some Moments are meant to be frozen in time. After that, we had a Sidewalk on that highway, under streetlight throwing dull yellow light, under shadow of moon and stars.

She pulled off her heels and walked on bare feet. She had threaded fingers of her left hand into fingers of my right hand, her right hand clutching my left arm. We walked slowly, silently. We spoke in languages, I had never heard before; soft moans and labored breaths carried meaning more than speech ever could.

"Why you tied your hair, you look more prettier with open hair," I said to Aahna, and swiftly I free her hair from the cage of her hair band. She blushed furiously at me. I rolled my fingers in her hair, and tucked a strand falling on her face.

****

CHAPTER TWENTY NINE

"*Are you ok, why are not coming to college?*" *:* I messaged Aahna.

"*No... I am not ok; I have caught into an accident. I got serious injuries. I can't walk. I am on bed rest,*" : **she texted.**

"*What? When did it happen?*" *I frowned,* " *and why didn't you inform me?,*" : I replied.

"*Chill Shourya.... I wll be all well,*" : she said.
"*I m coming to see u....,*" *:* I texted.
"*Noooo...... You can't, Dad is at home,*" : she sent.

"*Listen Aahna, I don't want any argument, I am coming right now,*" *:* I texted.

"*Oh....lord.., u nvr listen to me...*" **she frustrated,** "*ok come, but please come in evening. Dad and everyone are going to an event in evening,*" *:* she replied.

****

In evening, I drove to her home. Actually, not home, it was a luxury Bungalow of an ML. I entered into the Bungalow through a big wooden gate. The Bungalow was so luxury, and well decorated with colorful curtains, painting, sketches and party posters, banners. There was a big framed of Aahna's MLA Dad. Granting all this, I was nervous, as it was quite ghastly to visit your crush's home. It was empty, no one was present there, and I padded like thief.

"Aahna...," I called her name and padded slowly in fear, my eyes darting from one object to another, trying to find my love..

"Yeah...! Shourya...., Come upstairs..," "then all of a sudden a voice travelled in that empty space, "here Shourya," I saw Aahna

156

waving her hand. She was sitting mid of staircase; legs stretched on that one whole stair, and back leaned against the wall. And there was smile rippling across my face, as I clocked Aahna. I strode towards her, and sat in same posture; one-step below her.

She wore a black sort, and white thin stripped top. Her brownish hairs were floating with cool wind. She was doing nail polish on her left leg. And her right leg was covered with so many bandages at her knees, and ankle. She was appearing so cute.

"How are you?" I asked and gave white rose to her and some dairy milk chocolates.

"Wow! Chocolates! I was dying to eat this," she said with huge brownish eyes, and snatched chocolates from me.

"Easy Aahna," I bellowed, "you are injured, you should take care of yourself, and why are you sitting at such dangerous place, you can fall down," I frowned, and hit on her head.

"No, I wouldn't," she sneered, "I can take care of mine," she laughed.

"Yeah!" I gave gawkily face, "I am seeing, how much you care of yourself?" I grinned and pulled her both pink chaps by my fingers.
"Aaaauuuchhhhh! Easy you are hurting me," she threw my hands away.

Suddenly, an old woman in yellow saree, and white hairs, short height came to us. I gazed at her; she had loose skin with so many wrinkles. She narrowed her eyes to recognize me.

"Shourya, right?" said, that woman.

I looked at her in surprise. And nodded.

"Shourya. Meet my best friend, my Dadi," Aahna introduced her.

"Hello! Dadi," I touched her feet.

"Aahna always talks about you," Dadi said.

"Yeah.... Literally Dadi, she talks a lot," I teased Aahna, and Dadi and I laughed.

"Beautiful rose," Dadi said excitedly.

"This is for you Dadi," I smiled and gave that rose and chocolates to Dadi while snatching them from Aahna.

"Dadi, he is lying, he had brought this for me," Aahna shrieked. And all three of us laughed.

"Ok, Baccho, you enjoyed, and Aahna take Shourya to your room, I will arrange coffee for you," Dadi said and left.

Then, we got up. Aahna leaned against the pole. She couldn't walk. She gave me weird smile, I responded her smile. She tried to step next, but she was about to slip.

Quickly I held her. I leered deep into her brownish eyes. She was with pondering face. Then fleetly, I lifted her up and carried her in my arms. Aahna wrapped her arms around my neck and nestled her face in the crook of my neck.

"Where is your room?" I asked.

"There." she said politely and pointed towards right. She wrapped her arms around my neck, and put her head on my chest.

"You are so heavy," I Said and padded slowly.

"And you are so sweet," she whispered slowly with blush and love.

And I entered into her room. It was too pretty, and flashing as like bedroom of any Royal Princess. Its walls were painted orchid pink. So many paintings, framed photos, flowers, curtains, and fair bouquets were decorated on every wall and corners.

I put Aahna on her luxury Round pink and foamy bed. I helped her in climbing on her bed, rested her head against the headboard, legs stretched straight on the bed.

I felt so nervous and awkward, as sitting on bed of your crush makes hot climate. She gauged my expressions_ lifted her eyebrows to me.

"Nothing," I shook my head. She giggled, and thereupon, she showed me her paintings, books, gifts and her childhood photos. She showed me her movie collection.

"Shourya... Look here. This is my teddy Aaru," Aahna said and kissed her teddy. I did the same.

"Let Me do...," I said and opened her bandages. I gave her massage on her leg. Her knee was still swollen.

"Aaacuuuuhhhh.......," she exasperated, "it's hurting," she groaned in pain.

"Don't worry, it would be fine," I said and blew air on her knee.

"Aahna, you didn't paint your nail properly," I said and held fingers of her injured leg.

"Yeah, I can't do it properly, I am injured naaa," she said, regretfully with cute and innocent face.

"Let me do, I am a good painter, you know?" I quipped and we both cackled.

I kept her barred leg on my lap and started polishing her nails with varieties of colors.

Her legs were so flossy, and soft. My hands shacked, I felt deceived, when I touched her leg.

"Show me your hands," I sat next to her, and put her soft hands on my palm and started polishing them.

Then, we caught so much fun; having snacks, watching movie. And we were exhausted now. We were lying on the foamy bed, arms spread across bed and facing the ceiling; we made ourselves comfortable. We were breathing so much air. We could hear our breaths only in that silent room.

I turned my face to her. I propped myself up on an elbow and observed Aahna. Her eyes were shining, her lips were slightly open, I could hear her slow breathing. I tucked a strand falling on her face behind her ear, and blew air on her face. She squinted her eyes. I leaned towards her lips, and put my lips on her soft lips. They touched and stayed there for a Moment. Our breaths were mingling into each other's. And I pulled her lower lip by my lips. Then I looked at her, there was surprise in her eyes. I smiled at her and went for another kiss. I rubbed my lips against her, and sucked her upper lip. She responded with a moan. She put her palm on my cheeks. Our noses were brushing against each other. Then I rested my lips on top of her, and held her lips together between my lips, paused for a Moment, and nibbled them twice.

I rested my weight on her chest for a support_ feeling her heart beat under my chest. And my mouth slipped from her lips to her cheeks, and then her ears, and then her neck, kissing slightly, leaving wet of my tongue on them.

I licked her collar bone_ and then moved down to her chest and licked there.
Moving up, I hid my face in her brown hair, my cheeks grazing hers. I kept on smelling her hair, moving my lips in her hair gently, as if I was searching for something there.

"Aahna..," I whispered.

"Hmmm...," she nodded.

"You smell so good," I said, and inhaled her hair long, before biting her ear slightly.

"Aaahhh.., you are tickling me now," Aahna groaned.

Again, I came back to her lips. She shut her eyes deeply, and breathed on my face. Her lips were quivering. I swiftly pressed my lips on her, and held them tightly. On impulse, she grabbed my head by one hand, and her other hand was on my jaw. My lips moved against her, sucking, nibbling.

And my tongue made its way into her mouth; compelled her to open it further. And my tongue met her tongue, twisting her tongue first and then sucked it smoothly.

My left hand was wrapped around her hair, right hand moved down to her bare thighs, her knees and further down to her ankle, and yet again travelled up in the reverse order passionately.

I rested my hand on her waist, and it found a naked space between her top and black shorts. I rolled my fingers in circle at her belly and pressed it to tease her.

It killed Aahna; sent shiver down her spine. She wanted to breathe, so she tried hard to free her lips from mine, but I didn't let her move for a second. She rose her face up to meet my lips. And she sucked my tongue furiously, and again she bent down to get some air. And I let her breath for a while and kissed again.

We peeked into each other's eyes, still panting for air.

Kissing Aahna was something like MEDITATION. I could feel my every breath, every second. I could feel myself alive.

"Aahna, I want to ask you something?" I asked and heaved on her lips.

"Say it. I am hearing," she replied and kissed my nose.

"Aahna, I want to know, which deodorant? You use?" I asked.

"What?" she narrowed her eyes?

"Which deodorant you use?" I whispered on her face.

"Are you idiot?" She annoyed. And here we crackled loudly, jerkily.

Unexpectedly, a harsh knocking began on the door, and broke our laugh. Swiftly, Aahna pushed me away, and I slipped down the bed. We both were startled. She arranged her top, and stroked her hand on her hair. We exchanged our gaze; we were caught terror, as the knocking was going louder with every second. And yes! Aahna opened the door.

I beamed a middle-aged man in white Kurta and yellow sleeveless jacket. He entered into room.

"Dad," Aahna said is wobbling voice, and threw me away from her. We got up hastily.
Aahna's Dad looked so infuriated; he was grinding his teeth like angry lion. He strode horribly towards me. He glowered at me.

"How dare you entered into my house," he hissed, and straightaway, slapped my right chap. I was in great shock.

"Dad, it's not like that, its misunderstanding. Leave him Dad," Aahna got dreaded, and she defended me. But her Dad collared me.

"You bastard, I will kill you," he barked.

"Sir, listen, we are friends only, you are getting wrong," I annoyed and protested.

"I very well know, such boys who play with rich girls, abuse them and them leave," he squelched, and raised his hand to slap me.

"Dad, it's enough," Aahna said heatedly, "he is my friend, and you can't hit him."

"So, now you will stop me, you bitch, you screwed my name," he roared and abused Aahna, and he moved his hand to hit me. But Aahna stopped his hand.

"How dare you?" he grinded his teeth, and raised his slap wrathfully to smack Aahna, but now I stopped him and depended my love.

I peered at Aahna, she was so threatened she was shuddering terribly. Her eyes were filled with tears. She was biting her lower lip to control her cry.

"You can't heat her," I frowned disastrously. I wanted to kill him at that Moment. What if he was an MLA, I didn't care. I would care for Aahna only.

"Leave my hand," he groaned, and glared at me.

"Shourya," Aahna snapped, "What are you doing? Leave his hand," Aahna said in vibrating tone. She could barely stay audible as she said that.

Thereupon, her Dad clutched me by my collar, and dragged me violently and threw me out.

"Stay away from her, otherwise I will kill either you or her," he frowned and shut the gate on my face.

I was in severe shock, I didn't get what to do, my brain got choked, I just wanted to run heedlessly for miles to burst out my anger and anxieties. My body, my mind were numb, my heart had been ripped out of my body. My whole world continued to shatter around me.

I rushed at hostel, and locked myself in my dark room. I was not confirmed that I was in anger or in pain or in fear. I couldn't help but I wanted to hurt myself as I was so sheepish.

"I lost her, I lost her, it was my mistake, I shouldn't have kissed her, I shouldn't have loved her," I murmured to myself, and blurted absurdly, and walked round and round in my room. I was extremely frightened.

I was so scattered, not because that her Dad slapped me. But I was sad and concerned for Aahna. Now she would have to suffer because of me. My body fired in severs fever. But for an instance, I was shocked that, how could her Dad slap her.

Admitting, any Dad would react, if he sees her daughter is being kissed. But Aahna's Dad was horrible. He seemed like he would kill us.

And the more torturing was that, Aahna didn't protect against her Dad. She was so brave and strong girl, so why she was bearing such assault.

My mind was crippled by so many fearful thoughts. The more I thought about it, the more deeper I pushed myself into depression. I sensed that, if I let such thoughts come into my mind, they would paralyze me. I couldn't help myself, I just lay on my bed, hoarding myself under the blanket, squeezing my hands between my thighs. I just needed a deep sleep.

****

CHAPTER THIRTY

That worst incident brought some changes in my life. But it brought me more close to Aahna. My soul started feeling for her. Some part of me wanted to know about the real life of Aahna, and wanted to accept her life as my own life.

Though, we didn't meet after that stuff. We didn't even talk. As we, both were scared that her Dad would ruin both of us, as his eyes were on both of us 24X7.

I would stay away from Aahna, only for her sack, whereas my heart was not ready to accept that separation. I had a faith that with time everything would be normal again. But can't wait, I just wanted to confirm that she was ok or not.

I wanted to ask, "Are you ok? Do you need me?"
I thought, things won't be normal again. I contemplated that I have lost Aahna.

The constant feeling of losing someone is more heart breaking than actually losing someone.

One day, I got chance, I saw Aahna driving her car towards Shiv Mandir near her home. I followed her, and approached to her car after 10 minutes. Aahna wasn't in the car. I marched towards temple. And I gazed Aahna's Dadi, sitting on stair of temple.

"Hello Dadi," I touched her feet. She gazed up at me. I noticed her eyes, which were sad and concerned for me.

"Why you came to us beta?" She clutched my hand, "Aahna's Dad will kill you," She sobbed.

"Dadi, I don't care," I patted her hand and lay on her feet, "I only care for Aahna, I want to know about her. Why she is in such gloom? What she is hiding from me? I want to know Aahna," I gestured my heart to Dadi, and gasped.

"Shourya, Aahna's life is hell. She is living like a dead body in her own house. Her Dad is an MLA, and he is a corrupt politician, and an unkind man. He does every evil to gain profit. And for that he can do anything," Dadi sighed, her voice shivered, "He spared his whole life in politics. He didn't give time and love to Aahna's mother. He tortured, disrespect, and humiliated her Mom.

So her Mom was exhausted of his evil. She became weak and alone day-by-day. And then Aahna took birth, when her mother was dying. So this made even worst condition of her Mom. Her Dad wanted a boy, who could lead his party. And when Aahna borne, her Dad lost his seat and Aahna's Mom died few days after her birth. So her Dad blamed Aahna for all these anxieties. He started treated her as bad luck. He even tried to kill her. But I saved her. But he made Aahna's life hell. He hates her a lot. He never paid attention in her growth. Everyone in family hates her and treats her as slave. They have controlled Aahna's life. She has been locked in cage in her own house. While, she has every luxury of life, all these pleasures are tasteless as she doesn't have love." Dadi said, and tears rolled down abundantly. I put my hands firmly around her shoulder, and clutched her.

I felt so embarrassed of myself. And I felt so much generosity or pity or sympathy for Aahna. I was feeling mercy for Aahna, that she didn't even see her mother. I didn't know, she held such sorrow in her heart. All pain and grief was less in front that bad of Aahna. My eyes filled with tears. I just wanted to hug her tightly, warmly.

She was so strong, despite of such exploitation she would smile to hide her malaise from people. How could God do such bad with such cute and honest girl? Aahna was that pretty that no one couldn't even shout at her. She was so adorable.

While, I had no idea about her miseries, but I had decided to cure her pain, to bring smile, a real smile on her face.

"Dadi, I am feeling so sorry for Aahna. I don't know why? And I don't know how? But I want to help her. I want to see her always smiling. I can't see her in such pain," I said with Ruth in my voice.

"Beta, I don't know what is between both you. But I noticed Aahna likes you. Only you can make her to smile, only you can get breathe back in her dead body. Please take away her from such sorrow," Dadi sobbed again.

Hence, I saw Aahna padding towards us. She was in white long kurti, and white thin, flared salwar, and a yellow and white dupatta across her upper body. Yellow and green bangles were jingling in her left hand. And as she walked close to us, I heard a breathe taking sound chhann.....chhann... of her payal in her both feet.

She was so adorable and mesmerizing, and astonishing in that simple look, and with waving Brown hair.

I was shocked that, how could her Dad assault her. Was he had no heart. Was these no kindness and humanity in him?

He was punishing Aahna for the mistakes, which she didn't do. I ask you, to the reader, is that her mistake, that she born as girl, God made her a girl. No, it's not her mistake. We all are borne by a woman. We can't think about our life without a woman. God gifts girl only to lucky person, and to one, who can take care of her.

So why Aahna's Dad treated her as bad luck? Why did he think, Aahna can't make him to feel proud, she can't lead his party?

Let me tell you, in India there are so many girls who are MLA, MP and a politician, so why Aahna can't be a MLA?

Come on! We are living in 21st century, where girls are at top in every field, in -Science, in politics, in economics, in art, in army, in civil service, and even girls are representing India at global world.

But I am pained that, cruel thinking still exists even in 21st century. We are exploiting girls. We don't allow girls for higher education, for job, for going out.

We are still discriminating girls. We think boys are best than girls. We treat girls as minority. And I am shocked and frozen, when I heard about villages of 21st century.

There still exits great miseries for women. They are being exploited for child marriage, dowry, Pardaah.

Women are being sexually harassed. And more embarrassing is that, there is no one to help them. They are helpless. And because of their poorness, they have to do suicide.

I just want to know that, who we to decide girls as minority are. They are also human being; they too have life, and dreams. They also get freedom in 1947. So who are we to torture them as like slave?

We, the man exploit a woman and then we feel proud, we call ourselves brave man. Bullshit, I fuck on such people. 'A real man, don't ever hit a woman, he always respect and worship Woman.'

I am so guilt that at one Side we worship goddess Laxmi, Saraswati, sati, and at the other Side we humiliate the real Laxmi, the real goddess of our home.

I alarm, that we shouldn't forget that Kali is also a form of woman. When a ruined woman got into avatar of Kali, then, no one can stop her. She can destroy whole universe. Whole world have to sick for mercy. There is no greater power than that of the sun, the moon, and a woman that knows her worth.

But in Defiance of that, women are so silent.

But it's not the time to be silent. When we will change our thinking? When, we will change our sensitivity? When we will be conscious? India has got freedom, but not the women of India.

'India is developing, but Indians are not.' And it's all because of corrupt politicians as like Aahna's Dad, and because of poor thinking of society. A corrupt politician is more worse than a serial killer. He can even cheat on God for his benefit.

"Shourya, you are here?" Aahna surprised, and sat next to me, shaking me out of my thoughts.

"How are you, Aahna?" I asked and smothered her palm in my both hands.

"I am good," She smiled. I felt a punch in my heart when I saw how much sad and wistful she looked

But I knew, she was not at all good. Her smile was fake. Her eyes were clearly saying to me, "Shourya, please help me, please take me away from this evil world, and please hide me in your arms."

I could see hope and trust in her Brown eyes.

"Shourya, I am so embarrassed because of my Dad's evil. And you had to pay for my mistake. I am so sorry --------," she was whispering but I stopped Aahna's words, by putting my finger on her lips.

I got up, clutched Aahna's hand, padded inside the temple, and stood up in front of lord Shiva.

"Aahna, you don't have any idea, how much you mean for me," I looked into her eyes, "Aahna I don't know why? But I promise you that I will be with you at every stage of life. No one can hurt you now," I said and held her both hands. She beamed, chuck under my chin. Her eyes were shining with revolving tears in her eyes.

Quickly she faced Shiva to pray. I was still looking at her cuteness. I too prayed to Shiva to give me power and strength to take care of her, to keep her happy always.

****

CHAPTER THIRTY ONE

Time plays most significant role not only in our life, but also in whole universe. We all are bounded with time. So we should respect time.

We can't race with time, as one day we'll be tired, and will be stopped. But time would never stop. We should just keep changing to the time. We should maintain a good relation with time. And then we would find only happiness in our life.

We can't change some things. But those things will change when we change our mindset, attitude and energy.

It was 20th march, it was a fabulous day of my life it was Aahna b'day.

At one Side, I was so much exhilarated. As on, that day had gifted me Aahna. Aahna took birth to honor my life.

But I was anguished too, as I couldn't celebrate her b'day. Even thought I couldn't wish her, because of her Dad.

Her Dad didn't allow her to go out. Though her Dad had arranged a luxury party for her, but I couldn't go her home. As, I had already, screwed myself in front of her Dad.

I still wonder that, things would have been different if I wouldn't have visited to Aahna's home, if I wouldn't have kissed her in her bed room. Then might her Dad wouldn't have been angry with me. So someday, I might have told him directly that I love Aahna, and I want to spend my whole life with her.

Sometimes we want to go in past to erase the worst day or think of our life.

I wanted to erase that day .As I had planned so much for her b'day. I indeed wanted to make her b'day so much special. As it was her first b'day with me. But it's all game of luck and bad luck.

My friends had already reached to her party. And I was sitting alone with my emptiness, in my dark room.

"Dude....whr d hell u r getting fkd. Jst come to MG Road metro station. It's urgnt. Come fast," : Rohan texted me at 8 'o'clock of night.

I drove towards MG road in dull shirt, and damaged blue lee Cooper.

I leaned against my bike, on one Side of Highway.

At 8:30 p.m. I saw Aahna's Audi coming to me. It stopped on other Side, just opposite to me.

Quickly, my friends stepped out of car, they smiled at me, in next second, and they left away by cab.

I was wondering, in sudden confusion, that what was going on? I shouted and waved my hands to them, but they had been disappeared.

Immediately, I pierced, Aahna stepped out of car.

"Oh my God!" I shocked. My friends made my day. They snatched away Aahna from her Dad, and got her to me.

This is the power of friendship, that your friends can hook your love even from God, only for you, and your friendship.

Aahna peered at me, and hence our eyes lost into each other. Our smile became more brighter and winder with every second. Our eyes turned more bigger.

Swiftly, I waved towards her that I was coming to her Side.

But she protested that, she wanted to come my Side. And she strolled to cross the road. But the road was so busy by vehicles.

Regardless of that, she ran unsteadily towards me. And consequently, she lost herself in middle of highway; she was looking

170

towards the loud horn, severe lights. And she surrendered, and starred at me, helplessly. I vellicated, and rushed rapidly towards her, and grabbed her tightly in arms.

She was in casual outfit, in light blue short sleeveless top, and more white levis' sort the blue top was labeled, 'I am bad girl.' Today she was forlorn. Her face was addled. But when I blew air on her tedious face, she started chuckling, her dull face started flashing. She smiled more glistening as like twinkling of stars. I touched her cute dimples. She tickled.

I gaped deeply into her brown eyes, which were clearing saying that she didn't at all want to celebrate her b'day, as I wasn't with her.

I was drowning in her love. But rapidly loud horn, and harsh head lights of cars, and shouting of people broke our romance. We had jammed whole Highway.

Hurriedly, I pulled Aahna to me and we crossed the road. She was stuck to me, as I pulled her to me. I don't why, but she buried her hand in my chest.

I chunk under her thin, "Happy b'day Aahna," I mumbled and caressed her forehead by my lips. I was watching her closely it made her conscious. She curled her lips inwards. Hence, we both again lost in unearthly silence. We would keep on stealing glimpse.

"Aahna, something is missing on your face," I quipped to start our stupidest.

"What?" she asked in haste, with wider brown eyes.

"I can't see your dimples. Did you lose them?" I asked innocently.
"Yeah! May be," she said with deadpan.

"Don't be sad, I will find, let me," I said in mischievous tone and touched her unclothed soft waist, and started tickling on it. She would protest and burst into laughter, furiously.

I sensed so much peace, by her cute dimples.

"Look, I found you dimples," I would excite. She beamed at me.

"Shourya actually, I was downtrodden. Just because of my unkind family. I hate their fake love for me. They arranged that fucking party, only to impress bloody politicians, and businessperson, just to show off. But the truth is that, they didn't even wish me. They were aborting my b'day. I literally wanted to celebrate my b'day with you only." Aahna gestured her heart, and squeezed my hands.

"Sorry Aahna," I mumbled, "but I brought nothing to celebrate," I said in dull voice.

"hmmm....., it's fine," Aahna buzzed.

"One minute, I have surprise," exasperated, "close your eyes."

"Why?" she deflected.

"Just shut up, and close your eyes," I frowned; she rambled something and closed her eyes.

Rashly, I wrapped off Dairy milk silk and placed it on my palm, and fired my lighter.

"Now, open your eyes," I said. She was surprised; she smiled longer, and beamed at me with wider eyes. I signaled her to assuage that fired lighter.

I started singing happy b'day song, and she would blow air to lighter. And she fed me a bite of dairy milk, and I fed her.

"Where is my gift?" she demanded.

"Nothing," I shook my hands empty.

"Penny pincher," she muttered.

I pulled out a locket from my neck, and put it around her neck.

"Aahna, my Mom had given this locket to me she has conviction that this locket will always save me. It's very close to me. But now it's yours. I wish, this will always save you too," I said.

"I promise, I will always keep it close to my heart," she kissed that locket, and crowded her fingers into mine.

Abruptly, it started drizzling, as might be; God of rain is welcoming and blessing Aahna and me. He also wanted us to be together.

"Did you ever dance in heavy rain, in middle of Highway, between horns, lights of vehicles?" I asked to her in excitement.

"What?" she panicked, turning her big eyes into small one?

"Let's dance," I said and lay on my knees, forwarded my hand to her.

"Do you know Mr. Shourya Sharma, that you are totally mad," she said and put her hand on mine.

"Yeah, I know. Miss Aahna kapoor," I giggled and pulled her into middle of Highway.

Little- Little rainy drops showered on us. And we got wet in few minutes water drops would roll on Aahna body, from her face to her pink lips. Then on her naked shoulders, and hence on her exposed soft waist. Her top stuck to her wet body. She was getting too hot, even though in cold rain, her wet hair sticking to her cheeks, neck and chest. I moved my finger on her forehead, and removed hair from her face.

Therefore, I made her to dance. We would dance some salsa steps, which we had prepared during fresher party. But agilely, we would dance like fools, while shaking our whole body unmannerly.

She lost herself in other world. She was enjoying a lot in rain. She was jumping, and kicking water on the road. She was shaking her hair frantically, to spray water on my face, her hair tickling my nose.

I became clam. I just beamed at her. I was amazed by that real Aahna. The whole world around me went silent and stopped.

Everything, cars, bikes, and people started disappearing from my front. I could peer only Aahna. She looked in such a way, that she was flying in sky. She was glistening in dark night. I sense so much love and peace by her happiness.

Now I didn't have any regret with anyone, I could die happily now. It was memorable b'day for Aahna and me also. I found my destiny in Aahna. I didn't know about our future; as we were living best in present.

And now no one could ruin her happiness. I was with her and we had the supreme power 'love.' Everyone has to sick for mercury, in front of love.

Some days, I wish I could go back in life. Not to change anything but to feel a few things twice.

****

CHAPTER THIRTY TWO

So finally we completed our first year of M.A., in the end of May. However, our exam was not so good, but we had expected that we would clear all subjects with passing marks.

Everyone was so much happy that they all were living for home for one-month vacations. No place can give you peace, if it's not your home. But everyone were drained also as they would miss each other a lot. Sid, Rohan, Ashvini and Yash had already left.

Only Ruhi and I were left in hostel. She was too not going to home. She said that she would stay with me, as I too was not going. While, I would insist Ruhi a lot to go, but she snapped on me that she would stay with me.

How strange and unexpected is that, Ruhi was from Bangalore and I was from Mumbai. We had such different places, culture, and people and Society.

But in contempt of, such variation we got so much attached with each other. Ruhi accepted my family, my life as her own life. She would always take care of me more than myself, without any expectation.

On next day, she enquired me that why I was not going to home? I lied to her as I had no answer of her question.

As years ago, I had decided that I would never ever confide my secret to myself also. I was lying on my bed, completely soaked in emptiness.

My Mom called me.

"Beta please come back home, it has been more than a year," she sobbed.

"No....... Mom, it's not so easy to gulp everything, and move on," I said in sotto voice, "and I left home, it was my decision, now I couldn't came back," I gasped.

"Beta please.....," she sniffed with gasp, "you just come back, everything will be ok, he will forgive you, I will insist him to accept you," she exasperated.

"Huh.....," I grinned in anger, "He will forgive me for what Mom? For the mistake which was not mine. No Mom now I can't live with him. I will never come, where my Mom has no love and respect, where I can't live according to me," I said, trying to arrange the sentence, but I could hardly speak, as I sobbed.

"Please beta, for me only," She begged like a kid, "I haven't seen you from a year," she said and burst into cry.

"Mom, I am too missing you and I love you. I don't want to make you cry, but I am doing this only for you. You are a doctor and even though, you are living in such remorse and guilt. Sorry Mom I can't. I can't," I said and switched off my phone, as I was losing control over my sobs. I would have burst in cry if Mom would have spoken once more.

I sank into my bed, hid my face inside a pillow to muffle my cries, and that worst nightmare flashed into my eyes, once again.

"Shourya, I have gathered all the enquiries of Oxford University. And I have registered your application for admission in MBA. Soon, you have to leave for USA," Dad said, flipping his laptop down. Dad, Mom, and I, we all three were sitting on couch in drawing room. Dad and Mom were just in my front couch as if they were there to interview me.

"Dad," I stammered. I was terrified.

"Yeah! Say, if you have anything in mind," Dad sighed and looked up at me carefully. That made me shattered; my words were not coming out of my throat. I knew that my Dad would freak out after hearing me. But I had to do it; I couldn't go on with that for my whole life.

I pressed my feet hard against the floor in an attempt to get the courage to speak.

I marshaled whatever strength I could and murmured mostly to myself, "I don't want to do MBA," I said still facing at floor.

"What? What did you say?" Dad asked narrowing his eyes to confirm what I said.

"I don't want to do MBA. I don't want to go USA. I want to be writer," I squealed, straightaway, staring at him.

And abruptly, there appeared a death killing silence. Dad and Mom remained stunned, with parted mouth. Dad gulped the whole glass of water in a single gasp.

The silence persisted in the living area. No one dare to speak a single word till 10 minutes. Stillness in the air was palpable. By that silence, I felt like a stab in the stomach.

"Do you know what you are saying?" Dad broke the silence, and it was like disaster to hear him.

I couldn't look up at him; I was twisting my thumb, pacing at my slipper.

"You are saying that you won't do business, and want to write, how could you even think of that," Dad shouted but I cut him off in mid.

"Dad please understand," I pleaded, " I can't live without writings, I really want to be a writer, I want to travel, I want to observe life of people I want to write for youngsters, I want to write for people to make them happy. I want to write for social cause. I want to write Dad. I want to meet new people every day. I want to explore their stories. I want to live many lives in just this single life. I want to write_ not so people would see me. But so I could see myself," I was gesturing my feelings, holding his palm. But my Dad chocked my mouth.

"Shut up, you have just gone mad. You will destroy your life," he hissed, "you are son of Sharma Industries, you will screw my name, and how would you survive by being road chhap writer," he sniggered.

"Dad money, name and frame are not everything in life. Humanity is also our responsibility. I want to work for people," I squelched.

"Hahaha...," he shrieked, "this world is full of evil people. They will ruin you. Don't know how bad people are, you have to cheat them, if you want to survive," he bellowed.

"Yeah, you are right Dad," I said, "today I have come to know that how bad people are when I saw your this Side. How greedy and egoist you have become Dad. You are killing poor people for making money. You even lost your soul, such a inhuman you are," I shouted the truth, I was hiding in my heart.

"What? What do you want to say?" Dad thundered. He got up and took a step towards me. Mom went to him and stood between Dad and me. Then she turned to me.

"Shut up Shourya, what are you muttering," Mom snapped.

She was in dilemma. She was between devil and deep blue sea. She had to keep both Sides. She couldn't choose between her son and her husband.

"Dad, I hate your business, because it's corrupt. And I can't be like you and I don't want to be like you, you are not a good father, neither good husband," I was bursting disastrously.

"Shut up Shourya, right now," Mom hissed but I didn't shut my mouth.

"Why Mom? Why I shut up?" I cried, vehemently, "look at you Mom, you are a doctor and you have no respect in this house. Why are you suffering Mom? Why? Tell me when did he dinner with us? When did he talk to you last? Mom he doesn't care whether we live or die," I was saying, abusing my Dad.

My Mom was trying to shut my lips. Amid, Dad pushed her aside, and in next second

Hastily a harsh slap, I felt on my left chap, which moved me unsteadily.

"Just get out of my house," my Dad grinded his teeth.

And that nasty slap got me out of that evil scene. My face was steamed in tears, I was swimming in sweat, my lips were quivering, I was breathing more and more through my mouth. I was startled, frazzled, and unaware of where I was. I didn't blink a single time. My eyes boll were pocking out my eyes.

Impromptu, Ruhi entered into my room, and so quick she got frozen, lips parted.

"Shourya....," Ruhi shocked when she detected my tears. She ran to me and forth me in her arm as tightly as she could. She rocked my back. And I wept freely, in her chest like a kid. And in that

Moment, I felt a warmth spread in my chest and heart felt lighter as I kindly let it go.
She cradled my face in her palm, wiped my tears, and she asked, "What happened Bhai...?"

Admitting, that I had decided that I will not confess my evil to anyone. But I don't know why I gestured everything to Ruhi. I told her that why I was not going to home, why I left my home.

"Ruhi, you tell, is that my mistake? I just wanted to live my dreams. I just wanted to write. And for that, how easily he threw me out," I gasped, sobbed, "he didn't care for Mom, that how she would live without me. She is dying Ruhi," I said, and tears flowed out abundantly and ceaselessly from my red eyes. And I armed Ruhi and cried.

"It's ok, it's ok, don't cry, everything would be fine, please don't cry bhai," Ruhi grabbed me tightly into her chest. She pampered me like kid. She rolled her fingers on my hairs; her eyes were shining with tears. And I don't know when I fell asleep in her lap.

When Dad threw me out of his life, I came to Delhi next day, to my Mama. I hoped that things would be ok after some time.

But that didn't happened. I was exhausted, I didn't know, where to go? What to do now? Day by day I was annihilating myself. I was not getting over of that bloody stuff.

So my Mama suggested me to take admission for higher education in a good College of Delhi. My mama esteemed that I would be remorse free and would get over of that bullshit, if I would get busy, if I would meet new people in college.

I too envisioned that, so I accepted his idea. So thereupon, I contemplated to start a new life.

So, I took admission in 'DCAC ' in good hope.

And I was right. I started legging behind my evil past. I forgot about my past life, when I got such trustworthy friends.

And when I glanced Aahna, I completely lost in her. I again started live alive. But wherefore, I became blind towards my dream. I completely darned my writings and my dream.

179

I started wasting my precious time in Delhi. I already knew that there was nothing for me. I didn't aware of what I was doing there. I became so vagrant that I didn't care and comprehend about my future.

Years ago, writing was my love, my passion, and was my everything. I was writing to explore all the things I was afraid of. I was writing to find my voice, my muse. I was writing, to listen my heart, to spread love, to bring a change in thinking of people. I was writing to live the life, I dreamt of.

But when I came to Delhi, things changed, and I too changed. I gave away my dreams. I forgot my past and started skidding my future in love and friendship.

Now here I shouldn't blame anyone. It's not Aahna. But it was I, who was responsible. It is the human mentality that we just only look for the excuses, to hide our guilt, our failure, and we collapsed our life.

Literally, when someone falls in love or any relation, he completely loses himself in it, that he gives away his present life and destroy his future.

Here I protest that, who told that person to sacrifice his dreams, his aim, and his duty because of love. As love doesn't do this. Love never requires any condition; Love doesn't become cause of any destruction. In fact, love leads us towards progress.

You can win the world, if you are in love. You can fulfill your aims easily, if your love is with you.

'Love doesn't change people; people change themselves and blame love.'

Admitting, that I also did the same bullshit, I too gave away my dreams. So consequently, I was living like dead. As Robin Sharma says, 'when we give up on our dreams, we die while still alive.'

But today once again, I faced my evil past. Today once again, my Mom put mirror in my front, and I faced the fictitious life that I was living from a year.

Today, I faced the authentic, truth that I was a guilt son, who has been thrown away.

Sometimes it's good to face the genuine, as it shows the mirror to bus. And mirror never speaks lie.

Today, my past life stood at my door, and knocked some questions at my door that who I was? Why I was there? What I was doing there? What I wanted to be, but what I was becoming there in Delhi?

From one month, these questions had cramped me. I was grabbed by these thoughts.

I spent lost one month while wandering alone in corridors till late nights. During day time, I would sit on edge of roof of a ruined fort near a lake with Ruhi. It was our favorite place.

'Sometimes, we need to lose our way, to find our way.'

And sometimes it's good to be hurt and grieved. We choose isolation, and we March in silence. We twist the connection with the existing world. And at that instance, our mind connects with the Supreme power, The world power or the cosmic energy.
The universe listens and responds to everything we think and feel.

'The cosmic energy' exits everywhere. Whole universe, planet, starts, human, atoms, and everything is bound by the cosmic energy. And when we feel that cosmic energy, we get answers of every secret of life.

That's why we should go in deep thinking, to get answer. Silence is the place productive people go to think.

As much, we reckon about our dreams, as much more we move towards our dreams.
Sometimes, we just have to die a little inside in order to be reborn and rise again as a stronger and wiser version of our. Sometimes we need to slow down to eventually go faster.

In spite of all these, I found it too tough to think about my life, to start a new beginning. But if you ever loved your dreams, if you ever had assent in your dreams, if your dreams were true; then one day they will come to you again.

"Journal-789

only the one deserves the taste of success, the one who dares to do sacrifices."

****

CHAPTER THIRTY THREE

More than a month had been passed. Our college had been started once again, everyone got busy in new session with new energy. I was still stuck on that same day. I was still wandering in depression. I started to abhorrence my bogus life, which wasn't giving me place. So, I lost myself somewhere in dreadful crowd.

It was 1st of July, it was my b'day. I envisaged that I had wasted 23 years of my dull life. I found and got nothing, in post 23 years. I was downtrodden. So I wanted to live in loneliness. I wouldn't pick any one's call.

But my friends noticed my pain. They forced me a lot, and they took me to our favorite and peace giving place, 'The ruined fort near a beautiful lake, in outer Delhi.'

We all were sitting in a queue, on the edge of ruined short boundary wall of that roof; our legs were dancing precariously from its edge, towards lake.

There we used to sit silently for hours. We would just praise the natural, miraculous beauty of that environment. The sun was half dipped in the water, spreading beautiful shades of blue, red and purple at the horizon. The waves of lake were so calm in such a way that they had been tired of whole day heavy work. But some couple of ducks was disturbing the silent waves. The sun was sating down in lake just to rise again next day, with new hopes.

A flock of birds was revolving round and round above the Lake. The birds were literally giving cool and fresh air by their wings

We would always tickle so much internal peace and bliss by

merging with by that environment. We would find some familiarly with that environment.

So, we had occupied that ruined fort as treasure house of pirates. We would scratch every wall and stone of that fort by our names and memories of our friendship.

"Shourya, it's your bday yaar...," Ashvini said, "and you are as indolent as like backchod cat," Ashvini shrieked and hit my shoulder.

"Nope... I am ok," I uttered in law tone.

"Oh! Now I caught you," Rohan exasperated, "you wanted Audi Q5 as your b'day gift from your Dad, and he must had denied, right?" Rohan grinned at me.

"Shut up, Rohan," I frowned, "it's not funny; I am not in mood," I muttered and glared Rohan. But he kept on torturing me.

"Don't be sad, let me call your Dad, give me his contact," Rohan said and snatched my phone, and tried to call my Dad. I lost my sense in anger and frustration. I was stampeded; I snagged my phone back and, threw it on a stone furiously.

"It's enough now, you crossed the limit Rohan," I hissed like snack, "I told you that it's not funny, when will you be serious, just grow up man," I snapped, and gasped. Everyone was in sudden shock. They eyed at me like statue without any blink.

"What do you know about me, about my life? Do you want to know, why I am sad? You are asking my Dad for fucking Audi. But you know, he didn't even wish me my fucking b'day. Do you know, he didn't talk to me since years? We both just hate each other, "I shouted atrociously and moved my body with agitation. I got down, and turned my face away from everyone_ and began to speak.

"And you know, why we rancor each other? Because my Dad wanted me to screw my life in his bloody business. He wanted me to be like him, to live according to him. But I couldn't do that. I wanted to be a writer. Writing was my dream, my life. And when I told him about my heart, then do you have any idea what he did with me?"

184

I held Rohan's collar, "he just kicked me out of his home, and he fuck my life, my dreams. He screwed my happiness. And now I don't know, why I am here, I am only spoiling myself, my career with you idiots. But you will never understand in my pain. As you are lucky that you don't have father like me," I shouted in quavering voice, and pushed Rohan aggressively.

I don't know, why I was saying that bullshit, I don't know, what was going in me. My pain, my words, wrecked everyone, they actually sensed my grief.

Aahna looked directly in my eyes there was generosity for me. She could feel my gesture. I eyed towards Rohan. He looked despondent. We kept silence; there was tense in the environment.

"You are right Shourya, I will never understand your gloom. You are right that I am lucky," Rohan muttered sadly and turned away from me, and leaned his head against the ruined wall, "I am lucky that I don't have Dad like you. But you are lucky that at least you have Dad and Mom. You don't know how much painful it is to find ourselves orphan." Rohan sobbed, tears rolled down from his eyes to roof.

"What? What the fucking you are saying" Sid and Ruhi squawked in shock, struggling to get right word to spit out.

"Yes, it's true," Ashvini grabbed Rohan and wiped his tears, but her eyes were also crying, "when we both opened our eyes, when we grown and realized world, we found ourselves in an orphanage near Delhi. We never sensed the love of mother and father. We don't know what a family is. Uncle and aunt who look for that orphanage gave us so much love so to speak, we are their own children. That orphanage house is our home. They gave us our growth they educated us. They are our family," Ashvini gestured, and clutched Rohan.

"But now that orphanage house is bankrupt. No one helps us. So uncle and aunty took loan for our education. They visualized that, after higher education, we would prefer for a good job, and so that, we would help them, save that orphanage house," Rohan sighed, "but it's too late, bank already has given us time for 4 months. They would throw out all little orphanage kids, they would auction our orphanage. And once again all kids will be orphan. You have no idea, how much we are agonizing. Despite of that, Ashvini and I are endeavoring. Ashvini and I are together. We both have assurance in each other, and the love, we have. We both are striving our hardest to save our family.

You guys don't know, every evening we go to orphanage house, to teach those kids, to look after them. And every late night we both go to night sift duty at a call center. Even being a girl Ashvini takes risk to visit out in late night in Delhi.

But still we couldn't arrange money. We are last hope of uncle and aunty. But we broke their trust, we had no hope. It was our dream to work for those kids, for that orphanage. We both don't want any car, job, money etc. We just want to devote our life to that orphanage. But now we are hopeless. We are wasting our time here. We would die, if we couldn't save those Kids." Rohan said, his voice oscillated, and he could barely stay audible. His face was steamed in tears. Ruhi, Sid, Aahna and everyone armed Rohan and Ashvini. We never saw Rohan such somber. Everyone's eyes were shining in tears. Everyone showed grace for both of them. But they patted Rohan and Ashvini in proud.

But I was standing away. Hastily, I lay on my knees in feet of Rohan and Ashvini I was so remorse that I hurt such true spirit.

"Maf krdo yaaraa...," I joint my hands to Rohan and Ashvini, "I am so embarrassed, I actually hurt you. You both are so great. You are such human being. And I abused you. God will never forgive me, and I will also not get over of this remorse------," I was saying in guilt, but Ashvini interrupted.

"Shut up, You jerk," Ashvini frowned, and Rohan and Ashvini pulled me into their arms.

"I am with you guys, everything would be fine," I whispered.

"My life is also same as your guys," Sid said, his voice cracking with desperation and turned towards lake, and gazed towards red sun, "I am also convulsing by same sternly tribulation," he gasped. We all turned and listened to his grief, "I am from a backward village near Allahabad. You have view that how much poor it is. It has no electricity, no transportation, no education, and no advance life. There still exists cruel thinking, old evil and lousy rituals and customs, as like during pre independence period. Villagers don't obey any law. They don't believe in system. As government did nothing for their development. But the truth is that they themselves don't want to develop. There exits corrupt and harsh Panchayat system. And for them nothing is above than the evil of caste system. They have completely bewildered themselves in their evil Panchayati system. They have pounded their life in their small village. They don't want any connection with city life. They are hatred of advance life. They have phobia of city people.

My father is also in illusion like other. But in fact, he loves me so much. My family is poor. My father works as 'pandit' as we are 'Brahmns'. He Travels to Allahabad for 'kriya and yajmani.' My uncle works in field. So when I grown up, everyone envisioned that I will study hard for them, and I will become a big man, I will ruin poverty and infelicity of my family. And whole Samaj (caste) presumed that I will make them proud. So because of pressure and misbelieve, and fear, I blindly believed their deceptive hopes.

But in reality, I had fealty to my father, I love him so much. So I studied hard for my father. I cared only my father, not for the Samaj. But my father never asked me, that what I want to do?

When I was 17, I don't know when, how, and why I got my dream. I don't know when I became addicted of playing Cricket, and when it became my life, my dream. But I couldn't confess my dream to my father and Samaj also.

One day, a member of a Cricket Club of Allahabad, pierce my talent. He took me to his club and worked on my training. I would practice hard whole night in flash of streetlight, as I couldn't practice in day. Every day I wrangled badly and soon selected in Allahabad team.

It was very important match for me that day. But God didn't want my happiness. So an old Panch of my village saw me, playing Cricket. Soon he took me to the Panchayat. There whole Village and Panch, abused me, and my father. They said that it was not in our blood to play. We are Brahmin. We are superior class on earth. If I would play Cricket then it would make me bhrast, impure my dharma.

They said that I was doing a sin, and God would never forgive me. They threatened my father that if I will play, then I would meet discriminated people. I would have to travel to other people's land.

And they shouted at me that I would drink madira, eat meat, and play with sluts. Panch, blamed me as like people blamed Gandhi ji for going South Africa. But I couldn't protest like Gandhi ji. Panch charged punishment for my mistake. They snatched money from my father. They forced for my purification. As in their eyes, I was impure by Cricket. They warned my father that if I would play Cricket. Then they would throw us out of caste and village. My father couldn't help, he forced me to take his oath that I will never play again.

And I swear of my father, not because of terror of Panch, but for respect of my father. I can't see my father in sorrow. I can't see someone humiliating my father for my mistake. So, on that day, I murdered my dreams, my happiness for sack of my father. And I came to Delhi for higher study so that I could get job for making money for my family, and my Samaj." Sid signed, and downed his tearful eyes.

Sid snorted and turned away, but not before, we saw his clenched jaw shivering ever so slightly and his eyes releasing a single drop of tears. He wiped it by his sleeve.

I felt another pang in my heart, I grabbed him, he dig his face in my neck, sobbing.

"I am proud of you bhai, you screwed your happiness for your father. And look at me. I gave away my family for my selfishness," I divulgence, in shame. I found myself so small in front of my friends.

"Guys I am happy and lucky that I don't any Dad. Why all Dad are so bad, and became cause of destruction of our life," Rohan wondered, and patted Sid.

"No Rohan, all fathers are not bad," Ruhi sobbed and put her hands on ruined short wall, and leaned against it, and gazed the lake, "I have best Dad in world. He loves me so much and I too. I had a cute and sweet family. Mom, Dad and me, we all were so much glad and blissful together. They would fulfill my every demand. My Mom always wanted me to be an IPS. And I literally accepted her dream to be IPS. I would study hard not for me, but for my Mom." Ruhi confided and sat near Sid on that wall. She looked into Sid's eyes.

"You are blessed Ruhi with such parents," I was saying. But she chopped my words.

"No, I am not...... Even I am worse luck," She exasperated and turned her face. She was crying.., "When everything's goes best in our life. Ergo, impetuously evil enters in our peaceful life, which shatters our happiness like dry leaves. In a car accident my Mom died. It was evilest day of my life. After that our rapturous life turned into hell. It wrecked our thrilled. We lost everything. My Dad went in severe shock. He couldn't get rid of that evil. At that Moment my cousin uncle and aunt took advantage of us. They transformed my Dad under their evil eyes they snatched our business, our property by betraying my Dad. They controlled our life. They treated Dad as a servant, and they exploited me. They would hit me like slave. They banned my education, my dreams; they made me to do all household works. They used to hit me in front of my Dad. I was dying day by day. They started torturing me to marry a stupid boy. So you know what I did?" Ruhi sobbed and panted once, "I ran away from my home in dark night. I didn't care of my Dad. And I ran to Delhi, too away from my home, so that no one can find me. So on that night, I lost my Mom, my Dad, my dreams, my glee, and my everything," Ruhi gestured and her knees buckled, and she slumped to the floor, her back propped against the wall. And she gave up and let the tears flow freely down her face. She vented out all the agony, she was bearing on her small heart.

Aahna and Ashvini assembled Ruhi, but Ruhi was trembling, her tears were not allowing her to stop.

When I heard Ruhi, a dead weight was stuck in my throat. A sharp pain shot through my body. My throat was chocked, so I couldn't speak a ward to Ruhi. I was so feared, and cold feet still that I have no words to utter and to elucidate my feelings for her.

I conceived that how God could hurt such cute girls. Girls are his beautiful and spectacular creation; So why he don't save them from monsters? He has no kindness and clemency for Girls. I knelt down in her front, and pulled Ruhi in my chest. Her long braid was touching my neck. I literally wanted to touch her feet. I wanted to solute her soul. My sorrow was nothing in front of her.

I had at least my Mom as my family. But Ruhi had lost everyone. She had no one, who could take care of her. Even her Dad didn't know that whether she is alive or dead. I pampered her forehead.

189

I observed, Sid's eyes were wet. There was so much benevolence in his eyes for Ruhi. Sid wanted to say that he was with Ruhi. He will take care of her always. He could die for Ruhi. He loved her so much.

Thereupon, ghastly, there appeared an ominous silence, the silence that was deliberating our miseries, the silence which showed us our defeat.

I put my hands on my face, fractured, and scattered on roof. Deadly, fast and shoring wind started blowing very fiercely. And dry leaves of tree made a rustling sound, which took us to queerer estimations. And the sky opened in thunderstorms and a cloudburst and I have felt the more matching whether to what my heart was feeling like. The weather was changing drastically. All of a sudden, it was getting dark. Black clouds hovered in the sky

We everyone had dreams, and once we everyone had loved our dreams. But we went through evil tragedies. And we everyone lost everything we had screwed our dreams, our happiness, because of our family, because of cruel thinking of backward villagers, because of selfish and inhuman people.

But I was surprised that, why we were uttering our pain, our failure today. We everyone had decided that we would never confess our anxieties, our grief to anyone ever.

But today something unearthly led us to confide our truth with each other. There was a reason behind our confession. Someone wanted us to mime our truth with each other.

"Guys, we everyone had a dream, and we loved our dreams once. And we ruined our dreams because of other. And now we all are enduring through same morose. We are living simulated life," I said in sad tone, and eyed down on floor, "Guys we all know very well, we are just wasting our time here. We are running away from ourselves, from our truth, from people, from our fear, from our dreams." I sighed and starred at everyone.

"What do you want to paraphrase?" Rohan exasperated.

"I am gesturing that we can't do this to ourselves. Guys did you notice, why we are discussing our bother today? Why we everyone ran away and came to Delhi only from such varieties of places? Why we met here in DACA?" I bellowed briskly and clearly and got up agitatedly.

"Why? Ashvini smacked and everyone turned to me in concern.

"Because destiny wants this; it's all game of destiny. Destiny wanted us to meet, to confess ourselves, because we all are same, we all are true, and we all are undergoing through same trouble," I freaked out.

And expeditiously the whole environment and sky burst into horrible noise of thundering of clouds. Whole sky was taken over by dark clouds. It made tense and fearful, and suspicious climate. It started vicious lightening and thundering. And stormy wind started to tempest hastily, which trembled our bodies to sweep away our fear, our remorse.

"The Supreme power wants us to complete our dreams again, to live alive again. The cosmic energy wants us to change our past by changing our present. Guys our failure, our same tragedy, our same gloom, our meeting at Delhi, and then our confession here, all this are not a co-incidence. Everything was pre planned, and already decided by Destiny," I said, and provoked them, "Guys in everyone's life a day comes which change their life. So today, this 1st of July, my b'day, this is our day. Today God gave us a chance to rise up again," I said in exasperation to give breathe to dead bodies of my friends.

As I completed my words, It started heavy and beastly raining. Our bodies got wet in big and cold and severe water drops.

In Defiance of that, we didn't move away to shelter, because that energy was not allowing to shatter away. That energy forced us to wonder, 'what I just said.'

"Shourya, what do you want?" Ruhi annoyed.

"Let's start it again. Let's do it again. Let's fight again," I spat out each word clearly, loudly, with a good rhyming. And we all got in sudden shock. My friends' eyes became bigger. They went in sudden COMA by my poisonous words. It looked like, whole world around us stopped.

"Ha ha ha....," Rohan laughed at me, "Ruhi look at him, he has gone mad. He is saying us to fight again, its rubbish. Guys Lets go, Shourya has lost his sense," Rohan ridiculed, and muttered absurdly, without any sense.

"It's not a joke, Rohan," I frowned, but Ruhi raised hand to me, to stop me.

"Shourya to whom we will fight for? We have already lost everything. We are dead now," Ruhi squelched and held my face and looked into my eyes, "look at me, and tell me can I fight with my own uncle," she said in quavering voice.

Apace, Sid jerked my hand, "and tell me Shourya, how could I play Cricket? How can I strife my villagers, with my Dad?" Sid snapped at me, and looked away, and it started more nasty thundering and raining.

"Look at us Shourya," Ashvini turned my face sternly towards her, "How can we get money to save our orphanage? Answer me Shourya," Ashvini murmured.

Abruptly Rohan snatched me, "Shourya, you tell us, can you go back to your home, and tussle your Dad that you will live according to you, you will write," Rohan roared in hatred, "no Shourya, you can't. You have just lost sense, you have gone totally mad," Rohan shrieked loudly and pushed me away.

Everyone showered their frustration on me, just to hide their fear they still wanted to run away from the truth.

"Shut up... I haven't lost my sense... I am not mad," I snapped with fully energy, and flamed at them with burning eyes, "I know it's not so easy, we have nothing, we are powerless. I know, we can't fight with our own people. I very well aware that, we need our parent's blessings and support to complete our dreams," I frowned, froze for a second and then stammered, "But guys we can't make excuses to hide our fear, our failure. We can't waste the remaining part of our life in thoughts about other people. I know we are feared. But the biggest leap towards freedom is declaring our fears and mastering them. We can grow fearless by walking into our fears. Guys, we all are our family. We have power and weapons of our unity, our entrustment in each other, and our assurance in each other. Guys we have supreme power and that are the power of love, Guys God is with us. Look at this rain, feel this harsh wind, this stormy lightening and thundering, these all are not co-incident. God is gesticulating us. God is awaking us. Guys please try to understand. We can't let the others to destroy our life. If we don't have any dreams in our life, then we are living dead bodies. Guys, trying something is better than trying nothing. Guys Michael Jordan said 'I can accept failure, but I can't accept not trying.' Guys don't limit our aspirations, dreams and vision of our life based on the current circumstances. Guys, don't let our dreams, just be dreams," I said in energetic and motivational tone, I padded towards Ruhi and squeezed her hand, and looked into her eyes in a new hope.

"No, Shourya.... It's inconceivable, we can't do it. And tell me Shourya, for whom we will do it. We have lost already everyone," Ruhi said in shaking tone and faced towards furious lake.

"Yeah! Ruhi, you are right," I said and put my hand on her barred, wet shoulder, "we have no one, for whom we will live. But look at me. Am I not your brother? Look at Aahna, look at Sid, Rohan and Ashvini, are they nothing to you? Ruhi we have to battle for each other. We have to encounter for our friendship. We have to wrangle for the youth like us, who are dying from same deteriorating as like us. Guys we have to present an example before them. We have to present an inspiration before them. We have to scramble for the change in society. We have fight to change the cruel thinking of backward villagers. We have to grieve to lesson your uncle. We have to break ego of my Dad. We have to writhe ourselves just to voluntary the power of youth to the world.
Ruhi we have to do it for your Mom. We will fight to bring the change in the society. And guys I would happily die, while performing my karma," I gestured my heart desperately.

"Ha, Ha," Rohan smirked," leave it Shourya. There is nothing to change. Everything is just a crap. No one cares for this situation. Poor has to die and rich will survive. And nothing will change Shourya, here we start, and there will be our end. This was to be happened, and this will be happening," Rohan freaked out, feeling disgruntled, and punched his fist into wall.

"Rohan, everything will change, we will change Rohan," I said, put my hand on his shoulder.

"But Shourya, how we will do this?" Ashvini asked in concern and a bit of excitement.

"Till I don't know, how we will do this? But I know that we can do this, if we are together," I signed,

"Guys I can't do this alone. I genuinely need all of you... Please," I pleaded in grief, and flashed to all of them. My body was oscillating in server cold rain.

Sky was thundering and lightening repellently, as might be, sky's anger was at its zenith.

For next 10 minutes, we all were frozen like statue. We were so silent. I was peering at then like a beggar. But they were still wondering, they couldn't decide because of abhorrence. Suddenly Ruhi gathered herself. She looked so energized.

"Ok, it's enough," She exasperated, "it's time to fuck my uncle, it's time to show power of girls, I am with you Shourya," Ruhi snapped desperately.

"Yeah, it's time to brain wash those backward villagers," Sid frowned and got up hastily. And abruptly there appeared a revolutionary environment. I saw a revolutionary fighter in each one of us. Our bodies were feeling a warm and irrational cosmic energy. Our bodies started vibrating. We didn't know what was happening with us.

Sarfaroshi ki tamanna..., Ab hamare dil me hai....., Dekhna hai.... Jor kitna...., Baajuyein.... Kaatil me hai..... those were the lines that my breaths were releasing.

We gathered ourselves; we all were like revolutionary heroes. We were feeling like most powerful creature on earth. As my friends were with me, no one can stop us.

Sudden, I noticed someone, who was glimpsing at me in hope and assent. She was Aahna. Quickly, I realized that I had to fight for my love also. I couldn't leave my love, because of my dreams. Aahna was my life. And without Aahna, my dreams were like body without soul.

Aahna was in black sleeveless top, and velvet black and red short skirt. She was sizzling in wet clothes, and wet hair. She was gazing deep into my eyes by her brownish eyes she wanted to say something about her heart to me.

But she was afraid. She was feared of her Dad. But I wanted her to destroy her fear by herself. I couldn't help her until she herself wouldn't brush.

As I knew that one day, she would have to fight with her fear. She had to stand against her Dad. We grow fearless, by walking into our fear.

"Guys," Aahna Whispered, and came closer to us, and clutched my hands. "Guys, I don't have any dreams as like yours. I have every luxurious, and pleasure of life. Still I am poorest person. I am living like a prisoner in my own house. I am in a great grievance. No one loves me. I am dying day by day in my home," she looked into my eyes. There were so much hope and assurance in her brown eyes, "guys I just want to be free as like you. I want to fly away, screwing my precinct. I want to shine like sun. I want to be part of your journey. And guys I promise, I will never cheat you. Please accept me," Aahna said, her Diamond eyes were shining by unshed tears. And her face was glittering with twinkling smile. I could see abundant tears in her eyes, even in heavy rain.

"Aahna, of course, you are part of our life. You are our sweetest girl," Ruhi shrieked, and we all hugged with so much energy, while holding tears in our eyes. We all were still in-group hug.

"Guys, guys, I have important to say," Sid exasperated, "Guys, today on 1st of July, it is very special say for us. 1st of July is our turning point. This date will decide our future. What we will be in life would only because of today, 1st of July. Now we will struggle hard for our dreams. And this battle will bring many ups and downs in our life. This may lead us towards separation in our life. In coming day we may not be together. But you all have to promise me, that in any deteriorating condition we will stay together, as we could fulfill our dreams, only when, if we are together. Our unity and our love is our strength. Despite the fact, I know it will take long time. And we have to separate for some time to exertion for our dreams. But I want all of you to come back together again. I veritably don't want to lose you guys. You are my life. I can't live without you guys. I again want to be with you. I again want see this sating sun. I again want to sit at edge of roof of this ruined fort, with only you guys. I want to feel the peace of this lake again. So promise me that two years later, where ever we will be, but we will come back on 1st of July. We will meet here at this ruined fort at 5 p. m. I want all of you to come here in any condition. And we will again do Masti. We will plan for tour of Paris on that day. This is my first and last wish from all of you," Sid signed; he uttered what was in his heart. And quickly, we all promised to Sid.

We signed a deal with Sid, that we will come back in any condition. And as a guarantee and proof of our promise, we collected everyone's special things. I gave my watch, Rohan and Ashvini gave their same bracelet. Ruhi gave her locket, and Aahna gave Payal of her left foot. And Sid gave his leather brown jacket. And we buried all these as our sign in wall of that ruined fort.

"On the name of Sid," we all cheered up. And we had taken flight, while screwing all the fear, limitations we had.

****

CHAPTER THIRTY FOUR

To start something is the strenuous task but, once we start, then the whole universe works according to us. The cosmic energy opens ways towards our triumph.
The secret of getting ahead is to get started.

With this conviction, we had taken off towards our battle, for our dreams.

Supposing, I was the leader, I inspired my friends. I bewitched them by my words. I galvanized them to live again, to source again. But in reality, I was unaware that how we would do that? And whether we would be successful or not, but I just knew that, we had to fight despite of every stuff.

Sometime, we shouldn't look for the result or consequences. We should just perform our karma, and letting go result on the God.

Our battle was going to be so horrifying, as we had to exertion with a corrupt politician, with an egoist greedy, inhuman businessman, with some cruel thinking villagers and with some rapacious bankers. But it's too true that a calm sea doesn't make a skilled sailor.

And we had no weapon, no power to strife, except our unity and assent. And more worst was that, we had to battle with our own people, with the people to whom we ever loved. So in de facto, no one was going to win this war. There would be only lose and defeat of relations and beliefs.

But at the same instance, there would be victory of love and friendship, and truth. No one can win from a corrupt politician, and arrogant, and unkind capitalist. No bomb, no gun, no troop, no sword, that can defeat them, they are evilest person.

But only one Supreme power can force them to sick for clemency, and that is the power of 'love. '

For me, love is above the God. And even God also have to surrender in front of love. Love has the power to complete transformation of heart of even corrupt politician and ungodly businessman. Love has power to pure the soul of even evil people, and can bring humanity in cruel and unearthly people.

It is the love only, which can bring a revolution for change in whole world. Change may the constant of the universe, but love is the one thing in the universe that changes everything.

It is the time for 'Yug Parivartan' or ERA – transformation. Now only truth will survive. Now it is the time for victory of good over bad, positive over negative, truth over false.

And the Universal power had selected us to lead the world, and people towards that Parivartan. God selected us to spread the love. God wanted us to step first towards that 'Yug Parivartan', because we were true soul, and followers of love. And God wanted next 'Yug' to be 'Yug' of love and happiness.

So, we accepted God's wish, and gave away everything, our happiness, our grief, our agitation, our sleep, our time, our Peace, our day and our nights to our dreams.

Our first and most important task was to save that orphanage house. We had to gather a large sum of money as soon as possible.

But it was seems like in executable. We were close to accept our first inadequacy. But thanks to the very talented and creative minds of Aahna and Yash. Aahna and Yash innovated staggering ideas.

They suggested for initiating a donation campaign and named it **"Project Smile"** to save those orphan kids. So for two months, we all led a campaign in our hostel, our college, and other colleges of Delhi. We would organize seminars, and events in every college, every department we would ask to all the students to save, to donate for poor orphan kids, to save their childhood, and to bring smile on their faces.

And Aahna and Yash's ideas worked with the very energetic and powerful speaker Rohan. Rohan would preside every seminar.

He would say, "We are not begging to you for donation. We are asking for borrowing money today. And in future these poor kids will return your money with interest by serving mankind, County, and you."

People actually moved by Rohan's words. They were petrified to donate. We would energize all the students, "it's the time to show student power to world."
And every evening we used to visit that orphanage, to teach poor kids, and to pamper them. Rohan, Yash and I had joined call center. Every night we worked to bring smile on innocent faces of kids.

Therefore our next mission was Ruhi. We exhilarated Ruhi to square her preparation for IPS.

We got Ruhi admitted into a civil service coaching. Ruhi endeavor hard. She would study whole day and whole night. And we would support her. Her every need, her books, her food, her coffer, her assignments, her newspaper, and everything were my duty. I packed her whole room with books, maps, charts etc.

In daytime, Sid, Aahna and I Would be with Ruhi to take care of her. And in night Ashvini would awake whole night to support Ruhi.

We wouldn't allow Ruhi to waste a single second. We would scold her to focus on her study and aims. And our writhe showed its color. Ruhi was performing well in all level of test at coaching classes.

Wherefore, after Ruhi, we had to deal with Sid's battle. We took Sid to a cricket club of Delhi. Ad he screwed all the levels and skills of test. He was storming batsman.

Now Sid's practice had started. Sid indeed practiced hardly. He didn't care for the injuries and wounds. He was so devoted that he would practice even in night under the lamp of hostel courtyard. He played powerfully for his Dad, for himself and for Ruhi. And it was the power of love and fealty of Ruhi that Sid crossed every stage of his battle.

There month had been passed, and every day we were stepping

towards our dreams, and our fruition. But there was something that was not letting me move towards my reward.

It was 1 pm of cloudy noon. I was with Aahna in college garden. We both sat, leaning against each other's back. I was narrating Williams Shakespeare play Romeo and Juliet: Aahna was earning my words with concern. And she was playing with my left hand fingers, trying to match my nail size with her. She always used to do such stupid.

And Juliet says, "o comfortable flairs I where is my lord? I do remember well there I should be. And there I am. Where is my Romeo?

"Then again she says 'yea, noise? Then I'll be brief, a happy dagger "! She snatches Romeo's dagger. And she stabs herself, and says

"This is thy sheath; there rust, and let me die" she falls on Romeo's body and dies.

I narrated whole play to Aahna and gasped

Then I closed that book, lay straggled, and lay on greenery. I closed my eyes, stretched my arms on greenery and exhaled deeply to relax myself.

Aahna wore a sleeveless white transparent Kamiz and dull white bloomed Salvar. Her right hand was full of blue bangles, and her brown hairs were drafting furiously in cold breeze. Although she had braided her hair in simple knot braid, she looked like she rolled out of bed effortlessly.

Despite of that, she was gleaming in sun light.
She put her head on my left shoulder, facing towards me. She was rolling her fingers sometimes on my left cheek, and sometimes on my jaw.

She wiggled her finger at my collarbone. Then she pressed my nose with her finger and thumb. I was like a toy for her.

"Aahna," I buzzed.

"Hmmm..." she hummed sleepily, and closed her eyes.

"Aahna, do you trust me, that I can fulfill my dreams," I asked inevitably.

"Shourya," she squeezed my hand, "I blindly trust you," she uttered and smiled with twinkling dimples.

"Aahna... At first, I roused my friends, I showed them a dream, I gave life to their dead bodies. But the fact is that I am powerless. I am unworthy I can't do anything miraculous. We all are in illusion," I sighed, "Aahna you don't know from last 2 month, I haven't even started my writing. I strived my hardest, but I couldn't write even a single line. My mind, my heart, and even my pen are not with me. I lost Aahna, I lost," I was explicating in sadness, and hastily Aahna stopped me.

She got up infuriately.

"Shourya," she frowned, "I don't believe this Shourya. You are talking this bullshit. Shourya You are our leader. You taught everyone to live our dreams. You are our power, our inspiration. And now you are saying that you lost. How could you say that?" she squelched and gasped, "Shourya, I know it's not so easy. But it's not inaccessible. You should just start. And I am with you, I know you can do this," she clutched my palms.

"I know Aahna, but it's beyond the bounds of possibility, to write again. And I am afraid; people will not like my book. And you know, there is no scope in writing now. So how would I survive," I muttered in irritation and looked down.

"Shourya, you have gone mad," she snapped and chuck under my chin, and starred into my eyes, "tell me Shourya, what you afraid of are? Shourya death is the worst thing in world that can happen to anyone. And if you don't despair of death, then how can you afraid of implosion. Don't be afraid to fail, be afraid to stay same.
Second thing is that, you can't compare your dreams with money or any fucking stuff. If you are living your dream life, then you are the richest and happiest person in world. Your dreams are precious, just because they are your dreams. So don't think so much, God will help you, you just write," Aahna said, with glistening smile, and blinked her brownish eyes in loyalty.

"Aahna, you know why? I do want to write?" I said, and looked into her eyes, "I want to write because, I live alive by writing. And I don't want to change. I know my value in my world of writing. I just don't want to piss in crowd of millions of people in outer world."

"Shourya, don't worry, I am with you. When you can't look on the bright Side; I will sit with you in the dark," She said, looked with the same faith in my eyes.

"Ok, ok, I got that madam. You won," I surrender myself in her feet, "but now tell me, how will I onset? What I write? I have no clue," I said.

"You should just pick a pen and paper in your hand, and write what you perceive," Aahna braced herself and removed a lock of hairs from her face, "You should write about Ruhi, Sid, Rohan and Ashvini. Write about our friendship. Write about you and me. Write about both of us," She maunder, clutched me tightly, I peered into her browns eyes. There was so much love and faith for me.

"Aahna...," I whispered with same love and caress, "Why do you esteem that I can write? Why do you believe me so much?"

Aahna put her head on my shoulder and snuggled close to me.

"Shourya....," she said politely, "you can write, because you listen to your heart. You can write because you are true. You always live for others. You live for friends. And I am damn sure that you will write impressive, because you will write what you heart feels. So now shut up or I will slap you, and just write," she quipped and turned her face close to me. She blinked twice briskly.

I was surprised by Aahna's words. I was searching my energy, my inspiration here and there. But my inspiration was near me, in Aahna.

She was source of my energy. Every day she would help me. She would give me the reason to write. Every day when I would glance her, my pen would begin writing itself.

Every day, I would write about Aahna, about us, about our assurance in each other, about relation, which had no name. Aahna was the reason of my fortune. She wasn't my love; she was my God, my life.

Our relation wasn't like others. Many times, a relationship between two leads them towards disorientation. Many relations don't work; reach at its fortune because of distrust, misunderstanding, and jeopardy.

And many couples destroyed their future because of miss-running of their relations. Even sometimes, it leads to evil of suicide.

But for me Aahna was my luck, my dream, my grind, my grand slam. Aahna was my cosmic energy.

"Aahna, I may be the writer, but you are the one who gave me my story," I said, "Aahna, *you are the author of my story,*" I squeezed her palm and kissed it.
She down her eyes in the shy.

I blinked at her in love and spoke politely, "Aahna you put me on my track. You ruined my anxieties, my horror. But Aahna, look at you, what are you doing to yourself? You are destroying your life," I held Aahna's face and pampered her chaps, "Tell me Aahna, why are you languishing so much? Why are you putting margins to your winds? What are you afraid of," I asked and removed hair from her face. And looked at her with such intensity in my eyes, she didn't blink, but I could see grievance in her brown eyes.

Ghastly, she got up from my arms, clutching her legs, her hands tightly wound around her knees, and she dug her head under her knees.

"Shourya......," she mumbled in pain, "I can't answer you, so please let me be on my own," she sighed, her voice was vibrating, I put my hands firmly around her shoulder, "Shourya, I promise, one day, I will screw my limitations and will fly away with you," she buzzed and leaned her head on my shoulder. I patted her head.

******

"Journal-675

We are living with Time. Everything is just moving with Time. Time is the only thing that is responsible for all the occurrence. Time is present and Time is which we have just lived was past and the coming next seconds are the future.

The thing is that there is nothing like Past, Present and Future. Actually it's the point from where we decide the conditions for the Past, Present and Future. We are standing on a point from where we can see the going Time and coming time, but we can't see present Time. We have to realize that there is nothing like Past or Future. It's just the Time.

What we have lived was Time, and what we will live, would also be Time. And time never changes, it's always same things. Time just cross us. But what changes is our position. When time crosses us it just shift our position that creates differences between Present, Past and Future. But reality is that everything was time and everything will be time.

We are on a journey with Time. And that journey never ends. Time will be always with us that race so how can Time be different. So we breath in Present always. We are dead in the time we have live, we are unborn in the time which will come, and we are alive in the time we are living.

We are connected to that cosmic energy in the universe, and that energy move in wave with our breaths, so we are all powerful when we are alive, when we are living in present, when we are honoring Time. We can do anything when we are in our present. And our present situations declare our future, our present power in our heart writes our future, and our past was set of circumstances that has made us powerful in present.

We can change our future by doing fair with our past and present. We are here to change our positions with time.

In our life we would never reach on the point where we can say "Yes! Here is my life. Here i wanted my life to reach."

Yes we would reach to that point, but we can't stay there for whole of our life, as Time is always travelling, and we are in bond with Time. Even we can't stop after our death, as we would travel in form of soul in the universe. Time is universe.

Our soul is always in present, as it's always awaken. Our body makes difference with time. Our soul is always moving with Time and that makes our soul all powerful and eternal."

****

CHAPTER THIRTY FIVE

Wherefore, we hassled hardly, we enjoyed our battle. Every day passed with so much ease. And we had completed 2 more months of our labor.

Every day we stepped forward without any difficulty and obstacle. We were so much close to our destiny. But when we are about to win our savvy, when we are about to snatch our dreams; at that time we find ourselves at front of caves of so many formidability, and obstacles.

Our actual wrangle starts when difficulties knock at our door. At that time, we should stay calm and strong. We have to face them without any fear. We have to stay stable instead of panic even in worst circumstances. And after that hard agonizing, we would feel the great peace and joy of real victory.

Predicaments, difficulties, and sufferings, come in our life to teach us, to bring out our best, to snatch our hidden qualities.

Diamond only shines more bright after hard finishing. Obstacles, challenges and failure are part of the success equations. We had to embrace them as they are our vitamins to success.

So we had to stay, strong and united in our worst time. But we didn't do that. We lost our faith, power and unity. The obstacles and up streams broke us, screwed our love, and crashed us, and snapped us like dry twinges.

Our worst time started with our first lose that is we lost our Sid. It was very blissful and special day for us and for Sid. Sid had prepared himself, and got entered into Ranji-team of

Delhi. He was leading Delhi against Haryana in Ranji -Trophy. Delhi had already won 1 match, and Haryana also 1 match. Today Delhi won, and it's all because of spectacular performance of Sid. Sid played too good, that he was the man of the match. Now to win the series, Delhi had to win next match after 4 days.

So today, we all were celebrating Sid's victory in hostel with bands, Dhol, Nagada, firecrackers, colors etc. It seemed like any Hindu festival. Everyone was dancing out of tune. Rohan and I had lifted Sid on our shoulder, and we were dancing. Sid was enjoying a lot. He was until in Cricket kit.

Impromptu, Sid shouted, "Rohan stop.... Stop..... Drop me down," so precipitately we got him down.
He was looking towards a man, in fear and concern. Sid padded slowly, as if he didn't want to move toward that old man. That man was in yellow dhoti, and dull white Kurta, a red scarf over his body, and a big Tilak of Chandan on head. He appeared so to speak, he was Pandit.

I noticed that man was in so much aggression. His eyes were burning red. He strode horribly and rashly towards Sid, as if he would stab Knife into Sid.

And that happened; he slapped Sid harshly twice. And he turned whole atmosphere of courtyard in harsh sound of slap. We all were in sever and rapid shock.

"You had taken my oath, that you will never play cricket," he roared and threw Sid's bat away.
Sid eyed down in fear and remorse.

Immediately, I quipped that he was Sid's Dad. We all were so much paralyzed, stunned, and stoned. Ruhi grabbed my hand tightly to stop my quiver. I was wondering, that now what would happen next.

"We work hard in field, day and night for your education, and you are doing such fucking, while playing again, you ruined my name, now Samaj will humiliate cruelly." Sid's Dad showered his anger on Sid. Sid gazed at me. But I was caught by so much terror that I couldn't spat out a word. I felt ashamed to look up at him.

"Uncle, it's not his mistake," I gasped, and assembled my words, "Actually I forced him to play, and uncle, he plays too good, he has a talent, so why are you --------," I bellowed to defend Sid. But his Dad raised his hand to me.

"Oh... You are right, it's fault of you, educated advance people. You brain washed Siddhu, You unkind, unworthy people," he snapped at me.

"Uncle it's not like that, Sid have dream to -------," I exasperated.

"Shut up, and get away," he hissed, "Actually it's my fault; I shouldn't have sent Siddhu between you inhuman city people. I shouldn't have sent him to study in Delhi," his Dad grinded his teeth, "but today I will correct myself. Now Siddhu will not stay for a second here," he smacked and dragged Sid into hostel.

"Uncle... Please...," Ruhi and I begged. But he screwed our begging by showing his hand, and pushed us away.

And within few minutes, He was back at hostel gate, with all the luggage and Sid. They were leaving towards gate of hostel. It was so sudden that we couldn't protest him. We were dazzled and blank mind.

Every boys and girls crowded them, to stop them... But we miss stepped. Sid was looking at Ruhi and me. His eyes were red and feared. They don't want to go. They were starting at me in need.

His eyes were saying, *"Shourya, Please help me. Please stop me. Please don't let me go. You have promised, you will save me, Please don't be like statue."*

I couldn't match Sid's eyes. I was so guilt and opprobrium that I broke my promise that I would be with him always. I cheated Sid. I padded backward like coward, when Sid needed me. I just let him go.

****

It was noon of next day. Ruhi, Rohan, Aahna, Ashvini, we all were sitting outside of canteen. We all were distressed, and, were crying on our implosion. It turned our happiness into sorrow.

I couldn't look at anyone. I was like skeletons in the cupboard. I was panged that Sid was not with us only because of my fault.

Everyone was staring at me in Fidelity that I would do anything. But as a matter of fact, they all were in illusion. I was nothing. I couldn't do anything. I was the green eyed, who dodged everyone. I showed them unreal dreams, which couldn't be achieved.

"Wow, Shourya... Wow....," Rohan grinned and clapped at me, "what a game planner you are," Rohan shrieked at me.

We everyone turned at him in shock.

"Awesome Shourya, you proved yourself, you did shit on our back and look still you are safe, what a safe game, you played?" Rohan quipped and glared at me.

"Shut up, Rohan, what rubbish you are uttering?" Ashvini squelched at him.

"Oh! You find rubbish at me?" Rohan said snidely, "look at him Guys, our leader. My fut." he frowned at mp, "we followed him blindly and he stabbed our back," Rohan sniffed.

"Are you mad? You know, what are you maundering?" Ruhi squelched at Rohan.

But Rohan didn't stopped his maunder.

"Shourya... Where is your bloody cosmic energy now? Where is your those motivational words? Where was your power of unity, when Sid was going? Because of you, Sid is not with us today," Rohan infuriated.

"Shut up... You rascal?" I cut him off, "Do you think? It is my mistake," I roared.

"Yes. Of course, you ran away cowardly, when Sid's Dad was dragging Sid. You didn't try any effect to save Sid," Rohan got up hastily and viciously, and threw plates from table to ground. "You, bastard," I grinned my teeth and collared Rohan.

"Stop it both of you, did you get that, I said just stop it," Aahna burst in shouting, "Do you have any idea, what are you d------," she was Barking but suddenly she stopped her words.

As rapidly, a black Audi rushed towards us and horned repeatedly at us. We glared at that Audi. Rapidly, we saw, a handsome boy in white v-neck -t -shirt covered by black blazer, stepped out of car and leaned against the car. He smirked towards us briskly; he took out his black goggles.

"Oh my God.....! Shambhav....," Aahna shouted in surprise or shock or in exasperation I don't know. Her eyes become like Diamond. Her face became more sparkling and blazing. Her dimples became more deep and twinkling.

She was taking my breaths. I never saw such astonishing and mesmerizing beauty of her. She was in sleeveless short white -top, which had so many black horizontal lines. And black skirt up to her knees, which was flared, and had so many white, red and yellow big dots.

Rapidly, she ran towards that so called guy Shambhav hastily, while stretching her arms to hug him.
And within a second, they both were in tight hug. Shambhav lifted Aahna in arms and waved her round and round, in air.

Ruhi, Rohan, Ashvini, and me, we all were in grimly shock. Our eyes were abundant, mouth were fully opened.

We wondered that, who was Shambhav? What was going there? What was their relation? It seemed like a sudden dream for me. A dead weight was stuck in my throat, my throat felt parched, my mouth dry, I was scared, paranoid. My body started burning in sever fever, my lower lip quivering, my frail heart giving up.

I don't know, what was going in me? Suddenly, Shambhav kissed Aahna's chaps. I felt like someone stroked my heart by hammer.

Yes! I was jealous and possessive. I mauled that someone stole my heart. Shambhav appeared as villain in my and Aahna's love Story. Who came to snatch Aahna from me?

Shambhav, ruined my every plan, every dream with Aahna. I was wanted to kill him or myself by the dagger lying on table. Actually, I know, I was over reacting.

But I was hurt and down hearted that Aahna found someone more important than me. Now she wouldn't love me.

On the ground, 5 minutes later Aahna sat in car and they fly away together. I sensed so pain that Aahna didn't even glance at me. She didn't even say bye.

She left us alone, when we were in worst condition, when we were in need of her, but she didn't care for us, even when she knew about Sid.

Aahna too broke her promise with me. She also cheated me. I was so angry and frustrated. I mused, everyone was deceiver, everyone hatred me. Everyone was selfish. Everyone hurt me. And heedlessly my head started bursting in evil thoughts and aggression

"Ha...ha....ha....," Rohan laughed like beast, "look Shourya, even your love didn't trust you, because you are a asshole," he taunted me.

"Stop Rohan....," Ruhi snapped.

"You lost Shourya, you are also like your Dad, you are also egoist, in human us like your Dad," Rohan was showering at me. I was losing my patience's, I got up horribly, fumingly and slapped Rohan's left chap.

And here was deadly environment, everyone was frozen. Everyone's breathing got stuck in throats.

"So, you think, it is my fault. Ok then, I will bring Sid back before next match," I grinded my teeth, and hooked his collar, "but after that, I will never see your anyone's face again," I spat out each word like poison, and rushed away, while jolting Rohan.

****

CHAPTER THIRTY SIX

It was 10p.m. of dark night. Ruhi and I were at New Delhi railway station. We were going to Sid's village, to get back Sid. I had to prove myself. I had to get my power back. Those 3 evil accidents, tragedy annihilated us. It snatched away my love, our unity, and our dreams.

I had lost loyalty of my friends. I had lost my love too. Already Rohan wasn't talking to me. Admitting, it was my fault, and I didn't apologize to him. We didn't even face each other.

I was so much bothered about Aahna. She didn't call me and text me from two days. I was broken hearted because her ghastly behavior. I logged in and saw her online. She stayed online till later. But the status never changed from online to typing.

So I decided not to call her and text her. But only my heart knew how much tough to stay away from her. I was missing her badly. My heart was dying to massage her, but, I severely control my hands. Heart and mind never listen to each other, but they couldn't live without each other.

Even though, I checked my phone in every two minutes, in hope of Aahna massage.

Time was running so hastily, train was about to leave. My eyes were waiting for Aahna, that she might come to see off us. As Ruhi had already informed Aahna.

I just wanted time to stop; I wanted time to wait for Aahna. I mused; she might be stuck in traffic. But it was my illusion, as she was busy with Shambhav.

At 10:30 pm train left for Allahabad. I sat on my berth and Ruhi was in my front.

Ruhi was also gloom. Actually, I didn't want her to come, but she denied. She rendered that she had to be with Sid. Sid was in great need of her.

I comprehended about Sid. My face was appearing dull in concern. I would wonder and fear that what would happen? When we would reach to Sid's village? What would we say to his Dad? Whether I would be able to bring him back or not? Even the thoughts were too sad to comprehend.

And I was scared about Aahna too. I literally loved her too much. Every second, she was in my mind and heart. I was feeling so lonely without Aahna. I was pretending to be strong. 'As a broken heart is most powerful heart, he can do anything'.

But I actually wanted to breakdown. But I so bad luck that, I couldn't even cry out my pain. Only Ruhi could feel my malaise and helplessness. She came and sat next to me and rested her head on my shoulder.

"Ruhi, do you also think it was my sin?" I whispered.

"Shouray, I said you my 'Bhai.' You are my everything. And I know you more than yourself. You are a pure soul, you can't hurt anyone. It's all game of destiny, so don't estimate too much," Ruhi chuck under my chin.

"No, Ruhi, I am a decoy, I lied to all of you. I led you towards wrong dreams, which couldn't be fulfill. I kept you in darkness. I am a looser. I can't do anything, we can't achieve our dreams, which are not real," I blurted absurdly.

"Shourya...calm down," Ruhi gazed into my eyes, "it's not like that, everyone believe you, you are our leader. You showed us true life. You taught us to live, and we all know; only you can lead us towards our dreams. So please don't lose yourself. You have to believe in yourself. I know we will prescribe our triumph," Ruhi deciphered exasperatedly, impetuously, to console me, rubbing my arm.

"Ruhi, I don't know, what will happen? But I want to thank

you," I sighed and snatched her both hands in mine," Thank you for being with me always. I really need you. I am paralyzed about next day. But we have to get back Sid at any condition. I have to cure my sin, I have to say sorry to Sid," I rambled.

"Don't worry; I am always with you Bhai," Ruhi blinked in assent, "we will get back Sid. And he will play last match. Don't stew, and sleep," she caressed me, and put her head on my shoulder and covered ourselves with a shawl.

I patted her back, checked my phone, and peered at Aahna's pics, and sometimes scrolling up and down our late nights conversation, and smiled at her jerkiness.

"You are missing her naa..," Ruhi mumbled.

I beamed half heartily, and again starred at Aahna.

"Hmmn...Don't worry, I will slap her, and get to you. How can she do this to my Shourya. She is only yours," Ruhi tickled and, ruffled my hairs.

In morning, at 7'o clock, we reached Allahabad. We were as tired as we couldn't sleep whole night. And now we had to take bus to Sid's village, Sitapur.

We took a ruin, and damaged bus, which all ready stuffed with school kids, some old men and women. Even some goats and hens were also travelling with us.

Thankful to God, that, we got seat. But bad luck was that bus was not in condition to ride, and worst was road, full of mud, and ditches. Ruhi was snoozing on my shoulder again and again.

Everyone starred at us as might be we were alien. I would give creepy smile to them, and they would giggle away from me. It was my first experience in Bus that was horrible.

It took us 3 hours to reach at front of Sitapur. But now we had to pad 3 km. to reach Sitapur. There was no transportation. We were almost frazzled, we were struggling ourselves. But we were padding unsteadily, much slower than an ant.

Now our feet had given up, they had refused to move a single step.

"Shourya...please...," Ruhi panted and threw her bag furiously, "I can't move more. I will die," she gasped and lay on vestige in green grass.

"Get up Ruhi, it's too long more. We have to get there before dark," I also sighed and held her palm to get her up.

"I can't...," she panted, "you have to carry me," she muttered.

I flopped next to her for 15 minutes in greenery. And we counted down again. I would hold Ruhi by her arms to make her walk. Then, we crossed a high hill, and we reached a river. We drank water hastily and abundantly. Again lay near its shore.

Unexpectedly, Ruhi got crazy, she ran inside of Silent River. She smacked water waves, making splashing sound and showered water on me, and I was soaked in water.

"You idiot," I roared, and rushed to catch her. I grabbed her from behind by her waist, lifted her up, and then threw her into river. She fell down, and was wet in water.

We did so fun. We laughed freely after long time. That cold water ruined our bothersome.

And finally, we strolled into Sitapur. We padded inside of village through a narrow street. The village was too small, 100 house, with 3000 population.

Every house was contrived with mud and bricks. There was no sign of plaster. The village was like unreserved region; there was no road, no electricity, no communication, no transportation, no S.T.D etc.

It seemed as if it was not a part of our country land. As we entered into village, everyone glared at us, as if we were riots.

Some kids in indolent, and unhygienic clothes and hair, followed us. Sometimes they would snatch our bags. Sometimes they would touch us, and then laugh.

Even dogs didn't like us. They started barking at us. Some women, in long Ghoonghat up to their neck, were bringing water in pots. There was a big temple; so many people were gathered and performing rituals. They all gave us freakish look.

214

Some young guys at a corner glared Ruhi. She was in blue denim sort and green short top. They started passing vulgar comments to Ruhi. I tempered to stop them, but Ruhi grabbed my hand, to don't mess with those jerks

We asked about Sid to some old men, smoking Hukka at one corner of street.

"Siddhu...ka ghar...?" A man excited, "come I will take you," he said.

And Thereupon, we follow him to Sid's house, which was too small. Whole village gathered outSide of Sid's house; starring at us strangely.

A boy ran inside to call Sid.

"Oh my God! Ruhi, Shourya..," Sid shocked in terror, as he strode out, "why you came here...? I mean how could you come here?" He asked. He felt exhilarated, relieved, and terrified at the same time. He gave half hug to me, and felt shy to hug Ruhi.

Abruptly, Sid's Dad rushed out, agitatedly.

"Why did you come here?" He snapped.

"Uncle we came to take Sid back to Delhi," I said.

"How dare you?" An old man in white Dhoti and Kurta, and a big turban on head, shouted, "How dare you step into my village?" he roared.

"Who are you to stop us?" I squelched, and flared at him.

"I am Rameshwar, the Panch, and head of village," he barked, "And you can't take Siddhu," he hissed.

"Why we can't?" Ruhi smacked, "it's our matter, and you can't interrupt."

"I am head of Village, and Siddhu is part of our Samaj. He has to be under my order," he maundered.

"Ha..Ha..Ha..," I snickered, "Samaj, Bullshit, what the hell this Samaj, which stop someone to fulfill his dream, which bind someone in harsh limitations," I wriggled.

"Shut up...., you cheap. You don't know power of Samaj, so don't mess with me, and my Samaj," he collared me.

"Oh, Really...ok then...come on...show me power of your fucking Samaj, come on I want to know your power," I grumbled, and pushed him.

"So you want to battle with us, ok. Now Siddhu's case will be placed in Panchayat today evening," he shouted at me.

"Ok, let's fight with us in front of whole village. And if we lose we will leave the village next day. But if you____," I grinded my teeth and went to close to that man, gasped on his face, "I will ruin you in front of everyone."

****

CHAPTER THIRTY SEVEN

Panchayat sat at 8 PM, under the Banyan tree. Every man and woman stumbled out of their houses towards Panchayat. There was a bridge around the Banyan tree, where elder men sat, in white and Yellow Dhoti- Kurta respectively. Some kids were playing around that bridge.

Ruhi, Sid and I were standing close, to that bridge, and in front of whole village. Sid's Dad and his family were just in our opposite.

I found myself so alone against whole village. Sid was so cold sweat. His hands were trembling. He had alarmed and requested us to don't mess with those illiterate, cruel people. I mused now, that he was right, as even I was feared too now

But we couldn't give up, we had to get Sid back to Delhi and we were prepared to battle with anyone. Hastly, Rameshwar, the head of village, strode into Panchayat, browned through the crowd.

Everyone stood up to respect him. He glared at Ruhi, and me as he passed by us. He stood up on that platform.

"All mighty Villagers, Today we are gathered here to save caste, our culture, our village, our dignity," Panch Rameshwar announced his villagers and then fixed his eyes on us and pointed us, "These city people came here to take our Siddhu with them, they wanted him to play that bloody game. They came to brush with us, so I am asking to you," he lauded and stood up that bridge, "would you allow them to take away Siddhu?" He asked to all villagers, raising his right hand.

"Noooo......," whole mob buzzed...

"Would you allow them to demolish our custom and principles?" he yelled.

"No... Never..," Every one shouted heatedly.

"Through them out of village, or we kill them," crowd roared madly. We got shocked bit, but paralyzed more.

"Hear them, what they want? Now get lost from here, if you love your life," Rameshwar Panch grabbed me by collar, then pushed me, and turned away.

"Wait, wait....," Ruhi sniggered at his back, "we heard you but, Now you have to listen us also. Even a idol justice hear both the Sides," Ruhi shrieked and squeezed my hand in her to volunteer her.

"We want a strong reason, that why can't Sid play cricket? If you have the strong reason just say it and we will get lost from here." I grinned with Ruhi, recklessly.

Panch gave us hatred look, and rushed close to me.

"So you want to know, why he can't play cricket." Panch steamed at me, "he can't play because he is a Brahmin. He can't play because our Samaj don't allow him to play cricket. Brahmins are the highest class from the ages. We are having a superior status. And playing such game would ruin our status. Our caste, our religion, our culture, our rituals don't allow us to do such evil and embarrassing. It is game of lower class as like you. So if Siddhu will play then he would be abandoned by our caste." Panch squelched at me, as if he would struggle me and lifted his scarf to brace himself.

"Bullshit...Are you kidding us?" Ruhi laughed jerkily and franticly, "uncle, Shourya and me also a Brahmin, but in our caste there is no such principles. And what caste, are you talking about. Uncle caste system has been abolished in 1950, when our Constitution was established. Under Article 19 in part of Fundamental rights everyone is equal. No one can be discriminated based on caste, race, religion and sex. Everyone has freedom to live, express, growth. Everyone in our country has right to take their own decisions. So how can you stop Sid to play?" Ruhi smacked at Panch. Ruhi paraphrased breathlessly.

But Panch got more irritated. He frowned close to us.

"We don't believe in your country, and it's Constitution," he screamed terribly, and rolled his red shot eyes, "for us our village, our Samaj, our society our people are everything. We live in a peace and unity. We work for sack of our people. We have truth on God, we have assent in our custom and rituals. We are honest and innocent. We are not so clever like you. We just stay away from your bloody city, where corruption, murder, rape, terrorism, theft are your customs. You are cause of deterioration of mankind," Panch abused us by his maunder.

"Yeah, you are right. Villagers are good and peace loving and cities are evil. You are right that cities are the cause of rape, terrorism, corruption and all the unkindness. But gaze at your own village. Your village is even more worst than a city," Ruhi let out an elaborated, frustrated sigh, and turned around towards villagers, "Your village is until not developed. You have No education, No electricity, you are still believing and performing cruel rituals. And you are blaming cities for raps, thief etc. But you don't know that women are more unsafe in your village and proof is that all the rascal youngsters of your village try to assault me, they made me to feel embarrassed. Second proof of your destruction is that, some kids snatched away my bags and money. So what is the future, they have? In which way your village is like heaven?" Ruhi untangled, firefly and hazardously. She padded towards women.

"Look at these pure soul women; they are deteriorating because of your customs of child marriage, dowry, Pardhaah, and many more fucking. They are living in cage. And even you bastards men exploit them horribly," Ruhi showered angrily.

"What rubbish? They don't assume our custom as sufferings. They do it with happiness, and do you think we are exploiting them?" Panch shrieked stupidly to hide his defeat.

"Ha... Ha... Ha...," Ruhi laughed at him, "don't ask to me, ask to these women. Come on Ladies, don't fear, and just say out the pain, you are bearing. Come on combat for your dignity and freedom." Ruhi energized to every women. They were shocked by the truth. They started musing and buzzing with each other, in their long Ghoonghat.

"Shut up... you shameless girl," Panch groaned in pang, "what are you trying to prove? What you will get by diverting my people?" Panch sighed furiously at Ruhi.

"Oh! You just Shut up, you old man," Ruhi quipped to Panch outrageously, she looked so horrifying and dangerous. So that Panch stumbled backward, away from Ruhi. Today she was in full power; her eyes were burning red. No one can defeat her today; because today she was fighting for her love. And when love is your weapon, then you are the most powerful girl like Goddess kali.

"You bad mannered girl, I was right about you evil civilize morons. You don't care for us. You are selfish. You destroyed us___," Panch frowned and spoke senseless. But Ruhi interrupted him.

"Oh! Uncle...Do you think, we ruined you? But the fact is that, you are already destroyed. You never developed. You have No roads, No power, No communication, No Internet, No government, No proper planned village. Your village is below development," Ruhi smacked and gasped.

"Ha... Ha...it's not our fault you idiot. It's because of your evil government, and corrupt officer. Your government didn't try to develop us," Panch shrugged.

"What the F____." I stopped and giggled, "Uncle, we and you all very well know, who is corrupt? Your mentality is not allowing you to develop. Your brutal thinking is not allowing you to develop. The truth is that you didn't cooperate with the system. You didn't allow government to lead your towards progress. Actually your caste system didn't lead you to development. Your hatred for city people screwed you," I uttered the truth of Panch.

"So, do you mean that, we are evil? Every village is bad? And so that all village should be destroyed," Panch grinded.

"Wait, wait. I didn't say that," I shrugged, "I am just trying to elucidate that, your way of living is not good. I am saying that, we should change with time. As change is the rule of Nature. We should move towards modernization, while holding our traditions. No village neither city is evil. But it is we, the people who are evil. It's our bad cruel thinking and our wrong deeds that create difference between the people," I said politely in flat voice.

And there appeared a dreadful silence. But it was a silence that was bringing a new ray of hope. Everyone looked convinced by us. They wondered on our words. And there appeared a subterfuge within the villagers.

Panch Rameshwar got shut and silent. He was speechless. He had no words to fight with us.

I gazed at Sid's Dad. He was upset and feared. He was digging his eyes into earth. But there was a shine of positivity on his face. It was correct time to provoke him.

"Uncle...," Ruhi approached to Sid's Dad, "Uncle we all know you work hard. You agonize a lot, day and night, only for Sid, for his education, fir his happiness. And you want that Sid should get a good job, so that he would cure your grievances. You want him to make you feel proud. And you are irrevocably right. As every father, want his son to study well, to get job, to grow a big man. But Uncle, Education is not only about to get job, and to collect money. Education has such wide mean. It's the only supreme power, which can pure soul of a person. It removes all the evil in a human to make him a good human being. Education is to grow intellectual, economically and spiritually. Education transforms a man into a good man. It is the only way to build an idol society, to build an idol Nation, Which spreads only feelings of unity, Nationalism, and brotherhood. Education is invented for development of mankind and to develop consciousness and renaissance. Education is not limited to earn money only. Education is the most powerful weapon one can use to change the world," Ruhi gestured, intellectually.

"And Uncle," I gasped and clutched Sid's Dad's hand, "Sid can also fulfill your wish by playing cricket. Uncle Sid had a unique quality. He is made for cricket. And when he will play for Nation, he will be famous; he will also ruin your poverty, your miseries. And I am damn sure, that on that day, you will be so proud of him, even everyone would be proud of him." I excited and beamed at Sid's Dad.

"No... You are wrong. He will not be a part of our village then," Panch snapped, again.

"Oh.. My God...! Why don't you understand," Ruhi groaned in frustration, and pressed her long mermaid braid and pushed it behind her shoulder with jolt, "When Sid will play, it's obvious that he will play for your village. He will serve your village. Your village will be famous through Sid. Everyone will come to know about your village, about your caste. And government would also pay attention to your village. It will work for your development. And then, every child will have Education. They would dream as like Sid," Ruhi was speaking incessantly, but Panch raised his hand, and cut her off.

"They are lying to us, don't wonder on them. They are putting mud on our eyes. They want to divide us. They want to destroy our caste and custom and religion," Panch blurted.
I muttered under my breath, "Crap."

"Shut up.... You buddee..," Ruhi roared like an angry lioness, "caste, caste, caste..., what do you know about caste and society? You are just cheating people by giving wrong definition and principles about society," Ruhi shouted ungodly, so Panch got scared; he padded away from Ruhi.

Genuinely I was too terrified by Ruhi. She heaved and turned towards villagers.

"We are students of Sociology. Every day and Night, we study about society and religion. Society is not to cage someone in limitations, and not to screw someone's freedom, not to stop growth of someone, and not to rule over someone," Ruhi exasperated and looked into eyes of every villagers.

"Society is a group of human being, who share common name, and characteristics. Society is an organization of all human beings not by an individual. Society is to provide equality, freedom, status to everyone. Society works for the growth of children, and to provide equality, dignity and respect to women in all sphere. Society has characteristics of mankind," Ruhi analyzed true meaning of society to innocent villagers. And everyone was surprised by the truth. They all were babbled.

"And religion is the basic principles which lead us to live an idol life. So society and religion works to remove evil in society. It provides a social control and social order for human growth," I drawled steamily, and stood near Ruhi.

"Shut up, and stop showering this kitaabi gyaan on us, you bookworms," Panch hissed at us agitatedly, "there is so much difference in theory and practical. You are just muttering, which is wrong," Panch quipped, and blazed at us.

"Oh! Now I got u, what is your crunch?" Ruhi shocked, "Actually, the matter of fact is that, you are afraid of city people. You are afraid of facing the truth," I ridiculed at Panch.

"What do you mean?" Panch grinded his teeth.

"You are terror of competition. You have phobia of city people. Actually, you afraid that if Sid would play cricket, therefore he would have name, frame, money and power, He will be of higher status than you. And that you wouldn't like, as it would collapse your fakism, your power, your control over innocent villagers. And this is not your cup of tea," Ruhi burst out, loudly.

We were trying to irritate and provoke Panch Rameshwar, to gulp out his truth from his mouth In front of everyone.

"Shut up... your evil words," Panch groaned in irritation. He was startled. He was becoming panic.

"Yeah... Actually Ruhi... You are right," I surprised, and put my hand on Ruhi's shoulder and glared at Panch, "Actually he is double crossing and then ruling over these unaware people. He is keeping these people in dark illusion, to gain power and prosperity," I shrugged and queered at Panch. He was not getting what we were doing.

"Actually Shourya, he is afraid that if every kid will get education and will become like Sid, then he will lost everything," Ruhi tortured Panch and Panch lost his sense.

"Stop it... Stop it ...You idiots," Panch blurted nonsense, terribly, "what you want to prove that, I am ruling? Yes I am ruling, I am cheating these jerks. And you are wasting your time here. These are the idiots without brain. They will not understand you," Panch squawked and pointed towards villager, "these all morons are under spell of mine. And they will be my slaves always," He grinned.

"HaHaHa... Great..," Ruhi laughed proudly and clapped, "Thank you so much you proved us right."

"Look at your head," I shrugged to all villagers, "he is ruling you from years, he destroyed your growth, and future of your kids. He betrayed you. Now open your eyes, wake up and find your freedom," I sighed.

"So Mr. Panch, what you have to say now," Ruhi teased him, "So, Sid can play or not," Ruhi laughed and whole Panchayat started buzzing and muttering gossips, there began a bustle in the crowd.

"Of course, Ruhi," I sneered, "we won Ruhi, we won_," I repeated, clearly thrilled too. Our eyes were shining with happiness. I armed Ruhi.

"No.... Who said, you won...," Panch frowned, "it's my village, I am head. No one can defeat me. I decide everyone's life. And Siddhu will never play and if he would play then his family will be thrown out of village. And you absurd, you have to leave our village before dawn. And that's my final words," Panch snapped and rushed away while cleaving whole crowd.

"It's fucking wrong. It's injustice. You can't do this," Ruhi and I groaned in pain, "Villagers please, help us. It's not fair," We begged and shouted, but No one heard us, everyone left us. "Fuck on you," I murmured.

****

CHAPTER THIRTY EIGHT

Therefore, It was our first and last night at Sid's village. We have had skirmished our hardest. We fight recklessly, but we lost. We failed to convince everyone.

Ruhi and I even tried to talk to Sid's Dad, and family. But they even didn't face us. So now we were completely exhausted, we were so alone. Now we had only one option, which was to fall into a deep nap. Sid had already arranged mattress on terrace. It was 12 AM of night, and Ruhi and I were still rolling on the mattress. We were lying on our bed, beaming silently at sky, and giggling in praise of its miraculous beauty, the beauty from which we were unknown, unaware from years. Sky was sparkling more and more moonlit with the moon and stars, as it was night of full moon.

Stars were twinkling as if they were twittering and talking with each other, and sometimes with us also. Cold breeze was blowing briskly to cure our grief. Leaves of trees were making bristling and whistling sound, as though they were sing a melody.

"Ruhi...," I whispered.

"Hmm...," she nodded and closed her eyes.

"Ruhi..., we lost today once more," I mumbled.

"What do you want to say, Shourya..?" She sounded in robotic tone.

"Ruhi, we labored a lot, we fought bravely, but these villagers are fools. They have such low and narrow-minded thinking. Actually, that Panch was right, these villagers are feeble, and typical minded.

Literally, they don't want to be free. They have become habitual of being ruled. They easily swallow all injustice and pang. They love to be ruled. They don't want to develop. Bloody......hell___," I snapped, and vented out my anger.

"Shourya...cool down; don't think about it," Ruhi muttered and then pointed towards sky, "Shourya, can't you see such beauty at sky. Just look there, we will not get such awesome night ever. Just observe the peace and silence of sky," Ruhi said, her face was glistening, and her lips were in creepy smile.

"Yeah...Actually yaar..," I surprised with big eyes, "Look at that twinkling stars, how much pretty they are!" I sighed.

"You know Shourya, we feel so much good when we look at outer beauty of these stars and moon. But we are unaware of the internal sufferings of these stars. They burn harder themselves, just to make people to sense well," Ruhi maunder, and put her head on my right arm just like pillow, and kept my free hand on her head. She snuggled close to me. She beamed as like a kid.

"You are right Ruhi, we everyone wants to shine like Sun and Moon. But no one wants to burn like sun and moon, for that shine. We human are so greedy and selfish," I gulped and closed my eyes, stroking my hand on head of my precious angel.

"Shourya, you know, when a pure soul dies, he become star," Ruhi said.

"Seriously!" I wondered.

"Yeah! Inevitably." She excited with big black eyes, "Look at that star, she is my Mom," Ruhi pointed towards a star.

"Which one," I asked.

"That bright one idiot," she quipped and pointed towards a big flashing star, "she is my Mom. She is always with me. I talk to her every night. And you know, I told her everything about you," Ruhi smiled amazingly, and threw her long braid aside, so that it hit on my right cheek.

"Hey! Aunty," I waved my hand to her, "By the way Ruhi, what did you tell her about me," I looked at Ruhi.

"Everything....Everything about you," she thrilled, "I told her that, Mom you don't worry, I am so much happy here, because you gave me a best friend-cum-a brother. He takes care of me more than you," Ruhi giggled and clutched my hand.

"Yeah, Aunty, you don't bother, because I am with Ruhi to worry. But she scolds and tortures me badly," I complained and teased Ruhi.

"Shourya, you know, my Mom always used to teach me only one thing," Ruhi said and got up, "she used to say that Ruhi, whenever you get into trouble and if you can't find any solution, then just close your eyes, and feel your heart, and then you will get answers of all the questions."

"But Ruhi, we lost every hope today. Next morning we will leave for Delhi, and we couldn't do anything," I said, and sat next to her, legs folded vertically, head bowed under my knees.

"No Shourya, we haven't lost anything," she quipped, and put her hands firmly around my shoulders, "Shourya, believe in yourself. Shourya, every morning comes with new hope, new beginning. Even these stars and moon will disappear in morning, but they will rise again in next night. So to rise and to set is the rule of nature. So don't think like loser. I know next morning we will get our answers," Ruhi unfolded, and pierced into my deep eyes. I sensed so much endurance in her black eyes.

"Oh my God Ruhi...How much, love you have for Sid. Look into your eyes," I teased her.

"Shut up Shourya...it's not funny," she frowned.

"No, No, just look at you, you are blushing. I think, now you should marry Sid." I laughed and tickled at her waist.

"It's enough Shourya, Now let me sleep."

"Ok, ok...But Ruhi just tells me, how many kids you will have?" I shrieked

"Kaminee....you mother fucker...," Ruhi roared and got over me and smashed me by pillows and her hands, and punched me to. We enjoyed a lot at night.

Sometimes, it's spectacular to behave like kids, to lost in our childhood.

****

The Sun had risen to shine again. It was already morning, but we were still in dark. We still didn't get any hope.

Ruhi and I was packing our bags and getting ready to leave. I was so much nervous, and Ruhi was too upset. Again I was pleading to time to stop, so that, we could get our answers. Now only a miracle could save us.

I sat on floor, closed my eyes, and listened to my heart, to get my answers. As I closed my eyes, only Sid's face was in my eyes. I was getting more and more deeper into Sid's face. It was so torturing, so I had to open my eyes.

And when I opened my eyes, I could beam at Sid. He was sitting in my front.

"Shourya.... I am so sorry; you came to such distance only for me. And you suffered a lot for me. Villagers and Panch humiliated you harshly. And I couldn't say a word in protest," Sid said, sadly.

"Guys we have lost. Now you should leave from here as soon as possible. Panch is bloody rascal, he will hurt you, guys please leave hurriedly," Sid blurted.

He was so panicked, fumed. He was trying hardest to stop his tears. His jaw hurt from clamping his teeth together to stop himself from breaking down. I knew a part of him didn't want us to go.

"It's ok, it's ok...," Ruhi and I armed him, and rocked his back.

"Please help me, guys. Don't go, leaving me alone," And here Sid cried openly.

"Sid, it's ok, calm down. I know, we strived a lot, and I know these villagers will not let you go with us. But Sid, why would you destroy your life for these bastards. Sid, for you, only your Dad matters. And we care only for his decision. If he would allow you to play, then we will kick these assholes," I sighed, and patted his back.

228

"Shourya, Baba will never go against Panch and Samaj. He would never let me go," Sid sobbed.

"Sid, I am sure, he will allow you, because he loves you, so much. You are his son and last night. I gapped so much love in his eyes. He cares only for you, and your happiness. He is just terrified of Panch. Sid, you have to talk him right now," I said.

"What..?" he shouted, "No..., I can't, and what will i say to him?" Sid asked, in hesitation, and looked into Ruhi's big black eyes.

"Sid, don't be panic. This is only our chance. If once Shourya and me left for Delhi, then you can never get back to Delhi ever," Ruhi said, "so, please Sid, just go to your Baba, and open your heart to him. Now only you can save us Sid. Only you can do this. As answers are within us, Sid," Ruhi whispered, poked his face in her palm. And wiped his tears, and blinked at him in assurance.

"But......," Sid mumbled, but we stopped him.

"Sid, just go to your Baba, close your eyes, listen your heart, and say out, what is in your heart," I consoled Sid.

And it worked, our words influenced Sid. We all padded in fear towards his Baba. His Baba was sitting on a charpai (bedstead) in courtyard.

"Don't afraid, I am with you," Ruhi grabbed his hand tightly.

Impetuously, Sid facture, and scattered in his Baba's knees, and held his Baba's feet.

"Baba, I want to know, do you love me?" Sid whispered and gazed at his Dad. His Dad was bewildered. He was inspecting Sid closely, to estimate the situation.

"Baba, please, don't do this. I know you love me a lot, you want only my happiness. Baba I also love you so much. I never disobeyed your words. You are my everything Baba," Sid gasped, his voice was shaking. He looked into Dad's eyes.

"Baba, today you have to listen to me. Today you have to listen my heart only once. And then i will happily follow your decision," Sid sobbed.

His Dad looked at him, in faith.

"Baba you work hard day and night for me. From my childhood, you always worked for my comfort. You fulfilled my every wish. You did a lot for me. And I couldn't do anything for you. You asked me to study, to get job, to make feel proud. And this time also I embarrassed you. I am not a good son Baba," Sid broke down. His tears were falling on his Dad's feet. He looked down in disgraced, "but Baba, I want to say that, I can't do job, my life is cricket. Baba I want to play, Baba please give me a chance to prove myself. I promise this time I will not break your trust. I promise, I will make you feel proud," Sid cried, and squeezed his Dad's hand.

"Baba, I will be happy, Baba I will live in peace, because I will do, what my heart wants. Baba I know you have no predicament with my playing. I know you just want my happiness. So Baba please let me go, let me play," Sid begged, his face was steamed in tears. Rapidly, his Dad got up and pushed Sid away unkindly.

But Sid grabbed his Dad's feet and stopped him.

"Baba please...., let me go..," Sid shattered in millions of pieces, "Baba I know why you are not letting me to play. You are concern about Samaj and Panch. But Baba you saw last night, that Panch is stabbing our back. Baba, don't destroy my life because of that bastard. Baba I don't care for any Samaj or Panch. I only care for you, because you are my Dad, not that bloody Panch. Baba you slept hungry to feed me, not that Panch. Baba I have taken birth to live my dreams, not of that Panch's. Baba please let me go," he pleaded like a kid. He was crying unabashedly.

"Stop it Siddhu...., it's enough, leave me, I can't let you go," His Dad broke his words, and shouted.

"Please...Baba..," he cried.

"Just get lost...you will not play anymore," his Dad snapped. But His Dad's eyes were in abundant tears. He really wanted Sid to run away from such evil cage. But he was helpless.

"Why he can't play...he will play..," suddenly, crowd of villagers stumbled into courtyard.

"Yeah...! Siddhu will play. Why are you screwing his talent for bloody Samaj and Panch?" they roared together.

"Siddhu will play for us, for our village, for our kids," some women said, while ruining their margins.

"But what about Panch? He will throw us out of village," Sid's Dad sighed.

"Panch is from us, we are not from Panch. Now there will be no more evil rule in this village. Now we are free. Now we will not endure. These Angel's opened our eyes. They showed us true meaning of society, and of life," some elders came to Ruhi and me and joint their hands to us.

"So Sid will play cricket," Ruhi surprised, excited, shocked, exasperated, "can we take him to Delhi," she said weirdly.

"Of course, he will play, beta," Sid's Dad touched Ruhi's head, "Go Sid go. Nothing is more important than your happiness," he cried out, and hugged Sid furiously.

"Thank you so much beta, Ruhi and Shourya," he sobbed and we got stuck to Sid's Dad.

Abruptly, and prematurely, Panch strode while tearing the crowd, with guards and lathis.

"What is happening here? Who are doing conspiracy here? And Siddhu where are you going?" Panch barked, and try to stop Sid.

But agilely, all villagers captured Panch and his army, and started hitting them with their own Lathi.

"Bhaag....Sid....Bhaag...," I shouted, and held Ruhi and Sid's hands.
And we ran away, while fucking our enemy. Finally we got triumph over our battle, and stepped towards our dreams while crossing all our boundaries. On that day I believed 'Yes! Of course! Miracles do happen.'
Interesting how dreams don't come true for people who don't believe dreams can come true.

****

CHAPTER THIRTY NINE

Finally, we were back in Delhi with Sid. Two days were left for last match. So Sid again got busy in his practice. Ruhi also got into tussle for his preparation. She had drowned into her books. Rohan was still inconsolable with me.

So I was completely alone. No one perceived my pain. Genuinely, I wanted to be alone. Though, I was missing Aahna so much. But I was hateful at Aahna. She didn't effort to meet me; she was busy in her rascal Shambhav. We both didn't texted yet.
 Some chat will never begin, if we don't text first.
I was still confused, that who the hell Shambhav was, and why did he come in our life?

"Hii... Shourya..., whr r u. Wanna catch u," : Aahna texted later. And quickly, I was feeling butterflies in my stomach, by just seeing her text_ this is what we call love.
But I didn't respond to her text straightaway. "Why would I call her? Why would I care for her, No, I will not see her face again," I was blurting to myself, absurdly. But no matter how hard I tried, I could no longer protest my heart.

I was sitting on the edge of roof of that ruined fort, besides the lake. My legs were dangling from its edge. I was throwing stones in silent lake, and starring at sating sun.

Sky was dancing with dark clouds. It was alarming of disastrous storm. But my heart was already battling with repellent storm. I was completely soaked in loneliness. I really wanted to cry out my anger, my pain. I wanted to burst out loudly.

Immediately, I sensed padding of high heels towards my

backside. And swiftly, I tickled a soft touch of hands on my both eyes. I could realize it was Aahna. I could feel her sweet redolence. Her head was over me. Her hair were showering on my face

Briskly, I filled with enthusiasm, and my heartbeat went faster. My face turned into creepy and stupid smile. I wanted to pull her in my heart.

But, I had to control my emotions. I had to fight with her first. I jolted her hands away harshly, gave her a dull and rude look, and turned back towards lake.

"Oh my God...Shourya...gussa....Hai..., How...Cute..." She grinned, "Ale bap le....ab to Shourya...ko manana palega...," Aahna mumble in weird and funny tone. She was just being childish to me. She put her soft arms around my neck, smothered me tightly, her left cheek rubbing against my right cheek, she was breathing in my neck.

"Shourya....Shourya, listen naa. I am really sorry....," she buzzed, in my ear, while snoozing over me. And she licked my cheek for long. But I didn't react, I was statue. So she bit my right ear cruelly. It hurt me. I protested and got up to leave.

"Sorry...Na...Baba...I am guilt... I will never do this again. Please forgive me Baba..," she knelt on her knees, touched her ears, and gave some funny expressions.
The cutest thing in the world is seeing your girl, saying sorry to you. I could rarely suppress my smile.

"Why are you saying sorry Aahna? And why you came here? Who I am to you? Why would you care for me?" I snapped upset.

"Shourya...it's not like this...you mean a lot to me," she said and grabbed my arms, and sat next to me on edge of roof.

"Oh really, then tell me, where were you when I needed you? You just left me alone; you didn't even text me once," I hissed, "Hhhh...But what's the mean of it now? Why I am expounding to you? You just get lost to your so called, Shambhav," I plucked and turned away.

"Shourya...again, you are getting me wrong. Shambhav is____," she stopped her word and looked at me with her huge

233

brownish eyes, "Oh my Goodness...Now I caught you. Actually, you are jealous of Sambhav," And Aahna burst into monster laugh.

"Shut up, why would I be jealous?" I hesitated to hide my envy.

"How would I know? Look at you, your face in burning in jealousy," she again laughed and she pulled my chaps to kiss on them.

"Stop it Aahna...," I angered ungodly, and snatched her tightly. She got paralyzed, "it's not funny. Do you have any idea, how much I missed you? How much I was in need of you," I spat out each word loudly, "but you will never understand me, just get lost," I frowned and pushed her towards lake, and turned around.

But I was jerk, I did evil mistake. Because of my sudden push, she lost her balance, she slipped from the edge, and she was falling down lake side.

"Shouryaaaaaaaaa...," she howled, and stretched her hand to me.

Immediately, I got sensed. I turned to her hastily, and jumped towards her; I held her one hand and stopped her falling. She was hanging on other Side of wall, towards lake.

I got so much scared, cold sweat ran into my body, my throat went dry. And heart was about to blast. I grabbed her more tightly. I put my extreme energy to pull her in my arms, and buried her in my chest tightly, like kid. I was so embarrassed, and rueful, that what I had just done.

I would have killed myself, if she would have got hurt. I was so panicked and I checked her again and again insensibly, that she was all right or not. I was panting dangerously.

"Aahna.....Are you ok? Please forgive me. Are you ok? You got hurt," I gasped and pampered her like kid.

"I am ok...Shourya...," she sighed.

"I am so sorry, I didn't know what happened with me; please forgive me," I blurted like moron.

"It's ok..., I am fine," she drawled.

"Aahna... I was just angry, so I vented out my anger on you, please don't get me wrong," I sobbed.

"Shourya...stop it....," She bellowed.

"You would have died, by my silly. I would never forgive myself," I spat out stupidly. I was getting more childish.

"Shoury...Shourya...Shourya.. stop it...behave yourself," she snapped and shook me violently. And I got calmed down.

"Aahna, I am afraid of losing you, please don't ever leave me alone," I said, and quickly she clutched me tightly in her warm chest.

"I promise Shourya..., I will never leave you till my last breathe," she whispered in my ears.

And we were in tight hug for 5 minutes. We felt so much peace and love. Abruptly, it started soft drizzling, which turned the Stormy climate into romantic one. In few seconds, we both were soaked in raindrops.

Water drops ran into her sleeveless deep cleavage black top, which had a flared dark yellow skirt. I grabbed her more tightly so I felt so warm of her body in me. We both were breathing hastily.

Suddenly, furious sensations borne in our bodies; our bodies were quavering. And we started sharing our energy into each other. We didn't know, what stampede ran into our bodies.

I looked into her brown eyes, which were so fainting like drugs. Her face was twinkling in water drops. She was appearing so innocent and nervous. Her pink lips were flashing so much hot in water drops. I moved my fingers on her exposed soft waist, and touched her Navel in sensation. I rolled my other hand on her soft wet hands, then on her shoulders, hence on her neck. Quickly, I put my fingers on soft rose like pink lips. It was killing her, she groaned in pain. She started breathing heavily and started swooning. She gasped again and closed her eyes.

Thereupon, I ruffled her wet hairs by my fingers and leaned my head against her. We both were panting. Our breathes were warm and were merging into each other.

We lost our control; we were allowing ourselves to cross our limits. We didn't want to care for anything. We wanted to lose in world of love and romance.

Smoothly, I rested my both hands on her waist and pulled her close to me. I downed my face to her, and went close to her lips. Aahna rose on her toes to meet my lips. We closed our eyes and put my lips on her juicy upper wet lip. And I sucked water drops of her lip.

I touched my nose to her, and beamed into her eyes. She was feeble. She closed her eyes. Then she rested her palm on my face, and pulled my face towards her for a furious kiss. She held my lower lip by her both lips and pulled my lower lip cruelly, passionately.

Now, we were furious, I was totally over her. I put my lips on her lower lips, and sipped. And she would suck my lips alternately. And we were smooching each other softly, and sensationally. Her lips were so melody and soft like rose.

I sensed a sweet smell of her mouth, many times our tongues met, and every time it was melodious and sexiest experience. We were so exasperated; we didn't think what we were doing. In fact, we didn't want to esteem on that. We just wanted to leave that precious Moment.

My body was weightless. I sighted as if I was flying in sky as if I was sinking into deep sea with Aahna. Aahna was more appalling. She put her arms terribly around my neck and pulled me tightly towards her lips.

I clutched her more tightly by her waist, and I lifted her up in air. Her head was above me. Her wet hair showered on my face, but she was continuously smooching, and biting my lips. she kissed me terribly, she didn't let my lips open for a second, I couldn't breathe. She was moaning and sucking water drops from my lips_ and she forced me to let her tongue enter into my mouth. She sipped my tongue for long, and released before biting between her teeth.
I peered into her eyes. Her hands were still hooked around my neck. I pushed her to a wall, she leaned against the wall, and I got over her. I slid my hands on her nude hands, and pressed her palm against the wall. I put my lips on her neck, and started licking it horribly. I moved my lips to her ears, cheeks, and paused at her shoulders. She was groaning, as it was so torturing to her. She was digging her nails into my back in protest.
Therefore, I reached to jip of her dress at the back, in one motion I

opened it. So, her dress slipped bit down the shoulders. And I put my lips on her chest, I nibbled her chest twice.

Unexpectedly, a harsh thundering of clouds broke our faint. Hurriedly, she opened her eyes. She was scared, she pushed me away desperately. Quickly, tears flowed out abundantly from her eyes. She started sobbing vehemently.

I noticed, she wanted to say out her feelings. But her voice was stuck in her throat. Briskly, she ran away, while wiping her tears. I was completely frozen; I couldn't get what just had happened. I couldn't mumble a word to stop her. I was guilt that we did wrong.

Literally, I was ashamed that I did a sin. I crossed my limits. I rescaled with an innocent girl; I broke her trust.

Dignity and self-respect is inestimable ornament for a girl. And I abused her self respect, grace, and honor. I couldn't face her again. I even couldn't face my evil face. I was embarrassed in my own eyes. I couldn't sleep that whole night.

****

CHAPTER FORTY

Finally the day come, we were waiting for the day of test of our friendship, our unity and our power. It was the day of final match between Delhi and Haryana, which was going to decide winner of series. But as matter of fact, that match was going to decide victory of Sid. Today Sid had to play best cricket of his life. If today Sid would play spectacular, and would lead Delhi towards triumph, then there would have chances that he would play for nation.

So it was best opportunity for Sid. He had to play with full power. He had to give his pain, sorrow, injuries anger, and everything to cricket. Today he had to play to prove himself, to prove ourselves. Give your best hours to your dreams is the valuable secret of success. Today it was the day of the examination of Sid's practice and battle, which he was doing from months, till every day and night.

Sid, Ruhi, Rohan, Ashvini were at hostel gate. They were leaving for the stadium.

"All the best Sid, Fadd dena...," I said and hugged him, all upset.

"Shourya, what is this? Are you not coming with me?" Sid asked in concern.

"No... I am not...," I rambled and dug my eyes down into earth.

"Shourya, you can't do this to me again," Sid frowned, "Today is such important day for us, and you are not coming, it hilarious," he hissed at me.

"Sid, please don't force me, I am not feeling well," I deflected and held Sid.

"Shourya...what's wrong? Is everything ok with Aahna..,"

Ruhi raised her eyebrows, "you are looking downed," she squeezed me..

"Yeah..yeah...everything is ok," I excited to hide my shame.

Actually, I was making excuses to go to stadium, as I knew; Aahna would also come there, to cheer up for Sid. And I couldn't face her; I couldn't match my eyes with her. I was caught by terror that what she would envisage of me. I was feared that what will I do? She would anger on me, or slap me, in front of everyone. I had decided that, I would never appear in her front. I was thinking too much.

"Shourya, you promised me that you will never leave me, and see you are cheating me second time. I will not play if you will not come." Sid shouted and lay on ground, and threw his kid down.

"Saale...Notanki...," I laughed and got over Sid.

******

We reached stadium, at last. Haryana had already played, and now it was time for Delhi to chess the big target. Delhi had already last 2 wickets. Delhi was suffering badly. Now it was Sid's time to rock.

"Guys, I am nervous," Sid whispered while wearing hid pads.

"What? What are you talking rubbish?" I snapped.

"What rubbish means?" Sid quipped, "I am nervous, that's it."

"Ok, listen, don't take pressure on mind, its only opportunity we have. Today you have to play for us. For your Dad, your village, for Ruhi," I said, and held his arms. Rohan was standing aSide; he was still angry and silent.

"Sid, today your victory will lead us towards our dreams. So don't be nervous, just play, play to win or to die. And we all are with you. So just go, close your eyes, and listen to your heart and play," I energized Sid and pampered his kits.

We all cheered up for Sid, as he entered into field. Sid continued the match, but the team was already in pressure. Even though, Sid started his game slowly, but he was apprehensive. He would take singles and doubles, and even he escaped thrice from being run out.

And Delhi kept on loosing wickets. Sid would encounter a lot to chess target. He was in need of a good partnership. And Delhi had left with only 3 wickets.

"What he is doing? What is wrong with him?" Ruhi bellowed in frustration.

"He is playing in pressure," I mumbled sadly. Actually I was still looking for Aahna.

"She is not coming," Ruhi teased me.

"What?" I shouted weirdly, and I gasped deeply. I felt so relax, I was like flying. Suddenly I started cheering up.

"Sid...Sid ..Sid...," I shouted powerfully with smile.

"What happened with you, rapidly," Ashvini shocked at me.

"Nothing...idiot...let's cheer up," I yowled.

Ruhi went close towards the field to cheer up Sid. She waved hands to Sid. She wanted to say something to Sid. Again she waved and yapped at Sid.

Speedily, Sid faced towards Ruhi. Ruhi blinked him, and smiled at Sid in so faith. Her eyes were saying, "I am with you, so don't be nervous, and just play with your heart."

Sid smiled back at her. And again he started his game, this time with more power and concentration. I don't know, what happened with him, that he turned the game in few balls. He was fierce and reckless. He would smack every bowler with 4s, 6s, 4s, and 6s.

On being frank, it was Ruhi's power; the power of love of Ruhi; the power of her glittering smile. It was like miracle, on that I actually started believing in miracles. Sid was unstoppable.

And we won over Haryana. Whole stadium resonated, and buzzed into hooting of Sidharth... We burst into joy; we shouted nonsensically, we hugged each other while jumping. We danced like kids. We lifted Sid in our arms.

Sid fulfilled our hope. He gave us new hopes and faith, that, "yes we can do this." Today once again, Sid filled us with confidence and cosmic energy to win our battle.

He proved that, we could do anything, if we are together. He pushed us forward towards our goals. Now we were unstoppable.

****

After the match, Rohan, Sid, Ashvini were celebrating with others at stadium. And Ruhi and I had left to do preparations to celebrate at hostel. I was driving my PULSAR, on highway, towards hostel.

Unusually, a black Audi Q3 blocked our way. Heedlessly, Shambhav stepped out of car. And I was bombshell, when I saw Anshul and his 2 guys also stepped out with Shambhav.

They looked so horrifying; they were red eyes. Their intension was not of good boys. They strode furiously towards Ruhi and me. I was still in muse. Ruhi was frightened, she grabbed my hand tightly. They approached us as if they would kill us. I got ready to fuck those morons.

"Shambhav...., he is that fucking bastard, Shourya...," Anshul snapped as they reached to us.

"Mind your words," I yelled, "or I would like to kick on your ass."

"You....," Anshul grinded his teeth and we both collared each other.

"Guys, guys...cool down, take it easy," Shambhav interjected us.

"What is your problem?" I glared at Shambhav, "why did you chopped my way?" I murmured.

"Actually Shourya...you are troubling me," Shambhav grinned, rubbing his jaw, "Actually you are coming between me and Aahna....so it is good for you to stay away, you son of bitch," Shambhav stormed.

"Mind your words at first, you pimp," Ruhi squelched at Shambhav with burning eyes.

"Oh, you shut up, you bitch....," Anshul was shouting, but I interrupted him.

"Anshul don't... I won't waste a second to kill you, if you said anything to Ruhi," I groaned in anger

"What the fuck," Shambhav sneered, "Anshul you told me that Shourya is in love with Aahna, but see, he loves this bitch," Shambhav said and laughed.

"Oh, yeah...Shambhav.. it means, he is playing with both girls," Anshul shrieked, "I am sure, Ruhi would have sleep with Shourya in his own room."

Anshul abused Ruhi, and laughed. When he said that, it hurt Ruhi. She was embarrassed. It abused her pure soul. And suddenly there was tinge of tears in her eyes.

"You mother fucker...," I roared and strangled Anshul's neck terribly.

And in few second, I was girdled by all the bastards. They grabbed me tightly. And they were about to hit me. But unexpectedly, Sid, Rohan and Ashvini approached to us. And without waiting for a second, they assaulted Shambhav and Anshul, horrendously.

Rohan and Sid stood up as a wall in my front to defend me.

"Now come..Who want to fight? Come on. Today I will gauge your blood, come you bastards," Rohan hissed franticly.

"Look, I don't want to mess with both of you guys. I just want Shourya...to stay away from Aahna...," Shambhav frowned.

"Why would I stay away? I love her and she loves me too. And for her I can die and also I can make anyone dead only for Aahna..," I said grumpily.

"You asshole.....," Shambhav crumbled his teeth, and raised his hands to hit me.

But Sid stopped his hands and twisted terribly.

"Don't dare please, I will kill you, if you ever try to hurt him," Sid said and threw him away.

242

"I will show you.. All of you," Shambhav barked and they ran away.

"Sid, you shouldn't mess with them, they are too dangerous," I said to Sid.

"Stupid.. don't worry... I will not die and also not let you die," he said and armed me.

Rohan was starring silently. I went to him.

"Bhai...maaf kr de yaar," I whispered. But he turned away from me.

"Bhai...please," I pleaded to Rohan.., "Achha chal tu bhi mar de chata, But don't behave like this to me. I can't see you like strange. I love you so much, Rohan," I mumbled, and held his hand.

"Bss kr saale..., I love you too my bebo...," Rohan shrieked, and jumped over me, and hugged me.

****

CHAPTER FORTY ONE

We were celebrating Sid's victory. Sid treated us with delicious dinner at one of the best restaurant of Delhi. Not with standing, I didn't want to go. But Sid and Ruhi forced me to come. Even they insisted Aahna too. So we both were helpless against Ruhi and Sid.

Aahna was sitting just in my front. She was in spring summer charming belted white black lace skater mini party dress. It was elbow sleeved white gauzy dress, and black flared velvet skirt up to her knees. She was illuminating in that white and black dress. She was astonishing, and taking breath of everyone there. She had made her brown hair into Lauren Conrad Side braid, and rest hair was left undone. She was dazzling. Her cute dimples were petrifying me.

Admitting that I had decided not to match eyes to her, but I couldn't control my urge to praise her.

Continuously, Aahna and I both kept on stealing glance at each other. And whenever our eyes collided, we briskly looked away. But it was so embarrassing. I felt so remorseful. I felt like someone straggling me. I couldn't breathe properly. Same was with Aahna. She couldn't eat properly. She was feeling so uncomfortable and awkward by my presence. So, I was rueful that what she was thinking of me.

"What happened Aahna? You are not eating properly. And why are you so silent today? Are you ok?" Ahvini asked and patted Aahna's shoulder.

"Yeah... I am good," Aahna delighted, then gazed at me. It was so terrible for me. I just wanted to run. So I stepped out of table, and strode to washroom rapidly. Sid and Rohan followed me.

"Bhai...Are you ok?" Rohan shrugged.

"Yeah! Of course...," I responded politely.

"So, what the hell you are doing here?" Sid bellowed and noticed me.

"I am planning for you idiot," I sneered.

"What do you mean," they both stunned, "what planning?"

"Stupid today. Wait Not today...even right Now...you will propose Ruhi. Got that," I sighed at Sid, and braces myself.

"What the F___," Sid swallowed his words, "Have you gone mad," Sid panicked.

"Yeah... I have gone mad. And I don't want to argue any stuff," I bellowed, "And please Now don't react as if you don't love Ruhi," I slammed at Sid.

"Rohan please tell___," Sid said to Rohan, But Rohan cut him off, "shut up."

"Shourya...," Sid again protested to me, but I killed his words.

"Shut up...," I hissed, "Sid, please listen, if you love someone, then you shouldn't waste your time. You should go directly to her and deliberate everything, what your heart feels for her," I said to Sid.

"Yeah...And if you missed this chance, then you will regret for your whole life," Rohan unfolded to Sid.

"But Shourya, I can't l," Sid hesitated, "I can't even say a word, when she comes in my front."

"Meri jaan...," I chuckled at innocence of Sid, "why are so much terrified of Ruhi. Sid you won the match, And Now, you will play for international match, and you should have some ego, arrogance. Why are you feared of a girl, shame on you Sid," I taunted Sid.

And Rohan and I provoked Sid. Although, it could be

dangerous, as Ruhi was horrible; but who cares when it comes to love.

"Yeah, you are right, I am the man of the match," Sid blurted in over confidence, "I will propose Ruhi, right now. Yes I will."

There upon, we started planning. So, when we finished our dinner, we walked out of restaurant. Rohan stopped us.

"Ruhi, Ashvini," Rohan said, "Can we have a walk over there?" He asked.

"Ehhh... What?" Ahvini shocked, "what happened to you today, Are you ok?" she grinned at Rohan, checking his forehead.

"Just shut up...Aashu...and tell me, do you want to have a walk?" Rohan frowned.

"Ok, ok, don't fight," Ruhi said, and our plan worked.

Ruhi, Aahna and Ashvini were walking before us in silent, cold, and Dark Street, which was flashing by yellow dim streetlights, both side cars parked, and some dogs were lying under the cars, and some were having pleasure at the roof of BMW, Audi, and Mercedes.

"Go...," I pushed Sid to Ruhi...and cleverly, Rohan called Aahna and Ashvini to us. And we paraphrased whole plan to them.

Now, Sid and Ruhi were walking ahead of us, lonely, kicking stones by their heels.

They would give queerer smiles to each other, as if they were strangers.

"So...," Sid whispered to Ruhi, and shrieked.

"Sooo...what...?" Ruhi beamed gawkily and nervously to Sid and raised her brows, while twisting her long bubble braid aSide.

"So... I want to say something to you," Sid stammered.

"Huh?... What?" Ruhi gulped, and starred at Sid. So Sid became more nervous, and feared.

"Don't give me such horrifying look Ruhi," Sid blurted in panic, "I am scared already."

"Ha..Ha..," Ruhi giggled; "ok sorry...sorry...say, what you want to say?" she shrugged, still grinning at Sid. Sid tried hard to speak, but he couldn't. He was fumbling nervously.

"Why don't you just close your eyes first, otherwise I couldn't speak," Sid said.

"What is wrong Sid? Say out Naa...," Ruhi irritated.

"Just close your eyes...please Ruhi," Sid pleaded.

"Ok, Baba, relax. I am doing." Ruhi said and close her eyes. Sid lay on his knees, joined his both hand to pray in front of Ruhi.

"Ruhi, you always say that we should listen to our heart, so today I am going to listen my heart," Sid said. We all were looking at both of them and giggling together.

"Ruhi..., I fell in love with you, when I saw you first, in my room. I don't know, what is love? But I know that, whenever I see you, my heart beats go faster. I feel so much peace. Every time I think about only you. When I see your smile, I started flying. Everything became so lovable.

I didn't tell this earlier, because I was afraid," Sid gasped and again gathered himself, "I was afraid, that you would leave me.

Ruhi, I want to live my life only with you. I want to chess my dreams, but only with you. I want to see Paris only with you. I want to die only with you. So Ruhi would you like to spend your life with me," Sid said and held Ruhi's hand in his hand.

Ruhi was surprised. She never touched so much special. She also loved Sid. But she was also feared as like Sid. But today her dream came true. Her eyes were shinning in tears, and her face was twinkling with glittering smile and bliss. She could spit out a word.

She made Sid to get up, went to close to him, and beamed into his eyes.

"I will accept you only, if you promise that you will never leave me," Ruhi sighed.

"I do....," Sid smiled.

"Idiot," Ruhi shrieked, and in next second, she pulled Sid and put her lips on Sid's lips.

We all were starring and tickling; I was so much gleeful for both of them. And I felt so relax, that finally I found someone, who would really care and love Ruhi.

Slowly and theft fully, I glanced at Aahna. Her brown eyes were shinning by unshed tears. She gazed at me. And abruptly, tears flowed out of her eyes, which spread her eyeliner on her face.

I tried to drown into her eyes.

My eyes asked to her, "Aahna, what is paining you? Why are you crying?"

"No... I am not crying...why would I cry?" Her eyes deflected.
"Aahna...please, don't do this to yourself, why don't you understand me?" My eyes asked.
"Do you understand me Shourya? Do you know what i want?" Her eyes blinked.
"Aahna...you don't ever give me chance to know you. Why are you not uttering your heart to me?
Please tell me what do you want?" My eyes would ask.
"Do you need more sign to know me? I kissed you, and now you are asking me that what I want?" Her eyes cried.
Suddenly, Ashvini and Rohan clapped for Sid and Ruhi. And we all hugged them.

Ruhi bloomed, but Sid blushed more than Ruhi.

Abruptly, Ruhi and Sid fell on their knees, and clutched my each hand.

"Shourya....thank you so much...you gave us our dreams, you gave us our love, you are our God...you are our parents, you are our everything." They gestured their faith in me.

"Bhai..., I can't expect a day without you. Today you gave me worthiest gift. Though, you already take care of me, but now it's your responsibility to take care of not only me, but also of Sid," Ruhi prayed like a kid.

I interrupted both them, "guys, guys, stop it...what are you doing this?" I excited and snatched both of them and armed them, "And I promise, I will always take care of both of you, and I wish both of you a happy and blessed life," I patted their heads, and kissed Ruhi's forehead. And we all shouted loudly, so that interrupted dog's sleep. They started barking at us and ran to us, but we ran faster than dogs. And they followed us to Hotel.

"Guys, guys..., it's too late...we have to leave for hostel...and Sid and Ruhi, you guys can kiss again at hostel. Even you guys can make out, I will allow you in my room," Ashvini shrieked.

"Shut up...shameless, Ashvini," Sid hit Ashvini's chap softly.

"Shourya..., you drop Aahna at her home," Ruhi shrugged.

"No..No..," Aahna and I denied, yowl, together, "Rohan will drop...," I mumbled and starred at Aahna.

"No..No..I am too tired..., Shourya..., you have to drop her," Rohan exasperated.

"No...Rohan.. You drop me...please," Aahna said hastily, and hold Rohan's hand.

"Shut up...you.. Idiots, what is wrong with both of you?" Ruhi thundered, glared at Aahna and me, "Guys let's go hostel, and leave both of them here. They have whole night to decide, leave them their own," Ruhi roared, and gazed at Aahna and me like hungry lioness.

And they all left hastily. Veritably, they wanted Aahna and me to spend some time in alone, to solve our problems and bothers.

I walked slowly to my bike. Aahna followed me silently. I leaned against my bike, and dug my eyes into the earth. Aahna approached me, and stood up in my front. She was looking here and there. We didn't dare to catch each other's gaze. It was too cold and dark night, wind was so brisk.

She was shivering in that gauzy dress. She rubbed her hands on her body to get hot. I pulled out my jacket, and forwarded it to her. But she didn't take it, and turned away. I exhaled in irritation, and went to her and covered her stripped body by my jacket. I kicked my bike, and waited for her to be seated.

She sat behind me, although after wasting 10 minutes, and my petrol. And I drove towards her home. We both were so silent. We sensed so uncomfortable, gawkily, and it was killing when our bodies collided. She allowed air to pass between both of us. And that's why she was jittering furiously.

"You will get cold, get close to me," I muttered rudely. She pretended like dumb, and duff.

"Aahna...please...you will get fever...sit close to me," I sniffed. She obliged me, and armed me tightly from behind.

I sensed so warm, by her hug. It was heavenly peace. I still feel that touch of Aahna.

Few more minutes later, we reached her home. She got down, and padded slowly in hesitation to her home, without whispering anything. She didn't even give back me my jacket.

"Aahna....," I whispered at her..And she turned briskly as if she was also waiting for me to call her. I walked towards her.

"Are you ok...?" I asked. she nodded.

"Aahna... I can't do this anymore, I am really sorry," I mumbled.

"For what?" She whispered first time and eyed at me.

"For that day, I misbehaved with you. Actually I was not in sense, so I actually did wrong, it was my mistake," I was blurting like moron. But Aahna stopped me.

"Do you think? It was a mistake, do you think, I kissed you by mistake?" Aahna squelched and looked away while gasping.

"Aahna...let me clear...what do you want?" I screamed in frustration, "if it was not a mistake, then why are you behaving rudely, you didn't even talk to me, after that," I sighed.

"Did you talk to me?" She quipped, and gazed at me. Her eyes were shining with unshed tears.

"Shourya...Actually you don't understand me ever. You care for everyone, but not for me. I cried a lot, because you didn't talk to me," Aahna sobbed.

"Oh! Noo..., please..," I buzzed, "so you tell me Aahna...what I do to care for you?" I muttered.

In next Moment, she stopped my lips by her fingers. She kissed my left chap, and ran inside of her home.

****

CHAPTER FORTY TWO

"Whr r u, how mch more it wll take," : Sid texted to Ruhi.

Ruhi, Rohan, Ashvini and I were at that orphanage house, to have check on the kids. It was already 10PM of night.

"Jst relx Sid..., wll catch u after a while," : Ruhi sent.

"Com soon, I hv smthng to shw u," : Sid messaged again.
"Sounds awesm, bt wht," : Ruhi asked.
"Cn't tell, jst come fast.i m missing u bdly,": Sid texted.
"I m too missing u already," :Ruhi sent.
"Awww so sweet, don't ever leave me alone,": Sid typed.
"I won't. N u too proms, u will b with me forever," : Ruhi said.
"I do. Jst come early, i m waitng for u," : Sid replied.

A little over an hour later, we headed towards hostel, Ruhi on my behind, on my Pulsar 220. I was feeling a ghastly malaise. There was so awkwardness, and silence in air. Everything on environment was signaling of something bad happening.

The fear that something worse would come up again still persisted deep inside me. At an instance, Yash called me, he was furious, his voice was vibrating, and he was sobbing terribly,

"Shourya, where are you? Come fast. Come fast. It's an emergency. Worst happened here," He cried, and cut off.

My heart lurched as I heard the terror in his voice. My throat felt parch, my mouth dry. My heart rose faster, my hands trembled; So that I couldn't even drive properly.

And the first face came up to me was of Aahna. I was worried sick about Aahna.

So many ifs and buts raised in my mind that is she ok? What if she is not ok? What would have happened to her? Even the thought of it gave me jitters.

But I had already noticed my heart, who was saying everything was not ok. So, I speeded up my bike, without saying a word to Ruhi.

We got at hostel. As we entered into gate, I saw huge crowd of boys and girls was gathered. They were wondering in round circle. They all looked feared and tensed. I accelerated towards them,

"Shourya.... Shourya....," Yash shouted as he gazed me from crowd.

I eyed towards him, and I saw Sid was lying on ground near Yash. Sid was swimming in blood.

When I observed Sid my head started revolving, darkness appeared in my eyes. My breaths got stuck in my throat, my body was shuddering, but my soul was like statue. I lost my balance, and slipped with Ruhi, and we fell down.

I pushed my bike away, and got up. I couldn't estimate anything. My body was powerless. My head was aching, and my body was fatigued. My brain was numb, but my heart was pacing as if it will jump out of my mouth.

"Sid....," I screeched loudly, and push away my bike hazardously, and rush incensed towards Sid, and slipped near him unsteadily.

He was completely stained in blood, as it was running out abundantly from his head and hands. His eye bolls were pocking so big from his eyes. I pulled him in my arms like a kid. I was so frightened. Sid was breathing hardly. I didn't guess, what had happened? And now what to do?

"Sid...Sid....," I mumbled at him and furiously and cradled his face panicky and fearfully in my palms.

Hurriedly, Rohan, Ruhi, and Ashivini rushed towards us. They all shocked. And when Ruhi saw Sid in blood, she couldn't handle it. She got fainted, and scattered in feet of Sid. And she didn't open her eyes again.

"Shourya...," Sid whispered and heaved, he tried to open his eyes.

"Yeah...Sid...Look, I have come," I said in stuttering tone, and grabbed him tightly, "someone please fetch the water...please fast," I bawled in vibrating tone. I wanted to let it out, but I couldn't even cry.

"Sid.... Look at me... it's ok...," I blurted and pampered Sid.

Rohan got water, and helped Sid to drink. I stirred my shirt and bandaged it on Sid's head to stop blood.

"Sid...say something...., Are you ok?" I chuck under his chin, and my face steamed in tears. Everyone was gazing at me. I was going mad, I was shouting without any sense.

"Damn it! Someone please call the Ambulance," I barked to crowd.

"Yeah... I am calling...," Rohan sobbed and said.

"How did it happen Sid...?" I asked, and clutched his head to my chest.

"Shourya...Sid jumped from terrace," Yash gasped and cried.

"Shut up...you fucking idiot...do you know what are you saying?" I roared, "Sid is my bhai...he can't do this," I yowled at Yash.

"Shourya...Sid attempted suicide," Yash sobbed, and whole crowd buzzed in evil talks about Sid.

"Shut up...you," I hissed at everyone, "someone please call the Ambulance, please take him to hospital," I begged.

Therefore, in few minutes Ambulance came hurriedly, with its loud Siren. Two men stepped out of Ambulance, placed a stretcher near me. They pushed me away and placed Sid on stretcher and got him into Ambulance. They were too quick, that I was unaware of what was going there.

Rohan held me and we both jumped into ambulance. My shirt was soaked in red blood. Rohan and I snagged Sid's each hand.

"Sid.... don't worry...we are with you...nothing will happen to you," I sighed.

"Ruhi....," he whispered, but his voice was not coming out of his throat.

"She is ok...she is coming with Yash," Rohan said.

Ambulance was running apace. And so many boys followed us with bikes. Within few Moments, we reached to 'Health and Care Hospital'.

As we stopped in front of gate of hospital, 4 ward boys in white dress ran towards us, and quickly, they translated Sid on a wheeled stretcher. They drove that wheeled stretcher, so browned, inside of hospital.

Rohan and I were running with Sid, while holding Sid's hands. Then they ran into elevator to take Sid to OT. Rohan and I took stairs, all wobbling, climbing 3-4 steps at a time. We reached to OT before the elevator. As we reached to Operation Theater, those men stopped us outside of OT.

"Sid, don't worry... I am with you," I shouted. I was trying to look into OT through black glasses. Immediately, so many Doctors rushed towards OT.

"Dr. Please save him...please save him..," I pleaded.

"Don't worry...we will take care of him, now you just calm down," Dr. said and patted my shoulder, and strode inSide. I panted, and turned to Rohan. And quickly tears flowed abundantly out of our eyes. I rushed to Rohan, and got stucked to him furiously, and I cried loudly terribly.

"Rohan, what has happened with us? Rohan you saw our Sid, our Sid___," I mumbled while sobbing.

"Calm down...calm down," Rohan patted my head, "we are

good naa, so God will not do bad with us, Sid will be ok," he whispered.

Abruptly, our friends entered in corridor of OT. Then, Ruhi strode towards us. Aahna, Ashvini, and other girls were following Ruhi and trying to stop her.

"Shourya..., now stop crying. Ruhi is coming, we have to stay strong for her, we have to handle her," Rohan said and wiped my tears.

Ruhi was running towards me, blinking her eyes rapidly, breathing through her mouth, her steps were measured confident. I too rushed towards her. And in next Moment, she got stuck to my chest furiously, as like kid. And she burst into scary cry.

"He's ok...don't cry...don't cry Ruhi..," I whispered in her ears. Aahna and Ashvini also armed her. She was panting terribly.

"Bhai...where is Sid? I want to see him," she cried and howled. She was getting faint, and furious. She was crying more louder and louder.

"He is ok, Ruhi...please don't cry," I said to console her.

"No, you are lying, I want to meet him, he needs me," she snapped and cried. She pushed me away. And tried to go inside of OT.

"No.... you can't go inside...Ruhi..," I grabbed her and said.

"No..Bhai...please let me go inside...please let me see him once...," Ruhi blurted loudly.

I held her by shoulders and shook her violently, "Ruhi...., behave yourself, he is ok....," I snapped.

Ruhi got feared by my anger. She got relax, and she looked at me with her big black eyes, innocently. And I pulled her back into my chest.

"Bhai...what is this happened with us? Please save him. Only you can save Sid, bhai," she sobbed and again broke into tears. She gave up and let the tears flow freely down her face. She was crying without making any sound.

I put my hand on her head in benevolence. It was too much tough for me to control my tears. Suddenly, she was exhausted, so she again got fainted. We made her to sleep on long bench.

Aahna and Ashvini took care of Ruhi. I couldn't suffer more, I turned towards wall and leaned my head against a poll and freed my tears to flow furiously.

Aahana come to me and put her hand on my shoulder. I turned to her and hugged her tightly.

I was too exhausted. Aahna's warm hug was like a deep nap for me. Time stood still, minutes passed like hours, hours like days. With every second, I was moving more closer to fear and despair. I was still in shock, wondering it all that was real or jsut nightmare. I felt crippled with the pain in my gut. I bent inwards, holding my arms together, clutching tightly against my stomach.

One hour passed, a nurse rushed out of OT, and asked us to get treatment. And we were lucky that we Rohan's blood matched with Sid. So he strode towards blood camp to donate blood to Sid.

I was sitting in one corner. Aahna was sitting near Ruhi. Ruhi was sleeping in Aahna's lap. Aahna was rocking her head in her lap. I was praying silently again and again.

"God...please save our Sid, please God, it's my last wish. I will not ask for anything again. God please take my life, and escape Sid. God please escape him for our friendship, for Ruhi, for their love. God today is time for a miracle. Please God, if there is your existence in universe, then please give symptoms of your existence. Please save him."

It was already 3 am of evil night. We all were crying for hours. And Ruhi had got fainted thrice in 4 hours. Unforeseen, and hastily Dr. came out of the OT. We got up fearfully and quickly. We went towards them.

"Dr. How's he?" Rohan asked.

"I can't say anything, we did our best, but his head almost destroyed. There are so many blood clots in his entire braid. His condition is critical. We have to wait till the dawn, and then we have to shift him to AIIMS," Dr. Mathur said.

"Sir, can we meet him?" I asked.

"No," he denied, "you can't..."

"Sir please, it's very important. Just one minute time. He needs us. Sir he will be ok, just when he will see Ruhi," we all begged, and cried. So Dr. allowed us to meet Sid. And we ran inside.

I felt so generosity for Sid, as I saw Sid. There were scars, big and small, on his face. He was completely covered by plasters. He was breathing on oxygen mask. He was surrounded by machines.

The computer was showing Sid's heart beat on screen. There was only sound beep from ventilator. Two nurses were checking him again and again. We stood up around Sid. I held his right hand and Ruhi his left hand from other Side.

"Sid...," Ruhi whispered Sid's name.

Sid opened his eyes slowly, and looked at Ruhi.

"Ruhi...," he murmur, and tried to open his eyes slightly to Ruhi.

"Yeah...Sid...I am here...," Ruhi tried hardest to gather his voice. She was biting her lower lip to stop her cry. Sid looked at her with squinted eyes. And Ruhi broke down loudly. She surrendered herself on Sid's chest.

"Ruhi, have you gone mad? Why are you crying? Look at him, he is absolutely fine. He will play cricket next morning," Rohan and Aahna bellowed to console Ruhi. But their voice was already shaking.

"Shourya...," Sid hardly opened her mouth.

He was saying something to me, but he couldn't speak. He squeezed my hand tightly. He genuinely wanted to tell me something very important.

"Yes...Bhai...don't worry...I am with you. I will save you. We have to go Paris. We have to fulfill your promise. And you have to marry Ruhi, you had promised me," I sighed and tried to smile and to laugh but I was helpless to sob.

Unusually, Sid started panting ghastly, he was breathing hardly. His chest was rising too high and then down at times. He was so fierce and extreme frightened. His body was getting harder like stone. He was stretching his hands and legs franticly. I noticed his heartbeats on computer screen, which were skipping.

"Dr...Dr..," I shouted disastrously, and I tried to handle Sid. Quickly Dr. rushed to Sid.

"Dr. Look, what is happening with him, please save him," Rohan and Ruhi Cried.

"You stay away, let us check," Dr. said and held Sid. Nurse prepared injections back to back and handed to Dr. Mathur.

Rohan and Ashvini held Ruhi and me, aSide. We all were crying silently. And suddenly, I beamed at screen. It was a single horizontal line without any zigzag. It meant, Sid was not breathing. He was dead.

His eyes were down, But Dr. was still giving him electric shocks, to get his breathe back. But it was hopeless. Dr. turned to us, and put his hand on my shoulder, "He is no more. I am sorry."

When Dr. Said that, cold sweat ran into my body, I was powerless, I stepped backward unsteadily. My body had given up. I couldn't stand myself. I straggled near Sid's feet, Ashvini held me. Something heavy stuck in my heart, my eyes widened.

"No...This can't be true...they are lying," I muttered and held doctor's coat.

"You are lying, I know he is alive, he can't do this to me. You try once more...you are not trying properly," I huffed with tears at doctor.

Rohan, Aahna, and Ashvini burst into loud cry. Ruhi was silent, she sat near Sid.

"Sid, you can't do this to us. You had promised us," I shouted and hit his chest, "Sid, Please say something Bhai...," I chuck under his chin and cried. I was getting faint like kid.

"Aahna..., you say to him, please tell him to talk to me. Sid always listened to you," I held Aahna's hand, and she again cried furiously on my shoulder.

"Dr. please save him...please do something," I blurted absurdly at Dr.

"Shourya...control yourself," Rohan yowled, and shook me, "Shourya, Look at her," Rohan pointed to Ruhi. She was smiling and rolling her fingers on Sid's face.

"If you will behave like this then who will handle her? We have to be strong for her," Rohan said and ruffled my hairs. I again got stuck to him and cried, "we lost our Sid, Rohan. We lost."

There up, some nurse and compounders began to remove all the machines, oxygen mask, and series from Sid's body.

"Hey! What are you doing?" Ruhi grumbled, and pushed them away, "can't you see? Sid is sleeping, he is tired, he has to play in morning," Ruhi cradled Sid's face in her palms. She was out of earshot.

"Ruhi...let them do...and come here," I hooked Ruhi..

"No..Bhai.., they want to kill Sid, they are removing oxygen. Sid can't breathe properly," she whimpered like jerk and snuggled to Sid tightly.

"Ruhi.. He can't breathe anymore," I screeched at Ruhi, "he is dead," I shook her abhorrently.

"No...you are lying...he can't die," Ruhi smacked at me, "he can't leave me alone. He has promised that, he would never leave me," she flopped on Sid's body.

Nurses were striving hard to get Ruhi away. But Ruhi was offensive, she clutched Sid more powerfully.

"Ruhi.....," I pulled her and slapped her harshly, "Ruhi, he is dead, he will never speak again to us," I said in quavering voice. And I pulled Ruhi in my arms, and we broke down.

We padded out of OT. And everyone armed us for clemency. Ruhi's face was steamed in tears. Her eyes were swollen and drowsy.

"Bhai.. Why did God do this to me? God snatched my Mom already and now he snatched Sid from me," Ruhi sobbed and buried her head on my chest, "only a month had been passed of our love. Was our love of only one month? Is that only power of love?" she said...,"Bhai..., please help me. I know only you can save Sid. Bhai please, you had promised me," she cried and again got feeble.

I couldn't handle it. I was frazzled; I just wanted to lie on my bed, to pull the blanket completely over me, to curl up there, to squeeze my hands between my thighs. I just wanted to fall asleep; I wanted to see a worst nightmare I could ever afford. As sometimes nightmare are good. Although, they scare us in the night, but in morning when we wake up, we find everything ok. And that gives us so much peace. So I wanted the death scenario of Sid as a nightmare. So that when I would wake up in morning, I could find Sid playing cricket. But things don't turn out as we want.

And the morning came, and nothing of that sort happened. Police investigated and took for Sid for PM, and they filed case of suicide.

In morning Sid's Dad and uncle came, they were taking Sid back to their village. We all wanted to go, but Sid's Dad alarmed us not to come. They blamed us for Sid's death. They threatened us, not to come to their village ever. They were right, if Sid wouldn't have come back to Delhi, he would be alive.

****

CHAPTER FORTY THREE

A month had been passed of Sid's death. Days were going so fast, but our life had stopped. Sun would rise and sat at it's right time. But we couldn't even see the rising Sun. We still couldn't accept Sid's death.

Everywhere we would perceive Sid's presence. We would touch that Sid was with us. Our life had stuck at Sid. Our life had become nightmare. We had lost our delight, our beam, our chuckle. We had no reason to laugh, to smirk.

That incident had destroyed us, and cracked us like dry leaves. It turned our life upside down. Every day, every second, we would muse, and contemplate of Sid. Every day, we would cry for him.

We gave away our study, our college, our joy, our friends and every pleasure. And the worst was that, we gave away our dreams. We broke our oath, our promise with Sid. Once, we could die for our dreams, but now we didn't even anticipated about our dreams.

Our dreams were mean less without Sid. We were powerless. We had lost our most powerful and intelligent person. We were exhausted and broken down.

'We should stay strong enough, in hard time'. But we were screwed already.

We all were exerting our hardest to stay glad, to get involved in people around us. We struggled not to envisage about Sid. And that's why? We would always remain together. As we were dismayed that if we would stay alone, then people would hurt, assault us. So everywhere, Every time, we would go together, in reliance that we would move on, we would stay optimistic.

However, we again started going to college. But unluckily, in college, in classroom, in canteen, in garden everywhere, all boys and girls would give us ghastly look, and would buzz about Sid's suicide. Supposing, some of them showed forbearance, But we had to prove in their front that, Sid can't do suicide.

But No one showed loyalty to us. It was so much torturing for us. So we would spare whole day in garden, sitting silently for hours.

Many times, we would sit on edge of that ruined fort, and remember sweet memories of Sid. But we would cry again then. I was much effected by Sid's death. He was so much close to me. He was my responsibility. He was like my younger brother.

Whenever, I would enter in my room, I would cry. Every thing in room, Sid's bed, chair, his cricket bat, shoes, his statue of God would remind me of Sid. It was horrifying to live therefore me.

Many times, I tried to write about Sid, But in few seconds pages of my diary would get soak in my tears. Much as I scrambled a lot to stay strong and radiant in front of Ruhi and everyone. But in fact, I would go to that ruined fort and would burst and loudly there. Only Aahna would be always there with me.

"It's ok...don't cry...I am with you, we have to be strong, we have to look for everyone. Everyone is your responsibility," she would console me, and wipe my tears. Hence, I would sleep in her warm lap for hours.

Literally, I was anxious for Ruhi...I would feel so tribulation for that pity girl. God had done such evil and remorseful with Ruhi. How could God do that with innocent girl? How could be he so cruel to Ruhi. Only one month had been spared in their love. Is love has such minor? They had decided to travel Paris. Ruhi had already planned so much for her marriage with Sid.

From that day, I lost my credulity in God, and universal power. As God was not helping my Ruhi; She was dying every day in infelicity of Sid. She had stopped talking to anyone. She locked herself in dark room. We could hear her howling inside of room.

She would cry silently whole night in pillow, hiding her face inside the pillow to muffle her cry. She would sit for hours in empty corridors and courtyards of hostel, unblinkingly. She chose silence as her painkiller. And she had done friendship with emptiness, loneliness. She had lost her beauty and glittering smile. Her face was daffy. Her eyes were swollen and darken spotted. Her tears had dried up on h her cheeks.

She won't eat properly. She was getting weak day by day. She had lost her soul with Sid's death. She was now a living dead body. She still had last messages of Sid_ 'come soon; I am waiting for you, I have something to show you.'

She got such weak, that we had to admit her in hospital for 10 days. Doctor asked us to take care of her, and to divert her mind from Sid, and to start again, to get her normal. So, we all friends, would effort a lot to get back her pretty smile, and flash. We forced her to meet people, to get involved in college. We would punch silly and absurd jokes to make her laugh.

We would take her to canteen, to dinner, to movies. But she didn't react. She remained in silence, that sometimes we couldn't even notice her presence. We never left her alone. Every day, every second, we would with her to take care of her. Every night, Ashvini would awake whole night for her. Ashvini would make Ruhi to sleep in her lap.

"Please, Ruhi...this is last, you have to eat this," I said to Ruhi. And tried to feed her one more spoonfuls of rice. We were sitting in my room.

"Shourya..., you have said that, thrice," she smocked and shook her head in protest.

"Ok, Now, it's last.... Pakka...eat this or I will also not eat," I said.

"So, mean, you are," she mumbled rudely and opened her mouth.

I gave her medicines and then, she put her head on my lap and wrapped her arms tightly around the pillows. I was trying to make her laugh by cracking funny jokes of whatsapp and facebook. She was laughing out loudly and freely and hitting me by pillow. I was amazed by looking her glistering laugh after a while.

"Ruhi...do you know? Aahna and I kissed once," I sighed.

"What the f____," she got shocked, and frowned, "when? And did you proposed her," she blurted in excitement. Her eyes were so big.

"Yeah, I did, but she refused me," I lied to her, "so, I think we have to kidnap her."

"Have you lost?" She shrieked

"No...yaar...I am serious.. I am tired of Aahna, Now I want her at any cost, so I decided to ran away while kidnapping Aahna," I muttered and giggled.

"Yeah...I got that," she wondered," Shourya, I have plan".

"What,"? I surprised.

"You run away with Aahna, and I with Sid, and we all would live in forest together. We will make our nest near a beautiful river," she was saying, so much excitingly. She forgot that Sid was no more and again she blurted in exasperation, "we will do so much of masti, you, Aahna, me and Sid_____," suddenly she stopped and gulped her words. Her lips were trembling furiously; she was biting her lip to control her sob. But she gave up and let the tears flow freely and abundantly down her face.

"Sid... Why, you left me?" She shouted and broke down terribly.

I grabbed her in my arms, patted her back.

"He promised me, that he wouldn't leave me ever," she sobbed, her voice was quivering, "why? Why God is so rude to me? What is my mistake, for what he is punishing me? Is there no mercy for me?" She said fiercely.

"It's ok...stop crying...Look I am with you," I consoled. My eyes were in tears, but I couldn't let them flow out.

It was so mournful for me to hold my tears. I ran towards that ruined fort, lay on my knees, and vented out my agony under open sky. I observed a soft touch on my shoulders. Aahna was again there to pamper me.

"It's enough. I can't do this anymore. I can't look Ruhi in such miseries," I sobbed and leaned my head against Aahna's head.

She wiped my tears and made me to sleep in her warm chest.

****

CHAPTER FORTY FOUR

These were the days of February. With the time, we all were getting rid of Sid's grievance. We had again started going to college, and got busy in our study. But our door was again knocked by the demons, who collapsed our remaining soul and body.

It was 17th of February; I wished that, that evil day shouldn't have come in my life. I was repairing my bike in hostel courtyard.

Impromptu, I saw someone entering through main gate of hostel. He was running unsteadily towards me. I got up agilely, and starred at him. He was Atul, my fucking senior.

"Shourya... Shourya....," he was shouting fumingly.

He strode and scattered in my feet. He was injured, and his clothes were stained in blood. I held him in my arms. He was breathing hardly.

"What happened to you Atul? Are you ok?" I asked and gave him water.

"Shourya.....," he gasped.

"Yeah....! Who did this?" I asked again.

"Anshul and Shambhav hit me. They attempted to kill me," Atul signed.

"What?" I bumped, "but they are your friends, why did they want to kill you?" I asked to Atul.

"Because, I have known their truth," Atul uttered.

"What truth? What do you want to say?" I sniffed

"Shourya...., Sidharth hadn't done suicide. He was murdered," Atul whispered, and my mouth got opened, and my head revolved in so many unusual thoughts.

"Shourya..... On that night, Shambhav and Anshul stamped into hostel to assault you. But they couldn't find you in your room. So they faced Sidharth. Sidharth messed with them to save you. They fight beastly. And while wrangling with those bastards, by mistake Sidharth, slipped down from terrace. They killed Sidharth, in spite you," Atul muttered in shaking voice.

At an instance, I touched so mildness for my innocent Sid. I was filled with the fillings of irrelevant. Because Sid died only because of me. But it was not the time to feel remorse. It was time to fuck on those motherfuckers. My anger went to its Zenith. My body was burning viciously.

I was blood thirsty of Anshul and Shambhav. I threw away tools; I had in my hand and started kicking my bike frenziedly, vindictively, and hastily. My anger had reached tipping point.

"I will kill you, rascals," I pissed my teeth and accelerated towards the gate.

"Shourya..... Stop.... They will kill you....," Atul tried to stop me, "Shourya, please stop."

I was so offended that I couldn't hear Atul. I just wanted to gauge their blood.

I drove towards college campus, and I luckily found Shambhav and Anshul at a beer bar, it was their familiar place, they would always spare their health to that bar. They were sitting on bonnet of Shambhav's audi, and pouring beer into their mouth.

I accelerated towards them furiously, and threw my bike on the Audi, so it clashed with that disastrously. Anshul slipped down off the bonnet. I rushed to Shambhav, who was in sudden shock -cum -fear.

I snatched him violently by his legs, and threw him from bonnet like a ball. I couldn't see anything, but only death in my eyes. Anshul got up terribly and jumped over me, but I kicked him away.

In next Moment, Shambhav cracked beer bottle on my head. Blood ran out freely from my head. My head was spinning, and darkness appeared in my eyes. I clutched my head by both hands, and fell on my knees.

Speededly, Anshul kicked on my chest again and again. And he was ready to Kick, but I defended, and twisted his leg, so Anshul slipped down by my Side. I dug my elbow in his chest obnoxiously.

I got up hastily, and punched Shambhav. I crashed his ribs in next punch. Thereupon, I glommed him by his hairs, and crashed his head sternly against the head lights of his Audi

Quickly, Anshul kicked me on the bonnet of car; I flopped on bonnet. Anshul and Shambhav jumped over me. They punched me fiercely again and again. I was shaking my hands outrageously. Shambhav straggled my neck, I couldn't breathe.

Unexpectedly, Rohan paced and attacked Anshul and Shambhav.

"Are you ok?" He gasped, and held me.

Again, Shambhav ran to me, and attempted to hit me, but I escaped by his shot, and was about to hit Shambhav. But Aahna, stopped my hand, and jerked it down.

"Stop it.... Guys... Stop it," Aahna howled. Atul had informed Aahna, Ruhi, and Rohan about the whole fucking garbage.

"What are you guys doing?" Aahna hissed.

"Aahna, I will kill him. He had...," I grinded my teeth, "you bastard," and I lifted my punch to hit Shambhav.

"Stop it... Shourya, behave yourself," Aahana smacked me, "what is wrong with you? What is the matter? Why are you fighting?" She muttered bitterly.

"Aahna, this ashole has killed our Sid," I braked in throbbing voice.

"Are you kidding? Aahna, he is lying. I don't know, what is wrong with him? He just came and started fighting with me," Shambhav signed innocently.

"You mother fucker, don't be smart, tell every bullshits to her, otherwise, I will shove your hands into your ass," I squelched.

"Aahna, he has gone mental," Anshul shrieked and wiped blood from his lips.

"Shut up, you bloody smug," Aahna stopped Anshul.

"Aahna, listen to me," Shambhav said, "why would I kill Sid. I mean, I didn't even know him. So, how can he blame me?" Shambhav shrugged.

"Oh shut up you unworthy," I sneered, "you didn't know Sid, but you know me," I boiled over at Shambhav.

"Actually Aahna, he wanted to kill me that night, but by accident, he killed Sid. I was lucky, but Sid wasn't," I gulped.

"Ha, ha, ha....., look Aahha..... What he is kidding?" Anshul, and Shambhav laughed at me. They were provoking me. They were proving me absurd in front of Aahna.

"It's enough Shourya, What the hell wrong with you?" Aahna exasperated in frustration, "why he will try to kill you?" Aahna mumbled, "Shourya, you are going mad, because of Sid's death. You should _____," I raised my hand to stop Aahna's words.

"I am not mad, did you got it," I frowned at Aahna, "You want to know, why he want to kill me? Because, he knows that we both love each other, he wants to kill me, so that he can get you. He wants to snatch you from me," I groaned and flamed at Shambhav.

"Shut up Shourya. Do you know, What the fuck, you are muttering?" Aahna smacked me, "who said that I love you? And how dare you to mumbled this stuff to me," Aahna fumed at with red eyes.

I was shocked by that gawkily attitude of Aahna. She screwed my anger, my heart started losing its breathes. I freeze for a second, and then stammer, " Aahna, please, don't say this, I will die, " I whispered in teetering sound.

"Aahna, we have been in relation since last two years. And if you don't love me. Then why did we kiss? What was that promise you did with me?" I sobbed, "no Aahna, I know you love me a lot. But you are brain washed by this bloody pimp. You are just frightened of bloody Shambhav," I roared and tried to hit Shambhav.

But Aahna defended him, and slapped me harshly back. Everyone was frozen. Harsh sound of that slap was still drifting. I briskly put my hand on my slapped, red chap.

I beamed at Aahna, by shining eyes by unshed tears. My mouth was parted half. A dead weight was stuck in my throat. I felt muddled, unsure of where I was. My lips were quavering.
My heart beats were racing with each other, my legs were giving up as usual.

"It's hilarious. I didn't expect this from you, I thought, we are best friends. I started just talking to you sweetly and you took it in wrong way. What you have thought that, I will sleep with you. Such cheap You are. Actually you don't deserve anyone. You always cheated your friends. You always hurt your friends. You are such a shit. And Sid also suicide only because of you. You killed Sid. You are a shame on friendship, "Aahna blurted, and abused me. She spat out each word like poison.

She was pressing her lips against each other to keep away from breaking down. But her brown eyes were already shining by almonds like tears.

I couldn't speak a word, my throat felt parched, my mouth dry.

"Just stay away from me, and please never show your face me again," she pushed me away, and held Shambhav's hand and turned around.

I was breathless, my breath was stuck under my throat. I was just looking at Aahna's back, like statue.

She was in green short sleeveless casual dress, which was flared at bottom. And that thin green dress had so many Floral work of yellow and white colors. She was going away from me. And with her every step, she was getting miles away from me.

Every memory with Aahna was disappearing from my eyes. She was taking away her love, her promise, and everything's we had. And she left only feelings of hatred to me for her.

Today, Aahna hurt my soul. She slapped my heart. And this time, she was not coming back. She was striding away while screwing all my dreams, promises, we had, in just one second. She ruffled my everything. And made gimmick in my life. I couldn't decide what to do?

Ruhi attempted to handle me. But I Prodded, and rushed away with my bike. Tears rolled down, as I closed my eyes. My heart was sobbing, but no one could hear it. I kicked door furiously, as I approached to my room. I was so horrifying.

"Why did she do this with me?" I shouted, I threw away my books, frames from table. I destroyed every gifts of Aahna.

I cracked Aahna's photos; I cracked lights of my room. I hit myself with mirrors. My head, my face, my hands all were stained in blood.

"She played with my heart, with my emotions," I hissed, "she used me, she stabbed me. I loved her a lot, more than my life. I did everything for her happiness; I worshiped her as my goddess. I gave her my life, my every breathe. But she was a bitch, she was betrayer, she slapped me for that bloody Shambhav," I roared, "even I wanted to free her from cage. I wanted to fly away with her. She was my inspiration. Even I wrote for her, I gave her my dreams. But she abused my love, my friendship," I was shouting unfortunately, and scattering everything here and there. I was in trepidation.

"Shourya..., Stop it, what are you doing? You will get hurt," Ruhi bellowed and grabbed me. But I jolted her away.

"I am already, hurt, that bitch ruined me," I hissed.

"Shourya, you have gone mad, you don't know what are doing? You are abusing Aahna," Ashvini said to me.

"Now, You also assume that I am mad. But can't you notice,

what she did with me? She kicked my ass, my love, only for that motherfucker Shambhav. She is saving murderer of Sid, our Sid," I squelched and glared at my friends.

"Shourya...., She is not saving Shambhav we all know that she loves you so much. But there may have some misunderstanding to her. There may be her reasons, that's why she did that," Ruhi said.

"Ha.....ha....., what the fuck," I grinned, "she is not a child, and she clearly alleged me as murderer of Sid. And you are saying that she has some misunderstandings, I am not that absurd Ruhi....," I frowned.

"Shourya... You are getting mad in envy and anger. You are just over reacting," Rohan said.

"Yeah, I am mad," I screeched at them, "just leave me alone, I don't need any of you, just get lost," I smacked and shut the door on their faces.

I didn't know what was happening with me. I was just howling at everyone. I wanted to vent out my anger, my frustration on someone.

Hastily, I rushed into washroom, and stood under the shower. Blood was flowing out of my head with water drops. I squeezed so heavy hearted I was completely exhausted.

It was so ignominy that Aahna did that to me. Every hug of her was fraudulent. That love for me in her brown eyes was only bluff and illusion. Her cute smile, her dimples were fraud. My every Moment with her was fake. Her every promise was betrayed.

"Why you did this...., Aahna?" I whispered in shivering voice, and I allowed myself to breakdown. And freed my tears to flow abundantly with water drops. Standing under the shower, you will cry hard but no buddy will hear up.

****

CHAPTER FORTY FIVE

After that harsh humiliations and tragedy, my everyday and every night had turned worst and sluggish. Her harsh slap was still resonating in my ears. My Heart was still groaning in remorse. I was scared, paranoid. My condition became more pathetic than Ruhi.

I used to spare my whole day in dark room. Rohan and I would drink whole night while sitting on the edge of the terrace of hostel roof. I was getting so scummy, my face was addled with big beard, and hairs were dull.

One could find me standing unlinking on empty balcony and walking listlessly through empty corridors late at night.

Once we got betrayed, then we got afraid of being cheated by everyone. Whole night I would play game of tossing and turning in my bed.

Sleep doesn't help if it's our soul that's tired. I hatred Aahna. Once my love was my strength, but now she was my weakness. Once she was the reason behind my writing. But now, she was the cause of destruction of my writings. I spoiled my manuscript in animosity of Aahna. I gave away my dreams, for which I had sacrificed my parents.

Now, for me love was like poison. Once I had worshiped love. As it was most powerful thing in world. And without recourse, Once our love led us towards our dreams. But now we were close to our destruction, because of love.

I started frosting the word love. It was only bluff and phony for me. The tribulation of Sid's death hasn't cured, and Aahna stroked with harsh hammer on my heart. She had ruined the remaining power and soul of mine. She made me to lose myself somewhere in crowd of people.

And because of me, my friends were also effect. As I was their only hope. So when I gave up. They inevitably last the battle. But the good Side of my grieve was that Ruhi had gathered herself stronger. She had got over of Sid's malaise, through little bit. Now, I was in great need of Ruhi, she had to.... Look after me. 'A broken heart was consoling the heart, which had hurt that same.'

"Shourya....... I think you should talk to Aahna once," Ashvini said to me, and smashed the waves of that lake by one more Stone.

"Are you jerk? Don't you know, there is nothing to talk? Every stuff has been finished, and she did it. It wasn't my mistake," I roared in pain, "and tell me Ashvini, was it my mistake, that I loved her a lot? Guys she fucked my life, she turned my jubilant into sorrow," I exasperated and smashed my fist into ruined wall.

"Shourya...., why are talking so arrogantly, you are just stretching this stuff. It's just a cute fight between cute birds," Ashvini shrieked, "You are just blaming her. Actually you want to prove Aahna as culprit of your worries," Ashvini patted my shoulder.

"Why shouldn't I abuse her? Guys look at yourself, look at ourselves, what we have became? Where our happiness has gone? Where our unity, our power has gone? Where our dreams have hidden? Guys It's all because of that bitch," I crumbled my teeth, and smacked water of lake.

"Shourya......, Don't do this please..," Ruhi whispered her eyes were swimming in tears, "please Shourya, talk to Aahna and solve your misunderstanding. If you lose her today, then you will have regret whole life. You will sicken in evil gloom. You will die in harsh pain of separation from Aahna. You would die every day," Ruhi sobbed and put her hand on my shoulder, while ruffle her big braid.

"Ruhi, I am ready to agonize from that pain," I uttered, "Ruhi it's my punishment. Because of me, you all are in bothers. And Sid is not with us, because I killed Sid," I said and looked down in embarrass. Guilt is perhaps the most painful companion of death.

"No, Shourya, what are you taking stuffy? You didn't kill Sid," Ruhi yowled and Chuck under my chin.

"No... Ruhi... I am a bloody murderer of Sid," I drawled, "I am the reason of your harsh miseries. If I wouldn't have loved Aahna. If I wouldn't have messed with Shambhav. Then Shambhav wouldn't have killed our Sid," I bellowed, and panicked, "Ruhi, I am your victim, I snatched Sid from you. Kill me Ruhi, then only I could get peace, kill me Ruhi.....," I blurted fiercely, and straggled my neck inconveniently by Ruhi's hand.

"Stop it Shourya... What are you doing? Just stop it," Ruhi squelched, and shook me terribly, "Shourya, you have no mistake, you can't hurt anyone. You can't kill Sid, even if god will come to me and says that you killed Sid, even than also I will not accept god's words," Ruhi howled, and snuggled to me.

There appeared so dreadful silence. We didn't know why we were behaving like that. Our grief was just getting us mad. We gazed at red sun; half deepen in Lake.

"Guys, look at ourselves, what we were? And now what we have become?" Ashvini groaned in gloom, "how much overjoyed we were. We were at the zenith. But how easily destiny smacked us to ground, and strewed us like dry leaves of spring," Ashvini mumbled, what a game destiny played with us? What a game?" Ashvini sneered and looked at sky.

Ashvini was so sincere. She would always talk intelligent. We all gaped at her. She was muttering out the truth as poison. But it was the only truth of our.

"Guys it's enough, we had cried a lot. We had mourned a lot on our sorrow and inadequacy," Ashvini gulped, "But Guys now I can't see this anymore. Guys we have already allowed a lot our enemies to fuck on our happiness. But now we will not allow anyone to shit on our life. We have to be strong. We have to be happy. Guys stay strong, make them wonder how we're still smiling," Ashvini bellowed atrociously. We all were still starring down.

"I know it's not so easy. We have to focus with full power. We have to concentrate on our study. Guys we have to do it.

Our final exams are coming closer. We have to got busy into college, and our presentation," Ashvini said, and eyed towards us. There was so much Fidelity and desires in her eyes.

"Yeah...! Shourya, she is ineludible right. And if we will get busy in our study, we will automatically move on," Rohan said and held me.

Literally, they were true. Getting busy in our work and our future is best way to forget someone. We again, dawned, and started going college. We would study hardly.

But, everyone in college would glare at us, as if we were the untouchables. They would blaze at us as if we were minority. But now, we were braced to smack everyone's ass.

But I would get weaken, when I would head Aahna. Every day, she would come college, at beginning of class, and would leave at the end with Shambbav.

We both never beamed at each other. We would behave like stranger. There was no existence of both of us for each other. And we would change our ways, if we were close to collide. We would disappear like illusion, from each other's eyes.

Much as, I was scrambling hardest to hate her, but I couldn't find a single stuff to scorn her. After all, she was my first love. And first love always remains special till our last breathe.

Everything, which was connected with her, was so much close to me. Her brown eyes, her soft pink lips, her cute smile, her dimples were still mesmerizing me. Her Brown hair was still blowing on my face, I still could sense, feel, her sweet perfume. Everything of her gorgeous beauty was still revolving in my eyes.
The deepest pain I ever felt was denying my own feelings.

Finally, our exams started in next month, and ended in last days of march. We studied hard. Day and night together. We completed our exam. So, in only few days we were getting post graduated.

****

CHAPTER FORTY SIX

It was 4ᵗʰ of April, the last day, the fare well day. Everyone was so much excited, but was bereaved also at other Side. As after that day everyone was going to be separated. They wouldn't be together anymore. And no one knew whether they would meet again or not ever.

"No guys, I am not coming, I am not feeling good, you go," I said, my voice was flat.

"Shourya.... It's fare well," Rohan yowled, "you have to come. We will not meet to our friends after Farewell. Shourya you have to say good bye to everyone," Rohan said to me.

"Dude.... An absurd farewell can't asunder us. Guys we will always be together," I said and held Ashvini and Rohan.

"Yeah...! It's obvious gadhe. We all are going to live together," Ruhi quipped at me, "but we are talking about our classmates. We probably meet them ever," she said.

As a matter of fact, I didn't want to face Aahna. I couldn't see her while saying good bye, and couldn't catch her while going away forever. To see someone for the last time is worse painful.

But my friends wanted me to face Aahna. They wanted us to patch-up again. So, I was handcuffed in front of my idiots. So, I had to go farewell.

At 8'clock, we approached to Farewell party. The event was held at college garden. The night was garnished so beautifully and flashed with so many dim and chromatic lights, flowers, and curtains. It was so fascinating.

At one corner, D.j. Was playing his re-mix. And in front of D.J. bar was arranged. Dinner was embellished in just right Side of the bar. A huge stage was renovated at the heart of the garden. Event was already going on.

As we strode into the event, our juniors welcome us with flowers and glittering smile.

Regardless of such fantastic environment, I scattered myself in one corner table with daffy face. My crazy buddies had already jumped into the event. Some were dancing on vulgar songs with D. J. While, other were dancing gracefully with ex GF or GF or crush, which was making me to feel envy.

But I darned them, and started my eyes towards crazy guys, who were troubling, dancing and eating people.

I turned to my left, and I clocked that, Aahna was sitting at just two tables away from me. She was dressed in silver transparent low waist saree, which had backless, silver blouse. Her saree was embellished with gold stones and squints. I couldn't suppress my urge to gaze her astonishing beauty. I was obvious sick of her sizzling look.

In next Moment, we captured each other's gaze. We beamed deeply into each other's eyes, without blinking. We couldn't break our eyes.

"Why, you did this... Aahna?" My eyes asked to her eyes.

Impromptu, Aahna turned away her face in fear.

I blazed, Shambhav was next to Aahna. He glowered at me, and put his arms firmly around Aahna's shoulders. He kissed Aahna's barred shoulder, and grinned at me. Shambhav was making me to feel jealous. He clutched Aahna tightly, and kissed her cute dimples.

Aahna was wearing his assault and smirked half heartily. My blood wents ups, as Shambhav touched Aahna. Aahna was pretending, as though, she was glad with Shambhav.

But, I couldn't see that shit. I got up hastily, shattered my table horribly, and paced towards bar counter. I poured myself with one shot of wine... Then one more. I was getting furious. I noticed,

Aahna marching towards me. And heedlessly, she snatched my right hand infuriately. She was so violent.

She pulled me nastily towards a dark corner. I was infirm against her anger. She jerked my hand cruelly.

"Why are you doing this? What do you want to prove?" Aahna snapped, her nostrils were flaring with every breathe she took. Her eyes were rolling in tears.

I didn't react to her, and turned around to leave. Rapidly, she pushed me to a wall. She collared me by her both hands, and got over me.

"Answer me -----," she bawled at. Her word clear, but her voice trembled.

"just leave me, " I grinded, and battled to remove her hands away from my collar. But she was horrifying.

"No.... You can't do this to me. Just talk to me," she dispersed like poor beggar.

"Why I would talk to you? What is there to talk now? And who am I to you? I am bloody bastard to you, so just get lost to your B. F. ," I roared to her and push her hands away, and strode. But she grabbed me by my hands, pulled me to her.

"Why don't You understand my pain? Just listen to me once," she sobbed. Her breathes were coming in gaspe.

"Yeah... You are right Aahna kapoor, I can't understand you ever. But now I have caught your green eyes. You are actually a good game player, as like your corrupt MLA Dad. You very well know how to use and throw a guy. Literally, Aahna kapoor, you," I sneered at her and clapped to embarrass her.

"Shourya......," she cried and dug hed nails into my neck.

I grabbed her by her brown hair violently and went close to her eyes.

"Just leave me alone, or I will kill you," I threw her away.

She fell down on her knees and burst into harsh cry. Tears were dropping abundantly from her brown eyes like pearls.

I rushed towards hostel back. I was pressing my lips against each other to control my breakdown. Only I know, how much mournful and rueful to hurt Aahna. I made that pretty girl to cry. I was so remorse.

But I had no other option, I couldn't uttered my feelings, "Aahna I am so sorry, I trust you, I love you so much, I can't live without you, please take away with you,"

I stumbled into my room, and flopped on bed, covered my face with my hands. From last months, I was hassling hardest to get strong, to forget Aahna, to gulped Sid's pain. But I was a failure.

Every time, when I would glance Aahna and Shambhv, everything, I would get frightened and betrayed. Day by day, I was getting weak. My mind and heart were chocked. I would muse that if Aahna is not in my life, then there is no life, of mine. I liked to die, instead of hating her.

And my second guilt was that, when I would stare Shambhav, again my blood boil. I got panic and spiteful. Shambhav killed my Sid, and despite of that, I couldn't do anything worst to Shambhav.

I couldn't see Shambhav enjoying in front of my eyes. It was so embarrassing to me. And the last guilt on me was that condition, bad condition of my friends.

They all were grieving because of me. They lost their bliss, their fun, their warmth because of my bothers. They gave away their dreams, their future just to solve my anxieties. And I was the only cause of Ruhi's malaise. I destroyed her life. Sid was murdered because of me. I always stabbed back of my friends. I was so sinfulness.

I couldn't go on with my life with a twinge of guilt or remorse. I was dying, I couldn't live while facing the wistful faces of Ruhi and my friends.

Aahna, Shambhav, Anshul and all other bastards were straggling me. I couldn't breathe within them. I was huddling in myself. I just urged to live in peace. I couldn't wear it more, anymore. But I was feeble, I didn't know, how I would get cure.

Suddenly, I got up hastily from my bed. I was continuously

stroking my legs against the floor, again and again, and wondered panicky.

When everyone was enjoying the Farewell, I decided to run away. I decided to run away from everyone and every bullshits. I decided to stampede, to melt away so far, in deadly dark night.

So, I didn't want to inform anyone, where I was escaping. I had decided to screw every contact of my past two years. I destroyed my contact number, and everything of my memory. So that no one could reach to me. I wanted to disappear from my past life. I wanted those two years to skip from my life.

On that Farewell night, everyone was clicking selfie, and pictures with each other, as a memory. But I was twisting every memories, I had with my friends and Aahna.

Everyone was heavy hearted, and crying and hugging, as they were separating from each other, from their besties, from their trust worthy, with whom they had lived, cried, enjoyed for two years.

And now, they were going to miss severely each other. But I had decided that, I would never miss anyone, actually, I didn't want to miss anyone. Everyone, was wishing each other a good life ahead. They were promising that they would meet again, they would remain in contact. But I was going to break my promise, with my friends. I was never going to meet them again, ever. But before that, I picked out my diary and pen.

"Journal-649

This is my last journal. I am writing for the last time. As from today, for me, there is no existence of you Aahna. I must unlove you Aahna.
By loving you, I have hurt myself. I love you, I hurt myself_ it is the way this tale unfurls. I must find it in me to unlove you; like a wound which closes and heals, like a sun which sets, like the final breath which is swallowed whole by the mouth of death___ I must. I must unlove you.
I liked you, but you belong to completely different world. I want to love you, but your world don't allow me to do that. I want to be with you, but there is no place for me in your world.

I want to know you, but I myself find stranger in your world
I loved you and that destroyed me."

I packed my bags, but I left that diary in my room, and left with my bike. I had left only a piece of paper for my friends.

"Dear friends,

When you will be reading this, I would have gone so far, I would from all of you, forever. You were always my best buddies ever. You all are still my life, and will be forever. I will miss you a lot. You were always there to help me out. Whenever I was about to fall, you all always held me.

But I am not so good to you. I am again going to deceive you, as always I did. And sorry for that, but I am prostrate, I have to do this. I have to leave you. And I will never meet you again.

Please try to understand me. I am leaving you alone, because you all are not safe with me. I am bed luck to all of you. I troubled you a lot. And only because of me, You are endure, by scarifying your happiness. You lost your dreams, your smile your everything because of me.

So it is good for you, that I stay away from you. Because if I will be with you, then you all will be always straggled by bastards, pain, sorrows, troubles and evil luck, I can't give you happiness.

Ruhi...... Please forgive me. You are my life. I love you a lot. I promised to you that I will be always with you. I had promised you that I will always take care of you.

But I am actually, extremely sorry. I am a bloody defrauder. I am responsible for Sid's death. I am your guilty. I am so much disgraced, guilt stricken. But I can't see you in such agony conditions. I am so shamed that, I can't show you my face. I can't move on with this sin.

So, I have to escape from you also. I know, you will never forgive me. But genuinely, I am not so innocent to forgive. So, I want all of you to gripe me.

Guys, I want all of you to start a new life. I insist you to live again you dreams, to look forward towards your future. Ruhi I want you to flight for IPS.

Guys, I don't know, where I will go? What I will do? But I know that where ever I will be, I will miss you a lot. I pray for your happiness.

Love you, my idiots........ Shourya.........."

So, on that night, I left behind two years of my life. But I don't know, where I was going? I just wanted to run on the silent road, which has no destination.

I was driving my bike since hours, without any stop. At 5am I reached near Ajmer. I don't know why and how I reached Ajmer? I don't know, why my feet padded towards shrine of Baba Moinuddin Chisti? I don't know, why I was so mouthed towards shrine?

Even though, I went to shrine, but in spite of that, I didn't go close to samadhi of Baba Moinuddin Chisti. My feet trembled every time, when I padded towards Baba. I was afraid, afraid of my sins.

So, I spared two days in shrine with beggars. I slept with beggars, and faryadis. I ate with them. I sat silently in mandli of Sufi Saint.

But with the sun rise of next morning, I found myself near the Samadhi of Baba. I lay near samadhi for hours, and starring silently at it. Suddenly tears flooded out of my eyes. My tears were praying for peace. I asked Baba to show me the right path, to answer of my questions.

After few minutes, I don't know, why I called my Mom from S. T. D.

"Hello..... Mom.....," I whispered.

"Shourya......... Beta.... Where are you?" Mom gasped. She recognized me in a second. I touched so much peace by her voice.

"Shourya... Where are you? I am calling you from a week. And why? Your phone is dead?" she showered hesitatingly, swiftly. Her voice was fluttering. She was one step behind to burst into cry.

"Maa, I love you maa..," I sobbed and my face got streaked in severe tears. I couldn't speak a word then, I didn't stop the sobs that were shaking me.

"Shourya..., Beta are you ok?" She sobbed once.

Only a mother can understand us, and only she can cure our pain and miseries.

"Maa....., everyone is so bad Maa. People are so evil," I complained to her as like 4 year kid, "maa.....please save me," I cried while snorting and wiping my tears, "maa.....I want to sleep in your lap. Please let me fall in deep nap."

"Shourya... Don't cry... Please beta...," she mumbled in cry, "Shourya.... Beta.. please come to me, please come home... Please come.. For me only... Please come back," She said.

****

CHAPTER FORTY SEVEN

Next day evening, I reached home, while skidding all the connections and memories of my past two years life. I was back to home, in a bright Side, in new fortune that I would find peace there. I would forget about all the stuffy, about Aahna, about Shambhav.

I held, I desperately needed some time away from all of the messiness. I hoped that, I would gulp the things; I was trying so hard to forget. I wished that I would be able to move on. May I would get deep sleep at night. May my hands wouldn't oscillate when I would sense about Aahna.

So finally, once again I stepped my foot on threshold, which I had left 2 years ago. Once again I was back on the same place, which I had boycotted to strife for my dreams, to live my life on my rules.

But as a matter of fact, Once again, I was there with harsh defeat. Coming back to home was sign of my downfall.

I was so scared; my hand trembled, when I rang the doorbell. Aasha aunty, our made, opened the door, and shocked, with wider eyes, and opened mouth.

"Shourya Baba....!" She fumbled, which paralyzed my body more.

She gave a space to enter. But my feet touched so heavy, they denied to move. But I had to battled with them to move in. As I had no other option, I was infirm, I couldn't run away again. So after defeating my feet, I padded into house.

Suraj kaku our driver, Shyamlal our watchman, Gopi our

Gardner and Mom's helping hand, they all stood up slowly while starring strangely at me. For a minute, I was glad that everyone was still there even in my absent.

I was soft hearted that things were still same as I had left. Everyone looked so familiar to me. So I over excited that Dad would also be same as earlier years ago. He would sound my name loudly and hug me. He would have forgotten every bullshit.

But I judged Everyone wrongly. Everyone glared at me, as if I was the serial killer, came to stab their master. They reacted as if I was a guest in my own house, between my own people.

"Who is there Gopi..?" Dad asked, he was sitting on the same couch, on which we sat last together. His eyes were glued into his laptop.

"Sir, Shourya Baba," Gopi paused and then stammered.

Rapidly, Dad looked up from his laptop, his brows were furrowed in frustration or concern or shock. He widened his eyes to recognize me.

And thereupon, for few minutes we fixed our eyes at each other, as if we didn't know each other. But rashly, his shock turned into sever anger. I myself stopped my breathing in terror. I didn't want to do any action, I froze myself. But I downed my eyes in shame. I was embarrassed.

Two years ago, I fought with Dad, and ran away to fulfill my dreams. And I was back with my failure, So, I was already, unworthy in his eyes. We both were already stumbled into cold war. He flopped down screen of laptop alarmingly. He got up horribly, and went into his bedroom.

"Suraj...." he bellowed from inside. I was so cold feet. I puffed in relax as Dad emptied the drawing room. I felt so bad and poor. I found myself so alone and helpless there.

Every faces were same, but their souls were changed. Their relation to me had been changed. Their love had been collapsed for me. I was like stranger in my own house. Everything had been changed in interior of house.

Two years ago, I myself had enhanced whole house. The couches, sofas paintings on wall, paints, curtains, LED screen, flowers and everything were of my choice. But now everything was replaced by Dad.

It symbolized that Dad had already thrown me completely out of his home, his life, and his heart. I was standing in middle of drawing room. There was so gawkily silence in my house. No one was there to love me, to welcome me.

But I realized, that I was standing there for only for one person, who loved me a lot, and will always do, she was my Mom, whose love never going to change for me.

"Shourya..... My son.... My Baba has come... ," all of a sudden, a voice traveled from kitchen. I saw Mom running briskly to me. And in next Moment. I was in her warm chest. She clutched more and more tightly like a newborn baby.

"Shourya...., where were you? I love you so much beta, I missed you a lot. Where you have gone?" Mom pampered me like a kid. She was kissing me furiously, and again hugged me panicky, as if I was running again.

"Sorry, Mom, I hurt you a lot, please forgive me... I am not a good son to you Mom," I whispered in her ears.

"I was so much scared, you didn't care for me ever. But now promise me. You will never leave me again," she sobbed, "two years passed, and I didn't see you. I was dying beta..," she mumbled, her voice shook. She gave up and cried openly.

"Mom, please don't cry. I am ok. And I will never ever leave you, I promise," I kissed her forehead, and wiped her tears, "look how bad I am? I made my beautiful girl cry?" I chuck under her chin, there was a hint of teasing in my eyes.

"Shut up, you idiot," she said and smirked, "get fresh, and I will serve dinner."

After dinner, I strode to first floor into my room, I was so tired. I shattered my bags in one corner, and sprinkled my body on my foamy bed.

I was staring incessantly at the ceiling. My room was on first floor. And it was still as it is, as I had left. Blue and red colored walls. My so many books were still there on my study table. And every wall was decorated with frames of my favorites. Robin Sharma, Paulo Coelho, Mr. Harivansh Rai Bachchan, and Swami Vivekanand Ji.

In my typewriter, there was still the lost word was same, which I had typed years ago. Everything was same, as no one touched them after my left.

For a second, I left myself wonder how things would have been if I hadn't loved Aahna. If I hadn't messed with Shambhav, Sid would have been alive. On moving more deeper in my thoughts, I gestured that, if I hadn't confided to my Dad about my dream, and if I would have join my Dad's business, then my life would have been different. Everyone would be so happy, so what if I wouldn't. Because my happiness have no space on earth. So to dream something was my worst mistake of my life.

I was so frustrated, I wanted to fall asleep, but my head was bursting. My eyes were not letting me to fall asleep. I was rolling terribly on my white bed.

"Nind nhi aa rhi.... Beta..," Mom whispered, and touched my head softly, and sat near me.

I put my head on her lap, and snuggled to her. She stroked my head with love. I sensed heavenly peace in her warm lap. Only our mother can give us such peace.

I knew, Only my Mom could handle me. Only she could understand my grievance. Whenever we get hurt, we call only our mother. As only she can cure our pain by just her warm hug. She can only make us to fall sleep.

'Maa', the word itself has greatness. She is the universe.

It was strange how that particular memory flashed into my head. It reminded me of how my Mom used to make me sleep in her lap when I was child. She would tell me fairy story, while rocking my head. Then I would pretend to her as if I have fallen asleep. To that end, Mom would cover me by blanket, kiss my chap, and switch off the lights. And when she was about to leave my room, quickly would wake up with jolt.

'Mumma, I am awakening still.'

On that night, I don't know, when I fell into sweet sleep in my Mom's lap.

"Good morning baba," Mom kissed me, "Get up fast."

"Morning maa....., I love you mumma," I muttered gruffly, and checked my phone with squinted eyes.

It was 11 at the crack of dawn. Sun rays flashing into my room, through curtains. I never slept so long and with so much Peace from two years. I got up, picked my coffee mug, and leaned against the front balcony. Sun had already risen too hot, but breeze was cool. There was so cessation in environment.

Suraj kaku, Gopi and Shyaam all were sitting in courtyard. "Good morning... guys," I bellowed and took sip of coffee.

"You are so late... Baba...., the morning is about to end," Gopi said, and they all came closer to balcony.

"Yeah.... I slept so well, after long time," I said.

"Shourya baba....., I am so delighted that you are with us again. I missed you a lot," Suraj kaku said, and beamed at me.

"Oh really! I don't believe you. You never made call to me," I grinned.

"No baba, believe me. You can ask Gopi," Suraj kaku hesitated, and swore.

"Baba, he is lying. He never missed you," Gopi said. And we all laughed.

"Baba, get down I have something to show you," Suraj kaku said.

"What?" I shrugged.

"Just come down. You ask so many questions," Suraj kaku annoyed.

Suraj kaku, was a man of 45. He loved me so much from my childhood and I too was his fan. He took me to garage.

"Look, I totally modified your car," he said, and delighted.

"Wow..... Kaku, I love you, you made it awesome," I excited, with wider eyes and stroked on my black Mercedes -Benz-A-Class.

****

I was doing lunch by Mom's hands.

"Eat properly Shourya..., look at you how thin you have become," Mom frowned and served one more paratha on my plate.

"Stop it, Mom. I am stuffed now. I have already done 5 parathas," I said gruffly while chewing one more bite.

"So, what? You have to eat one more. Can't you see, you are so thin," Mom giggled

"I am always thin for you Mom," I bellowed, "actually your eyes can't see my fat," I laughed.

"Shut up... And eat fast," she snapped.

My Mom was young and graceful lady. But now I noticed how tired her eyes looked, weary with dark shadows underneath them. She had grown much older. Her skin had become dull. She had become weak and thin, because of my pain of separation.

"Mom, Dad is still angry with us, he still don't talk to you," I squeezed her hand.

"Nooo.. Shourya. It's not like that, he loves me a lot," she said half heartily and looked away.

"Mom, I love you Mom," I said and hugged her tightly by her waist.

After lunch, I was getting bore. I had nothing to do. I sat on front of LED screen, and gazed some stupid T.V. Serials of Sas and Bahu drama. Hence, I decided to sleep again until dinner, and after dinner, I again went to sleep.

****

CHAPTER FORTY EIGHT

One month passed away so hastily that I couldn't see dawn and sat of sun. Every day, I would wake up late, after crack of dawn. I would take lunch, and sleep again after watching daily soap. I would never sit on dining table with Dad. I would do my dinner in my room. I would never face him. And many times when we were about to collide each other. We would briskly change our ways.

Thereupon, I started sparing whole day in my room. I was so silent. I didn't know, what I was doing there? Why I was there? What I will do next? I stopped speaking to everyone. I seemed to be lost somewhere else. Everyone was so concerned because of my miseries and weird behavior.

"Baba, what happened to you? You look so upset?" Suraj kaku and Gopi would always ask to me.

"No.... Guys... I am so glad....," I would always chunk and smile creepily at them.

"No.. Baba...we are dying to see your laugh. You look so cute when you laugh," they would tease me.

"Really... I don't think.. So," I would say. And would battle to laugh a forged smile.

I had come to home, in hope that I will start a new life there. I had hoped that with time I will be ok.
But time doesn't heal everything, it just teaches us how to live with the pain.

But day by day I was getting worst. I had no future plan to countdown. I had already screwed my writings. Every day I was getting alone and ghastly. I started again losing myself in Aahna. I was missing her terribly. I couldn't live alive without Aahna. She had stolen my smile, my joy.

Every Moment, I would think about her, about her cute smile, about her brown eyes. My heart wanted to cry out for her. But it was already dead without her. I lost myself in such worst that, I couldn't notice anyone around me.

Many times I would lose myself even in front of LED, while sitting on sofa silently for hours. So, I got fever because of weakness.

One day I was sitting on sofa silently.

"Shourya....," Mom called me from behind but I couldn't hear her.

"Shourya....," she shouted loudly, but I was lost.

"Shourya....," she frowned and shook me.

"Huh............?" I blurted in extreme fright. I felt mumbled, unsure of where I was. I was so paranoid.

"Where are you, Shourya? I was calling you from 10minutes," Mom said, and put her hands on my shoulders.

"Sorry Mom," I whispered. I dispersed in her lap.

"Baba... What is going with you? Why are you so silent? What's the thing that tumultuous you?" Mom mumbled and ruffled my hairs.

"No Mom. I am ok... I am just missing my friends," I gasped.

I was veritably missing Ruhi, Rohan and Ashvini. 'Friendship is such special that in few time, we get attached to someone that we can't live without them.'

"Shourya.... I want to say something to you," Mom said.

"Yeah..! Mom," I nodded and closed my eyes.

"Shourya, I think, you should go out with your old friends. You should go out for dinner with them. You should stay out of your dark room. You will feel good," she said.

Next day, Mom called my childhood friends to take me out for movie and dinner every day.

But it couldn't help me. I was more speechless and dull with them. They were not like Ruhi, Rohan, Ashvini. They were my idiots. So in some time, my old friends got irritated and bored of me. So they threw me back to my home.

So, now Mom would take care of me. She would take me with her to his hospital, then to shopping, then lunch at good restaurant in a good mall. She would try a lot to get my smile back. But I was still with sluggish face.

Although, I would follow her everywhere like robot. I don't want to hurt her anymore. So I would do everything, Mom said. I wanted to see her happy.

But the truth was that only Aahna could get smile on my face. The person that can make us feel better is the same person who broke our heart.

I got scared of things, I don't know what they were, but they wouldn't let me sleep. Often, when I would have been sleeping, I would feel like I am falling from a huge height. But I couldn't stop my fall. I would feel like someone is smothering my neck, I couldn't breathe at that time, I would just shake my hands and legs desperately. And then I would wake up with jolt, totally steamed in sweat.
At that Moment, in the dark, I felt like a child again, needing my Mom to protect me and tell me that everything would be okay.

****

One night I was sleeping in Mom's lap. She was stroking and making me to fall asleep. I don't know how? And why? But tears rolled down on my face, abundantly.

"Shourya.... Baba.... Are you ok?" she chuck under my chin. As she glanced my tears.

"Hmm..... Mom," I sobbed.

"Shourya.... I don't know what happened with you in Delhi? And I will not force you to tell me. But I can't see you in such malaise. I want only your smiling face," she whispered and kissed my right chap.

"Shourya, I muse, you should forget all the stuff. You know beta, when you left home, I was so alone_ I had lost my happiness. Though, I wanted to bring you home back, but I couldn't help. My life has been stuck between you and your Dad," Mom said. Her tear fell on my cheek.

I felt so much pang of guilt, as I never thought about my Mom that how she would do without me. Today, for the first time, I was seeing my Mom's Side things.

"Beta, when you came back, I hoped that now you will restore things between you and your Dad. But again, you are silent. But this time I want you to mend things with your Dad. I want you to say sorry to your Dad, and should help him in business. He has grown older now. And you have already hurt him a lot. If you will help him then his anger on you would be ended. And you will also feel good. You can divert your mind," Mom untangled hesitantly, "Shourya... Please only for me. Please join office," she pleaded.

****

On next evening, Dad and Mom were doing dinner. I came out and sat fearfully with them on dining table first time. But Dad didn't give importance to me. He didn't even beamed at me. And I also didn't dare to glimpse at him.

"Shourya, want to join office," Mom whispered to Dad. But he didn't react.

"He is guilty of his wrong. Now he want help you, now he will do, what you want?" Mom said in vibrating tone.

"It's my business, It's my house, I worked day and night for this power. And I don't need anyone to help me or whatever bullshit," Dad stormed.

"And he is not my son anymore. He can do what he want," Dad hissed and glared at me. He got up hideously to move. He had just stepped twice and I stopped him.

"Dad Please, give me a chance," I muttered each word after taking pause at each word, I was still starring in my plate.

"I know, I hurt you a lot. I was always against you. But I am self flagellating now. I will do, what you will say. Give me a chance to correct my sin, to prove myself," I gasped, in shame.

"Ha, ha..,"Dad grinned, "to prove what? That you are a looser, you are already an unworthy. You don't have anything to prove," Dad barked.

"Just give me a chance, and I will show who is looser," I screeched and got up from my chair, and fixed my eyes at him.

"Ok, so you again want a battle," he smacked, "ok then. 9 AM next morning, your fight starts. But if you do a single mistake, and I will threw you out of my house," he clamped his teeth.

CHAPTER FORTY NINE

"Mommm......," I screamed loudly, I threw my blanket, and jumped off the bed, as I checked the time in my bed. I got up hastily towards kitchen 8:45 AM.

"Mom, why didn't you wake up me," I snapped, sullenly, "Dad will kill me. I am late."

"I wouldn't help anyone of you," she slammed, "I wouldn't mess in your fight," she tickled.

"Whatever," I quipped at her, ran towards bathroom, and came out more hastily after taking half shower.

I dressed myself briskly in black trouser, white shirt.

"You are so mean. I hate you Mom," I kissed Mom, took a bite of cheese sandwich and ran.

"Run..... Shourya... Run...," Mom laughed.

So finally, I had decided to move on. Sometimes, it's very hard to move on, but once you move on, you'll realize it was the best decision. I stopped my car in front of Sharma industry. Sharma industry, was one of the most successful electronics company produced cell phones, laptop, TV, fridge etc.

I went up stairs on 3rd floor, towards Dad's office, while holding blazer in one hand and bag in other hand.

"Good morning Sir..... ," every employee graced me first, and suddenly they giggled with each other

I sensed so occult and nervous.

"Fuck off," I murmured and beamed at everyone. I didn't know why they were sneering at me.

Unsteadily I entered into Dad's cabin. He was already hot tempered as if he was just waiting to kill me. He fixed his flaming eyes at me, and stood up furiously. I downed my eyes in terror.

"20 minutes. 20 minutes, you are late on your first day," he hissed.

"Sorry Sir," I mumbled.

"And what the hell? You can't dress up yourself, look at you," he squealed and lifted telephone to call someone.

I gazed at myself like a school kid.

"Bull shit," I buzzed.

My shirt's buttons were done wrongly. And it was not properly in. Nod of my tie was made in stupid way. My hairs were so greasy. My face was dumb.

"Yes Sir..... ?" Kashyap uncle strode into cabin.

He was our MD, MD of Sharma Company. He had grown up older now. From my childhood, I liked him so much. He would always greet me with chocolates, when I was kid. Dad eyed to him, and Kashyap uncle took me with him.

"Here you go....," he smirked, "this is your office, this is your seat, this is your laptop and this is your phone," uncle said and braced himself.

I examined the whole cubical glass cabin. It was awesome, as I could sleep so well in AC. The big-glassed desk was embellished by laptop, telephone, so many files, award and certificates of Sharma Company. Dad had appointed me as senior most employee of Sharma Company.

I had my own office, and every bullshit. But I was unknown, of what the hell it meant? What was my work? And what the hell Sharma company famous for? On speaking truth, I was not qualified even for the lowest employee of company.

"Uncle, what I have to do now?" I asked innocently to Kashyap Uncle

"Wait.....," he delighted and left.

Genuinely, I was enjoying the new cabin, and jumping on the spring chair.

Rapidly, I pierced, that my Dad's cabin was just in my front. He would keep his eyes at me all time through glass. Few minutes after, Kashyap uncle entered back.

"Shourya... This is your work. There is whole data of Sharma company," he handed me a file.

"You have to read out it carefully. And this is your today's file," he gave me another file, "You have to read it and then have to prepare its report and submit to Anand Sir, I mean your Dad," I took those file by fluttering hands, as if those were time bomb.

"Shourya.., this is Nisha, she is to assists you," uncle said and cackled.

I gazed towards a girl. She was dazzling in short sleeved white shirt, and tight black pencil skirt up to her fair knees. She had dark black hair, which were falling on her white glasses.

"Hello! Sir," she said with pretty smile.

I was so timorous that I could speak out hello to her.

"Get on work Shourya, fast," uncle shrieked, "all the best," and he left me alone with Nisha.

I was feeling so ghostly with her. But admitting, she was to pretty just like Ruhi. I glanced at her, and smiled creepily at her. She responded same to me, stretching her lips to wide smile. I sat on my chair, she sat on my front. I unlocked those files and battled hard to read out them.

And in few second, my head started spinning. My face was wet in sweat even in cold A.C. I was so paralyzed; I had never seen such complicated files. I couldn't get anything. And the worst was that Nisha estimated my shrinking by her dark black eyes. I would smile half heartily, to hide my unworthiness.

I was flipping pages again and again, and pretended that I was busy in those files. But my condition was like a child of 6th standard, who has been asked to solve the problems of 12th standard. I login into laptop, and pretended as if I was preparing report. But I was busy in Facebook.

I was so belittled and awkward with Nisha's present. She had already caught me. She was giggling surreptitiously.I blazed at her. "What? What was that?" I angered on her.

"Sorry Sir," She stammered. I looked again into my laptop.

"Ok. Me Sorry...," I whispered.

"Ehhhhh....," She shocked.

"Nisha actually, I didn't know anything about this bloody stuff. I can't even read a single page. I was just trying to impress you. And I know, you caught me," I was blurting absurdly and viciously.

I gasped once and we both looked at each other. Suddenly, she looked here and there to control her laugh. But she again shattered into loud laugh. She became cute, when she laughed, and helplessly, I had to laugh on my jerk.

"Nisha, will you help me?" I asked.

"Yeah, of course, I am here, only to help you Sir," she again chuckled.

Thus, Nisha sat next to me. She was analyzing every stuff of Sharma Company. I was listening to her as like a deaf. I didn't get her words.

"So now I think, you have understood everything, right," She shrugged at me.

I beamed at her with innocent eyes, and shook my head fearfully.

"What?" she bellowed, "no... Please Sir don't do this to me," she mumbled in sad tone, "Sir from 2 hours I am continuously expounding. You can't do this to me, that's unfair," Nisha blurted, her voice was shaken, she was about to cry.

"Ok, Sorry... Sorry.... Please one more time, please...," I pleaded.

"No, I can't. My energy is vanished, I am exhausted," she frowned.

"Ok wait, I will get coffee for you," I said and rushed out briskly and return with more energy, while carrying coffee mugs and snacks.

"Sir.... Why you are doing this? Anand Sir will throw me out, if he will see that I am troubling heir of Sharma Company," Nisha sighed and laughed.

"Just shut up and finish your coffee," I tried to terror over her.

Hence, we finished our coffee.

"Ok Sir, let's do it, but this is last time ok," Nisha yowled and pointed her finger at me.

"Ha..... Pakka..... Pakka...... Last time," I said politely and swore.

And unsteadily, Nisha and I completed report and submitted it to Dad in two days.

"Ok... Bye..... Sir... See you tomorrow," Nisha said and emptied the cabin.

Rush, I submitted the report to Dad and ran to catch Nisha but she had already got into lift. I had to jump so many staircases unsteadily to appear in front of Nisha, when she padded out of lift. I panted on my knees and smirked at her.

"What....?" she shocked.

"I was thinking, I should drop you home," I wheezed.

"No..., no Sir, I will manage on my own," she panicked.

"Please Nisha, you helped me so much. I should do it at least. Please allow me," I pleaded.

"Ok.....," she giggled. And in few minutes we both were in my Mercedes.

"So, you are an MBA," I asked and gazed at her.

"Yeah...! I think so," she quipped, and we laughed.

"So, basically, you are a Mumbain," I said and tittered.

"No.... Basically I am from Pune. And I am here for job. And I live alone in Laxmi Apartment," she said.

"Lucky, you are," I shrugged sadly, "I always wanted to live alone in an apartment," I cracked silly jokes. And we reached at her apartment.

"Thank you Sir....," she said, as she stepped out of my car, hands resting on the window.

"Don't call me Sir, I am not your boss, I am your friend ok," I frightened her by my loud voice.

"Ok, Shourya," she shrieked.

"Oyee... Listen, I will pick you in morning," I said.

"No... Shourya.., I will get there myself really," she exasperated.

"Shut up... It's my order, and I am your boss," I squelched at her.

"But you just said, you are my friend," she gave a look at me and braced herself.

****

CHAPTER FIFTY

"Shourya... Where are you? It's 9:30, and again you are late. Your Dad is bursting at you," Nisha bristled on phone, and ruined my deep dreaming. It was my 25th day, and I was again late as usual. And I was running towards Dad's cabin as expected in dreggy dress up.

"When will you get on time? You can't be serious ever, and you batted with me that you will prove yourself," Dad burst out like volcano, as I stumped into his cabin.

"Sorry Sir....," I buffed under my breathe.

Thereupon, he threw a file on my face, "took this and I want it's report till my left," he shouted. I was peeing at him, and muttering.

"What are looking now, get lost," he roared.

Heedlessly, I rushed away and stumbled into my cabin furiously. I was with nonchalant face. Nisha faced me and she started chucking to tease me.

"Shourya... You were again going to pick me, what happened then? Gadi puncture ho gyi thi kya?" Nisha hurled a taunt at me.

"Shut up.... Idiot," I frowned.

But she came close to me, and made a proper nod of my tie, and closed buttons of my shirt in proper order.

"Let's go, we have to do lots of work," she agitated and grabbed my hand.

"Excuse me...!" I bellowed with a pause, "I don't need you, I can do this on my own," I grinned at Nisha.

"Oh really...!" She surprised with big eyes and braced her hands.

"Get lost," I pushed her aside, and mocked at her.

Wherefore, I started preparing report as Nisha had taught me. Nisha sat in my front silently. Sometimes, she would adjust her make -up, and sometime she would play with her I-phone.

In two hours, I completed report. And I was going to submit it to Dad.

"Shourya, don't be crazy, let me check it first," Nisha tried to stop me.

But I ignored her, and submitted report to Dad. After an hour back, Dad clumped furiously into my cabin. He threw that file on my face, "what the hell is this?" he heated. Nisha and I got up hastily in terror of my Dad.

"How many mistakes you did? It's waste and you useless," Dad grated his teeth and rushed out.

I felt so embarrassed. My Dad was the worst enemy even than Shambhav also. Nisha and I eyed at each other in fear. I threw that file on wall. All papers shaded on floor like dry leaves of spring. But in next second, I collected all the dry leaves, as my Dad was flaming at me from his cabin.

"I told you, but you never listen to me," Nisha taunted at me.

"Will you please shut up for all mighty," I roared, "I will kill either you or Dad."

"Don't shout at me. Give it to me I will correct it," she took the file and got busy herself.

"Oh my god...! Shourya... So many mistakes. How can you do this?" Nisha annoyed, "I think Sir should have slapped you," she angered.

"Nisha, I am hungry, let's go out for lunch," I squeezed her hand to lift her.

"Nooooo.. ," she frowned, "Sir wouldn't allow, and after this worst, never," she denied and jerked my hand.

"Don't dismay, I have a plan as usual," I laughed evil.

****

"Sir, I am not feeling good, I want to go home," Nisha lied to my Dad, innocently. I already knew that Dad will not say no to Nisha. So I fired gun by her shoulders.

"Ok, go carefully. And if you need anything, inform me," Dad said hastily in concern.

"Sir, can I take Shourya Sir to drop me. I can't go home alone," she again lied as I had trained her. She was a good student of mine.

Hence Nisha and I went out to a restaurant. We would enjoy a lot. I had started appreciating her company. Now I had a good friend.

"Shourya, do you know? You are crazy," she hit me and shrieked.

"Yeah! I know...," I quipped.

****

CHAPTER FIFTY ONE

I was so much tired of whole day work. I was in my room.

"This is file of our new launch of new cell phone. You have to give presentation on it tomorrow morning," Dad came in my room and placed file on my bed. At first I was babbled, as I was watching game of thrones, secretly. At the Moment, I flopped down my laptop, and pant.

"What?" I shocked, "are you kidding me? How can I? I mean, it's already evening, and how can I prepare presentation in just one night. And even without Nisha, how can I?"I howled briskly and absurdly. Stampede occurred into my body.

"I don't want to listen any massive. I want your presentation in morning," he said and left.

Actually, Dad was a good businessman. He took advantage of time. He very well knew that I couldn't do that alone, without Nisha.So, he had got chance to win over me. But I was more clever than him. I couldn't accept defeat.

At 7p.m. doorbell rang

"Nisha, you?" Dad shocked, "why you are here late at evening?" He asked.

"Sir, Shourya Sir called me. He has something important with me," Nisha said.

"What?" Dad frowned, chocking on his words," I mean, you can't help him. He has to do ____," Dad was blurting, but I cut him off.

"Nisha... You came. Ok come fast up stairs. We have so much work," I said and grinned at Dad.

He was frozen with open mouth. But still he gave me killing look. Nisha came upstairs into my room. She was still hassled in confusion, which we both Dad and I were throwing to her.

Nisha prepared presentation on the launch of new cell phone, intelligently. And now she was explicating me about how to give presentation. She was continuously muttering in my front while walking left and right. I was already exhausted. I was nodding in deep sleep on my bed.

"Shourya...," she steamed in irritation and sat next to me.

Her voice was so harsh that broke my nodding.

"Huh...? Sorry..., Sorry...," I uttered suddenly, unsure of where I was. I shook my head terribly to get up.

"You need a coffee," Nisha said and patted my shoulder.

****

"Ok, where is milk? Give me milk fast," Nisha ordered me. We were preparing coffee in kitchen.

"Sugar...?" she said without looking at me.

"Coffee...?" she again murdered.

I was obeying her rapidly. There up, we sat on sofa in drawing room. Nisha checked my laptop, while sipping the coffee. Suddenly she unlocked Ruhi's crazy photos on my laptop.

"GF?" Nisha raised her brows and cackled me.

"No... She is my sister, my life, my best friends, and my everything," I said in dull voice and sipped again.

Today, once again, I missed Aahna and Ruhi. I turned my face from Nisha, to hide my gloom. I gulped a dead weight and closed my eyes.

"Who was she?" Nisha put her hand on my shoulder and whispered. Actually, I had forgotten that Nisha was an MBA. She was so clever, so that she could even read people's faces. I beamed at her and told everything about Aahna.

"So, is there still anything in your heart for Aahna?" she asked softly.

"No, it's already over," I lied and smiled at Nisha.

She gave creepy smile and hence we both went silent.

"Shourya," Nisha held my both hands, "look, I don't know, I should say it or not. But I started liking you. I don't know how it happened. But I sense so bliss with you. I can't sleep well, because every time I think only about you, I think I really love you, Shourya," Nisha pleaded like a kid. Her eyes were dim in tears.

"Nisha, Nisha, relax, it's ok," I bellowed and held her shoulders.

She gave me shocking look, with wider eyes.

"So, it's fine to you, that I love you?" she babbled jerkily.

"Yeah! You can love me. But I can't I will be your friend always," I sighed.

"Shhh... Bad luck," she banged on my laptop and smirked at me, "so can I get a tight hug at least," she exited, and stretched her arms.

I wrapped my arms around Nisha, "idiot," I uttered and grabbed her tightly.

Unexpectedly, Mom rushed out. The big watch on the wall was telling, it was 12.30 AM. I don't know what the hell Mom was doing at that middle night.

"Oh my god! What is this happening?" Mom mumbled, stopped her words, and put her hands on her mouth in shock.

Quickly, Nisha and I broke our hug. We exchanged our gaze.

"Ma'am, it's my b'day, Sir was just greeting me," Nisha cocked her eye to me.

"Oh! I see," Mom buzzed, " I was scared that you both_, by the way, happy b'day beta," Mom blessed Nisha.

Actually, it was her real b'day. So, Dad, Mom and I celebrated her b'day. She cut the cake. I feed Nisha, then to Mom, briskly I was close to feed a bite to Dad, and my hand stopped.

We both starred at each other. But next second, I put the whole cake on Dad's face. I genuinely sensed so jubilant, and overjoyed. Dad too laughed and cleverly smashed my face on cake.

Today only because of Nisha, Dad and I had a good time after years back. We did dinner together. And first time, I felt that we are family, Dad, Mom and me. That night, I realized love in Dad's eyes for me.

And it was only because of Nisha. So, next day I took Nisha to shopping and got her a beautiful dress, heels, purse, and other so many stuffs, girls use. I was surprised that how I was letting go myself with the world around me. When we can't control what's happening, challenge ourselves to control the way we respond to what's happening. That's where our power is.

****

CHAPTER FIFTY TWO

It was unbelievable, that I had completed six months in Sharma Company. But my encounter was still on with Dad. I was working hard day and night to win over my Dad, to prove that I am not an unworthy.

Initially, I was getting fun to fight with Dad. And I forgot about Aahna, about my past life. And even I ruined the life, which I had dreamt of years ago. I had lost my dream.

But as time passed away I was getting irritated of that bloody stuff. Dad again and again attempted to defeat me. He kept on giving me harder task. I would feel like someone was straggling me. I couldn't breathe. I was dying because of stifle of that bloody business.

How much we effort to run away from reality, But it would never leave us behind. Again I lost myself. Again I started missing Aahna. Veritably, I allowed myself to lost in Aahna, because she was my only Peace, which I could feel. So, once again I reversed my life 6 months ago.

I again wondered about my friends, about my dreams. And that deep contemplation led me to in isolation. My mind wasn't accepting the world, existing near me.

And the hardest prison to escape is in our mind.

I would spare my whole day in silence. I would capture myself in my dark room. Day by day I was again getting weak. I wanted to breathe between books not within machines. My heart was dying to write. But I killed urge of my fingers of typing on type writer.

Admitting, I couldn't writer, because I was crumbling between my Dad's arrogance and my evil infelicity. I was actually in need of courage. I was in need of support of my Dad.

We sometimes feel like we can't talk to our own parents, even when we need help. At that time, we want our parents to ask us about our pain. They should know us without being known by us.

One day Dad informed that in two days a Japanese company was coming to deal with Sharma Company. They would invest in Sharma Company, if Sharma Company would convince them.

So Dad asked me to represent Sharma company, in front of Japanese. So it was a good opportunity for me, to prove myself, to ruin my Dad's egoism. So, I started working hard on that project.

It was late at night. Nisha and I were in office. Nisha was preparing data to represent Sharma Company. And I was searching all the details about Japanese company on my laptop.

I was working continuously from hours in my cabin. I didn't even care for my health. So, now my body had started to pain. My eyes were giving up. I was snoozing on my laptop. And I still don't know, when I fell into deep sleep on my laptop.

Abruptly, I felt someone stroked soft hand on my head. I got up prematurely.

"Huh?.. Who is it..?" I blurted in dread. I was unsure of where I was.

I turned my eyes furiously here and there. I was so fatigued.

"Shourya.... It's ok... Relax.. it's Nisha," Nisha pampered me, and sat next to me.

"Shourya, you are tired now. You sleep. I will do it," Nisha said politely, and ruffled my hairs.

"No, no, I can't sleep. I have to do it fast till morning," I stammered and raised my hands, head strongly.

"Ok, ok, don't be terror," she frowned, "wait, I will get you coffee," she smiled and left.

She got coffee from canteen. She sat near me. Nisha was peering at me in concern. She was doing efforts to read me.

"Shourya, what happened to you? I saw from last months, you look so sick at heart. You are not talking to anyone, even to me also," Nisha gasped and sipped.

"No, Nisha, I am alright," I smiled.

"Shourya, don't lie to me. Look at you; what you have become? You are not happy with yourself. You are assaulting yourself," Nisha yowled at me.

I couldn't say a word to her. I was just looking down.

"Shourya, if you believe in me as friend, please tell me. What is wrong?" Nisha clutched my hand and beamed directly into my eyes.

I couldn't neglect Nisha. She had so much loyalty in her eyes. I uttered to Nisha, everything about my past life, about Sid, about Ruhi, about Aahna and about Shambhav.

My eyes flashed by unshed tears. I told her about our friendship, about our love, about our dreams, about our destruction. I confessed to Nisha, why I gave away my writings. I confided the pain, I was suffering from. My voice was paralyzed.

Nisha came close to me, and put her arms around me. I leaned over her body.

"Shourya, I have no idea about your grievance. I know it's so much tough to move on," Nisha mumbled," but Shourya, you can't spoil your life in remorse. Shourya, you should start your writings again. Why you are aborting your life, yourself in this hell? Shourya don't stop dreaming just because you had a few nightmares," Nisha said recklessly,

"No, Nisha, you aren't right. I am glad here. Believe me, I want to do this work," I sighed.

"Shourya, I am with you from 6 months. Shourya, I love you so much. So I know you more than yourself. I know you don't want to do this business. If you don't love what you're doing stop wasting your time," Nisha gestured and Chuck under my chin.

312

"No, Nisha, you don't know me," I groaned.

"Shourya, I know you are in this company because of your arrogance, and stubborn to defeat your Dad. You are batting absurdly with your Dad. But can't you see, that you are also becoming cruel as like your Dad. You can't see, that you are annihilating your happiness for your Dad," Nisha exasperated, quickly, I prodded her away.

"Shut up Nisha...," I roared, "what you know about me? I am dead now. I can't write anymore. Did you get that?" I should and glared at her.

But Nisha didn't frightened.

"You are lying to yourself. You are convincing yourself that you are gleeful. But I know, you are not jubilant. Because you are borne to write, you are dying to write. Your heart, your hands are groaning to hold pen and paper," Nisha squelched.

"Stop it Nisha... Please..... I am dying," I grabbed my head by both hands and groaned.

Nisha cradled my face in her palms.

"Shourya, You want to fly away in world of books. But you are sending so down yourself in limitations," Nisha whispered, "looking back you realize that a very special person passed briefly through your life and that person was you. It's not too late to become that person again Shourya. Don't ruin yourself, you will die, you will not stay blissful here," she shouted on my face.

Suddenly, I was out of my control. My head started bursting in aggression. I don't know, rapidly what happened with me? That I slapped Nisha.

"Get lost, leave me alone. For god's sack please leave me alone," I thundered, and rushed out. I didn't go to home. I went to Marine drive, and lay whole night on the shore of sea.

And the morning came. Not with standing, I was not ready for the deal with the Japanese. But I braced myself unsteadily to win their heart. So I put my whole energy in that meeting.

And the result of my hard work came out positive. Japanese were gripped by my words. They showed credulity in me. They got ready to business with Sharma Company. Every buddy in conference hall clapped and graced for me. One by one everyone congratulated me. I gazed at my Dad. I impressed him. He looked dispersed by me. He smiled at me, and stamped towards me, while stretching his arms.

But rapidly, I rush out and marched furiously towards washroom. I unsteadily reached in washroom and threw my whole weight on wash basin. I was so fatigue, I was panting terribly in front of big mirror. I don't know how? But my face was steamed in tears. My eyes were red. I observed myself carefully in the mirror. I glared at my mirror image.

"Who are you?" I asked to my image, "Why are you here? Why are you killing me? Why are you battling with yourself?" I groaned in gloom. Again I starred at my illusion and grabbed my chaps.

"Just look at your face. This is a fake. You are living fabricated life," I mumbled innocently, absurdly. I was behaving as if I was talking to a kid. I was getting panic and mad.

"Recognize yourself. This is not your face. This is not real Shourya," I screamed and slapped my chap.

"Shourya, always wanted to fly. Shourya never lived on boundaries. Shourya never lived the life, with other decides. Shourya always wanted to live the life, which he had decided, so who are you? You are not Shourya," I sighed and flamed at the illusion.

"Where is that Shourya? Where is that will power of Shourya?" I hissed. But in next second I became calm down.

"Please free that Shourya... Please free him," I pleaded to my mirror image.

Suddenly, again I got horrible.

"Shut up.. Shut your mouth... Get lost.... Just leave me alone," I shouted disastrously, snatching my head by my hands.

Thereupon, I cried loudly and smashed my head with the mirror image.. "That Shourya is dead, he is dead, can't you get that?" I roared and gasped.

I heard someone's padding towards washroom. He was peering at me, from half opened door. He was my Dad. Hastily, I wiped my face with water and rushed out.

****

On that night, I was so enervated. I slid against the red wall and slipped down to the floor in my dark room. Folding my legs in front of my bed, I rested my aching head on knees. I closed my eyes and felt tears wet my cheeks. I let them flow abundantly.

Today I was again facing the grief. Today once again Nisha had put me in front of the truth, from I was running away. I was sobbing on my failure once again. Fleetly, I noticed someone poking through my half-opened door. He was my Dad. And when he pierced my tears, he drilled into my room, and he pulled me into his arms.

"Shourya, my son, what happened to you?" he said, his voice trembled. He was melted against his arrogance.

I peered at him for a second and buried myself in his arms like a kid. I grabbed him tightly as much I could.

"Shourya.. Why are you punishing harshly to us? Why are you doing this with us?" Dad said.

"Dad... Please save me," I said in gruff tone. And I stuck to Dad, and I gave up and let the tears flow freely down my face.

I cried loudly and horribly. I didn't respond a word to Dad. I was just crying more and more louder. I was holding Dad cruelly, that I tinched his shoulders. And that was only thing, which was giving me Peace.

I felt warmth spread in my chest and heart get lighter as I cried and vented out my remorse, which I was bearing in my heart from years.

"Dad, Please save me, you won Dad, you won, I am a failure Dad.. I am dying Dad," I sobbed.

"Shourya, Please forgive me, I hurt you a lot, I tortured you a lot only because of my greed and arrogance," Dad mumbled. He tightened his lips to control his cry.

"Shourya... Please tell me. What is troubling you? Why are you doing this to me? Shourya Please talk to me," Dad stroked on my hairs.

I still don't aware, what he meant? And I don't know, why I burst my heart to him. I confided everything about my life at Delhi after leaving home. I told him about Sid, about our struggle to chase our dreams. Hence, I told Dad about our defeat that how we lost Sid? How Aahna hurt me? How she left me to die?

"I lost everything Dad, I lost everything my friends, my dream, and Aahna. And I lost you and Mom too," I gasped and cried again.

When Dad heard me, he was guilty. He realized his sin. He strewed on my knees, and clutched my hands. Mom had already stridden into my room. She was peering at Dad and her son. She didn't interrupt. She wanted Dad and me to ruin all our misunderstandings and hatred.

"Shourya... What I had done with you beta? I ruined you. You are agonizing from such miseries, only because of my greed and suborn. I didn't care for you ever. I never understood you. I never gave time to you beta. I was lost in my money-making business. I demolished your happiness, only because of my haughtiness. I was killing you," Dad paralyzed and cried. His lips were shivering terribly.

"I am not a good Dad Shourya. I can't even ask you to forgive me. Because no Dad kill his own son's joy by his own hands. " Dad put her head on my knees.

His eyes were rolling in abundant tears. I saw Dad's tears first time in my life. And I felt so embarrassed that my Dad was crying only because of me. "No, Dad, please don't say this," I sobbed and wiped Dad's tears

"No, Shourya.... I am evil Dad. You were always exploiting yourself for my happiness to make me feel proud. Shourya, if something bad would have happened with you, then I couldn't forgive myself. Shourya, you are my life beta, you are my everything. This bloody empire is waste for me, if I can't keep you happy. This whole empire is bullshit in your front. I was insolent because of my power and business. I couldn't see the world by your eyes. I forgot about the humanity. And I smashed your dreams. I am bad father Shourya," Dad cried and peered at me.

"No, Dad, you my best Dad ever. I love you so much Dad. And I can do anything for your happiness," I cradled his face in my palms.

"Shourya, if you love me. If you forgave me, then please full-fill your dream for me. Please stay glad with me. Please write again," Dad gasped.

"No, Dad, I can't write. I lost Dad. I am a failure. I lost my friends, my love and my emotions. I am dead now Dad," I sighed, and turned away from Dad.

"No, beta, you can't lost. You are my son. You have to write. You have to write for your friends, for Aahna. And I am damn sure, that Aahna and your friends will come back to you after reading you," Dad said.

Today, Dad won my heart. He was motivating me, as I did with my buddies years ago. I hugged my Dad tightly; Mom's eyes were vellicating, at the same time. She was glad by catching our love. And I was amazed that Dad loved me that much. Today I was so lucky, as I had best Mom and Dad in world.

Today once again love won. Today once again love showed its power. Love transformed an ostentation nature of a businessman. And only love can do this.

Today I was richest boy in world. Now my dreams were dreams of my Dad. Now I could win the whole world, only if my Dad is with me. I grabbed him more tightly.

****

CHAPTER FIFTY THREE

On following days, I started my writing and once again I lost in the world of books. I had only one job, first to read and then write. I would write whole day and whole night. I would write on blank paper and then tear it then throw in scrap. And would do it again and again. Dad and Mom were always there with me. They would sit me with whole. Mom always cared me with coffee even in mid of night. Dad would help me with good vocabulary. He was a good reader to review my work.

Nisha would always visit to me. She was now part of my life. She would always take me to some good locations of nature. Bandra Bandstand, Juhu beach, Elephanta caves etc. were her favorite places. And i could easily write there while she would sit near me. I would write, what my heart said. I wrote about my love and affection with Aahna. I wrote everything Aahna that how I fell in love with her in first sight. About our fight with each other. About our accidental kisses. And then our love gone stronger with time. I praised her beauty, her magnificent brown eyes, her silky hairs with the hint of brown at the end and her cute dimples. All my words had heartbeats.

Then, I wrote my second part, my friends. About our unity, our funny fights, taste of beer at hostel terrace with Rohan and Yash. I remembered our past life once again in my book. That how we got a way towards our dreams. How we struggled to fulfill our dreams. How hard we did to get money to save Orphanage house.

And in my story the most important part was Sid. He was so much attached to me. I wrote about his dream, cricket. How we fought to his villagers and get back him to Delhi.

When, I was writing, I realized that I was nothing without my friends. My friends were my strength. They always stood there for me. They were ready to die for me. But what I did with them? I left them. I cheated them as always I used to do. I was selfish every time. Ruhi and I had so strong relation. She called me his brother. She was my life. But when she needed me, I ran away like coward.

I was feeling so guilt of my mistakes. My inner writer gave away to write a word. I stopped my writing. And I swore to correct my mistake. I told my Dad about Ruhi. And it took 2 days to get her details. She was back at her home in Bangluru. She was getting married to evil boy to whom her demon uncle and aunt had chosen. She was going to kill her happiness, only because of my mistake. So without wasting a second, Dad and I took off to Bangluru.
Though, we didn't know what and how we will save Ruhi? We just knew that we had to be there.

When we reached at her home, I was shocked as it was the final day of marriage. She was getting married in few hours. Everyone was so busy in preparations; whole house was decorated so beautifully with flowers, lights, curtains. Mandap was decorated in front of the house, which was so adorable. Priests were preparing Havan agni. Some people were busy in dinner and other were still dancing and torturing band master.

I asked a boy about Ruhi. He took us to first floor in Ruhi's room. I stood outside of room. I was feared to face Ruhi. My heart was beating fast, shaking my legs. I looked inside from gate. Ruhi was sitting in front of mirror. She was wearing red Lehenga, which was hand embroidered. She was decorated with jewelry on neck, hands, and head. Her hands were made in Mehendi. Some girls were doing her makeup, other were putting red Chunari on her. She was looking so pretty. My little sister turned into beautiful bridge. "Behnaaa...," I said softly.
Every girl turned to me. Ruhi looked up at my mirror image. And tears rolled down furiously and abundantly from her black eyes, which ruined her kajal. I don't know how? But I felt moisture in my eyes too.

She stood up terribly and ran towards me. In next second, she was stuck to my chest. She wept freely, furiously. And she started to punch my chest terribly.

"Where were you? Why did you leave me alone? Why did you do this? What was my mistake? You promised me and then you cheated me. why....?" she was shouting and sobbing loudly and hitting me continuously.

I was ready to be punished. Tears rolled down on my cheeks. I tried to hold her, but she was unstoppable. In few minutes she was exhausted, she started panting, but her tears couldn't stop. She leaned against my chest and I buried her in my arms.

"It's ok...., calm down...," I said and put my hand on her head.

"Why did you left me alone, Bhai....?" she whispered innocently. I felt so pain, when she said me 'Bhai'....

"Ruhi..., I hurt you, I am your victim. But look I have come back, to take you away from this hell with me. You have to be IPS na..," I said. And quickly, she got away from my arms. She down her face.

"No, Bhai..., it's too late. I am getting married, I can't come with you. You are late," she said while wiping her tears.

"Ruhi," I held her, "you have to come, you can't do this," I said.

"No, I can't hurt my Dad. It's his decision," she looked at me.

"Ruhi, remember, you have promised to Sid. Sid wanted you to be IPS. So for him, you have to come with me," I said.

"My uncle and aunt will kill you and me. They will not let me go," she cried again.

"Ruhi, you said me Bhai na, so do you believe me?" I chuck under her chin.

"Hmmm..," she nodded.

"Then just close your eyes and held my hand. No one can touch you till I am alive," I said. She held my hand, we ran out of the room, then through balcony, then through corridor, and then we ran down the staircases. We were about to end the second last stair and our way stopped by the fucking people. I faced a man of 45 in yellow kurta and a big turban on head. He

was Ruhi's uncle. A lady in yellow heavy saree, she was her aunt. And a young guy in red sherwani, he was Raghu, the fucking bridegroom.
Ruhi grabbed me tightly. I glared at them angrily, Dad stood near me in support.

"Who are you? And Ruhi, why are holding him? Where are you running?" Her uncle roared. Ruhi got feared. She tried to hide behind me.

"I am her brother. And I came to take her away from you bastards," I smacked.

"You mother fucker, how dare you?" Raghu shouted, ground his teeth and ran to hit me. but I defended and kicked him back.

"Stop it..., stop it...," Dad said. And suddenly, Ruhi's Dad, Hari uncle came. He looked so simple and weak. He was feared of Ruhi's uncle and aunt.

"How dare you touch her? She is our daughter," her uncle shouted, "Ruhi, what are you doing? How can you go against your Dad?" he glared Ruhi.

"Shut up, you_____, I very well know you bastard. You controlled Hari uncle and took away everything," I shouted.

"You poor guy, you don't know me. Leave her otherwise____," he was saying, but I cut him off.

"Shut up you..., I don't want to know you. I want to talk to Hari uncle," I said and looked at Ruhi's Dad.

"You shut up. You have no right over our daughter. Leave her," her aunt snapped at me.

"Shourya..., they are right. We have no right over Ruhi. Leave her," Dad said..

"But Dad," irritated.

"Shourya....., I said leave her," Dad spat out loudly. And I left Ruhi's hand, and glared at her uncle.

Dad went to Ruhi's father and pleaded, "Sir, let her go. Let her live her life. She is brilliant girl. Don't destroy her life and her happiness. Sir I was also an egoist and cruel. But I realized my mistake. Sir, our happiness is in happiness of our children," Dad was saying.
But her uncle pushed Dad away, "get lost."

I held my Dad, I wanted to punch Ruhi's uncle, but Dad stopped me.
And in next Moment, Ruhi was in knees of her father. She held him and started crying, "Dad, please let me go. I don't want to marry Raghu. I want to study Dad. I want to be IPS. Dad, please. They will kill me Dad, please let me go, please say something Dad," she wept freely, but her father didn't say a word.

Ruhi's uncle and aunt grabbed Ruhi's hair and tried to snatch her away from her Father.

"Dad, please listen to me. Don't destroy my life. Please save me Dad. They will kill me Dad," she was sticking to Her father knees. Then her uncle and aunt started slapping her furiously. They dragged Ruhi by her hair towards stairs. I couldn't see this anymore. I felt to kill every one of them. I rushed to them, pushed them away from Ruhi and clutched Ruhi in my arms as like a mother her child.

"Get away, you absurd," I cried and held Ruhi more tightly.

"Shourya leave her, right now," my Dad shouted, "if her father don't want to save her, then why we would care," Dad pulled me away.
I saw Hari uncle standing like statue, but his eyes were in tears. I ran to him and begged to him.
"Uncle, look at them uncle. They are killing her. Please save her. She is your own daughter. How can anyone hit her, in front of your eyes? Don't you have heart? Uncle, you just allow me to save her. And then I will take her away. I will bear all her responsibility. Uncle, she is my sister, please uncle," I said, but he didn't move by my words.

"Uncle, I don't believe this. You are stone heart. Ruhi's Mom will not forgive you ever," I grinned. I hurt him and it worked.
His face turned into anger, his eyes were red in tears.

"Stop it...," Hari uncle screamed, "leave her you bastards. She is my daughter. How dare you hit her?" he roared like lion. We all were shocked. This was the real father of Ruhi. Ruhi pushed away all the assholes and stuck to his father.

"Oh! So you also have voice. Don't forget, I will throw both of you out of the house. Don't forget, you are a servant here," Ruhi's uncle was shouting. But Hari uncle interrupted furiously.

"Shut up, you pimp. I will chap you right now if anyone touch my daughter," he snapped and looked at me, "Shourya, take Ruhi away from this hell."
And in next second, Ruhi was in my hands.

"Stop you bitch..., you have to marry me or I will kill you," Raghu ground and rushed to slap Ruhi. But I stopped his hand and punched his nose. I grabbed him by his hairs and hit his head on my knees, "don't even try to touch my sister. I can kill everyone right now," I sneered.

****

On next day, she was at my home. Now she was my official sister. But I was in loss by her coming, as Dad and Mom started sparing all the love to her. She took away my room, my car and my every thing. Even she got a good friend, Nisha. But we all cared her so much.

"Beta..., what happened? You look sad," Mom kissed Ruhi's head.

"No.. Maa..," she smiled, "just missing my Dad," she hugged Mom.

"Mom, this is not fair. You forgot me as you have got new daughter. You lost in Ruhi. No one loves me now," I annoyed.

"You are 25 now, you are not a kid. And she is my just new born baby," Mom grinned.

"Yehhhh...., Maa loves me more," Ruhi excited and showed me her thumbs down.

"He he he... very funny," I irritated to Ruhi.

"Whatever," she cut me off.

"Mom, you know, actually she is sad because, she is missing her so called Dulha, Raghu," I sneered and laughed at Ruhi to tease her.

"Shut up, Shourya. Maa tell him to don't torture me," she irritated and threw a pillow on me.

"Ha, ha, Maa ki chamachiii..," I said in loud.

"What did you say?" She frowned.

"Chamachiii...," I laughed.

"Kutteee... wait, I will kill you," She ran to hit me by her sneakers.

****

CHAPTER FIFTY FOUR

We can't judge the time. Whole universe is dependent on time. We can't control time according to our conditions, despite we should change according to time. We should do justice, respect with time.

Now everything was going well in our life. I got my dream back, I got my Ruhi back, I got my family back. These all were symptom of 'Yug Parivartan', coming of humanity, coming of good time. We should have faith in 'Cosmic Energy', that one day everything will be okay. That energy will open all the ways.

Ruhi took admission in a coaching; she was so much dedicated to her study. She had already done great planning for her UPSC exams. I was all the time with her. I would drop and pick her from her various classes. Then we would do our hard work. She would study whole night in my room and I would write in her company. She would help me in recalling our best Moments at Delhi. I was happy with her, but we would fight a lot. She would tease me on my awkward writing and I would torture her on name of Raghu. And then she would slap me 4 to5 times a day. But I got one more mother in form of sister. She would care for me a lot.

Her UPSC prelims was coming closer. She started even more harder study. Our room was getting packed day by day. Even books of history, politics, economics etc surrounded me. She replaced paintings of my room by various types of maps. She deepened herself in books. Her dream was looking clear to her. No one could stop her. It's her pain in deep heart which gave strength to her. And then result of her hard work came positive. She cleared her UPSC prelims. And now, she had to do more hard work for her UPSC Mains. I helped her for Mains exams, I taught her to develop good writing skills and time management for essay writing.

I was also almost close to complete my final draft. I was writing the climax of my story. Ruhi sat whole night with me. She would help me to know more about her and Sid. I was writing last chapter about Sid's death, about our destruction, about our separation and about our sorrow.

Tears rolled down through my cheeks and dropped on my diary when I was writing about Sid. I really started missing Sid, my hands started shivering. And Ruhi's condition was more pity. She missed Sid badly. Her every Moments with Sid appeared in her eyes. She cried whole night on my shoulder. But that was most important time for us. So we didn't let this pain to effect our work. Even, we got more stronger, and worked more hard for Sid.

While pursuing our dreams, there was the times when we feel like giving up. That's when we told ourselves it's days like these that will separate champions from ordinary people. And the best part was that we found fun in our work. We found our job as our fun. So we didn't exhaust of such hard work.

Now, after 6 months of my writing, final count down started. I gave away my sleep, time and piece for my writing. Luckily, I got a publisher. I worked with their editors for one more month. And finally the day came for which I worked all day and night. I got my book published and launched on 14 February. I dedicated my book to Sid. I didn't want my book to boom out to get terrific reviews. I just wanted that when anyone will read it, there should be smile and peace on his face. He should feel loved for his beloved, he should miss his friends while reading my friends. And yes it happened, I was overwhelmed by the readers.

****

14th Feb, Dad, Ruhi and I padded on stage with our publisher in discussion with the readers.
"First of all, congratulations Sir...," a reporter wished me.
"Thank you so much..," I replied with smile.

"So, first question is who inspired you to write? Who is there behind this book?" a reader asked from audience.

"There are so many people behind it, but if I am here in your front, and if you can read this book, is only because of my Dad. He is my hero. And my sis, Ruhi," I said and smile in thank you towards Dad and Ruhi.

"Sir, you are son of a businessman, so then why did you choose to write?" a guy asked.

"Yeah, you are right, every son follow his father's profession. But I choose to write because, I listen to my heart. I write because it gives me peace. I write to explore all the things I was afraid of. I write to express my feelings, my pain and my happiness. I write because, I want to be part of revolution of books. I write, because I have a story that only I can tell. I write to find my voice, and to work day and night for it. I write to be the characters, I thought of. So that I could live the life, I dreamt of. I write because some day that's the only way. I can stay same. I write so I could see myself," I exposed the writer in me and everyone turned to clap for me.

"Sir, from where do you get power to write?" a girl questioned with smile.

"I get power to write from love and friendship that you guys are carrying. I get power from the lovers. I get power from idols of love. Dasharath Manjhi, who even dug the hill for his love. The great legends of love, Romeo Juliet, Heer Ranjha, Laila Majnu, Shah Jahan- Noor Jahan all these are the great lovers to inspire people like me," I said.

"Sir, what do you mean by the word 'Love'?" Another girl asked.

"For me love is a feeling of caring and belief for someone. In this world there are things which we can only experience but can't define. And for me love is one of that thing. Love means progress, inspiration and good hope. Love never leads to destruction. Love doesn't mean to get someone, it is the feeling which makes us to lost deeply in someone. Love is craziness to ruin all the limits for someone," I whispered emotionally.

"Sir, is it your own story?" a boy asked."Yeah, of course, it is my story," I quipped, "it is your story too. It is story of every youth. As we all have some dreams in life. And also we all go through sweet situation of love too. And we every youth struggle a lot to get our dreams and our love both. And in this battle we need our friends, our parents. We can't get success without support our parents. And luckily, if we get success then that success wouldn't give peace to us as our parents are not with us." I said smile at Dad.

"So, Sir did you get your love in your real life story?" asked reader.

"No. Although, story in book ends. But my story is still on the climax, which will never end. As story ends, but love story never," I replied.

"Sir, you titled your book 'you are the author of my story' so here who is the author of your story?" a girl asked.

"Literally, my friends are the author of my story. I couldn't have come to this Side of mine, if I wouldn't have met my friends. And when I finally broke, they were my friends, who picked up my shattered pieces. Tearing themselves open on each broken shard as they put me back together again." I said. And it took one more hour to talk with readers. They really wanted to know more about my friends and me. And it was all like a dream for me.

"Any massage, you want to give your readers?" asked a reporter.

"Yeah..., I want to tell few things to the youngsters," I said and got up, "first, if you really love someone, then love her madly, faithfully, and carefully. Don't think much and love her truly. I am sure it will work. Respect her emotions; make her feel so much special with you. And go, tell her what you feel about her. Open your heart to her. She will accept you, and if not then also love her. One day she will come back to you. And second, is that I want all of you to see dreams, otherwise anyone else will hire you for their dreams. I just want you to live for your dreams. Respect your dreams. Do what your heart says. Break all the limitations and fly away and don't stop till your dreams are achieved. And every struggle you have done in your life shaped you into the person you are today. Be thankful for the hard times that can only make you stronger. And spread love as much you can. Stay happy," I energized and ended conference.

So, I had completed my first book. But this book once again threw me to my past and recalled all the memories with Aahna. She was my first love and first love remains special until we breathe last. I was missing her again. This book pushed me to the past, I was running from. Once again my dead love got breathe. I realized that how much I love Aahna still? I couldn't live without her. Even my book is meaningless, if she is not with me. Our souls were united, so how could our bodies live apart. After that, every second I would think about her. I would check my FB, emails and phone again and again, as if there would be Aahna's massage. I thought she would realize after reading my book that how much I had loved her. But nothing such happened.

Same was with Ruhi, when she read the book, she lost in Sid. She missed him badly. We both were upset. We were not getting peace. Once again this book threw us 2 years back and this book reminded us about the promise, we had done with Sid on my birthday.

****

"Shourya, I want to say something.....," Ruhi said softly and put her head on my shoulder. We were sitting on the last stairs, out Side of house.

"Hmmm...," I whispered.

"Shourya, your birthday, 1st of July is coming," she said. I gazed at her, she held my arm tightly,"Shourya, Do you remember the promise, we did to Sid," Ruhi gestured.

I was shocked and scared too. I wanted Ruhi not to talk to me about Sid. As I couldn't face her. I felt guilt, I was ashamed as I was the reason behind Sid's death.
"Ruhi.....," I frowned, "we had decided that we will not talk about Sid. You know that it pains both of us. And we wouldn't move on," I was saying but she snapped at me.

"What pain Shourya? What pain? And where you want to move on?" she jerked my arm, "look at you Shourya, and look at me. We are already in sorrow; we have forgotten to smile Shourya. We are not getting peace, can't you see?" she cried, a tear rolled down on her face.

"So, what do you want, what I do? Should I kill myself? That's the only way I will get peace," I smacked and stood up harshly.

"Shourya..," she squeezed my palms to calm down me, "Shourya, I can understand your pain. But my heart says we should complete Sid's promise. So might we get peace? I sense that something good will happen if we fulfill Sid's last wish," Ruhi said and looked in my eyes by her big black eyes.

"No Ruhi..., I can't, and I shouldn't get peace. And we have lost Sid, so there is no mean of his promise," I said.

"Bhai...., you are right. We lost him. But tell me, isn't he still live in our heart. My every heart beat moves for him only. And I am sure he always looks upon us. We have to do this for peace of his soul," Ruhi said and put her big braid on her right shoulder.
She was right, but I was bloody bastard. I was abused that I couldn't peace to myself.

"Bhai......., please, for my happiness. Please," she pleaded. But I was so strong like stone.

"Ok, fine. You die here every day. Sid sacrificed his life for you and you can't fulfill his promise even. You were right that you are selfish as always. You don't love me," Ruhi cried, "But I will do it, alone," she snapped.

"Drama queen, stop this stupid drama," I said and armed her from behind, "I will go, we will go."

****

CHAPTER FIFTY FIVE

"Why did we come here Ruhi?" I asked, stepped out of cab. She didn't respond, "Ruhiii..., I am talking to you dambooo," I shouted.

"Just shut your mouth, you idiot," she snapped.

We were in Delhi. And Ruhi brought me to that ruined fort near a lake, where we spent our two years. Ruhi dragged me by my hand towards terrace of fort.

"Shourya, we had decided our dreams here only. We find our main aim here. We had started our journey here. So we have to finish it here only," said Ruhi. It was 30th June, a day before my birthday. On 1st of July we were leaving for Paris to complete Sid's promise.

"Shourya.......," I heard a sudden voice and turned around more quickly. They were Ashvini and Rohan. I was shocked, it was completely unexpected. I gazed at them weirdly. It was all Ruhi's planning.

"You bastard," they roared and ran to me, they looked furious. And before I could sense anything, they were on me. They slapped me terribly, pushed me down, and kicked me uncountable time likes a football.

"Why did you leave us, you moron? Why did you cheat us? Didn't you think of us even once?" Ashvini shouted and punched my chest with her soft hands, but Rohan's punches were hard.

"Guy, please forgive me...., it's hurting now," I begged.

"Oh! Really, but that's why we are hitting you, idiot," Rohan slapped me again.

After furious dhulai, they relaxed. And we looked at each other while panting on our knees. Automatically our eyes were wet in tears. And I pulled them in my chest. "I missed you so much guys," I whispered and hugged them more tightly. Ruhi joint us. We all were sobbing. It was actually fabulous to meet our old friends after years. The whole seen there was looked like the climax of movie 'Three idiot.'

We sat silently on the edge of wall, facing the lake. Everything was as it was, as we had left. The sun was till setting down same, waves of lake were silent, a flock of birds was revolving around the lake. There was still that silence in cool breeze. I felt like nothing had changed, we were still in college, still doing fun with Sid. But I mused that things were same but we had changed. Sid wasn't there. The person because of whom, we had patch upped was not there with us.

Friendship is such ocean of emotions, sometimes I feel like years have been passed, and at the same Moment I feel like not a single Moment has passed.

The things we had buried in wall of that fort were still there, Sid's brown jacket, Aahna's payal of left foot, bracelets of Ashvini and Rohan.

"Guys, I can't believe, we are back together again," Rohan said.

"Yeah..., it's a miracle," Ashvini said.

"Sid always had believed that, we will meet again. He always wanted to be together," I whispered.

"Yeah...! But look how destiny played that he is not with us," Ashvini said in sad tone. Everyone's eyes were red.

"Guys, I know it's tough, but now we are back to live the life, which Sid had dreamt of. So now we will live these days only for Sid. And Sid don't like that we are crying. So cheer up for Sid," Ruhi assembled all of us.

"On the name of Sid," we all cheered.

****

It was late night of 30th June. We were at airport, waiting for flight to take off for Paris.

"Ruhiiiiiiii................., Ruhi...........," suddenly we heard someone calling Ruhi. We turned around, our gaze followed that voice.

And I was in COMA, my mouth left opened. I saw a girl waving her one hand to Ruhi, holding trolley bag in other hand. I pinched myself to check whether it was dream or any kind of illusion. But she was real, she was Aahna.

"Wow...... gorgeous..," I amazed. She had grown up more beautiful cum hot in all these years.
When I glanced her after two years, I felt same as I felt when I had seen her first time in Pub. And of course, the world around me felt silent. Music blew in my ears. And cool wind began blowing in me as always.

She was in black short dress up to her knees, which had floral effect, she had put white blazer on it with a pink purse across her body. Her hair were flying furiously, which were more longer and brownish. She was running to us while colliding with others. My heart started counting in reverse order as always, as she was coming close to me.

She hugged and kissed Ruhi's cheeks. She was so much enthusiastic. She greeted Ashvini and then Rohan with half hug and then quickly forwarded her arms to hug me, she was unaware of me. I was smiling to her like dumb. Her cute dimples, brownish eyes were taking my breathe. And then our eyes met, we captured each other's gaze. We were swimming in deep love.
But rapidly, I realized that she was the girl who destroyed my happiness, she had cheated me. And my love turned into hatred. I glare cruelly to her. I wished to kill her right there.
She also looked angrily to me and ground her teeth. In next second, we were going to kill each other. But cleverly Ashvini took her aside.

I turned to Ruhi and gave her harsh look. This was also Ruhi's planning.

"Excuse me?" Ruhi said, padded slowly and tried to avoid me. But I held her hand.

"What she is doing here?" I frowned.

"I don't know," Ruhi replied innocently.

"You liar. Kaminiiii...., I will kill you," I shouted and twisted her hand, "why didn't you tell me about her?"

"Because you didn't ask," she smacked.

"Oh! Really. Fine then. I am not coming, if she would," I said and jerked her hand.

"Shourya.. Bhai..please, don't trouble me anymore. Even she didn't know that you are also coming. It took 2 hours to convince Aahna. And she came only for Sid's promise. Sid's promise can't be complete without her. She is also Sid's friend. So she ran away from her home for Sid only," Ruhi pleaded.

"Great! Then I can kill here easily and no one will be aware about this," I shrieked like evil.

"Kuttteeee..., don't even dare to touch her. She is my responsibility," Ruhi hit on my head while adjusting her big braid. Sometimes I wished to cut her braid.

******

"Ruhiiii......," I bawled, as I saw my seat was by the Side of Aahna's seat. And she was already sitting there.

"What...?" Ruhi smacked, "why are you shouting?"

"I will not seat near her. Throw her elsewhere," I glared at Aahna.

"Oh hello! I will not move from here. Ruhi, if he has problem then throw him out," Aahna flamed with her brownish eyes.

"Listen Shourya," Ruhi gulped and held me, but I cut her off.

"No, No, No, I will not seat her and how dare you talk to me like this?" I frowned at Aahna, she got up and tried to tinch me , but Ruhi stopped us.

"Aahna, you please sit on my seat," Ruhi requested to Aahna.

"I will not move from here," Aahna grinned with pause.

"Look, you jerk. Don't mess with me, I will kill you," I roared.

"Oh really! Come then. Hath laga ke dikha," she collared me and I strangled her neck. And we both shouted loudly. It annoyed our fellow passengers.
Everyone eyed at us, and pursed their lips for us louts. Suddenly two airhostesses ran to us.

"Excuse me! Ma'am, and Sir, what are you doing? Plane is taking off, please take your seats. You are not supposed to disturb the other travelers," they snapped at us. And broke us. We realized that, we were in plane. We have to be in discipline. Helplessly, we sat quietly on our seats. But I was green eyes, I was burning to take revenge from Aahna.

So finally, we took off.

After 20 minutes, I was drinking coffee, and my evil mind knocked. Cleverly, I dropped my coffee Mug on her skirt.

"You rascal......," Aahna roared, and glared her brownish big eyes, "I will kill you," she stifled my neck.

"Ruhi.... ," I shouted, "save me."

"What happened now?" Ruhi stood up, she was before us.

"Ruhi....! See, he poured coffee on my dress,"

"Excuse me! I didn't do that intentionally, it was just an accident," I fumed.

"You......," Aahna barked.

"Aahna, Aahna please go, and clean it," Ruhi begged to Aahna.

"Disgusting," Aahna said and went to change in washroom. Ruhi murmured and blazed at me. I ignored her. After one hour, When I was sleeping. Aahna poured her drink on me.

"Ruhi..... ," I shouted, and broke everyone's sleep.

"Now what?" she asked grumpily.

"Ruhi, look she dropped drink on me to revenge from me." I complained to Ruhi. We were disturbing fellow passenger, and we had already tortured air-hostess and Ruhi and Rohan. So, Rohan, Ruhi and Ashvini got up finally and they showered on both of us.

"Are you both idiot? Can't you sit silently," Ashvini freaked out.

"God please take me up, I did a big sin. I shouldn't have called both of them. How I will bear both of you in 8 day," Ruhi groaned in frustration.

"Oh hello! I didn't know that she is coming. I am not interested to travel with her," I snorted.

"Oyeee, bastard, I am also not dying to be with you," Aahna huffed more infuriatingly

"Shut up....., both of you," Rohan, Ruhi hissed, "sit here silently," they pushed us on our seat. We were scared.

"If you said a single word now, we will throw both of you out," they shouted and threatened us. So after that, we didn't say a word in till we landed. We straggled ourselves in our blankets.

****

CHAPTER FIFTY SIX

In morning, we landed in Paris. After collecting our luggage, we went to the hotel, Relais Saint Charles, it was a 3 star hotel, which would give amazing look of Eiffel tower through windows.

We had booked one room for girls and another for Rohan and me. So, it was our 1st day of journey of Paris. We were finally close to fulfill Sid's promise. We had decided that, we will enjoy this journey as we had promised to Sid. And we had faith that we were not alone. Sid was always with us. We can feel his silence, his shyness, his honesty.

During whole journey, I would wear Sid's black leather jacket, which was only thing we had of Sid's memory. That gave me some peace, so that I could get rid of my remorse. But I had to bother about Aahna. I don't know why destiny brought us together again? But for me she was now only hatred. I would assault her a lot, and she would also exploits me during whole journey. That was giving us rid of our frustration and anger for each other.

In morning, as I padded out of my room, I noticed, Aahna was approaching towards washroom, which we had to share, as it was common between two rooms.

Hastily, I rushed towards her, pushed her aside and captured over the washroom for almost an hour. She was banging the gate, barking, and abusing me. After irritating her extremely, I got out of washroom, while walking in attitude and whistling at her.

"Ridiculous.... ," she kibbled her teeth, and glowered at me.

Our first task was , 'Musee d' or say, it is definitely one of the must see place in Paris. It is world's premier collection of impressionist paintings. But it also cover different art forms, including sculptures, engravings, photos, film, architecture and urbanism. It is gift of artist such as Degas, Monet, Van Gogh and many more.

We had so much, exhilaration and fun there, by capturing every art in our cameras and phones.

****

1st July, it's my birthday, in the late evening and dawn of night, we went to a beach Side resort, to celebrate my b'day. I blew the candles and cut the black forest cake. Everyone blessed me and fed me cake one by one, excepting Aahna.

She was starring from distance. She was so hot in black strip-less party dress up to her thighs. Her black - brown hair were spread over her barred shoulders. She still had that locket which I had gifted her years ago, on her b'day .

"Aahna, please come here, wish him at least. Don't be so rude," Ruhi insisted Aahna .

So, she wished me in hatred, I neglected her. So, as she turned around to move. She pushed me on the cake. My face was completely in chocolate, I frowned at her.

"You idiot," I shouted, and complained to Ruhi and Rohan.

"It's your matter, you both solve it. We will not mess with you morons," Ruhi and Rohan darned at me.

We enjoyed a lot that night. We were so bliss after such long time. We were down trodden also for Sid. We missed him a lot, but we didn't confide to each other. But tears in our eyes were depicting our pain for Sid. We toasted for Sid.

"On the name of Sid," we all cheered up.

Next morning, again I was waiting Aahna to pad towards washroom, and when she strode towards washroom, I ran while prodding her aside and again took over washroom. And stumbled out after an hour. She was sneering at me like devil. Her eyes were greened. When I entered into my room, I was shocked. Aahna had ruined my clothes and cut them into pieces.

But, thank God, she couldn't find her payal and her yellow scarf, which I had snatched from her in college. I relaxed and exhaled deeply.

Thereupon, I would tease her by kissing her payal, scarf, ring. I would play with her payal while producing sound of chhan chhan, in front of her eyes. She would hissed at me and battle to snatch her payal and scarf.

Now we would go to 'Chapelle de la Sorbone church' it is large chapel white building. We asked father to pray for peace of our Sid. We burnt candles, and closed out eyes and prayed for Sid. I really sensed so much peace there; my eyes were dipped in tears.

And as I opened my eyes tear rolled down. I turned my left, I glanced Aahna. She was in white sleeveless short casual dress, which had green and red floral effect and black belt. She was on her knees. Her brown eyes were shining in tears. She was twinkling so innocent. I was dying to bury her in my arms forever.

But in next second, I hatred that she was my cause of destruction. I was green eyed. I stole her camera, placed near her. And came back on my seat, and pretended innocent myself.

We strode out of church, and then we would give away our favorite things to poor, we would help poor people as much we could. And we would buy and take something as memory of Sid, which could relate us with Sid .

As it was Sid's humanity to help other, and collect such priceless thing from everywhere. He had made us to be kind, helpful and human being.

On that night, Aahna searched her camera in her room and my room also. I was whistling and playing with her payal innocently. She would glare and narrowed her eyes to notice me. Although, she had caught me but she needed proof.

On that next morning, we traveled to a religious site, 'Notre Dome cathedral.' it was a high tower building and finest example of

French Gothic architecture. It was attached to main city road, so it was so much crowded.

It was built by Romam to worship Jupiter. It had a gallery of kings, holding a stick and a crown. It has a architecture of lion 'Gargoyle.' I was capturing it by Aahna's camera. Suddenly she noticed me. She strode terribly to me.

"You, thief, it's my camera," she hissed and raised her hand to snatch it. But I moved her hands away.

"Excuse me, it's mine, I bought it yesterday," I frowned.

"Ruhi......," she shouted, "Ruhi, look he stole my camera, and he is lying now," Aahna gasped but I cut her off.

"Hello! Mind your word, I didn't steal it. This is my camera, and I don't lie like you, got that," snapped, and snatched it from her, but accidentally that camera slipped down, and destroyed.

She shocked in big brownish eyes.

"You broke my camera, I will kill you," she barked in vibrating tone. She got up terribly to tinch my face by her sharp nails, but Rohan and Ashivini grabbed her. She cried in her bed on that night for her camera.

Our next day task was 'Arc de Triomphe', which is one of the most famous monuments in Paris. It's made in memories of battle of Napoleon Bonaparte. It has an Arc dealt with data, description of battle and victories of Napoleon.

And then, in late night we went to Rex club which is most adorable night club of Paris. We drank there, and then danced absurdly with French girls. Ruhi, Ashvini and Aahna all three were in short party outfit, they really rocked the dance floor.

Next morning, we visited to our childhood place, not only of mine, but of every kid.

'Disney Land', we enjoyed there a lot like kids. We played with Mickey Mouse, bolt the dog, Donald duck, bear and so many more. We were lost in our childhood; Aahna was more crazy than 2 year old kid.

Aahna went to Mickey Mouse ride, and I followed her. She was jumping, slipping, rolling stupidity on that balloon ride. And when I got chance, I made her to fall down and she slipped from 12 feet high balloon slide.

She got injured, I was starring and laughing at from her up. Suddenly, Ruhi pushed me down and I also slipped down and rolled over Aahna.

"Kuttee....., Mar dala.....," she cried wrathfully, and slapped me.

After that, we went to roller coaster ride, 'Space Mountain.' It was so high and had so many dangerous waves. Aahna, Ruhi, and Ashvini got cold sweat. A dead weight stuck under their throat. They dreaded and denied to go on that roller coaster.

"Ha ha ha , such coward ...," I sneered. Rohan and I laughed at them, and challenged their girl power. And they got provoked, and dare to go on the ride. And Aahna got on her seat, I sat near her. And the ride took off. Actually, it was horrifying, I too started trembling and fearing, I felt so weight less.

And Aahna was close to die. She was shouting, crying, panting, stupidity.

"Mumma.....Mumma...... Mumma.... Stop it...stop it..., keep me down," Aahna cried like kid, unaware of her age.

Her brown eyes were in tears. And as the ride stopped, she walked wobbling and then fell down, in her short blue sort and white summer top. That was too much torturing to her.

I don't know, why were fighting? Why we were doing that? But I muse, we both were bursting out our frustration, our anger and our love. We were asking answers to each other, which had no questions.

But in spite of that, so much love, we had in our eyes, but we didn't letting it out. And the good thing was that, we both never changed. We were still same crazy, childish, and victorious as we were in our collage life.

On that night, we all were so much tired; we got into sleep so early. I was alone in my room, as Rohan was hanging out with

Ashvini. Suddenly, my door opened slowly, and someone padded like thief. It was so dark. I switched on the dim light and looked with squinted eyes.

She was Aahna. She closed the door and paced towards me. Her eyes were red in anger. I was flummoxed that what was in her evil eyes. What she will do now? I moved backward on my bed in corner, and hid myself in blanket, as she padded towards me. I was so terror.

And suddenly she pulled out a knife from back. And she strode towards me. I was wet in sweat; my heartbeat went reversed order. My voice didn't come out of my throat. I thought that today she would kill me.

"Ruhi.... Rohan .... Ashvini..... ," I shouted in trembling voice, "Ruhi save me, she will kill me," I was panting.

"Aahna sorry.... Please forgive me," I pleaded, "I will not torture you, please don't kill me," I prayed absurdly, and closed my eyes.

 And she laughed, and rushed out of my room. But I fell faint. And woke directly next morning. Everyone was laughing at me. Aahna too was laughing with cute dimples at me.

I was not in condition to fight anymore. I was silent whole day. I didn't troubled her anymore we. As I couldn't believe her, as she could kill me in real next time. She was crazy girl.

****

CHAPTER FIFTY SEVEN

I don't know how fast 8 days had been passed in Paris. Every day we enjoyed a lot. Every day we lived so alive. We lived every Moment which we had missed from 2 years. We laughed on our grief from which we all were dying from 2 years.

We realized that our souls were getting peace with the soul of Sid. We again started breathing, which we had last year ago. Sid was true that, we together can only stay happy. We thanked to him that he had taken promised from us to meet again.

But I was still searching for my life. Aahna and I still didn't have peace. We both were still in pain. After 2 days again we both were going to separate to never meet ever. We had only 2 days to decide our destiny, this time destiny couldn't decide our future.

It was 8 o' clock of night, we all were in a resort, enjoying the cool breeze and high waved of beach. We were playing 'Truth and Dare.' Now it was my turn to round the bottle, and it stopped at Aahna.

"Come on Shourya, give a task to Aahna," Ashvini excited. But I glared at her, and got up to leave. But Rohan and stopped me.

"You can't leave the game, you have to ask her to do something," Ashvini said. I jerked her hands.

"What I will ask to her Ashvini? She is already cheater. She very well knows how to win by stabbing backs of friends. She is a liar," I shouted and flamed at Aahna. And the whole environment turned into silence. And sudden, it twisted into wild. Wind became furious, as coming of a storm.

"Shourya...... What are you saying?" Ruhi said to me. "Please Ruhi, don't stop me today. What will I ask that why you played with my heart? Why you used me and then threw me? What was my fault? That I loved her. She slapped to me to save Shambhav. She saved Sid's murder," I shouted. Aahna looked tears down.

"I loved her a lot. I wrote for her, but she destroyed my life. She abused my love. I still cry for her. I still remember each and every Moment of her with me," I said in trembling voice, "I wanted to free you from yourself, from your cage, she forced me to live in cage. I hate you more than Shambhav."

"But now it's over. I will not cry more for her. And why I am muttering this bullshit to her. She is no matter for me now. Today is last night of our. We will be again separated till next night. And Aahna I promise you again, that I will never show my face to you. So be happy with Shambhav, but I request you that please don't cheat people who actually loves you," I said and tears rolled down from my eyes. I strode away towards hotel.

There was deadly silence. Only Aahna's sobbing was beating with waves of water. After my left, she cried a lot in Ruhi's arms. Rohan Ashvini showed sympathy to her.

"Ruhi you know, I didn't cheat him, you know why I did that?" Aahna cried.

"Yeah! Aahna, I know you can't cheat him. You love him. You suffered hard for his happiness. But Aahna he is unaware of the truth. Now it's the time to tell him everything." Ruhi said to her.

"No, Ruhi I can't. We don't have future. We can't be together. Destiny don't want us to be together," Aahna said, trembling voice.

"Aahna, why are you exploiting yourself? Why are you destroying your life? Aahna look, we all have dreams to complete. We all had promised to Sid that we would achieve our dreams. And Aahna I know your dream is to fly away with Shourya. So go and fight for your life and love to your Dad.

Aahna, look Rohan, Sid, Ashvini and Shourya, we all have battled hard with our parents. And at the end they surrender to us. So you have to fight against your Dad and Shambhav.

It's your life Aahna . So you have to fight for it. We can't help you. You have to face them. Running away is not the solution of problem.

Aahna, I know you love Shourya, then why are you marrying to Shambhav? Aahna, Shourya also loves you a lot. So go Aahna, it's last chance, don't miss it," Ruhi said to Aahna.

****

I was standing at the terrace and wondering about my pain. I was convincing myself that I didn't do wrong with Aahna. I don't love her.

Suddenly, my door opened hastily, she was Aahna, her eyes were red, brown hair were ruffled. She strode furiously to me, grabbed my hand and dragged me terribly into her room, without saying anything.

"Leave me, what are you doing?" I shouted and battled to escape my hand. But she didn't react. She pulled me terribly, threw me on the bed, and looked the gate.

It was dark and fear full night.

"What are you doing...?" I asked, and got up

"I want to solve something to you," she said.

"Get lost, I don't want to talk to you, or listen to you," I muttered and rush away towards gate. But she pushed me aside.

"Today you have to listen to me, got that," she frowned. She scared me.

"Today you have to listen the truth that I didn't cheat you. I didn't abuse your love. Today you have to listen, that you are wrong," she gasped.

"Huh! I don't care. I know you are a betrayer," I said but she cut me off.

"So, you think I cheated you, I broke your heart, I played with you. But you are wrong. You are wrong that you suffered and cried. You said I didn't love you, then what is this? Why I kept your diary still with me. Then why I wrote the journals you left empty, read it, you bastard," She pulled out my diary from her bag, and threw at me. it was that diary, I had left in my room two years ago. I am still shocked how it reached to Aahna? When I read the journals of Aahna, I found Aahna too loved me as I did.

"I am also suffering from the same pain. From 2 year, I cry every night for you. Yeah I know that I slapped you, but I had my reason that time. But you never understood me. You say that you loved me than, you would have believed in me. You would have respected your love, and me to understand my pain.

On that night of farewell, when I came to you to tell you everything. I hoped that you would understand me, because you loved me but I was wrong. You were not ready to listen me. And you even humiliated me. You had just believed what you had seen, but you never looked the truth into my eyes. And then you say that you loved me. But Shourya you are wrong, you hadn't trusted me ever. You never did effort to feel me, to know my pain, my reasons," she cried.

"Ha ha ha..... ," I sneered, "Aahna, I know what are your reasons, so there was nothing to understood. Your slap was proof that you don't love me. You love Shambhav. So now there is nothing to talk," I was saying.

"Really? It means, only that much trust you had on me. So that was only love you had for me, that a slap would decide our love. Shame on you Shourya," she said. I looked down.

"Aahna it's over. Now why are you muttering this? What do you want to prove that you are right and I was wrong, but it's mean-less," I said turned away to leave, but again she grabbed my hand, and she slapped me harshly.

"I am muttering all this because, I want to prove that I still love you so much bastard," she roared and cried furiously.

She put her head on my chest and cried. I was shocked, unaware of what she was saying. I mused that if she loves me then why she didn't accept me?

"Aahna, so why did you slap me that day? Why did you save Shambhav, who killed our Sid?" I said.

"Because, it was my Dad who killed Sid. He was blood thirsty of your. He wanted to kill you," she sobbed.

When I heard that, I was frozen but still wondered.

"Shourya, my Dad wanted me to marry Shambhav, son of business partner for money and power in politics. At first, I denied, so they tortured me a lot. And on that night when we kissed, Shambhav caught us. And he told every bullshits to my Dad. Dad got so angry; he planned to kill you to save his power and money. But accidentally they killed Sid. When I came to know about that. I fought with Dad, and pleaded to forgive you. So he put condition to me that if I would forget you and stay away from you then only he would let you to live.

So, I had decided to break every contact from you. But you were coming more and more closer to me. And you messed with Shambhav again. So, I had to slap you, I had to hurt you, so that you would hate me, and leave me away. So that Dad would let you live. But I killed my love, my happiness. I sacrificed my everything only for you. I left no stone un-turned to get you, but I couldn't help. But you never understood that how much pain I am going through, I am dying Shourya," she cried on my chest.

I was in sudden COMA. My body started trembling, my heart was broken, and it had given up. I couldn't breathe, I felt straggled. A sharp pain shot through my body, I padded unsteadily backward. I couldn't stand. Tears rolled out abundantly and ceaselessly from my eyes.

I was so guilt that what worst sin, I did with Aahna. I tortured her, and she saved my life by paying her life. I was the cause of pain of everyone's life.

I lay on my knees, "Aahna, I am really sorry. I did a sin to you. I led both of us towards destruction. I am not a good friend, not a worthy son, not a true lover. I stabbed everyone," I said.

"Aahna, you saved me, and in return I humiliated you. I tortured you harshly. But you didn't say anything. You are such pure soul. And I am evil. I am ruined in my own eyes Aahna," I said, she sat on me lap.

"Aahna, I can't face you. I am your victim. You suffered a lot because of me. I should kill myself Aahna," I sobbed and slapped myself.

"Shourya....Shourya...stop it...," she held me, "what are you doing? Who said you are not good. I know you are more pure than I am. You didn't know the truth, that's why you did that. It's not your fault. Why would you be guilt?" she said and wrapped her arms around me.

"Aahna please forgive me. I know I hurt you. But I still love you a lot, I can't leave without you. Please don't ever leave me. I will die without you," I cried on her shoulder and mumbled like kid to his Mom.

"Shourya...., stop crying ....," she said and wiped my tears, but her face was too steamed in tears.

"Stop crying, I am not going to leave you ever. I love you more than yourself. I will not let you go ever," she said and clutched me more tightly to her chest. She pampered me like kid. I was exhausted. She helped me to stand up. She cradled my face in her palms to console me.

I looked up at her and wiped her tears. She was still sobbing. I touched a strand of hair falling over her eyes. Our heads were resting against each other, our nose touching, and our breaths merging.
I moved close to her lips, and pressed my lips on her soft lips, waited there for a Moment, and sucked her lower lip. She responded with a moan, and placed her palm on my face. She moved her lips smoothly to kiss my upper lip. And I made way of my tongue into her mouth and smooched her tongue. She tasted so sweet. And here she got furious. She started sucking, biting my lips passionately, rubbing her hands on my jaw, and neck.

It was so much sensation when our tongues met. We both started rubbing our lips. Desperately while moving our heads in a good rhythm. I was touching a sweet adolescent of her mouth. That made us more furious. We didn't know what we were doing. We were losing ourselves.

We were two love birds who were fly in the high sky. We were ducks, who were drowning in deep river. She pushed me towards bed; I obliged her, and flopped on the bed, our lips never breaking contact. I was down. She sat on my belly. She bent over me, still kissing me cruelly. Her hair was falling on my face. I held her waist tightly for support, and tried to rise my head up to meet her lips. I wrapped my arms around her waist. She clutched my T-shirt in her both hands, pulled it off in one swift motion, and threw on floor. She ran her fingers on my shoulders, and chest. She leaned over me and started licking my jaw, then shoulders, and then chest, biting slightly, and revolving her tongue around my chest.

"Aaahhh.," I groaned, as she killed me. I pressed my fingers into her back, and stopped her. Now it was my turn.
I sat on my knees, facing her. I took off her top in one move. She was naked in my front. She was gleaming hot in black bra against her fair glow skin. She was glistening in the moon light coming from window.

These moon, stars, which cool breeze, those trees were attesters of our love. We both felt as if we were reaching in heaven while swimming in air. Tonight we had broken our limitations, our fear, our misunderstanding. Tonight, we didn't want to care for the evil world. I was staring at her, it made her feared. She clutched her body by her arms to hide herself. Her face turned red, eyes shined in tears. I made her to look up at me, and removed her hands from her chest. And rapidly, she melted in my arms.
I pushed away hair from her neck and bit her neck. She groaned heavily, and smothered me tightly. I ran my fingers down her back, on her silky skin. And I touched straps of her black bra. I tried to unhook that strap but couldn't.
She arched her back, and I supported her weight on my left arm. I grazed my right hand down on her neck, then stayed at her chest. My hand could feel her heart beat rising with every second.
I slid down my hand down to her waist, and I pushed her back on the bed. I bent over her. I felt warm as my body rubbed against her soft body. Her breast heaving against my chest.
I looked into her eyes; she smiled with faith in her eyes. I went close to meet her lips, and sucked her both lips together. Then I moved my mouth to her neck, and licked her neck from right Side. I moved down to her chest, brushing my lips on her chest. Then I skipped down to her waist.

I grazed my cheeks on her soft waist, and then kissed her naval. She dug her fingernails into my back, and she arched, moaning, as I sucked her navel. She pressed my head cruelly against her waist. I circled my fingers on her waist, just above her shorts. And I opened hook of her shorts. I folded her right leg, rocked smoothly on her thighs, and touched every inch of her skin. Again I came back to her lips, smooched her lips once more, and beamed into her eyes.

"Aahna....., will you marry me?" I asked to her.

"Of course Shourya ....., I love you so much ... Please don't leave me. Please take me away in high sky," Aahna said gruffly. I kissed her forehead, "don't worry, I will capture you from your Dad soon," I said. And suddenly she opened her brown eyes.

"What? " She shocked, "you mean, you will send me to my Dad again?"

"Aahna, we will not go against our parents we will marry on your Dad's wish," I said, she cut me off, and got up.

"Are you made? They will kill you. I don't know anything. We are not going to India back. We will live anywhere, away from my Dad," she said innocently, and put her arms around my waist, and hold me tightly like kid.

"Aahna, we can't ran away from him. One day they will find us. Then?" I asked evenly.

"So, what you want? And what you think? That my Dad will easily let you to marry me?" She said dull sound. I held her; make her to sleep on my shoulder.

"Aahna, you always wanted to fly away, so now you have to fight. You have to face your Dad, and tell them what you want. It's your life Aahna, no one can snatch it from you. You have to fight alone. I will stay with you, but I can't fight with your Dad, till you stand against him," I said.

"No Shourya. I can't face him, I can't go against him. I have no such guts," she gasped in fear.

"Shourya, I don't wanna argue. We are marrying here only.

And if I will go to him, then they will never let me back. And they will kill you," she hugged me.

"Ok, then, I will die happily for you," I said.

"Shut up, you moron," she frowned, "why don't you understand? I have already lived in cage. I already have suffered a lot. But now I want to live with you only. I want to spend a luxury time with you only. And I will not let you die. You have to live for me," she sobbed, tears in eyes. And hugged me tightly.

"Aahna, do you love me?" I asked.

"So much," she said and licked my chap.

"So, you should believe in me. Everything will be alright. Now you are with me, so I am most powerful person in the world. Just hold my hand and listen to my heart. No one can separate us. If you are with me. I can fight from whole world," I said and rolled my fingers in her hair.

"Aahna, Look at these stars and moon. No one can separate them. They are made for each other as like us. So don't worry and sleep silently," I armed her and we don't know when we fell asleep in each other's arms.

******

A harsh smash of water broke our deep sleep. We got up hastily in shock. And I saw, Ruhi, Rohan and Ashvini surrounded Aahna and me. They were glaring and sneering at us as if we did some wrong or guilt. Yeah! Actually, Aahna and I did guilt last night.

"How can you do this to her Shourya? You destroyed her life," Ruhi snapped at me. I was a bit of threatened.

"Oh my God! Aahna, and how can you allow him to do that? Didn't you feel shame?" Ashvini teased Aahna.

"Shut up...... Aashu ....don't trouble her, it's nothing like that. We did nothing," I said and held Aahna. She was afraid, and remorseful.

"Now Aahna, you will be pregnant," Rohan taunted to Aahna.

"Now, you both have to suffer hard for this sin. God will never forgive you," Ruhi snapped at us.

They tortured us a lot. So we both were scared and guilt, that actually we did wrong. We shouldn't have done that. Suddenly they all laughed out evil, at us.

"Bastards, you killed me. I was actually feared," I gasped.

Briskly Aahna face steamed in tears. She was so scared.

"Awww, so cute baby, she... is....," Ruhi and Ashvini said and armed Aahna.

****

CHAPTER FIFTY EIGHT

It was our last day in Paris. We were close to complete Sid's promise. And everything had been solved in our life. It was so special day for us. Today we had left only last but not the least place to visit. Today we had to travel to the heart of Paris the Eiffel Tower.

Although, it was our last day, but we didn't know what would happen next? How we will face Aahna's Dad? But we had faith in our love, that everything will be ok. And I was so energetic as Aahna was with me. She was my power. And this time no one can snatch her from me.

And today once again my friends were with me to defend Aahna and me from every difficulties. Now for them only Aahna and me were their dream. We were just under the Eiffel Tower. Suddenly, a car came and stopped before us. 2, 3 and then 5 people rushed out of it.

"What the f___," I gulped.

They were Aahna's Dad, Shambhav and their gang. Actually Aahna's friend Sanaya had told everything to her Dad.

"God please saves us...," Ruhi whispered. We looked at each other in terror. We all were frozen. My heart was rising faster. I glanced at Aahna. She was paralyzed, her lips were trembling, and she was gasping.

Aahna's Dad and Shambhav strode furiously, terribly towards us. Their every step was taking my breaths. Aahna clutched my hand and stood behind me.

"You unworthy bitch........., I will kill you," Aahna's Dad rushed and raised his hands to hit Aahna. But I grabbed his hand and jerked his hand down. And I clutched Aahna close to me.

"You bastard...., I will kill you......," he barked and tried to slap me again I stopped his hand and close to hit him.

"Shourya... Noo....," Aahna shouted and looked into my eyes. She put my hand down.

"You son of bitch......, I should have killed you," he roared and slapped my twice. I was bearing every slap like statue. Then, Shambhav grabbed Aahna and tried to snatch Aahna from, but I held Aahna's hand tightly.

"Dad please... Listen to me ...... I love Shourya so much... Please leave us, Dad," Aahna cried.

"Shut your mouth, you bitch..... I had already told you, if you want him alive then you have to leave him," Shambhav pulled Aahna terribly. She was crying desperately.

I got tempered now. I kicked Shambhav's belly and then smashed his head against my knees, and then dug my elbow into his back. And he scattered down on my feet. I glared at her Dad.

"Sir, if I can die for Aahna. Then I can also make anyone dead for Aahna," frowned.

"But I will not do that, because I love her. And in love there is no place of violence. Sir, my Dad taught me to respect elders. Sir, I promise to you. I will not touch anyone; I will not accept Aahna till you give her to me," I was saying, "Sir, if you want me to die. Then I will die but I will not leave Aahna ever," I said.

Suddenly, Shambhav got up horribly, and he pointed gun at me. He was so angry. I was scared for a second. My friends held me.

"No, No, Shambhav..... ," Aahna, "please don't do this.....," Aahna begged at Shambhav. And stood in my front to save me.

"Dad, you want to me to come with you, okay I will come, but promise you will leave Shourya.....," Aahna pleaded to his Dad.

"Aahna, what are you saying?" I said to her and grabbed her hand. His Dad also held Aahna's hand and pulled her.

"Please..., Let me to go Shourya...," she said and removed my hand away.

Once again Aahna left me. Once again she betrayed me. She had promised me that she would never leave me, but again she broke her promise. She broke my heart once again. I could see her going away from me every second, and I knew this time she was leaving me to meet again in next life. We all were seeing her back side.... And she turned for once towards us.

****

"Aahna..............," I said loudly so that she could hear me.

"Aahna..where are you going. Please come back Aahna," I said politely with emotion, "Aahna, I love you so much. And I know, you also love me so much. Then why you always leave me alone? You have promised me that you will not leave me. But again you left me. Why Aahna ? Why don't you understand me? Why are you so much scared of other? Why you are still living in cage, where you can't breathe? Aahna it's your life so why you are allowing other to rule over you? Aahna you always said that you want to live a free life, you want to fly in high sky like a free birds. You want to swim in deep sea like a fish. You want to blow desperately like cool and fast wind. Then what happened to those dreams of your life. Today you have chance to fly away in free sky. So why are you deciding limitations to your wings?

Aahna broke your limitations today. Aahna you have to fight from Dad, from Shambhav, and from everyone for your life. Aahna we all had promised to Sid that we all will complete our dreams at any cost and Aahna today once again you are breaking Sid's promise. You can't do this Aahna. At least think about Sid. Aahna, Sid sacrificed his life for us. So we can't letting go Sid's sacrificed in waste. Aahna we came to Paris to pray for Sid's peace. We had started our journey together. And today is last day of our journey. And this journey can't be complete without you, Aahna. So please come back. Aahna I love you so much that I can't think about a second without you. But Aahna you have to do effort first to get back your life. We can't do anything until you will not take step against your evil. Aahna just close your eyes and listen to your heart and then tell everything about your heart to your Dad . Pleaded to them for your life, for your love and for your happiness.

Aanha. If you loved me, then, just hold my hand and I will take you to the sky away from every evil. But just come. Please come Aahna," I said in sad and emotional voice, there was so much pang in my voice. People were looking at me silently; they were spell bound by voice, which depicted so much of pang.

I sensed so positive and good that unknown people even people of other county were helping me. They had humanity, which exists, all over the world. It's power of love that connect people of shows that we are same human being whether we are Indian or french. We all need only love. The love, which is same all over the world.

"Sir," I said for Aahna's Dad, "you say that I am playing with Aahna for money and other stuff. But Sir you are wrong as the truth is that you are playing with her life for power and prosperity. But I am playing with her for love. I love her so much. But actually you will never understand my love. Because you don't aware what love is."

"Sir I know you hated me a lot and I too hate you a lot. But Sir today we have to ruin our hatred only for Aahna's happiness. Sir today you have to listen to me only for Aahna. Sir, you are a politician, you have power, name, money and everything of the world. So you can kill me easily and No one will be aware of that. But Sir how would you kill my love, which exists in your daughter's heart. Sir you are an MLA. You have all rights to torture anyone or me. You killed my friend, but Sir he is still with us. Sir you are so weak against us. As we have power of love and friendship. Sir we can destroy whole world by our power of love and friendship. Sir you have every luxuries of life, but despite of those luxuries. You are the poorest man on the earth. As you don't have love. Sir you have such worst luck that you own daughter hate you. How embarrassing is this. And why you have such arrogance that you have power an respect. But Sir you are in dark illusion, that everyone respect you but Sir actually everyone's fears of you. Everyone follow your order because of fear not because respect and faith. Sir you don't know that your own daughter scared of you. She asked me to escape away from you. But I denied to save your respect and Sir I have faith in you that you will understand our love and will accept us. I didn't want to destroy you and to humiliate you. As you are Aahna's Dad, and she would get hurt if you got humiliated. Sir my Dad always teach me to spread love not hatred. I wouldn't do any violence. I will accept Aahna on your wish, if you will happily send her to me. Sir we can snatch our dreams, our happiness by fighting with our parents, but that happiness will not be a true happiness as that will not give us peace. No one can stay happy while hurting our own people. Sir I hate you a lot, you killed my Sid. You exploit Aahna, you assault helpless people, and you do every evil. Still, despite of that, I have hope that you will accept us. Because I know somewhere in your heart you also love Aahna. Just try to look at that corner your heart, and I am sure, you will find love, humanity and feelings for Aahna and me. So Sir for that hope please let her come and prove me right. Sir I will keep her so much happy and one day you will proud of me, I promise Sir don't destroy her happiness. Sir your happiness will be flashed when it will merge with our happiness."

"Sir please give us our life," I said, eyes in tears. Ruhi was crying furiously. Rohan would hold her while wiping his own tears. Aahna was crying desperately. She wiped her tears and turned towards her dad. she was pleading to her Dad .

"Dad, please let me go Dad. He loves me too much and I also love him. I can't live without him Dad. I will die without him. Dad, I will not go against you. Dad I will not do things, which hurt you and your reputation. Dad I will go to him only if you will allow. But Dad Just listen to me just once," Aahna held her Dad's hands and cried.

"Dad, I never asked you and demanded for anything to you. I lived always as you wished. I lived in cage for you. I gave my every breathe to you. And I myself lived like a dead body. Dad today only once. Listen to your daughter if you ever loved. Dad please become my best Dad for today, please Dad, please give a reason to love you. Dad please give happiness of saying 'I love my Dad.' Dad I want to live like alive not like dead bodies. I want to live a free life, which I dreamt from my childhood.

Dad this much anger, greed arrogance is not good. Dad these will give you pain only. Dad you are already living fake life. I know you are dying every day. Dad, if today, You will not let me go, then you will have remorse for whole life. You wouldn't be able to eye at eyes forever," Aahna sobbed but her Dad was cruel listen like statue.

"Shut your mouth Aahna," Shambhav roared at her, "uncle we have to leave as soon as possible," but Aahna knelled on her knees in her Dad's feet.

"Dad please, let me go Dad. Dad don't be such cruel. Dad because of such ungodliness of your. I hate you. Even Mom also hatred you always. Dad you don't know but you killed my Mom. She destroyed herself because of suffering you gave always to her. Dad you have already lost everyone, and Dad if today you don't let me go, then I will also destroyed myself. And you will be murdered of your own daughter." Aahna cried and grabbed her feel tightly. Her Dad was scattered, his ego, greed had ruined as his eyes were shining in tears.

But suddenly Shambhav lost his temper, he was horribly. He started slapping Aahna, and he tried to drag her by her hairs, and pull away her from her Dad.

"You bitch, shut your mouth. You have to merry me, and I will kill that bastard Shourya," Shambhav hissed and slapped Aahna again.

"Dad please save me. Dad please, he will kill me. Dad please let me go to Shourya. I can't live without him. I will be happy only with him. Let me go," Aahna cried and stuck tightly to her Dad while battling against Shambhav.

"Oh just don't be crazy, your Dad will never let you go. Your bloody shut, you have to live on my bed for whole life, you slut," Shambhav slapped again, and raised his hand to hit it against Aahna's chap.

But Aahna's Dad downed Shambhav's hand and smashed him back.

"She is my daughter, how dare you touch you. I will kill you, if ever touch my princess," he roared and pushed Shambhav away and pulled Aahna into his chest. Suddenly Shambhav and Aahna's Dad stampeded, and pulled Aahna recklessly.

"Shourya........," I heard a panting voice of Aahna. She was running towards me.

She was Aahna, in front of my eyes. She was panting on her knees. In just her one glace, my heart got its breathe. I again started living alive.

"Where are you going? Leaving me alone, will you not take me with you?" Aahna said innocently low voice. And she smiled with tears in her big brownish eyes. She was crying, smiling, and shaking at the same time.

I beamed at her and her cute dimples vanished all my pain and miseries as like water bubbles. I couldn't wait anymore, I stretched my arms and smiled at her. She was running towards me, briskly. Suddenly, I sensed a harsh smash of hockey on my head from my behind. I couldn't get my sense. My eyes were big. My head was spinning. Everything around me started revolving in my eyes and then everyone disappeared from my eyes and i was in deadly dark world. I fell down and closed my eyes. I was dead.

"Shourya........," a laud sound resonated from everywhere. I could hear that sound of Aahna, but I could react. I couldn't open my eyes. I was lost somewhere in other dreams of Aahna.

"Aahna...." I shouted, I opened my eyes slightly, and got up hastily. Shambhav was standing like between Aahna and me.

"Shambhav..... Leave him... Bastard...," Aahna roared and rushed towards me, but Shambhav's man grabbed her.

"Chhhh....chhhh....," Shambhav pursed his lips, and sneered at me and then turned to Aahna, "such a cute love ha Shourya," he laughed, "but now you have to die for her as like your Sid. I really enjoyed when I killed him by my hands, now it's your turn," Shambhav ground his teeth and hit on my legs terribly.

"You pimp, leave him," Rohan rushed to Shambhav and threw

him away. Rapidly, two more rascals captured Rohan, and they kicked Rohan harshly.

Shambhav got up aggressively and hit Rohan's chest by hockey.

"No.....Shambhav.....," I shouted, "your battle is with me, leave him. You want to kill me. Then come kill me. I promise, no one will touch you even I also," I mumbled while standing unsteadily.

"Yeah, you are right, you rascal. I will kill only you," Shambhav barked and hit my belly, then my shoulder, then my back, then again my head by hockey.   I
was groaning in pain and wobbling here and there, falling and getting up again and again. I didn't effort to defend myself as I had promised Aahna's Dad that I will not touch anyone till he will not allow me to accept Aahna.

"Shambhav......., stop it Shambhav....," Aahna was crying and begging to Shambhav, "Shambhav please leave him. Please don't hit my Shourya. I love him," She cried furiously on her knees.

"Look bastard...., what you did with her? She is crying for you. What magic you did on her? You snatched her from me. You mother fucker," Shambhav roared and broke his hockey on my shoulder and legs. I fell down and Shambhav too. He was exhausted more badly than me. He was panting harshly. My body was completely stained in blood. I was ready to allow my last drop of blood to flow out only for Aahna. I smile at Aahna and that gave me so much energy to laugh at Shambhav.

"That's it......," I sniggered at him, "see the power of love."

"She is mine.... only mine, you bastard," Shambhav kicked my face and I rolled down again.
Shambhav rushed towards Aahna furiously, he grabbed Aahna terribly by her brown hairs.

"See, now I will kill him in front of your eyes. I will kill him," Shambhav laughed and pointed his gun at me.

Aahna was so paralyzed; she looked at me with bigger brownish eyes. I gave smile to her and closed my eyes to die. Suddenly, I heard someone hit on Shambhav's hand. So that gun slipped down from his hand. I gazed up and was shocked that Aahna's Dad tried to free Aahna from Shambhav's cage.

"I did a big mistake to understand you bloody. How dare you hurt my daughter," Aahna's Dad shouted and pushed away Shambhav.

"So now you will stop me, you..," Shambhav bawled irrationally, and hit Aahna's Dad by hockey. And Shambhav again raised hockey to smack Aahna's Dad's head.

Briskly, I ran and jumped between his head and Shambhav's hockey. Resulting, hockey stroke with my head. I covered Aahna's Dad in my arms and endured all the smash of that hockey on my back.

"Shambhav... take Aahna and run away, cops are coming," Shambhav's boy barked and got ready in car. Shambhav grabbed Aahna's hand and started to run away while dragging Aahna.

I rushed towards Aahna. And grabbed her hand to stop her. Quickly, Shambhav turned to me.

"You bastard...., leave her hand or I will kill you," he pounded his teeth and moved another hand to hit me by his hockey. But I stopped his attack.

"Now, it's my turn," I surged and punched powerfully to Shambhav's nose. And I pulled Aahna towards me.

"This is only for you, Sid," I looked up at sky and attacked on Shambhav horribly.

Suddenly, two pimps grabbed me from behind. But quickly, Rohan snatched them away from me and destroyed them unkindly. I hit Shambhv's head against an iron pole, his face was soaked in blood. I kicked his stomach and then his head cruelly. He dispersed down on ground.
He battled to get up but I kicked his chest again and again.

"You killed my Sid. You...," I was horrifying, "what was his mistake. He was innocent. You destroyed Rui's life. You___," I got over his chest and punched his face repeatedly terribly. I was crying too in vibrating sound, "why did you do that? Now you have to die, I will kill you," I hissed and grabbed his neck and pressed to strangle Shambhav. But Ruhi, Rohan and Ashvini held me.

"No Shourya..., leave him.... leave him....," Ashvini said.

"No, I will kill him. He killed our Sid. He have to die..," I roared in trembling voice.

"NO, Shourya. Leave him, we are not like this bastard. And Sid didn't want violence. So what we will say to Sid. He will be so upset. So leave him, please," Ruhi said.

Suddenly, cops came and took away Shambhav and his gang.

Thereupon, there was a deadly silence, the silence after the furious storm. We everyone were only hearing our panting and sobbing. I was swimming in red blood. And still blood running out of my head and hands. But it was sign of good coming and happy ending.

I was standing just under the Eiffel tower. Aahna was at a distance from me. I gazed at her and opened my arms. She burst into cry, and was just about to run towards me. But her Dad stopped her.

"Dad, please let me go. I love him so much," she pleaded in trembling voice.
Her Dad smiled at her, pulled her into his arms, and hugged tightly.

"I am sorry beta, I did so sins and mistakes that I couldn't even say sorry to you. But today, I will do a good thing. Today, you are free to fly away in high sky with Shourya. Go Aahna, he is only for you", his Dad cried.

"I love you Dad. Today, you gave me the reason to love you. Dad, I was suffering for this love, I was dying to hug you from my birth. Thank you Dad. Thank you," Aahna said, hide in his Dad's chest.

And in next second, she started running towards me. When I beamed at her, I was once again spell bounded. She was running towards me in short casual black, half-sleeved dress, which was embellished with light pink and yellow rose floral effect.

Once again, I slipped in her love. A cool breeze began blowing in me. I sensed a soulful music in my ears. Whole world around me went stop. I could see only her, with brownish flying hairs and her cute dimples.

I stretched my arms and she got collided with me forcefully and stuck to my chest.

"Aaaahhhh....," I shouted, "you are hurting me," I said.

"Oh! Sorry... sorry... sorry...," she said and touched my wounds. She put her hands on my head and blew air on my injuries. I smiled at her, "idiot....."

"What?" she shrugged, raising her brows innocently?
I shook my head and hugged her tightly as much I could. I was feeling heavenly peace. I exhaled on her hairs. I sensed that she was only my destiny. And I got her finally. I looked at her Dad and he responded with a bright smile with tears.

Then, I turned to my life, my idiot friends, who were ready to die for me. They clapped for Aahna and whole crowd and I followed them while glittering smile on everyone's face.

My friends rushed and hugged Aahna and me. Now we were together finally as we had promised to Sid.

We had after all completed Sid's dreams. We proved our friendship. We won over a corrupt politician, a arrogant businessman, cruel villagers and unkind, greedy people of Ruhi.

Our unity, our love and faith in each other led us to victory. Our power of love defeated power of hatred. We transpired everyone's hatred and animosity into love and belief.
Finally, we ended journey of our dreams. However, it took away so many sacrifices from us. We had suffered hard. But we never gave up. We did it as we had faith in power of love and friendship. We were together and ready to die for each other.

My love, Aahna had faith in me that only I would take her high in sky. And I proved her faith right.

Today, everyone's face was steamed in tears. We were missing Sid today badly. We were in need of him. But today, we fulfilled our dreams only because of Sid. It was not we, it was Sid, who completed our dreams and gave us new life by sacrificing his own life.

"Thank you so much Sid," we all said and looked up at sky for few Moments.

And suddenly, Ruhi shattered into million pieces and let the tears flow freely down her face.

"Ruhi, what is this? Why are you crying? You are our power. You are so much strong. You always consoled us that we have to be strong. You said that Sid is in our heart always. So why are scattering now?" Ashvini said and clutched Ruhi.

"Please, let me cry for today. I was pretending to be strong from years. I buried my pain deep inside of my heart. But now I can't gulp more pain of Sid. Today, let me vent out that pain. Please let me cry," She sobbed, "please let me cry," she said in shaking voice scattered on ground. She wrapped her arms tightly around her body as if she was holding herself. And she cried loudly. She didn't even control her sobs that were shaking her body. We all armed her and cried with her.

"Sid..., where are you? Please come," she shouted, "I fulfilled your promise, now please come back to complete that promise, which you had done with me. Sid why did you left me alone? Please come, I am still waiting for you," she sobbed while looking at high sky and cried again, freely.

We tried to stop her cry and shaking.

Aahna's Dad came and put his hand on Ruhi's head.

"Beta, sorry, please forgive me. I am your victim. I know I destroyed your life. I couldn't get that boy back. But Beta, I will try everything to give you your happiness back. I will help you to move on. You are my second daughter now. And by this only I can get peace. So please Beta, stop crying for me. please....," Aahna's Dad said to Ruhi.

And she calmed down in few minutes. We looked at her weirdly.

"What are you looking, idiots?" she shrieked with red eyes, "come on its celebration time. Aahna and Shourya's love story has been completed," she said enthusiastically, "guys, our ShouryAahna is completed," she shouted with big black eyes while putting her long braid on her left shoulder.

"Not yet, Ruhi....," Aahna raised her hand, "Shourya haven't proposed me yet," She glared at me and folded her hands.

"Come on. Go on then Shourya," Ruhi, Rohan and Ashvini laughed at me.
I got down on my knees and held Aahna's hand in mine.

"Aahna, when I saw you first. You stole my heart. On that day I gave away you my every breath, my pain, my happiness, my dreams and my everything to you.
I know Aahna, I am not a good boy. I hurt you a lot. But believe me, I love you so much. I want to write only for you. I want to spare my every breath with you only. I want to dance absurdly with you. I want to sleep in your lap. I want to fly with you. So miss Aahna Kapoor, will you marry me....., please," I said and kissed her palm. But she jerked my hand.

"Chhiiii, Shourya..., so disgusting you are," she made weird face, "why I accept you Mr. Shourya Sharma? Give me a strong reason to make me feel special, to make me fall in your love," she giggled and raised her eyebrows in attitude.

"Ok, so madam Aahna..., remember, once you said to me that if someone propose you in front of Eiffel Tower, then you will accept him," I said, "so, just look around miss Aahna Kapoor, you are standing in front of Eiffel Tower. So now will you marry me," I said innocently.
She held me and made me to get up. She pulled me close to her brown eyes.

"Stupid...," she shrieked and slapped me.

"Aaauuucchhhh.., it hurting idiot. When will you stop slapping me?" I irritated.

"Never .." she said and put her soft pink lips on my blood stained lips. She took a deep smooch... it was so magical and exciting among all kisses. She just kissed me in front of her Dad.

She was slowly rubbing her lips against my lower lip and sucked my tongue twice.
Suddenly, she became notorious and bites on my upper lip unkindly.

I pushed her away, "idiot..., you bite me," I frowned.

"Its love bite gadhe...," she laughed and put her arms around my neck and kissed my cheeks.

****

www.ingramcontent.com/pod-product-compliance
Lightning Source LLC
Chambersburg PA
CBHW070840260626
47170CB00007B/2441